ONE MIL

Before turning to full-time writing, Andrew Gro... an executive in the sportswear business. Andrew has written nine novels, seven of which were Top Ten bestsellers in the UK. He has also co-authored five *New York Times* Number One bestsellers with James Patterson. He currently lives in New York with his wife Lynn and their three children.

Novels by Andrew Gross

Everything to Lose
No Way Back
15 Seconds
Killing Hour
Reckless
Don't Look Twice
The Dark Tide
The Blue Zone

By Andrew Gross and James Patterson

Judge and Jury
Lifeguard
3rd Degree
The Jester
2nd Chance

ANDREW GROSS

One Mile Under

HARPER

Harper
An imprint of HarperCollins*Publishers*
1 London Bridge Street
London SE1 9GF

www.harpercollins.co.uk

This paperback edition 2015
1

First published in Great Britain by
HarperCollins*Publishers* 2015

Copyright © Andrew Gross 2015

Andrew Gross asserts the moral right to
be identified as the author of this work

A catalogue record for this book is
available from the British Library

ISBN: 978-0-00-738426-6

Set in Meridien by Palimpsest Book Production Limited,
Falkirk, Stirlingshire

Printed and bound in Great Britain by
Clays Ltd, St Ives plc

THE CRADLE

CHAPTER ONE

Dani Whalen noticed the first slivers of whitewater ahead on the Roaring Fork River, the current picking up.

"Okay," she called out to the eight people in helmets and life vests aboard her raft, "it's been pretty much a nature hike so far. Anyone ready for a little fun?"

As if on cue, the young couple from L.A. decked out in their bright Lululemons, Maury and Steve from Atlanta, he just a month into his retirement from a sales job, and the family from Michigan with their kids in the bow, all shouted back in unison, "*We* are!" and "Let's do it!"

"Good to hear!" Dani said, catching the sight of spray up ahead from the opening set of rapids known as Entrance Exam, "'cause you've come to the right place."

Dani was a whitewater guide along the stretch of the river known as Slaughterhouse Falls, outside Aspen,

Colorado. And by "fun," she meant navigating the series of eight Class Three and Four rapids that were the main draw of the river's four-mile run. Not that there was much real danger. They were all well-protected, of course, and Dani had done this run hundreds of times with barely a hitch. But the first sign of froth rising usually did engender a blanched face or two—Class Fours had a way of doing that to first-timers. But Dani knew exactly how to get them going as well.

On any morning, she could point to an eagle soaring above the tree line, or a long-branch elk with its doe along the river's edge; or a silver trout streaking underneath them in the current, which was definitely picking up now. That's why she loved what she did. That, and the triumphant yelps and whoops that were always a part of being shot out of Crossbow, icy water cascading all over you.

But it was the thrill of whitewater that was truly in her blood.

She had been a geology major back in college, back east at Bowdoin in Maine, and she could easily have been in med school or doing fourteen-hours days on Wall Street like a lot of her friends, probably making more in one month than what she pulled in in a season out here. But this river was in her blood. She'd grown up on it. She knew most anyone who had anything to do with it. After college she came back for the summer, and started earning money doing for work what she'd always done for love, and entering a few competitions.

4

She knew she wasn't exactly building a real life for herself remaining out here—guiding in the summer, teaching snowboarding to the youngsters in the winter—certainly not a career. Her dad was an orthopedic surgeon, at Brigham and Women's Hospital back in Boston, but he was in Chile right now on a teaching fellowship. Her older sister, Aggie, was in med school in Austin, and her younger brother, Rick, the real brain of the family, was studying 3-D graphic engineering at Stanford.

But Dani loved what she was doing—not to mention she could make it over the Gallows, a Class Five on the Colorado River with a twenty-foot drop, as well as any of the guys. And for her there was no payback better than the wide-eyed thrill and the yelps of exhilaration from a family being shot out of Cartwheel, with its 180-degree spin, to remind her of how much happier she was out here than back east behind a desk somewhere. In her skin-hugging neoprene vest and Oakley shades, her sun-streaked curly blond hair up in a scrunchie, her blue eyes focused on the river up ahead, every day was a reminder, that for the time being at least, she'd made the right choice.

That morning, she was handling the early morning run. Out at eight, back by noon. It was one of those picture-perfect Colorado days: the sky blue, the scent of aspens filling your nostrils, whitewater biting at you from the late spring runoff. Megan and Harlan, nine and eleven, were up in front with their parents right behind them. Dani didn't want to scare them, though navigating the Falls pushing around two thousand cubic feet per second did require a bit of technique. Everyone was laughing, pitching in paddling, enjoying the ride. Her job was to give them the time of their lives.

As they made their way around Jake's Bend, for the first time they could see the froth from Entrance Exam rising into the air. That's when you knew you didn't come here for a nature ride.

"*Look!*" Harlan was the first to point up ahead.

"I don't know . . ." Dani said teasingly, "those Exams are looking a little angry this morning. I hope everyone studied up!" It was a bit of a performance, of course, to build the tension. The real trick was not letting them realize that. She always loved catching those first looks of anxiousness on everyone's faces about what lay ahead.

"We may lose a few of you over the side," she said, "so remember what I said if you end up going in." Feet-first, and not to struggle against the current. And if they got trapped in an eddy, to just relax, not fight it, and sooner or later it would pop you back out. Dani had to tell them all that—like a flight attendant pointing out the exits on a plane—but in three years of guiding she hadn't had an incident yet. "You people on the left, I'm gonna need a little help today, okay? I need you to paddle like crazy as soon as I give the word. Otherwise, we won't make it through. You all up for that?"

6

They all took hold of their paddles and responded with nods of determination. *"We are!"*

"Good," Dani said, maneuvering the raft down the left side of the rapids.

"So what about us . . .?" Steve, the retired salesman from Atlanta who was on the right side asked with some disappointment.

"Okay, you guys on the right, I didn't mean to leave you out . . ." Dani held back, timing it perfectly as they reared, about to go over the first big dip. "All *you* have to do is just hold on for your lives!"

The froth kicked up and the raft plunged about five feet as she traversed through the tricky S-curve at the top of Entrance Exam, a chute of three interlocking, swirling rapids. The large raft careened against a rock. Everyone screamed as they were thrown up and down, out of their positions. "Okay, left side . . . Get ready . . ." Dani warned. "We're gonna take on some big-time water in a second." The raft kicked sideways, bouncing up out of a hole like a rubber bath toy in a tub.

"Now, paddle, everyone! *Paddle!*"

They lurched forward, nine paddles propelling them down the chute, icy water spilling in from all sides. Everyone on the left side worked feverishly, letting out screams and whoops. Dani guided the raft around and they spun through the last part virtually sideways, a huge *"Whoa!"* sounded as they dropped down another four-foot dip and then bounced out as if ejected by a slingshot, water cascading everywhere.

"*All right!*" Dani hollered. Everyone was screaming and drenched. "Everyone like that?"

"That was so cool!" Megan shouted, as they made it into a calmer stretch in between rapids.

"We lose anyone?" Dani asked above the whitewater roar. "Look around. I get docked if I don't bring everyone back. Harlan, still with us, up there?"

The young girl was gleeful. Most fun ever. Her older brother, though, didn't seem to think so and looked about as white as a ghost. Dani called up front, "What's the matter, Harlan, you eat something that didn't agree with you this morning?"

"No, ma'am," Harlan said, blanched. "That was just really scary, that's all."

Everyone laughed.

"Well, now you're a pro. From here on, it's a piece of cake. And left side, that was great work! I want to thank you all for pulling us through. I did mention, didn't I, that this was my first trip down, solo . . ." They all turned back to her. "*No?* Gosh, I left that out. I thought I'd told you all that. Well, maybe not my first, actually. I did do a demo run with one of the instructors when they gave me the job."

Everyone was laughing. Barney's Revenge was next. A legitimate Class Four. Followed by the Falls. Then One Too Far, where after you're sure you're through and start to relax, there's this unexpected five-foot dip where your stomach drops along with the raft—the spot where Dani always yelled out, "Well, that's the one too far!"

By Hell's Half Mile they'd all been scared, exhilarated, bounced around like on a barroom bronco. Totally drenched. There were only a couple of more rapids to go. The Baby's Cradle and Last Laugh, both less challenging Class Twos and Threes. The river was slightly calmer down here. Flat water, it was called. Though because of all the rains of the past week and the late spring runoff, there was a ton of water pushing them around, so every rapid posed a little challenge.

"Coming up on the Cradle . . ." Dani called out, a series of five interlocking chutes that gave you the sense of being rocked back and forth, hence the name. The first one always took you by surprise. She said, "I know I kinda gave you all the impression that it was going to be a piece of cake from here on in . . . Well, sorry—" As if from nowhere, the current grabbed them. "You all better start to paddle, guys . . . 'cause I'm afraid I lied!"

The next sensation was your stomach plummeting like a jet that had just dropped three thousand feet, dipping and rising, water spilling in. The adrenaline was rising. Everyone screamed. It was slightly tricky here, bounce off a rock and come out of a turn the wrong way and you could capsize. Once, Dani spun around and had had to make it through Slingshot backward and had almost fallen out herself. This time she nailed it perfectly, excited whoops of "All right!" and "Piece of cake!" coming from Harlan, who was now clearly enjoying himself, along with a lot of water-soaked smiles.

"You guys are proving to be tougher than I thought. So next up—" Dani positioned herself to take on the next rapid.

That was when she saw something up ahead along the shore that didn't seem right.

It was just a flash of red at first, below the third of the Cradle's rapids, the easiest, called Baby's Rattle. For a second it just looked like an overturned kayak floating there, which happened occasionally. Everyone else was either paddling or laughing at their drenched raft mates and hadn't noticed it yet.

But as she drew closer, her worst fears grew real. It wasn't just a kayak out there, there was something inside. Someone in it. The flash of red she saw turned out to be the rider's wind jacket. Suddenly the people up front spotted it, too, pointing.

"Oh my God, what's that! There's someone in there!" Harlan's mother exclaimed.

"I see it," Dani said, feathering the raft closer. "Everyone just stay calm." Though inwardly she acknowledged that this wasn't a good sign. "We're gonna pull in over here and I'll go take a look."

She pitched the raft along the easiest route down the next chute, her heart beating anxiously now. She knew most of the people who rode out here, especially the ones who came out this time of the morning.

"I'm gonna pull in over there." She steered toward a shallow rock bed up ahead along the shore. "I want you to all get out." That way the raft wouldn't continue to drift downstream with her team still in it. "Steve, Dale," she said to the two largest guys, "I want you to help me drag the raft up onto shore. Everyone please wait here. I'm gonna go take a look. I'm really sorry you have to see this."

They disembarked and dragged the raft up onto the shore bed until it was secure. Dani grabbed the radio out of the nylon gear case and clipped it to her belt. "Everyone, please, wait here. The current's a little tricky and can take you by surprise. So whatever you do, don't wade in after me."

They all muttered, okay.

She ran along the shallow rock bed in her Teva sandals, until she got as close as she could to the over-turned craft. It was trapped in an eddy pool, water swirling all around. Some forty feet from where she was. The current was still powerful here, enough to make what she was doing dangerous. Dani traversed her way across the rocks, slick as ice from a few thousand years of water rushing over them, her rubber sandals seeking whatever traction she could find. If she slipped, the current would hurl her down the final leg of the Cradle. She'd be separated from her crew. Not to mention, it was dangerous. She had no helmet. This wasn't exactly smart.

Once or twice she almost slipped and had to catch herself, whitewater lashing at her legs. The overturned kayak was maybe ten yards from her now, on its side in the swirling pool. No sign of movement inside. The current tugging at her from all around.

Without a rope or a partner, she knew what she was doing really wasn't the smartest idea.

Finally, she made it across, straddling the eddy where the kayak had come to a stop.

"Can you hear me?" she called out. But whoever was inside wasn't responding and hadn't moved. She could see it was a guy, but his face was in the water, the current slashing all around. He wasn't wearing a helmet, either. Everyone always thought they could take this river without a care. Dani bent down, positioning her legs on the rocks for traction, and flipped the body over on its side.

Her stomach dropped, just as precipitously as if she had plummeted over the falls herself. She stared for a moment, shocked and disbelieving, denial, then sorrow filling her inside.

She knew him.

She stared into the dead rider's drained, colorless face.

She knew him well.

for a pulse, not finding even a hint of a heartbeat. *Oh, Jesus, no* . . . She rested him back down in the river.

Trey.

She knew he came out and did an early run before work sometimes, just to keep his feet in the game, now that he had a regular job. Regular, meaning off of skis, the mountain, or the river. She recalled how a few years back he and Dani had ended up together after last call at the Black Nugget, when Dani had come back after college after her mother had died. It wasn't much of a relationship, or even what you'd call a fling. Trey wasn't exactly boyfriend material back then. He was a quiet, rugged guy from a small town up north, and with his long ponytail, his washed-out, blue-eyed smile, and that easy, but confident way, women always seemed to flock to him. As Dani had a couple of times, maybe a little rootless and angry back then over her mom.

But somehow Allie Benton made all that change. Trey settled down, married, cut his hair. He even got a totally "straight" job managing the Outdoor Adventures shop in town. They had a kid. Petey. Who everyone said made Trey a changed man. Dani had last seen him a couple of months ago at the Post Net store in town. He was mailing off an application to the national ski trade show. He'd developed this custom mounting for those GoPro action cameras that skiers and riders put on their helmets, and which they were selling like crazy

14

in the store. Dani remembered thinking, *Who'd ever figure Trey Watkins for an entrepreneur?* Amazing what having a kid could do.

And here she was staring at him now. Bloodied and crumpled. Those washed-out blue eyes that looked like Roger Daltrey's of the Who stilled. It didn't make a bit of sense where they were. Trey could handle a rapid like the Cradle with Petey on his lap. He could do it blindfolded, even *with* this amount of water being pushed around. Dani inspected his kayak. She didn't see any gashes or dents. She looked at the oozing abrasion on the side of his head. She just closed her eyes and shook her head in disbelief.

Poor Trey.

She thought about trying to drag the body out and administer CPR, but he was gone. It was clearly too late. She took out the radio from her belt. The company bus was set to meet them all not too much farther downstream. It was already on its way there.

"*Rich.* Rich . . ." she called in. "Can you hear me? It's Dani."

No one answered. Only a scratchy static came back.

"Rich, get on the horn, quick, I need you," she said, trying again. "It's urgent. Something's happened here."

"You at the fords already?" Her tour partner finally came on the line. "God, you're early, Dani, it's only—"

"Negative, Rich. I'm at the bottom of the Cradle and we've got some trouble here. There's been an accident."

15

"Oh, shit," he went, imagining the worst. "Everyone okay . . .?"

"Not us," Dani said. "It's Trey Watkins. His raft flipped over. There's a gash on his head. He's not breathing, Rich."

"*Trey?* Oh my God . . ." Everyone knew him. "Any sign of a pulse?"

"Negative, again. I can't believe this, Rich." Trey could ride with the best of them out here. The most challenging water was all well behind him. She looked back and saw her raft team all gathered on the shore, looking on. "I'm holding him here, Rich. He's dead."

CHAPTER THREE

Chief Wade Dunn kneeled down on the rocks overlooking the river, as the Pitkin County Rescue Team pulled the kid out of the water.

Not a kid really. He was twenty-nine. One of those adrenaline junkies around town who did it all. Off-terrain skiing. Paragliding. Mountain biking. The on-site opinion of one of the EMTs who inspected the body was blunt-force trauma to the head and possibly a broken neck. Any one of those rocks could have caused it. No telling how far the raft had continued down. *Made you wonder.* Wade watched, lifting his Stetson custom cowboy hat. Trey Watkins was also a topflight river rider. This far downriver, he was way past anything that might have been thought of as a challenge. Wade knew his young wife. Allie. Pretty, and must be quite a gal to tame

17

someone like Trey. And things were just starting to take off for the guy. A new kid, and he had this camera-mount business that was just getting off the ground. Allie's father, Ted Benton, who owned a rib restaurant and a small hotel in town, once joked to Wade that his son-in-law was going to make them all look poor.

Wade watched the rescue boys do their job. *Look at him now.*

They lowered down a stretcher, then hoisted the body back up the slope, and cut a path in the brush to where the emergency vehicles had parked on the road. Wade stood up and looked at the body as they brought it by. It looked exactly like what it probably was: the kid must've flipped and struck his head on the rocks. Enough to cause that wound or to break his neck. Probably trying out some slick new move. Grab some air or a spin-o-rama, or whatever they call them today. And not wearing a helmet. Not as smart as ol' Ted thought, apparently. These kids, they all think they're invincible. Come here from all parts, think their life is a fucking X Game. They'd do a drug and alcohol test in the postmortem. Who'd bet on what they'd find?

Thrill junkie.

He was like that once, too, Wade reflected. Invincible, or he surely thought so. That was back when he was the sheriff in Aspen. Not Carbondale, the little commuting town thirty miles down the road where everyone lived who couldn't afford to live in Aspen. Shit, he could've pretty much run for mayor back then. Or governor. Anything he wanted. He knew all the big celebs—Don Johnson, Melanie Griffith, Goldie Hawn, and all the big CEOs flying in on their Learjets and Citations. Now look at him. Divorced. Twice. Widowed once, though they had been living apart. A couple of stints in detox. Running a police force one-tenth the size of what he used to, and lucky to have the damn job at that. Looking a whole lot older than his fifty-seven years. Basically broke. Now he was what, the mayor of the sober community here in town? Younger, more ambitious men all waiting in line for him to retire.

Then there was Kyle. His boy from Wade's first marriage. Came back from Afghanistan missing a leg and an arm, and his brain rattling around in his head like loose change. What did they expect *him* to do in life? And who was going to take care of him? His mom was down in Florida somewhere. Working on a cruise ship, last he heard. Kyle was still rehabbing in a VA hospital in Denver, where he'd been for two years. Learning to eat peas with that new bionic hand they've given him. Basically the same age as this kid, Trey.

Kyle had maybe five, six more months and then he was out. Who was going to watch out for him? What with the government cutting back benefits every day, and all the mess with the VA hospitals. Wade went down once a week to see him. Someone was going to have to help him in life. Pay for the kind of van to get him around, or retrofit his house to make it easy to live there. And all those bloody therapists . . .

"Wade."

Dave Warrick came up from behind and put a hand on Wade's shoulder. "Just letting you know, I closed down the river to traffic for the next few days. Until we get this fully figured out. I called into Denver." The Roaring Fork was in a state park. "Parks Service'll be sending someone around just to make sure."

Dave ran the Pitkin County sheriff's force in Aspen now. Wade's old position. They had jurisdiction here. He was nice enough. Wasn't his fault his old boss had been mixing bourbon and OxyContin he'd stolen from his own evidence locker. That had taken every friend Wade had left to get behind him. Not to mention every dollar too.

Wade agreed. "Seems like the right move, Dave."

"I think you know the family, don't you?"

"His wife's." Wade nodded. "He was from up north somewhere, I think. Maybe from around Greeley."

"I took a statement from Dani. She said the kid was quite the rider."

Wade shrugged. "Who knows what he was trying to do. Flips, three-sixties. These kids all watch Shaun White and think they're him, minus the red hair. Doesn't matter what they're riding."

"I hear you. So you want me to go with you? To see

his wife. These things are never easy. Never hurts to have someone along."

"Thanks." Dave never used his new position to make Wade feel smaller than he was. "But after twelve years in AA, telling people how their life is about to come tumbling down on them, I think that's one job I'm equipped to do these days."

"Well, let me know if I can help." They stood on the rock, looking. "Just seems like a big fat waste of a life to me." The Aspen police chief shook his head. "Funny, isn't it?"

"What?"

Warrick shrugged. "How it was Dani that found him . . .?"

"Chief, can you come over here . . ." One of the troopers interrupted them. Dave and Wade both turned, but it was Warrick they were calling. They were getting set to load the body into the van.

"As I said, let me know if I can help, okay . . ." Dave patted Wade on the shoulder. "I'll be in touch when we have something back from medical."

"Thanks."

Funny . . . What *was* funny was that for twenty years, Wade felt like his life was running down his own set of rapids. Lying to everybody. Hiding what he'd done. Losing his wife. Then his town. Knowing one will capsize you in the end, just like Trey here.

Charles Alan Watkins III. Sounds like some judge somewhere. Wade watched them load the body. You can only make it through so long, right? Riding through life that way. Without a helmet. That's the truth.

Wade scratched his head and headed back to his car.

He knew sure as anything, one time he wouldn't make it out of those rapids, either.

CHAPTER FOUR

There was a kind of memorial gathering that night at the Black Nugget, the bar in Carbondale where a lot of the river riders and top skiers hung out. A few of them had already gone over to the house and paid their respects to Allie. No one could believe what happened: the bottom of the Cradle getting the best of someone like Trey. Everyone agreed that it had to have happened farther upstream, like at the Falls or Slingshot, and the current carried him down. That was the only way anyone could see it.

Allie told a few people that her husband had gone out the previous night. A friend of his from the shop was getting married and a bunch of the guys took him to Justice Snow's, a bar in Aspen, for shooters and kamikazes. Apparently he made it back home around

23

midnight. Allie said maybe he was a little tipsy when he came to bed, but in the morning he was up at half past six pumped to catch a run or two before work. All that new water out there, two thousand cubic feet per second. "Be back before nine, hon," he said and gave her a kiss.

Same ol' Trey.

At the bar, a bunch of them were still sitting around after nine P.M., going through their favorite Trey stories. His good friend Rudy was there, whom he'd ski off-terrain with for years. And John Booth, a paragliding instructor and sometime river guide, and his girlfriend, Simone. Alexi, a ski rep, and couple of others sat around, everyone trading stories and pitching in for beers. Dani was on her third Fat Tire. Rudy was telling one how he and Trey were once skiing out of bounds behind Highlands, trying to map out some new terrain for a Warren Miller film.

"The snow was pretty loose back there. The mountain had issued an avalanche alert, but Trey said the powder seemed pretty firm. 'Anyway,' he said, 'Roots, you and I can outski whatever comes down that mountain. Look at it,' he said, talking about all the fresh powder. 'It's once-a-season quality, Roots. One hundred percent pure.'"

"That was Trey," said Alexi, lifting his drink.

"That was Trey, *pre*-Allie," John Booth clarified.

"Totally pre-Allie," Dani said. "Post-Allie, Trey wouldn't even cut to the front of a lift line."

"You got that right," John's girlfriend, Simone, said.

"So we're zooming down this fall line," Rudy went on, "and Trey's ripping down the slope at full speed, eight feet of air at a time. I'm just doing my best to keep up, maybe twenty yards behind. And suddenly the ground shakes and I hear this rumble . . . I look behind and it's this wall of white coming at me from the summit. I didn't even have a second to react. Only to think to myself, *Okay, Roots, this is the day that you die!* It just slammed into me and took me away. I figured I'm gonna hit some tree at a hundred miles per hour or be buried under ten feet of snow, and Trey and I are goners. Finally it stops. I'm completely covered up. Not a sound. No one around. I don't even know which way is up. I'm yelling, trying to make an air pocket around me and I got my GPS, but who knows if Trey's got his. Or if he's in the same boat. I'm pretty scared, but I'm also so f-ing mad at him for dragging me down there. I still had one of my poles and I'm jamming it in the direction I think up is, screaming holy hell, trying to show anyone around I was there.

"Suddenly, I hear someone calling my name. 'Roots. Roots? Are you there?' Guess who? I'm going, '*I'm here!* I'm right fucking here, you sonovabitch. You're alive!' I'm jerking my pole around like this." Rudy thrust his two arms in all directions.

"So he's standing right above me. Trey, bless his soul. I'm going, 'Get me out of here! Get me out!'"

25

The sonovabitch has got to hear me. Then I hear, 'Listen, dude, I'm sorry to leave you like this, but I gotta meet someone at Starbucks. I'm gonna head back up to the lodge for a bit. Hey, you want a latte, man? I'll bring one back for you. You like yours with or without froth . . .?' I'm screaming, 'Get me out!' I start jerking the pole around. I wanted to kill him. Suddenly I break through. Turns out I was only about two feet under. He said he could see my boots the whole time. Who the hell knew . . ."

"Just be glad that it was Trey you were with and not me," John Booth said, grinning; "otherwise you'd still be down there."

"Funny." Rudy sneered at his friend, taking a swig of beer.

"I actually saw him at Starbucks, just after that," Alexi, the ski rep, said in his French accent, but with a completely straight face. "He said he left you back there and asked should he go back and dig you out? I said, 'Aw, what the hell.' He asked if he should bring you a latte and I told him, 'Look, don't go all crazy now . . .'"

"That was Trey," Artie, his ski tuner in the shop, said.

They all clinked mugs again.

"It just makes no sense." John Booth shook his head. "Where this happened. The Falls, maybe. Or even Catapult. Trey could do the Cradle with Petey on his lap."

"Or why he was out there without a helmet?" Dani said.

"Trey didn't wear a helmet," John Booth said. "Off-terrain maybe, or if he was doing tricks."

"You're wrong," Dani said. "I saw him lots of mornings out there. Since Petey was born he damn well did wear one."

"Anyone find one?" John Booth looked at her. "The rescue team was all over the place out there."

Dani shrugged. She had waited around to see after she gave her deposition to the police. "No."

"So there you go. Probably trying a one-eighty or a rollover, or something, and all that water got to him. Maybe his reactions *were* a little dulled from the night before, who knows? Anyway, here's to my man." John raised his mug. "To Charles Alan Watkins the Third."

"To Trey!" Everyone at the table joined in.

Through the crowd, Dani saw Geoff Davies come in.

Geoff was the owner of Whitewater Adventure, where Dani worked. He was thirty-four, from Australia, had a master's degree in psychology, and had moved out here from L.A. after a divorce and bought the business. He built it up, with a clothing line and videos and state-of-the-art equipment. He and Dani had been seeing a bit each other for the last few months. Not a big thing, and probably not the smartest. either. Taking up with the boss. But it was only now and then, and Geoff was an upbeat, good-hearted guy, and smart. And anyway it wasn't like this was some Fortune 500 company and there was a whole corporate hierarchy where it could get around. Whitewater Adventures had eight full-time employees.

"I heard this was where you could lift one up to Trey Watkins?" Geoff came over to the table.

"That it is," John Booth said. "One more round," he said, motioning to Skip behind the bar. A few of them had already had four or five, and that was becoming clear. "Sit right down."

"Thanks." Geoff grabbed the empty chair next to Dani. "Hey."

"Hey." She shrugged back. Though everybody probably already knew, they always kept things cool and gave each other just a friendly kiss on the cheek.

"So how're you doing?" He gave her an affectionate stroke to her hair, which Dani had tied back in a thick ponytail. He had wiry brown hair and soft, gray eyes.

"Hanging in there. Everyone get back okay after Rich picked them up?"

"Not exactly how we normally like to end our deluxe Roaring Fork River Thrill Experience . . . But yes. I gave them all a full refund, of course. Not that anyone really wanted it. Up until then they all had a terrific time and they all said you were great. And how you handled it. They even left some tips for you. It just seemed the right thing to do. Especially with the kids in there."

"I think it was the right thing." Dani squeezed his thigh under the table. "That was nice." The new round of beers arrived and they all toasted Trey one more time,

Geoff as well. Dani downed a long swig, maybe a quarter of the mug.

"I heard his father's coming down tomorrow," Geoff said. "He's a farmer from up north somewhere."

Rudy nodded. "Trey always said he came from a small farm. He mentioned once that lately it had fallen on hard times."

"There's been a pretty long drought up that way," John Booth added.

"Two or three years."

"Sometimes your luck just runs out." Rudy shook his head, enough beer that he was growing melancholy. "He just hit a rock the wrong way and . . . Just a freakin' accident. Could happen to any of us the same way."

"It wasn't no accident." They all heard a voice ring out from behind them.

Everyone looked around. A guy named Ron was at the bar—Rooster, everyone called him, because he had long, straggly hair, a pockmarked face, and a pointy chin. He was a balloon operator for one of the sightseeing companies in Aspen that took tourists up for a view of the valley. Rooster was in his fifties, a heavy drinker, who was always running his mouth off somewhere. No one cared for him much.

"What are you talking about?" Rudy shifted around.

"Just that it wasn't no accident," Rooster said again. His eyes were bright and kind of intense, either from the beer or with mischief, and he sat there, looking at them, seeming kind of pleased. "All I'm saying."

"What do you mean, it 'wasn't no accident'?" John Booth said, mocking Rooster's grammar. "What the hell was it then?"

"Not for me to say." Rooster shrugged. "Just that he wasn't alone."

"*Wasn't alone* . . ." John shook his head and rolled his eyes. "And you know this, *how*, Rooster . . .?"

"'Cause I was up there. This morning. Just after light. And I seen it. I seen what happened."

There was silence. "You got something on your mind, Rooster, better let it rip," said Rudy, shifting around in his chair.

For a moment, Rooster puffed out his chest like he was about to. The guy was always a weird duck. He always said he'd been a roadie for the rock group Boston; clearly they'd invited him to the party room one too many times. He didn't have a whole lot of friends and mostly hung out alone. Dani had seen him drunk once or twice and it wasn't a pretty sight. He'd been let go from his job by the owner of the tour company, but one of the operators had quit and it was summer, so apparently he was back on a temporary basis. Mostly, she just felt sorry for him.

"We're waiting, dude . . ." Rudy tapped his finger. Rudy was large and had had a couple, and was known to have a short fuse. It had been a long day, and they had all lost a friend. It wouldn't take much for him to let it go. "Now would be the time . . ."

"All I'm saying is, you didn't see what I saw." Ron backed down. He glanced around, looking for a way to get himself out of trouble. "He just wasn't alone out there, that's all." He sat there, bouncing a leg against the barstool, as if thinking, maybe this wasn't the smartest thing.

"You're saying someone did this? So who was with him?" John Booth pressed.

Rooster saw that he was sliding headfirst into a mess. He cleared his throat, and stammered a second, evading the question.

"*Ron . . .?*" Dani pitched in, seeing he had gotten all nervous. "It's okay. What did you see . . .?"

"Nothing," Rooster finally said. His eyes hung, seeming both shot down and defeated, and they seemed to settle on Dani's with a kind of contrite, regretful smile. "Nothing more to say." He raised his glass to Rudy and John. "I'm sorry for your loss."

"C'mon, Rudy, that's the end of it . . ." John Booth pulled his friend back around by the arm. "Just Rooster being Rooster. Sit back down and have a wing. We've all had a bunch to drink."

"I ain't drunk," Rooster chimed in again. "Been clean for fifteen days now. It's ginger ale. See . . .?" He held up his drink. "Anyway—to your friend." He tilted his glass.

31

"To Trey . . ." Rudy nodded grudgingly, turning back around. Under his breath, he muttered, "Asshole."

"I think you're right," Dani said to Geoff, sensing the shift in the mood. "Time for me to move along." She went into her jeans pocket and came out with a couple of twenties.

"No way," John Booth and Alexi seemed to say as one. They pushed her money back. "Your money's not good here. Not after what you had to do today."

"Thanks," she said.

"You want to stay with me?" Geoff asked. "It's a long way back."

"I'm fine," she said. She put her hand lightly on his thigh and smiled. "Thanks. But don't worry about me. I'll be fine. Besides, Blu will get me back." Blu was her three-year-old yellow Lab, who went with Dani everywhere. She stood up and said, "It's a work night, everyone, or at least it is for somebody out there . . . Time for me to get back home."

CHAPTER FIVE

Blu got up from snoozing in the back as Dani climbed into her Subaru wagon. "C'mon, Blu, baby . . ." He stepped up to front, wagging his tail happily. "You're shotgun, dude. Time to get me back home."

Carbondale was thirty miles northwest up Route 82, and there were always a bunch of cops out at night. And Geoff was right, she'd probably had had one more than she should. She turned on a CD, a local cover band named Wet Spring. She made the turn onto Main and then went on through the rotary, heading onto 82. She settled in for the forty-minute ride.

Sure, accidents always happened, she knew. And that was likely what it was. John Booth was probably right, he could have been trying out some old spins or flips. He could have been going down backward.

There was so much beautiful water, he could have easily hit his head a million ways, with no helmet. You pitch into a rock, or get sucked under by an eddy or thrown by a hole. Anything could happen on the river. They all knew the risks. Trey more than any of them.

Dani sighed. "What did it really matter anyway, right, Blu?" How Trey died. He wasn't wearing a helmet. It's a lesson for them all. He was dead.

That's all.

Around the turnoff for Snowmass, she winced at the thought of Allie and Petey having to suddenly go it alone. To have their world ripped from them. Just like that. Like soldiers in the war, talking one minute, who drive over an IED. One day you've got a beautiful family and the sky is blue and the whitewater is rushing. The next day you're gone.

Her mind flashed back to Rooster: *You didn't see what I saw, that's all.*

That Ron was a hard one to like. An even harder one to put stock in and believe. But what he had said seemed to stay with Dani. *It wasn't no accident?*

Well, if it wasn't an accident, what the hell was it then? Was there another rider out there? Did someone else ram into him, and cause him to spill? Or did someone come out from the shore? There was that rock bed down there by the Cradle.

She tried to imagine Rooster in the air gliding by. Then she let out a sigh of disappointment, suddenly realizing he was totally full of shit. There was no way to see the Slaughterhouse Falls run from anywhere near where the balloons went up in Aspen. Even on a perfect day like yesterday. It was at least a couple of miles away. Whoever had said it was right: the guy was basically a quarter short of a dollar between the ears. And always starting trouble.

Rooster being Rooster again.

That was all.

Wet Spring was singing their hit, "Misunderstood," which she'd seen them do a couple of times, and Dani couldn't stop herself from singing along. Blu had his front paws on the divider and his hind legs in the backseat.

From there it was another fifteen minutes to Carbondale. She pulled off Route 82 and into town, which mostly dark now—nothing much happening here after ten P.M.—and turned onto Colorado Street and into her apartment complex: eight attached units facing Mount Sopris. She shared it with Patti, who worked at the yoga clinic, but Patti was away in L.A. doing some certification seminar. Her neighbor's calico cat, Cici, was slinking out on the lawn. She never strayed very far and sometimes walked along the fence that separated their decks when Dani was drinking her morning coffee or doing her sun salutations. And who, defying conventional wisdom, Blu seemed to get along with rather well.

35

"Hey, baby." Dani bent down and picked her up. Cici was purring. "How was your day? Mine was pretty terrible."

The door opened and Dawn stuck her head out. "Oh, Dani, sorry, she must've snuck out. We've been calling her."

"No worries," Dani said, handing the cat over. "I never mind a visit from my friend."

"We've got a zin open." Dawn was a massage therapist who worked at the St. Regis, and her boyfriend, Jerry, was a chef at the hotel, too. "You and Blu want to come over? Watch Jon Stewart?"

"Thanks," Dani said, "but I've had enough. Rough day."

"I know. We heard. So horrible. Did you know him?"

Dani shrugged, opening the door for Blu to go inside. "A little. More a while back than now."

"You're sure you don't want that glass of wine? It's a good one."

"Thanks, Dawn. I think I'll just crash. We'll do it another time."

"I understand." Dawn smiled. "Let me know if we can do anything for you, okay?"

"Thanks, doll. I will," Dani said back.

Inside, she peeled off the shell she'd had on since this morning and stepped out of her jeans. She threw herself down on the couch and took out the scrunchie from her ponytail and shook out her hair. She massaged her neck a little and blew out a weary blast of air.

36

Yes. Rough day.

She got up to make herself a cup of tea. Her cell phone vibrated on the counter. Part of her felt like she didn't even want to look who it was. She already knew who it was anyway. Geoff, making sure she'd made it home. He was a gentleman like that. Part of her just wanted to take a long shower and go to bed and wake up and better things would happen tomorrow. She listened to the buzzing a third time.

She looked at the screen and saw a name she couldn't place at first. *Ronald Kessler.*

Who the hell was that? Probably some marketing call. She was about to just let it go to voice mail when curiosity got the better of her and she just answered. "Hello?"

"Dani?"

By the time she put it together who it was he'd already told her. "It's Ron."

"Ron?"

"Rooster."

"Jesus, Rooster . . . *Ron,* how'd you get my number?"

"I had it once. Remember, you recommended some customers to us a year or two back."

"Oh, yeah, right." It struck her as a little creepy that Rooster had kept her in his phone all this time. "Listen, Ron, it's a little late and I'm just getting ready—" There was a lot of noise in the background.

"I know it's late, Dani. I don't mean to bother you,"

37

he said. "There was just something I had to say. About what happened back there at the bar."

"Look, we all had a little too much to drink . . ." In a weird way Dani always had a soft spot for Rooster. In the same way you might feel sorry for a stray cat. The guy was an outcast. But he didn't mean anybody harm. John Booth was probably right, he'd just taken one too many hits of something back in the day. "But Rudy was right, Ron. Trey had a wife and kid, and you can't just go around riling people up making accusations that you can't support."

"I wasn't making anything up. And I wasn't lying. About what I said I saw out there this morning."

He hesitated just like he had at the bar. She put on the kettle for her tea.

"Ron, if you've got something to say, just say it. Or else take it to Chief Dunn." She knew Rooster knew Wade. Wade was once his sponsor in AA, and that didn't go so well. Rooster had slipped several times and had a reputation of not being honest in the program. "And just so we're real here, you can't even see that part of the river from where the balloons go up. You know that better than anyone."

"I can't take it to Chief Dunn. There are some things between us. I know he thinks I'm a few of bricks short of a wall. Everyone does. And maybe I am. Plus, I wasn't supposed to be where I was out over the river earlier. I was the only one up today and this nice couple, they handed me a hundred-dollar bill to stay up there a while longer and let it drift. That's why I'm calling you."

Dani started to grow impatient. "Me?"

"*You* can take it to Chief Dunn, Dani. He'd want to know this."

"Ron, please . . ." Dani put in the tea bag and poured water into the mug. "It's been a rough day for everyone. And I'm getting ready for bed. So what is it you saw?"

"All I can say is, your friend wasn't alone out there on that river."

"I know, that's what you've been saying. Look—"

"He was wearing a red windbreaker, right?"

That took her by surprise. He was.

"And his kayak was blue . . .?"

Dani didn't answer, but her hesitation seemed to give Rooster the sense that he'd struck something with that.

"So I'm not so crazy after all, am I? I didn't know it at the time, but it had to be him, right?"

"So who was out there with him, Ron?" Dani's attention was suddenly aroused. "Ron, it's crazy in there. You still at the Nugget?"

"How about you meet me at the balloon field in the morning." Near the Aspen Industrial Park where the balloons went up from. "I got a ride at seven and we'll be all tethered back by eight thirty."

Dani didn't have a tour in the morning. And, yes, she could take it to Wade. Whatever Ron claimed he saw. He did have the color of Trey's kayak right, and what he was wearing.

"Will you be there?"

"All right, I'll be there," Dani said. She suddenly felt the hairs on her arms stand on edge. She didn't even like the idea of being alone with him.

"I know he was a friend of yours, Dani. But you were always a fair person to me. Not like some."

"Yes. I know that, Ron."

"So I'll see you at eight thirty, then. After my ride."

"Okay."

"And Dani . . ."

"Yes."

"I don't care what anyone thinks, I wasn't drunk. I wasn't drunk tonight and I surely wasn't this morning, either. You believe me, right?"

"Yes, I believe you." Before she'd left the bar, she checked with Skip, the bartender. To be sure. Rooster had been drinking ginger ale.

CHAPTER SIX

The sun came up slowly over the mountains the next morning, covering the Aspen Valley in streaks of yellow and rose, as the four balloons rose majestically into the sky.

It was a picture-perfect dawn, light dappling the moss, peaks bathed in glinting sunlight. Ron revved the burner with heat, the blue flame shooting into the envelope with a loud hiss, sending the balloon higher.

On board, the four passengers oohed.

"Take a look over there," Ron directed them. "That's Aspen Mountain there shrouded in shadow, and as we get up, you can see those two peaks to the west, those are the Maroon Bells, two of over fifty-three mountains in Colorado that are over fourteen thousand feet."

In his basket was some big-shot financial dude from

Connecticut, who was trying to work it out that he and his bundled-up trophy wife could get a private, trying to buy off the launch manager. But it didn't work out. And a middle-aged couple from Japan, equipped with the requisite camera and one, long fucking lens, Ron admired. At five hundred feet, the four balloons cut a beautiful path across the morning sky, each of them a colorful design of reds, yellows, and greens.

By seven, they were at six hundred feet, the maximum elevation today because of the winds, and Ron cut off the burner, cooling the air.

The view was amazing.

"Wave hi to your mates over there," Ron said, pointing to the closest companion balloon, maybe a hundred yards away. The Japanese couple waved and the husband aimed his gargantuan lens. The financier and his wife were bickering about where they were going to have lunch later, the burger at Ajax Grille or sushi at Matsuhisa.

Suddenly Ron felt a thud from above. The whole basket rocked back and forth. Everyone looked up. "What the hell was that?" the financial guy asked, his wife clearly a little spooked and not happy in the first place to be sharing the ride with the Japanese couple.

"Don't know," Ron said. "Maybe we hit a thermal. It's kind of like a wind inversion. There's a breeze today." He checked out the other balloons to gauge his relative height and noticed he had descended slightly. He opened the valve and shot a blast of flame hissing into the balloon, momentarily lifting it to where it was before. "I think we're okay. So check out that river to the northwest out there." He pointed. "That's—"

The basket wobbled again. He noticed them losing more altitude. Air was definitely leaking from somewhere. He may have to bring this baby down. Then suddenly he heard a tearing sound from above them. The basket lurched again, swaying. Everyone grabbed the sides. Ron shot more heat in, but nothing seemed to be happening. Except that they were losing air.

And altitude.

"Is everything all right?" the financier's wife asked, looking a little edgy.

Ron looked above and kept pumping as much heat as he could into the envelope. "Don't really know."

A call came in on the radio. Steve, in the next balloon. "Ron, you got something wrong on your right side. You're definitely losing your pitch. Can you see it? You better get yourself down. Pronto."

"I hear ya," Ron replied. "Exactly what I'm doing, Sorry, folks, seems to be some kind of malfunction up there. I'm going to have to take her down. Shouldn't be a problem." He kept pumping in as much heat as the balloon would take. But still they kept coming down.

"Cole! Cole!" he radioed in to the company attendant at the landing field. "Something's wrong with the balloon. We're leaking air. I'm coming back. Now.

43

"Nothing to worry about," he said supportively to his passengers, who were now clearly anxious. "We've got a malfunction in the canvas. But I'll get you down. These babies are fit to—"

Suddenly he heard another tear. They all heard it this time. *Phhfft.* "What the Sam Hill . . ."

The basket lurched again, this time terrifyingly. Then there was a deep groan emanating from above, hot air leaking out, colder air coming in.

The balloon swaying and collapsing.

Over the radio he heard, "Ron, you've got a full-scale implosion going on! I can see it. Get your ass down as fast as you can."

"I'm trying, I'm trying," Ron replied. He continued to rev the valves, thrusting as much heat as he could into the envelope, compensating for the cold air rushing in through the tear, to bring them down at a manageable speed.

It wasn't working.

"What's going on? What's going on?" the financial guy was yelling. Their descent started to pick up speed. "Do something!"

"I'm trying, I'm trying," Ron said. "Everyone be calm."

They were still five hundred feet up. He looked up and saw the huge tear on one side, a flap in the material buckling and falling over, a huge swath of it suddenly falling down on top of the basket, and to Ron's horror, catching the flame and suddenly igniting.

The balloon became engulfed in flame.

"*Do something!*" the financial guy's wife shrieked, her eyes bulging in terror.

"There's nothing I *can* do!" Ron replied, continuing to rev heat into the useless, crumpled canopy. He grabbed the radio. "Mayday, mayday, we're going down!" They started to fall out of the sky, picking up speed. The ropes holding the basket could catch at any second and then . . .

The financier's wife was sobbing on the floor mat. Her husband gripped the basket's rim and looked down in disbelief. The Japanese couple huddled together.

Ron shouted, "You know a prayer, this would be the time to say it."

He always wondered what this would feel like. How he would react. In his dreams he had dreamed it many times. It was like a bad trip. And he'd had many of those. "Mayday, mayday!" he screamed uselessly into the radio as the basket began to plummet. "*Oh Jesus Lord, we're going down!*"

CHAPTER SEVEN

Dani saw it as she headed into town before her rendezvous with Ron.

Around the cutoff to the Aspen Industrial Park just after the airport, traffic was being slowed into one lane. She saw EMT vehicles, their lights flashing, and it seemed as if every cop in the valley was there. A throng of people, many out of their cars, were lining the highway looking on. In the large field which the Aspen by Air Balloon Adventure used as their takeoff site, a plume of black smoke funneled high into the air.

What the hell had happened?

Dani pulled up to one of the cops who was waving on traffic. She recognized him as a guy she had gone to high school with, Wesley Fletcher. She rolled down her window and leaned out of her wagon. "What's the hell's going on, Wes?"

"Balloon dropped out of the sky. Five people on board, Dani. Traffic's being routed onto Rectory Street into town."

"Five people." Dani felt her stomach tighten *"Whose?"* she asked, though she was sure she knew the answer even before the question even was out of her mouth. "Whose balloon was it, Wes?"

"Aspen by Air. Rick Ketchum's company. They're up every day."

"I don't mean who owned it. Who was operating it?" Dani pressed, a feeling of dread grinding in the pit of her stomach. "The one that went down."

"All I was told was that there were four tourists on board. And everyone's dead. And some guy named Ron."

"Ron?" Dani's heart went still. *Rooster.*

"I guess the balloon fell apart at five hundred feet into a ball of flames. But, look, I have to wave you on now, Dani. Gotta get these vehicles routed over onto Rectory, and as you can see—"

"Is that Chief Dunn's car over there?" She saw a white and green SUV with the Carbondale police lettering on it, among the many vehicles pulled up in the field.

"I think that's him. I saw him drive up earlier."

"Thanks, Wes." Dani pushed on the gas and caught up to the car in front of her. She got as far as the rotary until she realized she no longer had any reason to be here now. She pulled over to the side and let her head drop against the wheel. *Poor Rooster*. Her heart felt heavy as she tried to imagine such a grisly descent. Things like this just didn't happen here. But that was only part of it. Part of what was making her insides feel so worrisome. The rest was what Rooster had claimed he'd seen yesterday, and now he was dead. The fool was going around shooting his mouth off.

He wasn't alone out there. That wasn't no accident.

Dani looked one last time at the plume of black smoke. Hot-air balloons just didn't fall out of the sky.

CHAPTER EIGHT

She waited until the end of the day, until she saw his vehicle parked outside the station back in Carbondale. She couldn't remember the last time she'd been to see him at work. Years. Certainly not since her mom had died.

"He's on the phone," a female duty officer said. Dani didn't recognize her.

It wasn't a big station, tucked into a corner of the Carbondale Town Center. Three or four desks, and some workstations. A room with a vending machine that doubled as an interrogation room. There were one or two detectives; whatever they did, Dani never knew. Any real investigation or forensic work was handled out of Aspen. When Wade took the job—the only job he could get—he joked that it was mostly setting up DUI roadblocks and the occasional marijuana bust.

And now, new state laws had even taken *that* away from him.

"If you wait over there I'll tell him you're here."

"I'm his stepdaughter," Dani said. "He'll see me."

She went right past her, the duty officer standing up, surprised, going, "Hey!" Wade was at his desk on the phone, his feet propped up against a drawer. The ever-present python-skin boots and that large, turquoise, Indian ring. He'd probably die with them on. On the shelf behind him were a couple of photos. Wade in his glory days. With his arm around Antonio Banderas and Melanie Griffith. Another with a younger-looking ex-president Gerald Ford. There were a couple of Kyle. One in his army uniform while in Afghanistan; the other, he and Wade fishing up in Idaho. Apparently, Dani hadn't make the cut. There were a couple of AA books stacked on the credenza, and an empty bourbon bottle, which he always said he kept close as a constant reminder of worse days.

"Let me know when they finish up . . ." Wade was saying. He eyed Dani unhappily, as the young officer who had asked her to wait rushed in after. Wade waved her off with a *Don't worry about it* gesture, motioning Dani into a chair.

She didn't take it.

"I'll check in with the guy from the Parks Service as soon as he finishes up," he said. "Be talking with you then. Thanks." He hung up and took his feet off the open drawer.

"The duty officer out there didn't make it clear I was on with business," he said, scowling at Dani like she'd burst in to sell him a new cell phone contract.

"You've got a problem, Wade."

"Thanks for pointing that out to me, Danielle. Let's see, five people are dead. The whole world's gonna be breathing down our backs looking for answers. I always knew we did a good job by sending you back east to that fancy college."

"*Six*, Wade. There are six people dead. And just to keep the record clear, you didn't send me. Mom did."

He wheeled his chair around to face her. "Well, I sure took you, didn't I? So anyway, six. If you count what happened out on the river. You'll have to forgive me, it's been a pretty crazy twenty-four hours here. Not that the two are in any way related."

"But that's just the problem." Dani stepped up to the desk. "I'm pretty sure they are. Related."

Wade snorted a short blast of air out of his nostrils, his round, sagging eyes regarding her both skeptically and condescendingly. "I asked you to sit, Danielle."

This time she sank into a hardwood chair across from him.

"And what makes you think some hotshot kid taking a spill on the river would be related to a tragedy like this . . .?"

"I was headed into to town to meet with Rooster," Dani said. "Just after it must've happened."

"*Rooster?*" Wade shrugged.

"Ron. Kessler, I think was his last name. He was manning that balloon."

"I knew who was manning the balloon, Danielle. And I knew his name. I called him a lot of things, but Rooster wasn't one of them. All right, you barged in here, you've got my attention. I don't know why your paths would cross with the likes of him, but you were going in to meet with him why . . .?"

"He was at the Black Nugget last night."

"Now why doesn't that surprise me one bit." Wade snorted derisively.

"A few of us were having a little tribute to Trey. Rooster . . . Ron was at the bar and cut in about how he saw something yesterday morning from his balloon."

"He saw something . . .?" Wade rolled his eyes.

Dani said, "Exactly how I thought you'd react, Wade. And why Ron said he didn't want to come to you with it in the first place. He heard us talking and he said what happened out there to Trey wasn't an accident. That he wasn't alone out there. He said he had seen something, but he backed down because Trey's friend Rudy Thommasson and John Booth were a little drunk and got him all nervous. You know how Rooster gets. Anyway, he called me after I got home and asked me to meet him this morning in town."

"Asked you to meet him . . .?" Wade scrunched his brow. "To tell you that Trey Watkins wasn't alone on the river. Meaning, what, that someone was along with him? Or was there when it happened? You're saying someone was responsible for his death?"

"I don't know what he meant. Only that he said it wasn't an accident. He was about to tell me after his run."

"Look, Danielle." Wade squared around. "I don't mean to speak poorly of the dead, but Ron Kessler was a person who wouldn't know what was real from a half-gallon jug of rotgut vodka. And when he wasn't boozing he was just a fool who would say anything that came into his mind if he thought it would get a rise. I bailed his ass out in AA enough times and he was never once honest with me. I even volunteered to be his sponsor once, when no one else in the program would have him. I don't know how they even let him operate that balloon, but from all I heard he did his job and it wasn't his fault."

"He wasn't drunk," Dani said.

"He wasn't drunk?" Wade eyed her skeptically and snickered.

"Last night. He wasn't. I know everything you said. We all thought so. But he made a big point of saying he'd been sober for three weeks. And I believe him. He even showed what he was drinking at the bar. Ginger ale."

"Dani, I don't care if the guy was sober as a preacher, Kessler would tell you whatever you wanted to hear if it stepped him up one tiny notch in his own importance. Your friend flipped his raft five miles out of town on the Roaring Fork River. Even if something did happen out there, whatever the hell he meant—which I'm not saying, only making a point—no way he could have seen that from the air."

"He said he was the only balloon up that morning and he took some extra cash from the customers to stay up and let it drift a bit over the valley. That's why he didn't want to bring it up. He didn't want what he did to come back to his boss and bite him. That, and because he knew you'd say exactly what you did. Which was why he came to me."

"Well, I guess I never made it much of a secret." Wade nodded. "You learn to live with people's weaknesses in the program. God knows, I've had to own up to enough of mine. But let's just keep it that ol' Ron, or Rooster, or whatever the hell he went by, zigged when the world zagged one too many times over the years and the world hasn't been a straight line to him since."

"Then I'd guess you ought to understand that yourself," Dani stared at him, "and be a little more sympathetic."

Wade's eyes grew fiery, but then they calmed, and he let out a long exhale. "Yes. On that point you're right. I do. Understand. But I don't have the time to argue that with you now . . ."

"Wade, look," Dani pulled up her chair, "anyone who knows anything knows Trey could handle the lower Cradle rapids in his sleep. And even if what took place happened somewhere farther upstream, say around the falls, the raft likely would have washed up somewhere north."

"So you're saying, what? Someone killed him? Someone was out there with him, like this Rooster said. And then what? That what happened to *him* up there this morning, and all those other poor people, was *what* . . . to keep that gerbil from running off his mouth off or something? To stop him from telling the world what he claims he saw. You did start this whole thing off implying they were connected."

"I don't know what I'm saying, Wade. But balloons just don't fall out of the sky. A day after someone goes around saying that they've seen something. Whatever else you might want to say about him, Ron did know how to handle himself up there. He'd been doing it for a lot of years."

"I don't know, maybe there was a rip or a flaw in the fabric or something. Or maybe something flammable got caught in the gas jet. The right people will figure that out. Or maybe your poster boy there just did something stupid, which he was eminently capable of doing, Dani." He shook his head.

"So tell me, where was Trey's helmet, Wade?" Her tone was starting to grow a bit defensive now.

"I don't know about Trey's helmet. Maybe he wasn't wearing a helmet. I mean the same guy would hurl himself off the summit of Aspen Mountain with only a sheet of nylon attached to him, so to me, it's not much of a stretch that he would go out on the river without a helmet."

"Well, you'd be wrong on that. Not since he had his boy. I saw him out there a dozen times. And yesterday you were sure he was either high or hungover. So what did toxicology come back with? I know the first thing they would have done was check his blood over in County."

"Jesus, you're sounding like a cop now. The river's closed for a day or so, so maybe you can find yourself a whole new career."

"He was a friend, Wade." She kept her eyes fixed on him. "So I'm asking, what did they say? About his blood?"

"About his blood . . .?" Wade shrugged and rocked back in his seat. "They said nothing, Danielle. Hundred percent clean. I'll give you that." There was a pause, one that seemed to carry the weight of the many issues between them, until Wade shook his head. "C'mon, Dani, who the hell would possibly want to kill Trey Watkins? Honestly . . ."

"I don't know."

"And all this because of some news flash from a totally disreputable source that he wasn't out there alone. Or your belief that he could handle that section of the river in his sleep? Or not finding any helmet?"

Wade stood up and came over, and sat on the edge of his desk. "Listen, Danielle, I get that he was a good friend, but what we have here are two tragic, but separate occurrences. Trey Watkins probably tried some ill-advised maneuver that got his head wrung up against a rock. That balloon, it'll come out there was something going on. It imploded. That's what the witnesses saw from the other balloon. Rare as it is, it happens. We get one shred of evidence that says it's something different, I'll be the first to jump on it. They got some team from the Parks Service in today and looking around the accident site. And I damn well know they'll be going over that balloon shell with a fine-tooth comb to find whatever they can, though God knows what that would be as it's nothing but a burnt-up mess, I'm afraid. How about you let me and Sheriff Warrick do our jobs. For God sakes, you're as headstrong as your mother. And you saw how that went."

"Seemed to go fine, Wade . . ." Dani said, her eyes flashing to the bourbon bottle on the credenza. "God knows how. Till those bottles were full and not empty."

"Easy to blame me, I admit . . ." Wade nodded and frowned. "I know we got some unfinished business between us, Danielle, but I was always a friend to you."

store on Galena, then bought the building outright, and then over the years, the one next to it and the one next to that, even becoming the mayor in town for eight years. When Dani was twelve, her mother married Wade, who'd had a few reversals in town, and who became the country sheriff mostly through his father-in-law's influence. Whatever the glitzy veneer, Aspen was then and has always remained a small town at heart, where insiders matter. Dani recalled them happy at first, and Wade became kind of a sizable personality about town, strutting around alongside the rich and famous in his trademark cowboy hat, python boots, and flashy rings.

But when Dani was sixteen, a miscarriage made her mom depressed, and then she started getting headaches. And Wade, whose self-destructive nature took over, stopped taking the kids fishing and camping and started coming home drunk—from parties he used to call his "public responsibilities," but then seemed to turn into all the time. Once he totaled his car and another time he got into a public fight with one of his officers right in the middle of town. He went into the program—even went away once for a month—but then he started using stronger stuff, which only came out much later, and which came to a head when he pilfered a couple of hundred OxyContin tablets from his own police evidence locker. By then it had all fallen apart for him and he was forced to resign. Her mother grew worse and worse, and

Dani took a semester off to care for her. But in Dani's sophomore year, Judy just suddenly seemed to give up and died. Complications from the disease, it was called. Her mom was taking her own share of medication back then, and Wade was mostly at his worst, and not much of a caregiver. But Dani still always pictured her in her mind, smiling and pretty, braiding Dani's long, curly hair and singing "Sweet Baby James" and John Denver songs with her, with those Colorado blue eyes. Dani even tattooed an "Ai," the Chinese symbol for love, on her shoulder, with her mother's initials.

So maybe Dani did always blame Wade a bit for her demise. Or at least, for not helping. Dani was in the process of transferring back to Boulder when her mom just fell off a cliff. For years Dani blamed herself for not having been there at the end. The suddenness had taken everyone by surprise. Wade may not have actually killed her; Dani had finally come to terms with that. But his own problems surely sapped the strength out of her and helped her to decline.

Dani drove along the river to the spot at the Cradle where Trey was found, which was now blocked off by tape with a Pitkin County police van parked there. She continued down about a half mile to a spot they called the Funnel, where the various currents fed into a narrow channel, about a quarter mile up from the ford, where the rapids tour ended.

She parked in a small turnout on the side of the road.

She knew the narrow pathway that led down to the river, which this far down was wider than upstream, but not much more than a rocky, shallow bed on each side. She knew this river like the back of her hand. She knew the currents, where they fed. As a kid, she had once lost a backpack in the current all the way back above the Falls, and weeks later she found where it had ended up.

At the Funnel. *Here.*

Dani climbed down through the brush and onto the shoreline. The alluvial currents here had widened out a deep gorge in the aspens and firs. She knew it was kind of like finding a needle in a haystack. Without even knowing if the needle was even hidden here. She saw a beer can glinting among the rocks. A flip-flop sandal was nearby, which must have slipped off someone's foot. A waterlogged Penn tennis ball. She kicked over an empty can of beans, stepping over the small, loose rocks. Because of the depth, the water color changed here from a clear blue and white to a musty gray.

It wasn't around.

She kneeled in the shallow bed, disappointed. It was kind of a long shot anyway. If it had washed down, she was pretty certain it would have ended up here.

She scanned the opposite side before going back up to her car.

Something glinted. Nothing more than a fleck of color amid the rocks on the shoals. Across the stream.

White.

The river was shallow here and easy to ford. Except for the narrow channel in the middle that was still about two feet deep where you could still traverse a raft. Dani went in in her shorts and Tevas and made her way across. About thirty yards. Her sandals gripped the silty river floor, water rushing by her knees. The current was mild here. No threat of being swept away. Not like what she had to go through to get to Trey.

She crossed toward the object she'd seen, which was nestled amid the rocks.

Whatever hope she had that she'd found something faded.

All it turned out to be was just a white plastic drink container. She bent down, picked it up and tossed it farther off the riverbed into the brush. Probably someone's water container that had fallen overboard. It could have been sitting here for months.

Maybe Wade was right. It was possible Trey had been just riding recklessly and hit his head against a rock. It's possible he wasn't wearing a helmet. Maybe Rooster did just make it all up—for the attention. To be the big shot. Anyway, it was now all kind of moot. Both Trey and Ron were gone. She'd never know, though something still inside her said—

Something farther along the shoreline caught her eye. Half submerged amid the vegetation along the shore. She went over, the black composite almost completely blending in with the gunmetal water and dark green vines.

She picked it up by the strap. It was a little scuffed, beaten up from its ride downstream, bouncing off rock after rock.

Her heart started to race.

Trey's helmet.

But it wasn't dented. Dented in the way it would have been if its wearer had sustained blunt-force trauma to the head.

Which had to mean one thing. That it hadn't been on Trey at the time he sustained his injury. If he'd cracked it with enough force to kill him you would have surely been able to see it. Holding the black helmet, Dani knew *that had to mean something, right?*

Her blood surged. So she wasn't wrong, at least, not about that part. Trey had been wearing it.

So maybe she wasn't so wrong about all the rest of it, either.

CHAPTER TEN

Back in her car, following the river back upstream, she searched for the spot above the lower Cradle where she had found Trey's body.

The road narrowed there, barely wide enough for two cars to pass, with dense brush crowding in from both sides. The aspens and pines were so tall here Dani could barely see the sky. She came up to the clearing where the rescue vehicles converged when they pulled Trey out. It hadn't rained since, and tire tracks and footprints were still visible all over the dirt road.

Dani heard the roar of the river slashing against the rocks below.

It was clear, even in just Class Two or Three rapids, that Trey couldn't have just nested to a stop here. His raft must have been carried down from farther upstream and come to rest in the eddy. She heard Rooster saying, *You didn't see what I saw. He wasn't alone.* Now she was even *more* certain he hadn't been lying.

But just what did that mean?

Had someone been along with him on his run? That wouldn't be hard to determine. The ranger station would know. But if it was all just a terrible accident, surely that person would have called it in. And if so, they surely wouldn't have taken such a lethal reprisal against Ron in the balloon.

No, it had to be something else. *It wasn't no accident out there* . . . Someone had to have stopped him.

The police vehicle was gone now. Dani made her way down the slope to the ridge above the river and scanned upstream. The cold spray off Baby's Rattle lashed at her, the sun glinting off her shades. It was possible that someone else had climbed down here and intercepted him on the river. But that would've had to have happened farther upstream. Or they'd have to have made their way down along the shoreline in between the first two rapids of the Cradle where the currents slowed a bit, in order for his body to have ended up here.

There were rocks in the river near where Trey was found. The Raptor's Teeth, they were called. Three sharp, pointed rocks that protruded out of the water, four to five feet high. If Trey had sustained a crash hard enough to cause his death, surely his helmet would show the impact. And it didn't. So how did it come off? How did it end up all the way downstream?

Dani followed the rapids from the high rocks, twenty or thirty feet above the river. She had to climb up and then down in order to follow the edge, but she was pretty nimble, having done her share of trekking and climbing in these hills. Once or twice, she even had to jump from one height down to another in her Tevas. If she stumbled she could easily fall in and hit her head or break a bone and be carried away. It was slow work; it took about ten minutes to climb a hundred yards.

Finally she made it to the Teeth. It was calm enough here for Trey to have been pulled over by someone. If a person had come out, pretending to need help. Or with a gun maybe. Yes, it could have happened here, Dani imagined. But why . . .? It was Trey. Why would someone have wanted to kill him?

She turned and looked back up the shore toward the road, and spotted something in the woods.

The narrowest pathway, which seemed to cut through the thick brush, barely wide enough to even be called a path. Barely wide enough for just a single person. It wound down directly above Baby's Rattle, the second rapid in the Cradle, right above the Raptor's Teeth.

So someone could have climbed down there from here.

Curious, Dani went back and followed the narrow path from the river's edge back up the slope toward the road. Thorny branches slapped in her face and scraped against her bare arms and legs. She was no scout or tracker, but she had the feeling someone had been here recently.

As she neared the road, she noticed something. She kneeled, sweating slightly in the sun, peeling back leaves and crushed branches on the ground to see.

It was like a small clearing had been made. Low branches were flattened against the ground, within a few yards from the road.

Not by hand, she could tell. It looked as if it was done by the front wheels of a vehicle.

So someone might well have been here.

She cleared away some of the leaves and brush on the ground. There were tire tracks. Something had pulled in—and whoever was in it had continued from the road via that pathway down to the Cradle.

To the very spot where Trey had been killed.

Her blood surged with vindication. It didn't prove a thing. Any more than finding the helmet did.

It didn't prove that Rooster was right. That, *it wasn't no accident out there . . .*

But he was damn well right on one thing.

Trey hadn't been alone yesterday morning. Someone had definitely been here.

CHAPTER ELEVEN

"Who the hell would want to kill Trey?" Wade screwed up his eyes, staring at the helmet Dani dropped on his desk.

"I don't know who'd want to kill him. But I told you he was wearing a helmet and he was. You see any significant dents on it anywhere? Don't you think if he received a head injury severe enough to kill him, there'd be some evidence on it somewhere?"

Wade's response was laced with impatience and rising frustration. "I'm not sure *what* I'm supposed to think." He took off his glasses and looked it over. "And you're saying this proves what . . .?"

"It proves he wasn't wearing it when he sustained his head injury. And the next question would be, Wade, how do you explain it coming off?"

"Don't teach me my job, Danielle. And I don't know how the hell it came off. Maybe he hit his head aside a rock. Maybe he took it off himself for some reason. To breathe. To take a leak for all I know. But this is all starting to cross the line. You're coming to me with this helmet, claiming it was Trey's, and that someone made their way down the rocks and then did what, lay in wait for him, to *kill* him . . .? Not even knowing for certain if he'd even be there."

"I know how it sounds. But Trey did a seven A.M. run a couple of times a week, so it wasn't a long shot that he'd be there. And I was looking around on the ridge above where I think it all might have happened and I found something else."

"You did . . .?" Wade's look of impatience was now amped up into the range of exasperation. "Surprise me, Danielle."

"I found a path. In the brush above the river. Leading back to the road. From exactly the spot where Trey had to have been killed."

"You mean where you think he had his accident, Dani. And if I need to remind you, there are paths all over the heights above that river. You and I have been through dozens of them. I don't see what one more proves."

"This one leads directly from the road to the spot just above the Baby's Rattle."

"The Baby's Rattle . . .?"

"It's a rapid on the upper Cradle where I think Trey was killed. Look, I know how it sounds, Wade. But I also found fresh tire marks near the road where that particular path came out."

"Dani."

"Which means someone else was there, and—"

"*Dani!*" She stopped. Wade sat back down. "We're dealing with a lot here. And this is starting to strain my nerves. Someone kills Trey in the river and then sabotages your pal Ron's balloon to keep it covered up?"

"He's not my pal, Wade. He wasn't even a friend. But that's not even the point. The point is . . . I don't know what it is . . ." She sat down, trying to lay out her argument with everything swimming around crazily in her head. "The point is we all know Trey could have done that run with his eyes closed. So how does he just upend, lose his helmet, crack his head. And then couple that with what Rooster saw . . .?"

"What he claimed to see . . ."

"What he *saw*, Wade. He knew exactly what Trey was wearing. And with Trey's helmet not being on him . . . and those fresh tire marks on this path. I just think it's something worth looking into. If you're not so interested, maybe someone at the *Aspen Times* might be. Or Sheriff Warrick."

Wade stared back at her, and this time with a lot more than merely frustration. "You must be kidding, young lady."

71

"I'm not kidding, Wade."

"You know what you're saying?"

"I'm just saying someone else might find this all adds up to something. Enough to look into. Did you check the balloon?"

"This is really starting to cross the line for me. Did we check the balloon for what?"

"I don't know. For anything that looked . . . suspicious."

Wade glared. "Course we checked it, Dani. Teams of people who know what the hell they're doing have been over it all day. The outer fabric is pretty much a burnt-out mess. And what are we looking for anyway? A rip? A tear? If what you're suggesting is true, some person sure went to an awful lot of trouble and risk to cover up the death of a basically broke, adrenaline-junkie, joy rider."

"What about a bullet? That could have caused it, right? It could have torn right through."

"You're starting to sound crazy now."

"All I'm asking is if anyone heard what may have been a shot going off nearby?"

Wade stood up again, came over to her, and sat himself on the edge of his desk. "What the hell is it about this, Danielle? This has gone too far. I know he was a friend. I know there are parts of all this that don't somehow add up to you. But no one else is seeing it that way. What they're seeing is a guy who may have gotten a bit too reckless and maybe misgauged how much water there was out there, which is exactly what the investigator the Parks Service sent agreed it was today."

"I know that river, Wade. No one knows it better than me—"

"But you're not a cop, Dani. You're a river guide. A smart one, maybe, but you're way overreaching here. And when you say silly things like you just did, about bringing in the press, more than they already are, it's starting to strain my patience to even listen to you. There are families coming here to retrieve their loved ones and there's zero tangible evidence to get everyone riled up that says it's anything other than two tragic, but unrelated events."

Dani stood up. Frustration ran heatedly through her blood, too. It all made sense to her, at least to a point. But Wade had one thing right. One thing she couldn't answer. Trey wasn't exactly the type to have enemies, so why, why would anyone want to do this to him?

Wade's shoulders sagged and he let out a resigned breath. "I tell you what . . ."

"What?"

"I'll talk to Allie." Trey's wife. "I'll see if there was any reason anyone would want to do him harm. Not that I believe there was, you hear me saying. But that's a start, right?"

Dani looked at him. The blood eased out of her face. She nodded. "You could check out those tire marks, too," she added. Then finally she gave him an accepting and contrite shrug, even a smile. "Yes. It's a start. Thanks."

"All right then. But the only reason I'm even agreeing to this is for you to stay out of it from this point on. No more detective, okay? It's getting people riled up. Especially *me*. We're opening the river back up tomorrow. Please, get your ass back on it."

Dani nodded again, against her better instincts. "Just ask her, okay?"

"And I don't want to hear any more threats about taking this to someone. Or I'm gonna have to figure out something else, Dani. To keep you out of it. We agree?"

"What do you mean by something else, Wade?"

"I don't know. Just don't. Understand? I need you to promise me."

She looked at him. "Rooster wasn't drunk, Wade. He knew what Trey was wearing. He saw something. He just didn't feel he could bring it to you."

"I said I need you to promise me, Dani . . ."

Her face was still flushed and red. She kept looking at him and he didn't know what she was going to say. Then she finally nodded, the air going out of her cheeks. "All right. I promise." She reached for the helmet.

Wade put his hand on it. "Where do you think you're going with that?"

"Trey's wife. It was his. She may want it."

"Sorry." He pulled it over to his side of the desk. "That's evidence. It stays with me."

74

CHAPTER TWELVE

Later, in an oversize Bowdoin T-shirt and sweat pants, Dani sat polishing off the last of a beer, her second, Blu curled up on the kilim rug in front of the TV.

"What is all this about, Dani . . .?"

There were a couple of messages from Geoff that she hadn't returned. The first was business: "Okay to do the bus leg on the afternoon run tomorrow and give Rob a chance to guide?" The second was more personal. "Look, is everything all right, Dani? You've been a little distant since Trey. We haven't spent any time together, and you kind of brushed me off the other night. I know you're upset. I'd like to come by tonight if that's all right. We could catch a bite. Or I could give you the ol' down-under back rub and we could catch up on a couple of episodes of *House of Cards* . . ."

She started to text him back that she just wasn't feeling up to it tonight.

She really didn't want to make trouble. And not with Wade. It was true, he hadn't been much of a husband to her mom. There were always rumors of him screwing around and he didn't exactly shine with compassion when she deteriorated and really needed him. By that time he was either too drunk or too stoned to be of much help; then he was let go from the Aspen sheriff's office and had to call in every favor he was owed not to have been brought up on criminal charges.

But he'd always been nice to Dani. Growing up, he was like one of those larger-than-life figures who would come in your life every once in a while and was always involved in fun, cool stuff. He took her camping and riding. He introduced her to famous people as "his little girl." Then he'd go on a binge. She'd gone to a few Al-Anon meetings and the part about how addicts weren't even in control always hit home. Wade was at the top of the list. The only parts of his personality stronger than his charm and charisma were his urges to be temperamental and self-destructive. Dani had tried to forgive him for being such a shitty husband to her mom. And at times maybe she had. And then sometimes his betrayals and constant pushing her mom away when she needed him most crushed her and broke her will. The same will everyone said they saw in Dani.

But now this was Wade's last chance in life, and it

was clear he didn't want to rock the boat. To Dani, the mosaic all fit together. Trey. The Cradle. The path that seemed to have been made down there from the road. Rooster claiming he saw something and then his balloon crashing down in flames. Maybe she couldn't prove any part of it, but it was all there for anyone to see if they wanted to take a look. She knew she was pushing the line with him. Wade didn't like to be crossed and he surely didn't like his authority questioned. Not in this job, which was the last rung on the ladder for him. And maybe Dani had made him look small to his staff.

But she couldn't just walk away from it. She couldn't just pretend it was all just some unrelated incident so the Chamber of Commerce could still brag about what an idyllic valley they lived in here.

What's this all about? Wade had asked of her.

She got up and went out to the deck. The moon was bright. The crickets were buzzing. The sky was dark and wide, the shadow of Mount Sopris looming in the distance. It was like you could see every star on the sky.

She sat in the Adirondack chair and put her feet up on the railing and swigged her beer. Blu shuffled out and curled up at her feet.

She wasn't about to stop, no matter what Wade had made her promise. How could he understand? She owed Trey. She owed him big.

Maybe everything.

*   *   *

They were on the upper Colorado River in Gore Canyon, two Aprils ago. There were four of them. Chase Gould and Tom Twilliger, both expert rafters. The lure was the biggest early spring runoff in years, over a thousand cubic feet per second coming down the river, which turned a Class Four into a Five, and a Five into sheer heaven.

Trey heard about and he called Dani and they decided to join in. They packed up their gear in Chase's truck and made the ninety-minute drive to Kremmling. Gore was an unspoiled mountain canyon, lined with snow-capped mountains and jagged cliffs. The three-mile rapid run through it had some of the most challenging whitewater in the country.

Dani had done the run once before, but never with so much water. It started out moderate: Applesauce and Sweet Dreams, easy Class Threes, just to stick your toe in the water, as they say. The gems were up next. Scissors, which could cut anyone up or flip you over, and Pirate, with its deep holes and rocks the size of buildings, and a ton of water slashing around. It wasn't just good technique that got you down; this run was also about strength. In the hardest water Dani had ever had to push around. There were plenty of yelps and whoops of exhilaration, paddles raised triumphantly at every chute they made it through.

Then they hit Tunnel Falls.

Most people do Gore Canyon for the Kirshbaum, a

half-mile narrow chute of rocks and holes with a 120-foot vertical that builds up the speed like a raceway. But the Falls is its signature rapid. Massive rocks on both sides of a narrow chute and then over a twelve-foot drop. You have to navigate through it at just the right line; otherwise it's a headfirst wipeout. Guaranteed.

And that was with half the water the four of them had that day.

Chase was up first. The best and most experienced of them. He'd won a few competitions. The basin at the bottom of the falls had a ton of water thrashing about in it. He hit it just like they drew it up, the rest of them looking on from thirty yards upstream. He disappeared over the edge, spray and foam exploding around him, and from where they were they had no idea. And then ten seconds later they saw him reappear fifty yards downstream, his paddle raised high, his ecstatic whoops drowned out by the turbulent water's roar.

"*Whoooiieee!*" Trey lifted his paddle in appreciation. They all cheered.

Tom was up next. He was no slouch himself. In his red helmet and yellow raft, the back of his craft careened into a rock just as he went over and he didn't hit it right.

"Shit," Trey groaned. "Wipeout." Dani watched him go over and couldn't see what had happened below, other than seeing Chase, downstream, running his finger across his throat, meaning he'd capsized. It took a while

79

until she finally saw Tom again, hanging on to his raft, riding with the current, giving the thumbs-up that he was okay.

"You ready?" Trey asked Dani. "I'll pick up the rear."

It was Trey's way of saying, *I've got you covered if anything happens*, and were it anyone else Dani would have probably shot back, "You first. By all means . . ."

Instead she just nodded and said. "Up to you. Last one down buys the beer," and steeling her nerves, pulled into the chute. She never felt there was a run she couldn't make it down, even this one with more water than she'd ever handled. She knew the trick was to keep the approach steady and hit the falls head-on so that the crosscurrents wouldn't pitch you to one side, which was what had happened to Tom. Dani felt her speed pick up and strained to hold her line, but the whooshing current was stronger than she anticipated and pitched her around. As she got within six feet of the drop, she knew she was off-line, the back of her raft knocking against a rock, spinning the bow sideways. Her heart leaped up and she tried to correct, but there was no way she was strong enough to push this powerful a current around.

Fear gripping her, she basically went over the edge sideways.

To this day, she recalled the sensation of her heart toppling even faster than the raft, before being slammed by the icy water headfirst, as hard as if she had barreled into a wall. Her helmet knocked into something hard—a rock, the bottom?—and then the desperate, helpless realization that she was out of the craft in Class Five water.

Over the years, she'd wiped out a hundred times—everyone had. Tom had just a moment before. That's how you learned. Spread your arms and get your feet forward and try to hold onto the line to your craft, she told herself.

But the line slipped out of her grasp. She felt her kayak shoot off ahead of her and when she tried to position her legs forward, it was like they were caught up in something.

It took her a second for her to realize: She was underwater.

Her first mistake was to try to yell, which sent a rush of icy water into her lungs. She gagged. She quickly got her wits back, realizing, though the fall was disorienting, that she'd been caught in some kind of whirlpool—fierce water swirling around. And even with her senses dulled and the knifing sensation of icy water in her lungs, she knew to make herself as still as she could and not to panic nor fight what was happening. Let the vortex release her and lift her up. She'd practiced it a hundred times.

But this time it didn't.

A frantic fear began to set in. Being thrashed around, not knowing up from down, her eyes stung by frigid water like dozens of bees attacking her, the coldness in her lungs sapping her strength.

Stay calm, she told herself, *stay calm.* But in her agitation, seconds seemed like minutes. She had no idea how long she was under and she feared she would lose her breath. Her mouth opened, water spilling into her lungs. Numbing her. For the first time in her life she felt fear on the river. Her instincts failed her. It took everything she had to suppress the basic urge to scream.

Please stay calm, Dani. Somehow. Don't struggle against it. The eddy will free you. You know what to do.

She realized Chase and Tom were way too far downstream to help. No way they could make their way back up against that current.

And Trey, sooner or later, he would realize what had happened. Chase had probably already given him the sign. But how long would he wait to see if she came through? Or if, coming after her, he'd nail the run perfectly and be swept right past.

Panic started to rush into her blood like the icy water in her lungs. She began to feel the very real fear that this could be it for her.

Let me up. Let me up. Dani started to struggle against it, which she knew was the wrong thing.

Please.

On the deck with Blu, looking up at the starry sky, Dani was gripped by the same sensation as if it were yesterday. One she'd never felt until that moment.

And hadn't since.

The overwhelming feeling she was giving up.

That she was going to die.

In the river, she felt water all over her, icy and black, the irony that something she loved so much was now about to kill her. In that moment, her mind actually began to drift, to a scene from her childhood, her mother telling her she was too young to go out on the river by herself. She'd have to wait another year. She was maybe ten then. Then—

She felt herself being lifted back up. *It's working*, she remembered thinking, sure that the current was giving her up.

But it wasn't the current. It was Trey, a hand clamped onto her wet-suit collar, the other hanging on to a rock. Pulling her out. She broke free and sucked a desperate breath into her lungs. She gasped over and over, coughing out water, throwing her eyes back at the beautiful blue sky, heaving.

Free.

"I've got you, Dani. I've got you," she remembered Trey saying. "You were in an eddy. But you can relax. Breathe in. I've got you now. You're safe."

She clung to him like he was a buoy in the middle of the ocean, and she wanted to cry.

"Jeez, and all the really hard stuff is still a ways downstream . . ." He grinned at her, in that offhand way of his and with a wink that at any other time she would have wanted to throw a punch at. But this time she just smiled and hugged him, nodding, wiping away the tears. He positioned her on his chest, feet forward, between his legs, and they followed the current downstream back to her raft.

She stayed with them and finished the Kirshbaum as if it were a Three.

What's this all about? Wade had asked, not knowing what lay at the heart.

She owed Trey. Owed him everything. He hadn't given up on her.

No way she was about to give up on him.

Especially now.

That's what this was about.

CHAPTER THIRTEEN

That same night, Wade was in his home up the canyon in Basalt. Not where he used to live, on Red Mountain in Aspen. Those homes went for millions now. In a rented house, kind of a dilapidated eighties chalet, with a dirt drive and the garage filled with his things, so he had to leave his Bronco parked outside. He'd gone to see Allie Watkins at the end of the day, just like he'd said he would. First, to pay his respects; Trey's father had come down from up north to take possession of his boy's body. Then to ask her, just for appearance's sake, if somehow there was anyone out there who would want to see her husband harmed.

Her raw, red eyes looked back at him quizzically.

"Just a formality," he explained, "in these types of things. We're just crossing off a line of investigation."

She shook her head. She had her long blond hair wrapped back in a braid, and was in a kind of peasant dress with a shawl covering her shoulders. "I mean, there was someone who he had a dispute with over the patent they were applying for on his camera mount," she thought back. "Mark Conners. He and Trey went to school together at CSU. But he lives in Massachusetts now. He wasn't even here."

"Massachusetts," Wade said, nodding.

"Anyway, they seemed to have ironed it all out. Trey was giving him a small share of whatever he made. So no, no one, Chief Dunn. You knew Trey. Everyone liked him. I don't know what you mean . . ."

"I'm not meaning anything, hon," Wade said, putting his arm around her as he went to the door. "Now don't go worrying about it. You've got enough to deal with as it is. You go take good care of that little boy of yours, okay?"

Later, he scraped together something to eat and sat down in front of the TV with a coffee. Tonight was one of those nights he longed for something a whole lot stronger.

She's always been a tough one to rein in. Dani. Going back to when she was a kid. Whatever she did, she did as tough as any of the boys—rock climbing, hockey, snowboarding. Once she got on something, it was like a demon was in her head. One that wouldn't let go. She had that headstrong nature.

Like her mom. Wade hadn't had much luck in that department, either.

This time, though, just this once, he knew, he would have to back her down.

There were things she didn't understand. Things she would see in a different way if she persisted. A way that could cause trouble for him.

Things he had to make sure didn't come out and that couldn't get around. Too many things depended on it.

He drank up the last of his coffee and flicked on the TV. His cell phone sounded. He took a look and saw that it wasn't his office. The words on the screen, UNKNOWN CALLER, made the acid in his stomach shoot up. He didn't even want to answer, but, he knew, these weren't exactly the kind of folk you left hanging. "Hello."

There was no greeting, only a slight pause, then a firm but soft Oklahoma drawl almost hissing the words at him. "You said this would be a piece of cake, Chief. All buttoned up. So far, I'd say that's anything but the case."

"I know."

"I don't really want to hear that you know, Wade. I think you know the consequences of what happens if we can't contain this."

"I'll handle it," Wade said, though he saw the thing unraveling like a spool of thread in a cat's paw.

"You'll handle it, huh? You'll handle it how, Wade? We already thought you had it all neatly bundled up.

And now there's another person going around making even more trouble. Some girl . . ."

"Listen . . ." Wade said, his stomach tightening as if it were squeezed into a ball. "How do you know about that?"

"Don't you worry how we know about things. Just worry how you're going to set it right. This was all supposed to go easy. First we find the kid on the river. The same route he always goes. Tuesdays and Fridays, right? Bright and early. No one around. Other than some fool flying in a goddamn balloon who goes spouting his mouth off. We both better hope he didn't take pictures."

"He didn't. And you didn't have to do it the way you did. Now I have all kinds of trouble here to factor in."

"Sheriff, I promise you," the caller laughed, "your little town doesn't even know the meaning of the word *trouble*, if that's what it is."

"This time you stay out of it. I'll take care of it," Wade said. He also knew these were not the kind of people you lost your temper with. "I'll make it go away."

"*Stay out of it . . .?*" The person on the other end chuffed back a laugh. "How do you think you even got yourself reelected, Lieutenant Johnnie Walker Black? We stay out of it, you wouldn't have gotten yourself appointed to the prom committee of your local high school."

"It won't go any further. I give you my word."

"Damn right it won't go further . . . 'Cause if it doesn't, everything stops. Today. Not another dime. That boy of yours will have to find his own way back in life without our help. That understood?"

"It's understood." Wade gritted his teeth and swallowed the acidy taste back into his stomach.

"I want to be clear, Chief. Carbondale's a cute little town. But if we have to make another stop down there, it might just be for you this time. So factor that kind of trouble into your thinking, Wade." After waiting a moment to let the words sink in, the caller hung up.

Wade placed the phone back on the table, anger roiling inside.

He needed them off his back, but he had let them in. That he couldn't deny.

Yes, one long set of rapids to run, he said to himself. *No different than Trey.*

Dani better keep her trap shut, that was all there was to it. Or he didn't know what he'd be forced to do.

One thing he should've learned a long time ago, you deal with the devil, you better get ready for the temperature to rise.

CHAPTER FOURTEEN

Early the next morning Dani was back out on the river.

There was a ranger station at the beginning of the park road. Cammie was on duty. Dani knew her, of course; she was out here almost every day. She handed out maps and advised people on where to camp and the conditions.

And they also kept track of the car traffic. All day.

"No run this morning?" Cammie said as Dani drove up, leaning out of her hut. The river had just been reopened and Dani waited at the gate until a few vans and buses from both Whitewater Adventures and a few competitors went on through. There was no kayak strapped to the top of Dani's Subaru.

"I'm doing the bus pickup later this afternoon. Cammie, listen, you mind if I talk to you about something?"

"Not at all." The ranger leaned out and looked down the road, seeing no one behind them. "Lots of doings out here these past two days. What's on your mind?"

Dani pointed to the camera at the gate that recorded the license plates of all vehicles going inside the park. "You keep that thing on, don't you?"

"Twenty-four/seven. Even after the gates are closed. State law."

"And you keep the film here? From the past few days."

They'd known each other for years, even though Cammie was about ten years older. But she'd been part of the park detail for a long time and Dani had been coming here since she was a teenager. Her booth had a picture taped up with her and her female partner. "Just what date are you looking for, Dani?"

Dani looked at her. "Last Tuesday. The twenty-second."

Cammie looked back at her. "Tuesday was the day Trey Watkins was killed, wasn't it?"

"Yes, it was."

"That must have been rough." The park ranger stepped out of her hut. "I know the two of you were friends. He still came out here a couple of times a week. He always seemed like a nice young man. Always called me 'Judy Blue Eyes.' Like from Crosby, Stills and Nash." Cammie kind of blushed.

"Everyone liked Trey. And, yes, it *was* rough." Dani nodded. "Thanks."

"Seems kind of hard to believe. Happening where it did. That far downstream. Some people are saying it must have happened up around the Falls, and the current took him down. It sure seemed he knew what he was doing."

"He did know what he was doing, Cammie," Dani said. "That's why I'd like to take a look at that film."

The ranger's eyes widened a bit, as she got the sense of what Dani was asking. "Everything I heard said it was just a crazy accident. Even the state parks team was here."

Dani shrugged. "Look, I know this may not be one hundred percent by the book . . ."

"I'm not so concerned about by the book . . ." Cammie said. "It's just that, it's not here. It's been handed over."

"Handed over? Handed over to whom?" Dani said in surprise. "The Parks Service?" If everyone was so sure this whole thing was nothing but an accident, why would it dawn on them to take the film?

"Not the Parks Service. It was Chief Dunn who came and took it. Day after it took place."

"Chief Dunn?" *Wade?* Wade had it all along. All the while he was saying this was just an accident. Cut and dried . . .

He was either hiding something from her, or he believed it, too.

"But we take 'em when people leave here, too." Cammie pointed to another camera, this one facing the exit gate. "And he didn't ask for that one. It's all digital these days. Fine with me if you want to come in and take a look."

CHAPTER FIFTEEN

He had it. The realization twisted inside Dani. Wade had it when she went into his office yesterday. When he made that big scene about her overreaching and butting out. It meant either that he suspected she was right—that Trey's death was suspicious, and then Ron's, too. Or worse, that he was protecting something.

He'd had it all along. Before she even found the helmet.

Which, after what Dani and Cammie saw was on it, also meant he knew . . .

There was a meeting under way at the police station. Another officer Dani didn't recognize was manning the front, and Dani went right past him, the officer going, "Wait! Hold on. You can't—" And she pushed open the door and barged straight into the chief's office.

Wade was at the head of the small conference table

with his one and only detective and another officer around it.

"You took it." Dani glared at him.

"What?"

The two others at the table looked up in surprise.

"The camera roll from the ranger station at the river. On the morning Trey died."

Wade's face grew heated. "Dani, I'm gonna ask you to step out now, if you please . . ."

"Cammie said you came and got it two days ago. So you knew. You knew all along it wasn't an accident. You knew there was someone out there even before I brought in the helmet yesterday."

The air hung like lead. Wade put down his pen and cleared his throat. "I'm sorry for my stepdaughter's outburst here. You all mind giving us five minutes and we'll reconvene."

The two of them left with a series of eye rolls and awkward glances that Dani knew would be around the station in two minutes. She realized this time she'd gone too far. She couldn't help it. Wade had led her on. When the door finally shut behind them, he turned back and glared at her. "That's my staff you just embarrassed me in front of. You do that again, and I don't care if you're my stepdaughter or not, so help me I'll . . ."

"I'm sorry. I was out of line. But, Wade, you've had it all along. You let me go through that whole thing about Trey and Rooster and the helmet and the path I found . . . You know who it was, too. Who was out there that morning? Whose tire tracks I saw."

"First of all," Wade said, coming around the table, "it's my job to look at anything that might—"

"That's a load of bull, Wade. You told me Rooster was crazy. There'd be no reason to even request that film if it was all just an accident like you said. Unless you suspected there was something suspicious that went on out there. At least I'm damn well hoping that's the reason for it."

Wade leaned his hands against the table. "And what other reason might there be?"

"I don't know. That you're hiding something." Dani didn't back down. "That there was something on it you didn't want anyone to see."

Wade's eyes took on a hardened expression, a space between hurt and outright anger. "That's a mighty strong accusation, Dani, coming from someone who I've only been a friend to in life."

"So convince me it isn't, Wade. Who else has seen it? Who else did you show it to, if this was some kind of big investigation? I'm sorry if I don't exactly believe you, but there's a lot of recent history between us that doesn't exactly rule that out."

He swept his arm in anger, the papers on his table flying onto the floor. "I don't have to convince you, Danielle. I'm the goddamn chief of police here! And whether there's something there or not, that's my role to determine, not yours. Just let me do my job!"

"Well, then do it!" Dani's eyes lit up with accusation. "But next time you might want to requisition the exit tape as well. They keep it, Wade—just so there's a record in case people get lost or stranded in the park. So they know exactly who's still in there."

Wade's mouth opened a bit, and he stood there, as if he'd had a gun drawn on him.

Dani opened the manila envelope she had with her and removed the black-and-white photo. The one she made after she and Cammie looked at the film. She put it on his desk.

It was of a white Jeep Cherokee. Colorado plates. D69-416. "He came in at seven-oh-nine that morning. Just after Trey. And he left forty minutes later. *Forty minutes, Wade!* Just enough time for him to set up and do whatever he came to do and for Trey to take his first run."

Wade's fists dug into the table so hard Dani thought it was going to collapse. "You don't know what you're stepping into, girl . . ."

"This is him, Wade!" Dani jabbed her index finger onto the photo of the car. "That's who killed Trey. And if you don't act on this, so help me, I'll take it to the *Aspen Times* or to Dave Warrick or anyone else who will listen to me and makes sure it's in the hands of someone who will. You don't have six deaths here to worry about here, Wade—you have six murders." She pressed her finger on the photo again, right on the plate. "And here's your murderer!"

CHAPTER SIXTEEN

"I want you out of town," Wade said, his jaw twitching, his chest heating up with frustration and anger, everything about him suddenly different.

This whole thing had hit a whole new level of seriousness for him now. A combination of being threatened by this crazy girl and the fear of what might happen to her (or *him!*) if she continued on. His conversation on the phone last night had made it clear. *I'll handle it,* he'd promised them. *I'll make it go away.*

He knew he'd better damn well deliver.

"You're not taking this anywhere." He pulled the photo back to his side of the table and crumpled it into a ball.

"You think I'd be dumb enough to put my only one down in front of you." Dani leered at him. "I have more."

"Then I'm telling you, as the head of this investigation and as someone who cares about you, Dani, I want them all handed over now." He reached across and grabbed the envelope out of her hands. "You're going to get out of this town for a while and let me do what I'm paid to do. In the meantime"—he took her roughly by the arm—"you're coming with me."

"What do you mean, I'm coming with you?" She tried to pull herself away. He clamped on tighter. "Wade, you're hurting me!"

He dragged her into the station house and then through a door in the back where they had four holding cells.

"Are you crazy . . . ?" Dani glared at him, trying to writhe out of his grip. "Get your hands off me, Wade! You're doing what—*throwing me in jail*? This is insane. You can't stop me from talking to people. You're sitting on something. Just like you did with Mom."

"I'm putting you somewhere where I can make sure you're not interfering with my investigation until your father comes, or whomever the hell else I can get to talk some sense in you and take you out of here. Trust me, it's for your own good."

"My father? On what charge?" she demanded.

"I don't know what charge! Obstructing an official investigation. Illegally obtaining government property. On the charge that it's for your own damn good, Dani. Whatever I can think of that holds you here for a couple of days."

"Are you nuts? Wade, please, how long do you think that'll last?"

"As long as it takes to call your dad and get him to come out here." He pulled her into the area where there were four holding cells. None of them were occupied.

"I'm not gonna stay here, Wade."

"You damn well are going to stay here! You're over your head here, Dani, and I'm doing this to protect you, not hurt you. Whether you know it or not."

"Protect me?" He pushed her in an open cell and closed it with a clang behind her.

"Yes, protect you, Danielle," Wade said, breathing heavily now.

"You're making a mistake here, Wade. Not about me, but about Trey. And Rooster. And whoever that car belongs to."

"Maybe so." Wade walked away and hung the key on the wall. "But I've made 'em before. Sooner or later, one's bound to catch up to me."

ADRIFT

CHAPTER SEVENTEEN

It had been too long.

The muscles were getting weak, the stomach a little flabby. A month back, long about Frenchman's Cay, he'd stopped doing his morning crunches. The urge to find himself again, to get back into something, the next chapter, grew more and more restless inside him. He kept asking himself, what was next? To go back to his old job? To Talon, the global security company he was a partner in? He'd taken a month leave to nurse his wounds and bring himself back to life and just extended it kind of indefinitely. Now the wounds had healed; the dime-sized holes where the bullets had found him were now just scar tissue, mostly hidden by the tan. But what do you do when you've brought down a worldwide financial conspiracy whose reach led to the doorstep of the president's own cabinet? Become a talking head on the TV news shows? Go on the speakers' circuit? Just sail? These past two months, he couldn't answer that question.

The first month, he didn't even bring it to mind.

The month Naomi had joined him.

Hauck gazed out in his trunks and shades at the exquisite turquoise sea, white waves lapping gently onto the shore, from the tiny cove he was moored in with no other boat in sight, and didn't care that there was no breeze.

That first month they just drifted. He didn't want money or fame. He'd just wanted to help people. That's why he became a cop in the first place, right? After the death of his youngest daughter. That's how he put the pieces together back then. How he made his amends. But there were never enough amends. So he just sailed. Until it found him. He knew one day it would.

The day this came down:

"Ty, I'm not sure where this email finds you. But I need your help . . ."

He had spent the past two months on a thirty-eight-foot skiff he'd rented in Tortola, bonefishing and just sailing around, letting his beard grow out. After he and Naomi Blum exposed the Gstaad Group and helped bring down the secretary of the Treasury, Thomas Keaton, who'd conspired to mastermind the series of events that brought on the worldwide financial meltdown. He just couldn't take a slap on the back for a job well done and a bonus check, and go back to his desk in Greenwich, Connecticut. Even the high-profile job that it was, handling corporate and governmental security issues with global connections. He couldn't just sit in a larger office, gladhanding prospective clients, using his newfound notoriety to land new business like some ex-home-run hitter at a baseball card show. The money didn't mean much to him, either, a guy who always figured he'd retire on a detective's pension.

The first three weeks, Naomi was with him. From her small office at the Office of Financial Terrorism at the Treasury Department in Washington, D.C., they followed the trail of Hauck's friend April Glassman's murder all the way to the top of Naomi's very department, to the president's right-hand man. And once the dust settled and the headlines stopped, the wounds healed, they sailed for a month from isle to isle. They let the boat just drift in the open sea and made love on the deck, on the forestairs, under the stars, whenever the urge hit, and wherever it took them. They pulled into small, festive ports and ate spiny lobsters or tilefish on the beach and danced to reggae bands in thatched-roofed bars, full of Red Stripe beer and Pyrat Rum.

Sometimes they would just sit on deck and watch the sunset, or the sunrise. And wonder why real life had to be any different.

Then she went back to D.C. Now, head of the Financial Terrorism office.

And he just continued to drift. What was next? What had meaning to him? She would send him texts; some cute, recalling their time together. Some sexy. She would refer to his scars and the many times he'd been shot. He'd write back that he loved to play the five chords from the opening of Philip Glass's *Music in the Shape of a Square* that were tattooed on her butt. The result of a Princeton degree in musicology, before she went into the Marines.

Now he thought of her diving naked into the turquoise sea or dancing in cutoff jeans and a bikini top. He had the time of his life with her. Free. Neither wanted any attachments. She was a rising star with the world in front of her. He . . . he'd been around a bit longer and had cheated death more than one time.

Then the texts grew shorter and less frequent. She got involved in new cases. Told him to come back. And still he drifted. He'd received a ton of emails from people who wanted to meet with him. From Tom Foley, the CEO of Talon: *When are you coming back?* From his daughter, Jessie. Now sixteen: *How long will u b down there, Dad? Have you gone mental???* Now he only checked his email once a week. He stopped doing his push-ups and crunches. His beard got thicker. If it was another month, then it would be another month. He just fished and sailed.

And then this message came.

Ted Whalen was his roommate at Bates College, where they both played football. Hauck was a running back, set all kinds of school records; records long broken. Ted was a tight end who mostly blocked and rarely caught a pass. The two of them, along with Ted's pretty girlfriend, Judy, were fixtures there. Eventually they married. Ted went on to become a successful orthopedic surgeon. At first out in Colorado, interning at some famous clinic out there. Then after their marriage fell apart, at Brigham and Women's back in Boston.

The message said that his daughter Danielle had gotten into a bit of trouble in Colorado, where she was living. Hauck was Danielle's godfather. He remembered the day she was born, though truth was, he hadn't seen her in years. He had gotten word a few years back that Judy had died out west. Complications from cancer. The last, sad punctuation point stamped on his college career.

Ted wrote: "I'm in Chile on a teaching sabbatical, otherwise I'd be on a plane myself. But from what I hear this might be more in your field of expertise than mine. Please go, Ty, if you can. I think it's urgent."

The last time he saw Danielle she was doing snowboard tricks at Mad River Glen in Vermont, where she and her dad visited one year. She was maybe thirteen. He'd promised Ted and Judy he would always be there for her, should anything ever happen. And that was before Judy got sick. Then they all drifted apart.

He wrote him back. "I'm on my way." He didn't even ask for a reason. The mountains would be a welcome change, maybe help him figure it out. Plus he owed them; owed him. Once a Bobcat, always a Bobcat, right?

He had made a vow.

Anyway, he was ready. Hauck looked out at the lit-up, purple horizon. Another gorgeous sunset. His last. He felt the old flicker in his blood start up, like an old engine coming to life. That spark he always felt on the job when he suddenly saw the mosaic of something larger than what the facts showed start to come together; when through the fog of misdirection and cover-up he saw with total clarity where a case was leading. That second sense. His muscles ached; but suddenly they felt ready. He put down his Red Stripe and stretched out on the deck. He started doing crunches. One, two, three . . .

He stopped at a hundred. Then he went downstairs and looked at himself in the mirror and took out his razor.

It had been too long.

CHAPTER EIGHTEEN

The following morning, Hauck left his boat at a marina he knew on St. Kitts, caught an eight-seater prop for the half-hour jaunt over to St. Maarten, where he was the last one on the 11:30 A.M. to Miami, which connected late that afternoon to a United flight to Denver. He spent the night at the Aloft hotel near the airport, and by six the next morning, he'd rented a car and was on his way up Interstate 70 to Aspen.

He'd been out here a couple of times years before to ski. Once, back in college, where he and four friends crowded into a classmate's family's two-bedroom condo at Copper Mountain. Hauck's folks were working-class people, and at Bates he worked a twenty-hour-a-week job on top of studying and football. Back then, he couldn't have even afforded a cheeseburger in Aspen, never mind a place to stay or even the lift tickets. He remembered how beautiful the ride up was: the new airport cutting around Denver, passing Golden, where he always wanted to stop off and see the Coors brewery, then into the foothills with the old mining towns of Idaho Springs and Georgetown, their steep canyons and buffalo herd patches until he reached Loveland Pass at twelve thousand feet. Patches of snow were still visible as he emerged from the Eisenhower Tunnel.

He made it to Carbondale in just under three hours. Ted had said to talk to the chief of police there. A guy named Dunn. It was a small town in the shadow of a massive, lone mountain with outdoor shops and a ski-chalet-like Safeway on a quaint, main street. He'd put the location of the police station into his GPS, but after twenty years in law enforcement he didn't need a satellite to help him sniff out a station. His nose led him right to the parking lot filled with parked green-and-white SUVs with CARBONDALE POLICE on them, outside a one-story, redbrick building attached to the Carbondale Town Center. He parked in a spot reserved for visitors.

Hauck's beard was down to a growth, and in his floral Hawaiian shirt, jeans, and sunglasses, he didn't exactly look official.

Inside, he went up to a female officer in a khaki uniform behind a glass partition, her hair in two long braids. She smiled pleasantly at him.

110

Hauck folded his shades into his shirt pocket. "Chief Dunn around?"

"He's on the phone. I know he's got to head into Aspen for a meeting there shortly after. Anything I can help you with?"

"I'm looking for a Danielle Whalen. I hear she's a guest at the spa here."

"The spa?" The officer looked up at him with a laugh. "You her lawyer?"

"Do I look like a lawyer?"

She laughed again. "Some of the lawyers here, why not? Hell, in this town you could be the mayor. Why don't you take a seat; I'll see if the chief is off. I know he was expecting someone. What did you say your name was?"

He gave her his card. "Ty Hauck."

She got up and went to the back of the station past a couple of compartmentalized workstations. Hauck didn't see any detectives. It was a small department. She knocked on the door of a glass-lined office with drapes restricting the view and poked her head in. A minute later she came back. "Dani's a nice kid, but it'll be a boon to all of us, the sooner you get her out. You can go on back."

"Thanks, Officer." He smiled.

He went back to the glassed-in office and knocked on the door that was left ajar. A stocky, middle-aged man in a uniform top over jeans stood up from behind his heavy wood desk.

"Come on in. Wade Dunn," he said as he held out his hand. Despite the salt-and-pepper flattop, he looked no more than sixty, with a round face, a flabby jawline, a reddish complexion. He had an ornate belt on his jeans. His hands were thick, his grip was firm, authoritative, with a large turquoise ring. "Officer Jurgens said you were here about Dani . . ."

"Dani . . .?"

"*Danielle*. Sorry." He motioned Hauck to a burled wood conference table. "I thought Ted might have mentioned I was married to her mother for a while."

"No, he didn't tell me that," Hauck said, surprised. "He just said to look you up. I knew Judy a bit myself, back in college. In a way, I guess that makes us all kind of related."

"How's that?" The police chief crossed his legs. Hauck's eyes went to the fancy python-skin boots.

"I'm her godfather."

"Well, I'll be damned! I guess that does make us all something." The chief seemed pleasantly surprised. "Hell, I didn't know she even had a godfather. Can I get you something to drink? Water? Or a soft drink maybe?"

"Nothing." Hauck waved politely. "I'm fine."

"So where'd you come in from, Mr. Hauck?" The duty officer had given him Hauck's card. "Says Greenwich here. But you look kind of relaxed. L.A., maybe. You look kind of L.A., if you don't mind me saying."

"The Caribbean, actually. I was on a boat yesterday morning when Ted got in touch with me."

"*Caribbean?*" Chief Dunn's eyes widened. "Well, I have to say, you certainly do take the godfather role pretty seriously."

Hauck smiled back. "Ted and I go back a long way. He said Dani was in some kind of trouble. There was no breeze. Here I am. So is she . . .?"

"Is she what?"

"In some kind of trouble."

"Ty Hauck . . ." The chief leaned back and crossed his legs, and looked at Hauck's card. He narrowed his gaze back on Hauck. "Jeez, I know who you are. I saw you on CNN or something. You're the guy who was part of that investigation that led to that Treasury secretary's arrest."

"Thomas Keaton." Hauck filled in the blank for him. "But I was only the one who got shot up a bit. Others did most of the work."

"Not from what I heard. You look a little different," the chief said, drawing a hand across his chin, "maybe because of the . . ."

"Midlife crisis," Hauck said, referring to the growth.

"Well, I sure as hell know a lot about those." Wade Dunn laughed. "Though mine landed me in this job. I used to run the force over in Aspen. Well, how about that, Dani has a celebrity godfather. So you knew her dad?"

113

"Ted and I went to college together. Back east."

"Only met him a couple of times," the chief said. "You're one helluva friend to have, Mr. Hauck, if you don't mind me saying. To drop everything and come out here."

"So what's Danielle done? I understand that she's being kept here. Ted wasn't quite clear."

"It's a bit hard to explain exactly what she's done. Nothing really, when it comes to the law, except make my life a living hell. Professionally speaking. Personally, I like the gal. Practically raised her. But I guess you could say it's sort of for her own good, if you know what I mean."

"I'm not sure."

"Look." Dunn let his chair come back up. "We've had kind of some misfortune in the valley in the past week. Two things . . ." He told Hauck about the tragic, but likely unrelated, accidents. Dani's friend, Trey, on the river, and the hot-air balloon that caught on fire in the air.

"That's terrible . . ." Hauck winced. "How many were aboard?"

"Five." Dunn shook his head. "Including the pilot. Who Dani claims wanted to tell her something about the rafting accident before his balloon went down."

"What was that?'

The chief shrugged. "Claims he saw something on the river, but she never got to hear. The guy was a bit

114

of a lone steer to me, if you know what I mean. Not all there. But Dani seems to think it was important. Look, these two events would be terrible for any community to undergo . . ." The chief lit up a cigarette. "Hope you don't mind if I smoke, Mr. Hauck. Only real vice I have left," the chief said. "The rest have all been legislated out . . ." Hauck nodded for him to go ahead. "But for us, here . . . Aspen may seem like a big, worldly place, Mr. Hauck, with all the glitzy stars and private jets, but truth is, this whole valley is just three small Colorado towns. Everyone knows everyone else. I know Dani was close to that young man who was killed on the river. Seems she's gotten it in her head that these two terrible accidents weren't exactly that."

Hauck cocked his head. "Not sure I'm following you. Weren't exactly *what*?" he asked.

"Accidents," the chief said, taking a drag. "Worse, that they're both somehow connected."

"What do you mean by 'worse'?"

The chief seemed to be taking a read on Hauck, his granite gray eyes settling on his. "Look, we're both law enforcement professionals here . . . I may not have had the headlines you have on your résumé, and this is kind of a sleepy job now, but up in Aspen as you can imagine, I've seen a lot in close to thirty years . . ."

"I'm not sure I'm following."

"What I'm saying, sir, is we turned over both of those incidents from hell and back—there's been a state parks

115

investigator on the river and a national safety team all over every part of that balloon, or what was left of it. And so far there's not a stitch of evidence that says there's been any foul play."

"But Danielle is convinced that there is?"

"Dani's like a mule. She gets on something and . . . You said you knew her mother?"

"For many years. I was the best man at their wedding."

"You don't say . . . Bowdoin, right . . .?'"

"Bates. Nearby, though. It's—"

"I actually know where it is . . . I took Dani on her college trips when Judy took sick. I think she applied there, too. Could've gotten in anywhere she applied. She always had the quickest brain I knew. Maybe too quick for her own good. But there's another part of her. That's kind of her enemy. We all have those parts of us, don't you agree? If you knew her mom, then you know what I'm talking about, Mr. Hauck."

"Might as well call me Ty. If we're related."

Chief Dunn laughed. "Ty it is then . . . and I'm Wade. But what I'm saying is, that woman never once let anything stop her or get in her way if she had her mind set on it. Hell, I ought to know, I was married to her for eight years. Except the cancer, maybe." Wade shrugged. "That stopped her. Cold. And Danielle . . ." He shook his head wistfully and ran a hand across his hair. "Well, she's got her father's smarts and her mother's temperament. And I guess it's worth saying, she's never been the keenest fan of me."

116

"And why's that?" Hauck asked him.

"'Cause I was there. When her mom died. And best to say maybe I wasn't the most caring person to have around at that time of my life, going through some weak moments of my own . . ."

"I hear you," Hauck said. "I was sorry to hear what happened."

"Years ago now. But anyway, Dani's stirring up some wild accusations. Threatening to take what she found to the press, or to the police chief in Aspen. That's just not helpful now. It's not the way we do things here. I thought it would be better if we just took her out of the picture for a day or two, while the investigators were here. If you know what I mean?"

"You put her in jail?"

The chief shrugged. "We were fully vacant. The rooms were there."

"They still around?"

"Who?" the chief asked.

"The investigating teams."

Dunn shook his head. "Nope."

"I think I get the picture. Ted only said she was in some kind of trouble. Can I see her?"

"*See her?* You can take her if you want, be my guest. We're all hoping you will. Hell, for such a pretty thing, she eats more than I can afford anyway . . . You can see, we're only a small department."

Hauck stood up.

The chief stood up, too. "Try and talk some sense into her, would you? No one gains by her stirring things up like she was. Maybe let her show you the state for a few days. Until this all quiets down. I don't know how long you have, but it's beautiful country out here. Sorry to drag you off your boat, Mr. Hauck. For such a mundane reason. Can't say I'd be a happy camper if it were me."

"Show me the way. I'll see what I can do."

CHAPTER NINETEEN

Hauck went inside the small cell block, down to the last of four manually locked cells. The only one that was occupied.

Danielle was on her back on the cot, in jeans and a T-shirt, one leg resting over a knee. She didn't even look up at him. He could see right away that she wasn't at all what he remembered. The wiry, athletic tomboy had grown up into a pretty, filled-out, young gal.

"Whoever you are, I want to see Wade. You can't keep me locked up in here forever. I'll call a lawyer. I've got a job and you're keeping me from doing it. I have a dog that needs attention. And I'm sick of eating just Subway and Burger King. And I want a shower. And—"

"Calm down, and you might just get what you want," Hauck said, stepping up to the cell.

She rolled her head, her soft blue eyes narrowing in on him. Then she jumped off the cot and stared at him, totally disbelieving. "*Uncle Ty* . . .?"

"I'm not really a big fan of Subway and Burger King myself," he said. "Must be somewhere out here we can find some good Mexican food."

Her eyes doubled in size. "Uncle Ty! What the hell are you doing *here* . . .?"

"Not surprisingly, your father sent me."

"*Dad* . . .?"

It had been years, ten maybe, and Hauck took in the sight. Dani was now a pretty young woman. She was wearing a gray T-shirt that read, *What happens on the river, stays on the river*, and tight-fitting jeans. Untied blue Converse sneakers. She had her mother's wholesome looks—a rosy complexion, a few freckles dotting her cheeks, her hair between light brown and blond, and lots of it, thick, curls over her face, tied back in a bushy ponytail, and her mother's eyes, glacier blue.

"He said you'd gotten yourself into some kind of trouble out here." He grinned. "None that I can see, though."

She shrugged. "None I couldn't handle."

"Of course not. You seem right at home in here. He said you needed someone to bail your ass out of here, so c'mon, pack up. Amazingly, Chief Dunn has agreed to entrust you to my care. As long as you're a good girl."

120

"Who decides what that means?" Dani turned up her nose.

"For the moment, me. Basically, if you don't hit anyone on the way out or leave something vile in the toilet, you're okay to leave. Oh yeah, and that you talk to me about whatever it is that's got you all riled up and landed you in here, before you go on about it anymore."

"Wade got to you, didn't he?"

It had taken barely a minute, but Hauck thought he already had a sense of what it was the chief was talking about. The part of her that was more an enemy than a friend. "He didn't get to me," he said. "He talked to me. And if I was still a policeman trying to do my job with all that was going on here I might have done the same thing, too. Just to protect you."

"Throw your own stepdaughter in a cell? Keep her locked up for two days."

"If she wouldn't keep her nose out of an official investigation? Or threatened to go to the press? Maybe."

"Official investigation . . ." Dani chuffed and rolled her eyes. "Wade wouldn't know an 'official investigation' from a tractor pull. He's dropped the ball on this from day one. So that's the deal, then? I have to shut my mouth and let them bury what's possibly a murder of a friend under the rug, just so I can get out of here." She crumpled her sweat shirt up and tossed it back on the cot. "I'll stay."

121

"The deal, Dani," Hauck said, putting a key in the lock, "is that I haven't seen you in about ten years and I'm here. And that your father was worried about you. Which I would damn well be as well if it was my Jessie. And all I had to promise, as you say, was that you would keep your mouth shut and not do anything stupid until you talked it over with me. Now does that sound like something you can do, or shall I tell them to order you up another Foot-Long Double Philly Cheesesteak . . .? Onions and peppers . . ."

"No . . ." She shrugged, her voice finally softening. "Don't! I can't take it anymore." She finally broke down and grinned. "I think I gained five pounds in two days."

"Then grab your stuff. And look at the bright side of this. I see a couple of things . . ."

"What?"

"One, that you get to spend a couple of days with me. Which is something I would like very much."

"Me, too. And . . .?"

"Two—it's not everyone who can say they were thrown in jail by their own stepfather."

CHAPTER TWENTY

"It's been years." Hauck said admiringly, at a cramped table at Allegria on Main Street. "Look at you." He ordered the tuna melt on seven-grain bread and Dani a juice concoction of kale, celery, and zucchini that Hauck knew had to be over-the-top healthy given it was such an unappealing shade of green. "At least ten, I think. You're a beauty. All grown up."

"Since that time in Vermont. I was just a kid."

"We were up at your father's place at Catamount. And you weren't a kid on that snowboard. Now I hear you're rafting . . ."

"Whitewater guiding." Dani corrected him. "It's not exactly 3-D engineering, like my brother, but it pays the bills and keeps me in the fresh air. You ought to try it while you're here."

"We'll see. I think my wild days are behind me," Hauck said.

Dani scratched her chin with her thumb and index finger and grinned teasingly. "Not from what I see . . ."

"You mean the growth? Just a product of a bit too much time on my hands . . ."

"And the tan. You're looking pretty smokin', Uncle Ty, for an old dude. Some of my friends would be all over you. I'm gonna have to watch you while you're here."

Hauck laughed, still moving a little stiffly after being shot three times just a few months ago. But who wouldn't like hearing a woman say that, even if it was your twenty-five-year-old goddaughter.

It had been years. He had grown a little distant from Tom and the kids since the divorce and Tom's move to Boston. Then Judy remarried. "I was really sorry to hear about your mom," Hauck said. This was the first time they'd been face-to-face. "I'm sorry I couldn't make it out for the funeral." He was on a special case on the Greenwich force at that time and couldn't leave. "She was quite a gal."

"That's okay. I know you had your own loss you were dealing with, too," Dani said. "Dad told me. I never got to meet your daughter."

Hauck had lost his youngest daughter, run over in his own driveway with Hauck at the wheel as he backed out of the garage after a spat with Beth. The moment that had altered his life, leading to the Dark Ages, as he called it, when he and Beth divorced and he was treated for depression for about a year.

"I think you would have gotten along. Anyway, let's not get caught up in all those old stories, okay? You're a whitewater guide. Boyfriend?"

Dani shrugged. "I see someone. No one exactly special. We like to keep it that way."

"I get it. What about your brother and sister? They're good?"

"Aggie's in her residency in Austin. Burn trauma. And Tommy's at Stanford. Total nerd material. Turns out, he's the brainiac of the clan."

"The game's not over yet," Hauck said.

Dani smiled and drank down the last of her juice. "Hopefully that will neutralize three days of Subway and Burger King . . ."

"So Chief Dunn gave me a sense of what happened, and why he felt he had to make a point to you."

"Chief Dunn . . .? You mean Wade. Some point . . ." Dani rolled her eyes.

"All the same, I'd like to hear it from you."

She told him about what happened. Trey. How she found him out there, and how he could handle that level of rapid blindfolded, and about Rooster, weird as he was, but what he said he saw, and then what happened to him.

"Hot-air balloons don't just fall out of the sky, do they, Uncle Ty?"

"I don't know."

Then she went through how she had found Trey's helmet, when no one else had even believed he was wearing one, all the way downstream.

"Which proves what?" Hauck asked, finishing up his sandwich.

"It proves that if he was wearing one at the time he hit his head hard enough to kill him, it should have protected him, right? At the very least it should have shown the effects of the impact. Not to mention, how did it happen to come off if he was in his kayak? To me, it all says he wasn't wearing it when something hit his head."

"Go on."

She described the path she'd found above the river and the tire tracks by the road. And then the car that had been there not five minutes after Trey arrived—and then left forty minutes later. The same car Wade knew about two days earlier, and was just sitting on after he kept insisting that nothing had happened. "Why would there be a need to requisition these security tapes if all along he truly felt it was just an accident?"

Hauck shrugged. "Maybe he was just doing his job."

"Or maybe hiding something."

Hauck understood from his detective days how evidence can be slanted to look a certain way if you're inclined to see it through that lens. Especially when that evidence is all totally circumstantial. "Why would anyone want to kill this kid?" he finally had to ask.

"I don't know. Wade keeps asking me that, too."

"Chief Dunn . . . I mean *Wade*"—Hauck caught himself—"said Trey didn't have an enemy in the world. And this guy who was drunk . . ."

"He wasn't drunk, Uncle Ty. He was sober. He's back in rehab and I checked what he was drinking."

"Nonetheless, according to Chief Dunn he wasn't exactly someone who'd you'd put your trust in as a witness. And not to discount anything you say, but whoever did this, if it's as you're suggesting, would have had to go to some extraordinary lengths to execute it and then cover it up. So you're talking about someone who not only had the means and the capability to get it done, and the knowledge of what this guy Rooster said and did for work, but also the will. This is pretty serious stuff."

"I realize that," Dani said.

"Which means this wasn't some random act against your friend. But something far more organized. And likely with more than one person involved."

"I know how it sounds, Uncle Ty. But you've handled dozens of cases. Just because it's easier *not* to believe it, that doesn't mean it's not true. Am I right?"

Of all the big cases he'd been involved in, and some went high up into the government, it was always easier at first to doubt your reasoning. To even accept yourself that it was true. "You were a science major in college, if I recall?"

127

"Geology." She shrugged. "I'm like an expert on rocks and things."

"And in geology, if someone was pushing this theorem, one that had a way of making you believe it if you fit a number of things together, but was unsubstantiated by fact, only possibility, no matter how credible the thinking behind it seemed . . . what would you advise them to do?"

"I know where you're going with this, Uncle Ty . . . I'd tell them to test it. To corroborate it. With evidence. Both in the field and in the lab." She took out a pen and grabbed a napkin and wrote something on it, and passed it across to Hauck. "So there . . ."

It was a number. D69-416.

Hauck asked, "What's this?"

"Your corroboration. It's the license plate number of the car that went in there just after Trey. From the security film at the park gate. Just check it out. You can do that, can't you?"

"I don't exactly have jurisdiction to do anything out here. Plus, I gave your stepfather my word."

"*Ex*-stepfather," Dani said. "Look, Wade's basically a good guy. I don't know why he would have sat on this. But he's not exactly his own man these days. He's burned a lot of bridges and he's got a son who's in a VA hospital who needs every dime he has. I think it's fair to say, there's not another job for him after this one."

"So maybe he did check it out. And it went nowhere."

"If that's the case, then what's there to lose? Please, that's all I'm asking. If you can bring down the secretary of the Treasury, I know you can manage to get an ID on a license plate. If it leads nowhere, I'll drop it. I promise. I'll be a good girl."

Hauck nodded. He folded the napkin up and put it in his shirt pocket. "And if it does lead somewhere . . .?"

"If it does lead somewhere, it means that Trey and Rooster were murdered . . ."

"And we give it to Chief Dunn. That's the only way I'll do it. I'm not going around playing cowboy here, Dani. That's the deal."

"Fine." She nodded. "I agree."

"Good. So now that we've gotten past that, where does a guy stay in this place? On an ex-detective's wage. I don't need to bunk next to Jay-Z and Beyoncé."

"You're welcome to stay with me." Dani shrugged. "If you don't mind the company."

"Roommates?" Hauck asked.

"No. Long tail. Four legs."

"I love dogs, but maybe it's better if we keep this a working relationship," Hauck said.

CHAPTER TWENTY-ONE

"Brooke . . .?" Hauck called in from a room at a pleasant-looking motel not far from Dani's apartment unit.

His secretary back at Talon was silent, clearly startled. "*Ty . . .? Is that you?*"

He hadn't called into the office in almost a month. "The one and only."

"*Where are you? Still in the Caribbean? I have a ton of mail and some messages I was going to send in my weekly email.*"

"I'm actually in Aspen."

"*Aspen? Colorado?*"

"Nearby anyway. A town called Carbondale."

"*Jeez, you certainly win the prize on how to get the most out a leave of absence. What happened to the boat?*"

"It's in a marina back in St. Kitts. An old friend called me to get involved in something, something to do with his daughter who got into a bit of trouble out here."

"Everyone was expecting you to come back here."

"I'm just checking out a few things and then I'll be back. Which is the reason I'm calling. I need you to do something . . ."

"Ty, everyone here wants to know what's going on. People come up to me, as if I have some inside information. Even Mr. Foley asked." Tom Foley was Hauck's boss, president of Talon, who Hauck knew was using him, his name recognition at least, to attract accounts. "I'm not sure how to respond."

"Respond how I would respond myself. I don't know. Soon. If Foley needs to reach me, he knows my number, same as you."

"He said he's tried, Ty."

"Well, yes, in fact, he has," Hauck admitted. "Somehow I always seem to be at sea."

Brooke laughed. She'd worked at Talon when Hauck arrived there. But over time she had proven again and again how loyal she was to him. "Last I heard, Colorado isn't anywhere near the coast. I think he'd be pretty mad if I didn't connect you."

"I'd be mad if you did."

"Very nice of you to put your executive assistant in the middle between you. I didn't take this call, okay? So what is it you need?"

"I have a Colorado license plate number. I want to know who it belongs to."

"How do you want me to find out?" The company had several ways to go about it. Both above and below board. Proper channels was to put though a request through Motor Vehicles, but they would need to know why and that could take a few days. Hauck was hoping to clear this up and get back to his boat as quickly as he could.

Less transparently, they could lean on their various law enforcement contacts they had. In the police or FBI. That could get the information in an hour. Those kinds of favors were called in every day. But then there would be a trail. Someone would know. And sometimes, you didn't want a trail.

The third way was to just pay someone off. There'd be no trail. No one would ever know. They'd get the information in a flash. Just a ledger in the company's cash account.

"You choose. It's all aboveboard," Hauck said. "And it's not that kind of getting involved. At least not yet. I just want it back as quickly as you can. Being on land is making me dizzy." If Brooke was one thing, she was resourceful. And discreet. "Okay . . .?"

"I'll have it for you soon as I can . . . And what about Mr. Foley . . .?"

Hauck paused. He could simply take Brooke off the hook and just speak with him. "Tell Tom it's nice out

132

here if he'd like to meet me for a drink at the Ajax Tavern . . ."

"Oh, I'm sure he'll appreciate the humor. I'll be back with the information you're looking for as soon as I have it," Brooke said. "In the meantime, try and stay out of trouble. The mountains are beautiful out there. How are you spending your day?"

"On the water."

CHAPTER TWENTY-TWO

Dani took him whitewater rafting. She took her normal shift on the afternoon run. There were seven people on board, a myriad of ages, and Hauck went along.

"I want to introduce my favorite godfather sitting up in front," she said, as they coasted toward Entrance Exam. "Just want everyone to know, no special treatment for him . . . You gotta earn your place up there and paddle like everyone else . . ."

"Not a problem," Hauck called back.

"Well, he's just used to a desk job these days. So we'll see. The rest of you are gonna have to make up for him. And by the way, that's our first challenge up there."

Hauck loved it. The reckless feeling of speed and that you might career over at any point. The bumps, like doing the moguls on the slopes. The feel of icy whitewater against him. He even went in for a plunge at some point, at the end of the course when the water was calm.

"How's that water feel, Uncle Ty? Not exactly like the Caribbean, huh? Funny how the jet stream doesn't quite make it up here . . . The ol' Arctic vortex does, though . . ."

Everyone laughed.

Hauck saw what it was that spoke so personally to her out here.

On the ride back, he sat next to Dani on the bus and they talked about her life out here. She was pretty and funny, and seemed to cater to the younger kids, who no doubt thought she was about the coolest, sexiest counselor they'd ever had.

And she was sharp, pointing out some geological details—how the river was formed, the sturdy characteristics of the aspen trees that are always the first to come back after a forest fire and are all connected by the roots. The massive avalanche fields, and how they occur. Nothing like the brash, obstinate gal he had met in jail.

When they got back to the company headquarters, she introduced him to Geoff, the owner, who was behind the counter showing videos of the raft going over the falls, which his crew had already put on a disk. Hauck noticed how he looked at Dani in a certain way, and how he said, "Nice to meet you, mate," in that likable

Aussie manner, and how maybe they would run into each other later on. Outside, as Hauck and Dani went to get in her wagon, he asked leadingly, "So is that the 'no one special' . . .?"

Dani shrugged. "Geoff's okay, really. Though it's probably not the best thing in the world to take up with the boss, right?" She opened the door and stepped in, without giving him his answer.

He shrugged as he got in. "Seemed nice to me."

Inside, Hauck dug into his jacket and took out his cell. He kept it there while they were on the river. He saw that an email had come in from Brooke with a note: "I think this is what you're looking for. No worries about the trail."

He opened the attachment.

"You know anyone named Colin Adrian?" he said to Dani.

She shook her head. "Who's that?"

"The white Jeep you're so interested in seems to be registered to him." He looked at her.

"*Adrian?*" She leaned over and took a look. It was just a registration. No driver's license. Nothing else. "We could ask Allie. But I think she's already up in Trey's hometown with their son. The funeral's on Wednesday." Dani handed the phone back to him. "I don't know anyone named that around here."

"No reason you would. It says his address is on Tuttle Road. In Greeley."

"*Greeley?*" Dani's eyes looked over at his.

"That mean something?" he asked.

"I don't know . . ." But her face took on a pallor that suggested that it did. "But Greeley's where Trey was from, Uncle Ty."

CHAPTER TWENTY-THREE

"It doesn't prove a thing," he told her, over a venison steak and a long-overdue beer at Allegria on Main Street that night. Dani was clearly excited about what they'd found. "I looked it up. Greeley's got a hundred thousand people in it. There's even a university there. It's not exactly much of a coincidence that someone else might have come from there."

"I'll give you that," Dani said, over salmon in a tamarind glaze, "if you tell me what that someone is doing at the river for literally only forty-five minutes. He pretty much followed Trey in. He probably had no idea his car was being recorded. And he didn't stick around any longer than it would have taken to drive down ahead of him and head down to the river. He could have been waiting for Trey there. Not to mention everything else that doesn't make sense: the spot where he was killed; the missing helmet, the path I found."

"It could have been for any reason." Hauck cut a slice of his steak. "He could have just been driving around. He could have been taking nature shots for *National Geographic* for all I know."

"You're starting to sound like Wade," Dani said.

"Speaking of whom, it's my intention to hand this information over to him in the morning, just so you know."

"You're kidding?" She put down her fork. "*Why?*"

"Uh, because he's the police chief in town . . . Not to mention I gave him my word I wouldn't go around his back. I'm supposed to be keeping you out of this, Dani. Not getting you further in."

"But Wade already has this information," Dani said. "And if he doesn't, he's even more lame than I thought. He picked up a copy of that tape the day after it happened. The ten-thousand-dollar question is *why . . .?* If he thought this whole thing was just a stupid accident like he's been saying. So why hasn't he gone back up there to run this guy's name by Allie, and see if it means anything to her? Or find out who he is."

"I don't know."

"Truth is, Uncle Ty, he hasn't gotten off his ass, except to take the parks inspector out to lunch, or go to Aspen and stand behind Sheriff Warrick and try and act smart while they're looking at that balloon."

Hauck dipped a bite of venison into a chipotle tomato sauce. "I sure hope when I leave you have nicer things to say about your godfather than you do your stepfather."

"*Uncle Ty* . . ." Dani looked at him. "Besides, I don't really even know you yet." She gave him a crooked smile behind a bite of salmon.

"Gee, thanks." They continued eating for a while. Hauck asked her, "So what are you thinking the right thing is to do?"

"I'm thinking the right thing would be to drive up there to Greeley, or wherever Trey is from—I think the town's actually called Templeton, just outside of it. It's up on the plains north of Denver."

"And then do what?"

"And then see if this person Adrian has any connection to Trey. This is possibly a murderer, Uncle Ty. And like you said, look at what they did to try and cover it up. It might all be part of something much larger."

"Sorry." Hauck put a piece of venison in his mouth. "No way."

"*No way . . .?*"

"I'm not on board with that, Dani. Anyway, I gave my word. Not just to the chief, but to your father, too. Your stepfather and your father. Besides, if I land you back in hot water," he said with a grin, "I'll be out of a job."

"Some job . . . You know, don't you, if we don't do

that, it'll just get buried? That's why Wade kept me in jail. Not to teach me a lesson. To shut me up. The minute I said I would take it to Sheriff Warrick or to the news-paper, he got all crazy. I know the guy. He's sitting on *something*, Uncle Ty. You want to tell me what or why?"

Hauck couldn't, of course. Only that while he sat there for a while, chewing on his venison and polishing off a second beer, he knew in his heart that what she said was right. About what to do next. And right about one other thing at least. Why would Wade even go to the trouble of requisitioning that security footage, if all along he was certain that what happened was just an accident?

"What are you thinking about?" Dani stared at him.

"Nothing. A good night's sleep. I was up at five A.M., and I'm still on Caribbean time."

"That's all? You're sure?" Dani cocked her head. "All right, since you're taking me to dinner I won't tell anyone that the famous Ty Hauck can't handle a little jet lag."

"I can handle jet lag. What I'm having a hard time handling is *you*!" He took a last swig of his beer and signaled for the check. "Catch me tomorrow. I think better in the morning. And thanks for the trip down the river. That was really fun."

She dropped him off back at his motel room. It was 9:30 P.M. The sun had set, leaving a dark purple haze over the hills. He stripped off his clothes and washed up. His lids were sagging. It had been one long day. He sank into the bed and turned on the television. He found a local baseball game, the Rockies against the Giants, and watched for a while. He knew he wouldn't need an alarm in the morning.

His mind drifted back to what Dani had said: Why would Wade go and ask for the tapes? He might have been just doing his job, crossing off the possibilities, going through every possible angle. What any good cop would do. He probably had everything Dani was saying on a list: the spot on the river where Trey died, the helmet, this Rooster character calling her up—*and where the hell did they get these nicknames out here, anyway?*—in spite of what he was divulging.

It's all what *he* would do himself, Hauck knew.

But Wade was certainly right on one thing, though . . . Dani was a handful. *When she gets her mind on something* . . . He could certainly see traces of Judy in her. The way she seemed to single-mindedly get onto things and not let go. He remembered a particular incident back in college. Judy was petitioning the school about some company she said had been dumping waste into the nearby Androscoggin River. The owner was now looking to build a new hockey arena at Bates with their company name on it. Judy got half the student body to sign a petition against it, and a good slag of alumni, too. Hauck recalled how the administration tried to tamp

142

down her protest. They contacted her parents. Threatened to throw her out of school. She responded by organizing a rally directly in front of the president's office.

Eventually the college agreed not to name it after him.

Judy won.

A handful. Hauck smiled. Chip off the old block

The game receded into background noise and Hauck felt himself drifting off to sleep. The name kept popping back into his mind. Adrian.

Someone would have had to have gone to a shitload of trouble to kill that kid as Dani said, then cover it all up . . . Shoot down that balloon, Hauck thought, dragging himself back from the edge of sleep. And why did Wade sit on that tape? If he knew the same thing they did. What if he *was,* as Dani suspected, sweeping something under the rug?

He rolled over and took his phone off the bed table. Eyes heavy, he texted another message to Brooke. Knowing it was after midnight back east and she was likely asleep.

"Me again. When you get in I want to know whatever you can find on that car owner. Colin Jerrod Adrian. Greeley, Colorado.

CHAPTER TWENTY-FOUR

If he wanted something really thorough on Adrian it would have taken a couple of days.

They could have canvassed Adrian's phone records, his bank transactions, his trips in and out of the country. Talon surely had the means.

They could have gone to the Internet providers and tapped into his email account. Pinpointed where he had lunch the day before. Who his friends were. Whom he spoke to. Gone through his tax returns. All the things they say you couldn't do, but you can if you know the right buttons to push. Down to what color dress he bought his wife for their anniversary.

As it was, though, in the time allotted, they checked his criminal history, his military service, and credit history. Standard stuff. It still gave you a pretty good picture of the kind of person they were looking into. Who you worked for? Your banking arrangements? Where you went to school? Whether you were married or single? Whether you owned or rented your home. Whether you'd been sued or had ever declared bankruptcy.

Most important, given Hauck's reason for asking, whether you'd been in trouble with the law.

"That's what wasn't making any sense to me," Brooke said when she called him back that following morning. "Why I didn't send a driver's license along."

Hauck had already been out for a jog, four laps around a park the gal at the front desk directed him to. He went back and did his crunches. He took a shower and ate some oatmeal and fruit for breakfast. Back in the old routine. "What's that?"

"It's that it's all a blank. Colin Jerrod Adrian is a big zip. Zero."

"He has to have a driver's license?"

"Nope."

"What about a bank account or a credit card?"

"Neither."

"He doesn't write a check? He hasn't even filed taxes?"

"Not in the past four years. He hasn't had as much as a traffic violation. Basically, the only sign that the guy is even breathing I could find is that he registered a car. Other than that, he's a total cipher."

145

"No one's a cipher like that today, Brooke . . ."

"Someone is," Broke said. "The only thing I could find, Ty, and even this I'm not sure of, was in a hit in his military records . . ."

"And what was that?"

"There was a Colin Jerrod Adrian from Oklahoma City who was an Army Ranger in the 101 Airborne and served in Iraq. Date of birth: May 11, 1984. He rose to staff sergeant and deployed twice to Iraq, in 2003 and 2005. But it doesn't make sense. It can't be the same guy."

"And why not?" Hauck inquired.

"Because Staff Sergeant Colin Jerrod Adrian, DOB five, eleven, eighty-four, was listed as killed in 2006. In Fallujah."

"Run that by me again?"

"According to U.S. Army records, he's a casualty of war. Whoever it was that registered that car, Ty, he took this guy's ID. That's who doesn't have a bank account or a tax filing in today's world."

"*Damn*," Hauck muttered, dropping back on the bed, some major things suddenly coming clear to him.

Principally, that Dani was right.

"You want me to scan this stuff in and email it out to you?" Brooke asked.

"No, I won't be needing that. Thanks."

"So where are you going next with this?"

"I'm not sure."

"Let me know if you need anything else. And try to stay out of trouble."

"I always stay out of trouble, Brooke."

"Yeah, right," she chortled.

They hung up, and he sat there, his head buzzing. Whoever it was who had followed Trey Watkins into the park that day, he had assumed a dead Army Ranger's personal ID, which meant it was very likely something sinister had taken place, and all of Dani's fears might well be true.

He thought of the balloon tragedy.

All of them.

He picked his phone back up and hit the app for Google Maps, and charted out a course. Four hours' drive.

Where was he going next on this? Brooke asked.

He got up and started throwing his things into his bag.

Templeton.

Where the trouble was.

147

CHAPTER TWENTY-FIVE

"I want you to stay here," he told her in no uncertain terms.

Hauck knocked on Dani's door, around 11:30 A.M. He remembered her saying last night she had the 8:00 A.M. run, another later that afternoon. But she'd be around in between. She was just coming out of the shower when he came by, a towel wrapped around her as she peeked through the window next to the door, her hair still wet and thick with curls.

"Where're you going?" she asked with some hesitancy, as if she could read it on his face.

He didn't answer.

"You're going to Greeley, aren't you?" she said, her blue eyes flared.

"Templeton, actually. I'm just letting you know."

"You can't go up to Templeton," Dani protested.

"I thought that's what you wanted me to do?" Hauck said.

"I mean alone. You can't go without me."

"That's not an option," he told her. "Look, how about letting me in, please, just for a second . . ."

Dani opened the door, her shoulders bare, covered up in her towel. Her Lab came up and barked, and gave Hauck a welcoming lick.

"I'm just going to drive up and talk to your friend. Allie. Then I'm turning around and I should be back tonight. Depending on what she says."

"What do you mean, 'on what she says'? You know something, don't you?"

"No."

"Yes, you do. What did you find out? C'mon, Uncle Ty, you can't just keep me in the dark. I turned you on to all this. You do know something. I can tell."

"I didn't find out anything, Dani. I'm just gonna go up, like we talked about. And try and put this to rest. If I find something I'm going to report it to Chief Dunn. Like we agreed. Sorry, but that's just the way it is."

"Uncle Ty, you can't go up there without me."

"Yes I can. I promised Wade, not to mention your dad, that I'd keep you out of this."

"Out of *what*? You don't even know where to go up there."

"I'm a big boy. I have an idea. Charles Alan Watkins.

The town of Templeton. It's about four hours, give or take. It's already in the GPS."

"You have to take me! You don't know them. What are you going to go up and say, 'Uh, I know this'll sound a little weird, but you know that accident everyone's talking about . . . well did your husband know someone named Adrian, who might've had some reason to, um . . . *kill him*?' They're a simple farming family. They won't even talk to you. Trey's funeral is tomorrow. You just can't intrude."

"I've done this once or twice before, Dani. I think I can finesse the details. I'm not negotiating this. You just go to work."

"Screw work. I can get have someone to handle my shift in ten minutes. I'll be dressed in five. C'mon, Ty, you need me to go up there with you. Allie won't open up to you. You know she won't. At the very least, I can go to his funeral. Which I ought to anyway." Her towel slipped down, half exposing a breast.

Hauck turned away. "Besides, it could be dangerous. Would you put something over yourself, please?"

"Why, dangerous? I can handle myself." She tightened the towel back up. "Jesus, you're thinking I'm right, don't you! You learned something since I saw you last night and now you think I'm right! C'mon, Uncle Ty, what is it you know?"

His silence gave him away.

"Holy shit, I knew it! I knew it from the second I

150

saw him there, in that eddy. Poor Trey . . . He got caught up in something, didn't he?"

"I don't know . . ."

"Uncle Ty, I'm going! That's just the way it is. You wait for me, you hear!" She jumped up. "Blu, you watch him. Don't let him move." She ran into the bedroom, her towel flying off and exposing her backside as she bolted through the door. A tattoo on her shoulder. Before he averted his eyes.

He thought about just leaving while she was getting dressed, but now he knew she would only hop in her car and follow. Then he thought about maybe disabling her car. Disconnecting the battery or something. Or even dragging her ass back to Wade and throwing her back in a cell.

No, none of that would work, he realized. Other than the last thing.

She'd follow him.

Blu sat there staring at him, his large brown eyes sagging. "You take your job pretty seriously," Hauck said to him.

He yelled into her bedroom, "You do exactly what I tell you, you hear? This isn't a game, going up there. People are dead. You don't open your mouth unless I say so. And then it's only what I tell you to say. Understood?"

He could hear her opening and closing drawers, and running into the bathroom.

"You hear . . .?"

"Okay, I hear! I hear!" she yelled back, amid sounds of hastily throwing her things together.

"And when I say we come back, we come back. Whether you're satisfied, or whether you think I'm just another Wade. You just get in the car with your mouth shut and we come back. No argument. *Okay . . .?"*

"I said okay already, Uncle Ty! *Okay!"*

"Okay, then. I'm going to take a lot of shit for this if it comes out. Your dad's going to call and he's gonna want to know what the hell we're doing up there."

"He called last night. I told him you were great. We're safe for a couple of days."

"And then there's Wade. He's gonna wonder if I'm still around and what you're doing."

"He's the one who told me to get out of town! Anyway, I won't answer his calls. What is he going to do, subpoena me?"

"I would." Hauck stared at Blu with some deflation. *I must really be out of practice*, he thought.

She came back out of the bedroom. She'd thrown some things together in a yellow backpack, but she was wearing a waistless flax dress, V-neck, nice sandals, her golden hair long and brushed out, setting off her tan. "I know it's not a game up there, Uncle Ty. I just want to find out what happened. He was my friend."

Hauck nodded resignedly. He couldn't help but shake his head and say, "You look nice."

"I mean, we *are* going to someone's house. It's only respectful."

"You're right." Hauck looked at himself in a black polo shirt hanging out of his jeans.

"You were just going to show up looking like that and assume they would open up to you . . .?"

He shrugged, agreeing reluctantly. She had a point. "I'll stop and buy something on the way."

"Blu, let's motor, dude! We're going in Uncle Ty's car." The Lab jumped to his feet.

Hauck shook his head. "Uh-uh. No fucking way we take the dog."

"Of course he's coming. He goes everywhere with me."

"N-O. What didn't you hear . . .?"

But by then Dani had put together a plastic bag with his food and grabbed his leash, and was already past Hauck, with Blu, out the door.

"I'm only kidding. We'll drop him off at my friend's. She watches him if I have to leave town." Blu bounded into the back of Hauck's rented SUV. "Shut the door on the way out. It automatically locks. We better get moving, don't you think. Blu, in the back."

Way out of practice, Hauck muttered to himself, shutting the door.

153

CHAPTER TWENTY-SIX

Templeton was a tiny farming town in the eastern Colorado plains, an immense expanse of dry, seemingly endless brush and scrub about twenty miles east of Greeley, along the Cache la Poudre River.

This wasn't the Colorado of the ever-expanding Denver or the glittery Rockies. The land here was flat and dry. From the highway, brown and yellow fields stretched endlessly on either side. The road signs they passed advertised gun shows and summer potato festivals. One they saw showed the image of downtrodden American Indians being herded onto a reservation, with the ominous headline "Take Away Our Guns." Grazing cattle and livestock were visible from the road.

Once they got to Greeley they took Route 34, heading west along the river. The water seemed low, the level conspicuously below its banks. The fields on either side were brown and arid. It was clear the entire region was in the grip of an extended drought.

"Not much hope in being a farmer up here," Hauck commented sadly, remembering what Trey's family did.

"That's for sure." Dani nodded.

The town itself looked like one of those western towns time had forgot. One main street of washed-out, old brick storefronts: a bank, a café, an insurance co-op, a hardware store, and a feed center. All sandwiched around a couple of vacant storefronts. There was no one on the streets. It was clear the place had seen better days.

"I can see why Trey wanted out of this place as fast as possible," Dani said, as they stopped at the one light.

They'd input the Watkins address into the GPS, and it took them out of town and on a straight country road that followed the river, which continued to be extremely low on its sides.

The sky was vast and wide with a layer of thin, high clouds. Everything seemed bone dry. All they did see were the occasional isolated trestles and the military beige cylindrical structures of oil wells.

About ten minutes out of town, dried-up fields on either side, the GPS had them make a left and they drove along a long, wire-fenced farm, or what would have been a farm had anything actually been growing. Many of the fields were dug, but seemingly not planted with anything. The crops Hauck did see were small and intermittent—onions, maybe potatoes. Some early corn. It was June; they were trying to grow, but nature seemed to have another plan. Irrigation ditches were dug all around, and long, transportable watering trestles sprayed the best they could, but Hauck didn't see a stitch of real water anywhere.

At the end of the fence, the mailbox read WATKINS.

The house was a traditional red farmhouse with a couple of large barns: one for some equipment and tractors; the other, it appeared, for livestock. A few milking cows and some head of cattle ranged lazily in a field. Hay bales were stacked. A tall wind wheel sat at rest, as if waiting for a breeze. It didn't take a *60 Minutes* piece to see life was hard here.

"How the hell do they even scratch out a living here?" Hauck looked around gloomily.

"Trey didn't like to talk much about his family," Dani said. "He just said it was way different than in the mountains."

Around a dozen cars and trucks were pulled up either in front of the house or on the road. Hauck parked behind one and said to Dani, *"Ready?"*

She nodded. "Let me talk to Allie first. I'll introduce you to her."

"You're the boss. Let's go."

Two people were leaving as he and Dani stepped onto the front porch and held the door. They nodded hello.

The inside was austere and sparely decorated; comfort wasn't a big factor here. Utility was. Sparse, wooden furniture, a simple open kitchen, threadbare couches and chairs, a lot of tartan plaid. There seemed to be around fifteen to twenty people standing around the kitchen and living room, picking at meat-and-potato pies and desserts. A few vases of flowers put out.

Someone called out, "Dani!"

A pretty young woman rushed up to them, her blond hair pinned up, wearing kind of a peasant dress.

"*Allie!*" She and Dani came together in a warm hug. "I'm so sorry, Allie. How're you doing? What a stupid question . . . I can't believe this has happened. I'm just so sad."

"I know. I know." Allie Watkins put her face on Dani's shoulder and squeezed her. "Thank you for coming. I didn't know you would be here. I know it was such a long drive."

"Allie, I want to introduce you to my godfather, Ty. He's from back east. Connecticut. He's out here visiting."

"Nice to meet you." Allie looked up, a brave face, but her eyes a little swollen and red. "I'm sorry this is how you have to spend your trip. It was awfully nice of you to come."

"Allie." Hauck squeezed her hand. "Dani's told me a lot about your husband. I'm truly sorry for your loss."

She nodded bravely and sniffed. It was easy to see why people liked her. "Thanks. This is quite a place here, huh?" She shook her head at Dani. "The land time forgot. C'mon, let me introduce you to Trey's dad."

"Where's Petey?"

"With his grandma. Trust me, he doesn't exactly lack for attention here. I don't even know what to tell him yet. He's only two. He keeps asking for his dad."

Dani interlocked her fingers with Allie's. "I can only imagine how hard this must be."

They met Trey's dad, a tall, soft-spoken man with an easy smile but rough, callused hands, wearing a western pocketed shirt and pressed khakis, who introduced himself as Chuck. He was probably in his mid-fifties, but looked older, as such a hardscrabble life might do. They also met Trey's brother and sister: Nick, maybe eighteen, muscular and fit, short hair brushed forward; and Kelli, in her twenties, pretty, dressed a little more sophisticated than the rest of the family. She explained she worked back in Greeley, at the college.

Her father said she was going to be married in the fall to a professor there.

"Nice of you both to come." She greeted Hauck and gave Dani a hug.

"Dad, Dani's a whitewater guide back in Aspen," Allie explained. "She rode with Trey. In fact . . ." She stopped before saying what she was clearly about to, that Dani had been the one to find his son.

"He always liked to go fast," Chuck Watkins said with a shake of his head. "Years back, I caught him diving off that barn out there into a mound of hay as if it was a pond. That's a twenty-four-foot roof he went off of."

"How old was he?" Dani asked.

"I don't know." Trey's father looked at his daughter for confirmation. "Eight, maybe?"

"Something like that, Dad."

"Sounds like Trey," Dani said. "Bombs away." Both she and Allie smiled.

"Broke an ankle and his wrist to say he'd done it, though. And when it mended he went right back up and tried it again. Don't blame him much for wanting out of this place. He always lived on the edge. We always said, his first steps were down a flight of stairs. What was it he was into . . ." He looked at Allie this time. "Jumping off a cliff with a kite."

"Paragliding, Dad," Allie told him. "But it's safe."

"Sure, safe . . . Paragliding. Heli-skiing, the rapids . . . I always knew one day one of those things would catch up to him."

It was clear no one here was thinking in any way that Trey's death was anything other than a tragic accident befalling someone who had always pushed the envelope one step too far.

"Allie, I want to talk with you for a second if we can?" Dani took her arm. "Before more people come."

"Sure," Allie replied. "Excuse me, Dad, Mr. Hauck." She pointed to an open bedroom. "Why don't we go in there? Trey's old room. Where I'm staying."

159

The daughter and Dani excused themselves and Hauck was left standing with Chuck Watkins. "Any chance I can have a few words with you as well?" Hauck asked him. "Just for a second or two."

Watkins looked at him as if the two requests to talk were a little strange, but shrugged. "Why not." He led Hauck around near where some soft drinks and liquor were laid out on the dining room table. "Anything I can get you, Mr. . . ."

"Hauck."

"Sorry. I'm bad with names. Dani said you were visiting out here . . ."

"That's right. I'm from back east. Connecticut. I'm no farmer, but I can see things look tough as hell out here."

"These last three years . . ." The farmer shook his head grimly. "It would take an act of God to get something to grow here. Water tables are down eighty percent from what they were. We try to grow sugar beets, onions, potatoes. Maybe some baby carrots and feed corn. You see the result. That river used to be pretty good to us. For decades. Now . . ." He was about to add something, then stopped. "Now everything's working against us these days."

"Any chance of bringing water in? I've heard some farmers doing that in drought-stricken areas."

Watkins just looked at him and smiled. "Well, I *can* see you're not from around here, son. Anyway, you said you're not a farmer, Mr. Hauck. What field are you in?"

"Security," Hauck said. "And before that, law enforcement." .

"Law enforcement?"

"I was the chief of detectives with the Greenwich, Connecticut, police force for six years. And before that with the NYPD."

"Did you even know my son?"

Hauck shook his head. "No."

The farmer regarded Hauck with an evaluating stare, then looked toward Trey's bedroom. "I'm starting to get the sense you didn't drive all this way just to come to Trey's funeral. May I pour you a drink, Mr. Hauck?"

Hauck nodded. "Scotch would be nice."

CHAPTER TWENTY-SEVEN

Hauck asked Watkins if he'd ever heard of Colin Adrian. If Trey had ever mentioned him? If he knew any reason why someone would want to harm his son?

To each question the farmer just stoically shook his head, no, finally looking at Hauck a bit suspiciously, "*Harm him . . .?*"

"A person named Colin Adrian drove into the Roaring Fork park directly after Trey the morning he was killed and left a short time later."

"*So . . .?*" Watkins looked up at Hauck and furrowed his brow. "I'm not sure I understand."

Hauck took him through what Dani suspected. Deliberately, as to not upset him. As Hauck's intent became clear, the lines on the farmer's face grew deeper and more worn. "You're saying what, so as I'm clear."

Watkins put down his drink. "You think my son was murdered? And that this man, Adrian, might have done it?"

"I can't say anything for sure. I don't know if you heard, but a hot-air balloon went up in flames and crashed the next morning, killing all five who were on board. The operator of the balloon was someone who claimed he saw something the previous day when Trey was killed."

"Saw what?"

"I don't know. We never heard. Dani seems to feel strongly that it might have been connected."

Trey's father didn't seem happy and glanced toward the bedroom. "I thought you said she was a whitewater guide."

"I said I would follow up a lead for her. And the more we looked at it, the more it seemed credible."

"Credible? And your lead led here? To Templeton?"

"This person we traced led here, Mr. Watkins, Colin Adrian . . . He's from Greeley. Which is why I thought you might have known who he is."

Watkins nodded, glancing toward the bedroom. "And that's what she's talking to my daughter-in-law about in there?" His tone closed up like a fist.

"We didn't mean to intrude upon your family's grief, sir. We just wanted to see if there was any connection."

"I met with the police chief back in Carbondale . . ." Chuck Watkins said.

"Dunn. Yes." Hauck filled in the name.

"He didn't mention anything about any possible crime. In fact, he said even the Parks Department seemed to have come to a similar conclusion of what took place. That it was all an accident. And anyway . . ." He turned back to Hauck, a measure of distrust in his eyes. "Who the hell would want to murder Trey?"

"We didn't mean to upset you, Mr. Watkins." Hauck put his drink down. "If there's nothing you can tell us, we'll be on our way. If there *was* something, we just thought it would have been something you'd want to know."

Watkins nodded, running his index finger across his thin dry lips. "You see that boy over there . . .?" He motioned toward his younger son, Nick. Big-shouldered, boyish face, short-cropped hair, pumped-out chest. "He's got a scholarship to the Cowboys in the fall. CSU. He plays linebacker. Captain of his team. They won the league championships the past two years . . ."

"Good for him," Hauck said, impressed. "I played in college myself. Running back. Though not quite Division One."

"And where was that?"

"A small college in Maine called Bates. Division Three."

"All the same, you know what kind of commitment it takes. Nice as a choirboy, that kid, when it comes to people and schooling. But put him on the field and he

164

turns into something else. You mentioned the kind of life we lead here, and you're right, it tests even the toughest of souls. I inherited this farm. Lord knows why anyone would want it now. But that boy's got his whole life ahead of him. And my daughter, Kelli, I mentioned, she's engaged. To a young professor at the college in Greeley. They've got their whole lives ahead of them, too. Life around here, it beats you down in more ways than you can count. More ways than some math professor could conjure . . ." His gaze grew distant, fixed on no one in particular.

Then he turned back to Hauck. "My son was always one gust of wind or one loose snowdrift away from where we are today, Mr. Hauck. I knew it. Everyone in this room, if they were honest, knew it, too. He dropped out of school, lived his life the way he wanted, doing all those crazy things. It was selfish. Especially to that pretty young girl in there." He looked at his grandson. "And that kid. So don't come here and tell me my son died from anything other than his own recklessness or indifference unless you have something real solid to back it up with. He was gone ten years. I don't know who he knew and who he didn't. I knew he loved that river, though, and that mountain. I'm just not sure if they loved him back as much. And I think that's how I'm prepared to remember him, if it's all the same. You want to come here and bring stuff like that out, Adrian or whatever his name was, I don't care what your

CHAPTER TWENTY-EIGHT

Back in the car, Hauck asked Dani if Allie had anything to add, as they turned on the main road, heading back toward town.

She shook her head. "At least, not about Adrian. She'd never even heard of him. What about Trey's dad?"

"The same. Nor was he exactly pleased to even be discussing the subject."

"Allie said all this talk about if Trey was involved in something was starting to worry her a bit . . ."

"I can understand. And I'm afraid that's still all it is right now, Dani. Talk." He got back on the country road in the direction of Templeton. He knew he'd upset Watkins, a day before his son's funeral. At some point soon they'd have to make a decision on what to do. It was 5:30 P.M. If they just continued on home they could probably get there by ten or eleven with nothing to show for it.

"So where are we heading?" Dani asked.

"Into town. I could use a coffee," Hauck said. "What about you?"

She grinned. "You think there's a Starbucks there?"

"About the same chance we find a Williams-Sonoma." He slowed behind a pickup with a horse trailer attached. "We'll find something there and decide."

"Decide what?" Dani looked at him.

"Whether to go back tonight or not."

Chuck Watkins had shut things down pretty firmly. He also seemed to have written off his son . . . *Trey was gone ten years. I don't know who he knew or what he did.* He seemed a hard man and not fully understanding. And he clearly saved whatever he had inside for his two remaining kids.

"Uncle Ty, I want to go to the funeral tomorrow." Dani turned to him. "It's at ten A.M. Even if we go back we can still leave by noon and be back by five. Okay . . .?"

"We'll see."

"Uncle Ty, c'mon . . . It's only one night."

"It's not the night. It's that we don't really belong here, stirring things up. At least I don't."

"But I do," Dani said. "I belong here."

"*I said we'll see.*" Her eyes looked a bit surprised at his tone. Maybe he had come off a shade sterner than he intended. "You knew the rules," he said, trying to sound a bit more conciliatory. "Trey hadn't been here in years and we still don't have any connection between him and Adrian. We don't even know anything about Adrian . . ."

"We have an address."

Hauck looked at her.

"On the car registration, there's an address. In Greeley. Tuttle Road, right . . .?"

"Yeah, we have an address," he agreed begrudgingly. He continued on and they didn't talk for a while.

Finally Dani turned toward him. "Aren't you just the slightest bit interested?"

"I'm interested." He was interested in how Adrian wasn't Adrian, but someone who had taken his name. Which likely meant he knew him from somewhere. And it also meant he was someone who didn't want to be found. Hauck thought he was also interested in the odds of both Adrian and Trey being connected to this same area. He was interested in how Watkins had completely shut him down. "Question?" he said.

"What?"

"Which one of us is the internationally known detective here, anyway?" He winked at her.

That made her smile.

They were on the outskirts of Templeton again, coming back in. Hauck noticed the high school. Like every thing else around here it looked dated and run-down. A one-level-brick-and-glass building. Vintage seventies.

"Look at that . . ." His eye was drawn to something as they went past.

There was a big new football field with fancy bleachers and a state-of-the-art scoreboard. Large enough for everyone who lived in this godforsaken town, and half the county, too. A big GO MUSTANGS! sign at the top of the scoreboard. Maybe in Texas, Hauck was thinking, where Friday night football was king. Or one of those showcase high schools in Denver or Boulder. But what was it doing here?

My boy's captain of the team. They've won the league championship twice. He's heading off to play at CSU.

"*What?*" Dani asked, turning to see what he was referring to.

"Nothing." He looked at it again in the rearview mirror as they drove on.

The second time through, the town didn't get any less run-down. The main street looked as rickety as if a loud clap of thunder would bring it down. Which wouldn't necessarily have been a terrible thing, Hauck thought. Templeton was a town of ranchers and farmers, and there clearly wasn't a whole lot of ranching or farming happening. Ten years from now it might not even be on the map.

Except for the damn football field.

As they went through town, they noticed something

170

else, too. A beautiful park. It was clearly new, with pretty plantings, sloping down to the river. Almost like a town green. There was a large gazebo and an outdoor public stage, maybe for concerts. A cool-looking playground for the kids, with a skateboard park. More green than there was in the rest of the town all together. In fact, it was about the only thing of beauty in it.

"I bet it's the place to be during the Potato Festival," Dani joked as they went by.

"Yeah. Hard to figure why, though." Something just wasn't making full sense to Hauck. As Allie said, most of the town looked like it was the place time forgot.

"Why do you have to try and figure out the reason, Uncle Ty?" Dani turned to him. "It's just pretty. That's all."

He glanced at her and smiled. "You're right."

They stopped and had coffee. And a freshly baked apple crisp. Then they got back in the car and continued past a couple of motels. These both looked really run-down. They kept driving, toward Greeley, another sixteen miles, following the low-lying river.

"So where are we going now?"

"To look for a place to stay," Hauck said.

Her eyes lit up. "You're going to check out Adrian?"

"I don't know."

"You are, aren't you?"

He shrugged noncommittally. "One night. Long as we drove all this way . . . That's all. After the funeral we head back. Understand? After *you* go to the funeral. Watkins made it fairly clear, he doesn't want *me* there."

Dani nestled back in her seat, pleased. "Thank you, Uncle Ty."

"Just so you know the rules."

There was a slowdown up ahead on the road, some large rigs coming to a crawl, backing up traffic.

"There's a university in Greeley. There has to be somewhere decent to stay."

"The U of Northern Colorado," Dani confirmed. "I have some friends who went there. They specialize in—"

"Dani, hold on!" Hauck hit the brakes, throwing his arm out to restrain her. A large, eighteen-wheel tanker pulled out in front of them from a road coming up from the river, almost cutting them off.

"What the hell was that?" he said. As they passed the road, Hauck could see two more rigs, identical to the one that almost hit them, pulling up to the intersection about to turn. Each, a long, metal cylindrical tanker. The ones he had seen up ahead slowing traffic looked the same.

Hauck turned and looked down toward the river. "What do you think they're bringing up from down there?"

"Has to be oil." Dani shrugged. "Or natural gas, maybe. There must be a well."

Hauck sped up and passed the one that had pulled out in front of him. They all had the same large logo on the sides.

RMM.

"One helluva well," Hauck said. "Those things are all over the place here."

In fact, they'd passed several wells on the ride so far, some dug right in the middle of people's crop fields. Dani said they were called *pumpjacks*. A steel trestle and a large, bobbing drill head that resembled a *Tyrannosaurus rex*, but was actually called a horse head. Churning up and down. It operated by hydraulic power to pump the oil or natural gas back up from underground.

"How do you know all that?" Hauck asked her.

"I told you, I was a geology major in school."

The crops couldn't grow, so the farmers leased the land out to the exploration companies in hopes of something far more profitable. He knew new drilling advances had made exploration out here a lot more feasible.

Ahead of them, the convoy of big trucks picked up speed. Gleaming in the late-day sun.

He looked at the rig again. An arrow, circling through the letters *RMM*.

It was like the farmland had just been handed over to the oil and mining companies out here.

CHAPTER TWENTY-NINE

They found a place to stay at a Fairfield Inn on the main road leading into Greeley.

The next morning, Hauck drove Dani back to Templeton and dropped her off at the church just before ten o'clock. People were already filing in. He told her he'd be back to pick her up in a couple of hours.

"What are you going to do?" she asked as she got out of the car.

"Sightsee."

"Just watch out, Uncle Ty. I hear the sights can be a little dangerous here."

"I'll keep that in mind."

The address on the car registration was 4110 Tuttle Road in Greeley, which turned out to be several miles from town in the flat, expansive backcountry. Every once in a while Hauck saw a farm, cattle grazing, fields penned in by wire fences. Ford F-150s were definitely the preferred mode of transportation out here.

Tuttle Road was at an intersection off the main road, CO 49.

The traffic out here was sparse. Every minute or two a pickup or a Bronco would speed by. The homes he saw were white or red farmhouses and most had barns. He finally pulled up to a mailbox marked 4110 with just a hand-scrawled number on it at the end of a long, dirt driveway. A white pickup whooshed by and Hauck waited until it was out of sight. He turned in and decided to drive down the rutted road, dense brush crowding on each side.

About a hundred yards down he came upon a dilapidated house.

More shack than house actually. The front porch was askew and the stairs rotted and falling apart. The front door hung unhinged and slapped against the walls in the wind. It seemed totally abandoned. Clearly, no one had actually lived here in years.

Hauck got out of his car, the wind whipping through the creaking shutters.

His antennae began to buzz. Colin Jerrod Adrian. Who the hell was he? From near the same town as Trey. But Trey hadn't lived there in years. With no bank accounts, no taxes paid. No present at all. Only a murky, ill-fated past.

Staff Sergeant Colin Adrian was killed in Fallujah in 2006.

Hauck kicked around the deserted shack for a while, stepping onto the creaky steps, finding nothing there, just a dried-up well. Frustrated, he got back in his car and drove back out to the main road.

He considered going to one of Adrian's neighbors and asking about him. The nearest house was probably a quarter mile away, and this was clearly the kind of place where people wouldn't take to outsiders coming in and asking about their neighbors. It was quiet in all directions. The county road seemed to stretch endlessly into the hazy mountains miles and miles away.

A kid was dead. Five others, possibly connected. A police chief was withholding evidence. Why? To keep what quiet? *They'd have to have the means to carry it out,* he had said to Dani. *And the will.*

Who would possibly have the will?

Hauck looked around again and climbed out of his the car. The wind kicked up, carrying a few branches and dust in its path. He stepped up to the mailbox. It was a roomy, rectangular lockbox. A couple of unopened newspapers or phone books were on the ground, bundled in plastic. Hauck took out the Swiss Army knife that was attached to his keys. The road stretched empty in both directions. He inserted the tip of the pick blade into the keyhole and jiggled it around. He knew what to do. He could take a lawn mower apart and reassemble it with just a screwdriver. And this lockbox wasn't exactly built to withstand much of a challenge.

After a minute or so he felt the lock click.

Another twist, and the tiny lock pin released. He swung the box open. There wasn't much inside. A few envelopes. Local junk mail. A magazine or two. Mailers from Safeways supermarkets and Walmart. All were addressed simply to *Resident*. It didn't tell him much. Only one thing.

The magazines were current. Which meant that someone came out here on a regular basis to pick them up.

Finding nothing else, Hauck stuffed the stack of mail back in the box, ready to close it back up.

An envelope fell out that had been folded inside one of the mailers.

It was the only thing in there that even bore a name. And it wasn't Adrian's.

It was addressed to a John Robertson. From something called the Alpha Group. An address here in Greeley. Hauck jiggled it and held it up. This wasn't junk mail. There was a piece of paper inside. It actually looked like a check.

So someone did receive mail here. Adrian or Robertson, or whoever it was who had taken Adrian's ID.

The Alpha Group.

Hauck jotted down the address, 2150 Turner Street. Then he put the envelope back in the pile and closed it back up. The owner would know the minute he came back out here that someone was on to him.

But an hour or so from now that wouldn't matter anyway.

An hour or so from now he was pretty sure John Robertson would know exactly who had been here to find him.

CHAPTER THIRTY

He drove back into Greeley and followed the GPS to the location for the Alpha Group in a small office park outside town.

He parked outside the modern, redbrick building and stepped through the glass doors. The reception area was small, but upscale. A receptionist sat behind the front desk, a large logo behind her of an oil well trestle with lightning bolt running through it. Three words on a banner underneath it: INFORM. CHANGE. INFLUENCE. Hauck stepped up to her and she put some work aside and said cheerily, "Can I help you?"

"I'm trying to find a John Robertson," Hauck said. "Is he here?"

"Mr. Robertson . . ." The receptionist's reaction seemed to have multiple things going on in it: The first was surprise. Clearly, she knew the name, but it was obvious people didn't just come in off the street asking for him. But Hauck also detected some uncertainty, too. Uncertainty as to what to do. "Mr. Robertson isn't in the office right now. But I'll be happy to take your name."

"Does he work here?" Hauck inquired.

"He doesn't exactly work *here* . . ." she replied after a bit more hesitation. "I mean, out of this particular office."

"So how can I reach him? It's just on a personal matter." He could see he was making her a bit uncomfortable. However she'd been taught to respond to this particular question, it was getting beyond her training.

"How about I ask our administrative VP, Mr. McKay . . .? I'll see if he's busy. What did you say your name was?"

"Hauck." He gave her a business card.

"Please hold on a moment Mr. Hauck . . ."

She got on the line and said something in a low tone to what sounded like the manager's assistant. "He'll be right with you." She came back with a smile. "He's just finishing up a call." She pointed toward a couch with some magazines on the table.

"Feel free to take a seat over there."

"Thanks." Hauck went over. The periodicals were all energy related. Oil. Natural gas. There was a stack of company brochures there as well. Hauck picked one up.

It showed the same logo as on the wall. The same slogan too: INFORM. CHANGE. INFLUENCE. *Influence what?*

The brochure described Alpha as a company based out of Denver specializing in the energy field. It talked about "technical and crisis management solutions for today's critical energy and environmental issues." It showed a series of corporate executives, both in hard hats and business suits. Out in the field and in company boardrooms. There were photos of oil and gas rigs, rig workers at work, some fancy office buildings, a pretty park, reminding Hauck of the one they'd seen in Templeton. Even an upscale residential community with a golf course, as if all were examples of the happy world Alpha's efforts were achieving.

Hauck folded the brochure in his pocket.

A man stepped out from the back. He was average height, trim, fit-looking under his white dress shirt, like he lifted weights; mid-thirties, though he had lost most of his reddish hair to a high forehead. "Randy McKay . . ." he said amiably, reaching out his hand. His grip was firm, businesslike; out of some sales training regimen. Military.

"Ty Hauck," Hauck replied.

"Janet tells me you're looking for Mr. Robertson . . .?"

"Yes. Is he here?"

"I guess she told you John doesn't always work out of this office. Alpha has dozens of operational sites throughout Weld Country and the Wattenberg field . . ."

"The Wattenberg field . . .?"

"That's where we are now. Right smack in the middle of it. One hundred thousand barrels of oil a day and seven hundred and forty million cubic feet of natural gas from around twenty-two thousand active wells. Not all *our* clients, of course, but we have multiple projects going on, where John spends most of his time."

"I see. So what exactly does Mr. Robertson actually do for Alpha, if you don't mind me asking?"

"I don't mind at all." The manger smiled. "Though we don't normally give out that kind of information on our employees. Why don't we step in here . . . Janet, we're going to be in Conference Room A for a couple of minutes if anyone's needing me. Shouldn't be too long."

"Of course, Mr. McKay . . ."

The manager led Hauck down a hallway and into an antiseptic room with a polished wood table, a matching credenza; oil rig and mining photographs on the walls. It looked as if the room came straight out of some furniture rental catalog. "We're not normally so secretive, Mr. Hauck . . ." McKay motioned him into a seat. "But we do like to know who we're talking to before we divulge certain information . . ."

Hauck said, "I wasn't looking for any information. I just asked what one of your employees does."

"I understand. And you're right. Take a seat. Are you in the energy business?" He had a clear-eyed and direct manner. Even when he was diverting a question, he did so with a smile. "Your card says 'Talon.'"

"I'm not," Hauck said. "I'm in security."

"Security? You mean like with wires and alarms?" He smiled again. "Mr. Pettibone, our director of logistics, is out right now, but that sort of thing falls under his expertise."

"More like firm-to-firm," Hauck replied. "Or country-to-country."

"I see. Well, most of what we do is in the energy field. We're not so well known as some of the bigger oil service brands. I was actually in law enforcement for a while myself, after I got out of the service. Until I got tired of wearing the uniform, if you know what I mean. And where is it you said you know Mr. Robertson from . . .?"

"I didn't say I knew him. I just asked what he did."

"That's right. You did. Well, Mr. Robertson is what we call a senior coordinator of field projects. But like I said, he's currently away."

"Where is he?" Hauck asked, clear-eyed at McKay. "If you don't mind me asking."

"In the field."

Over the years, Hauck had been stonewalled by some of the best, and this guy was giving it his shot. "What exactly are 'field projects' for Alpha'?" he asked, his eyes roaming to the pictures of mining and drilling operations on the walls. "Are you guys drillers?"

"Not drillers, exactly. You might say we do field testing, handle certain site management issues that come up."

"Field testing? You mean like geological?"

"Similar to geological . . ." McKay nodded. "Just not in a lab."

"In the *field* . . ." Hauck said vaguely.

"That's right," McKay said again, that same stony smile. "The field."

"Your brochure seems to call it 'crisis management solutions for today's energy and environmental issues.'"

"Yes, I'm glad you were able to take a look," the Alpha man said. "You never know who actually reads through these things . . . But like any solutions-oriented firm, we like to think we take other people's problems and turn them into opportunities. Newer drilling techniques today come with equally new challenges for communities and local governments. We like to think we make those issues . . ." He paused as if searching for the right word.

"Go away . . ."

"Well, not quite 'go away.'" McKay smiled again. "But at least, become far more livable."

"Inform. Change. Influence," Hauck said.

"Now I see you *have* read up on us," the Alpha manger said. "And now what I suggest I do is that I take your card here, and when I can get in touch with Mr. Robertson, I'll make sure he gets it."

"And when might that be? I was hoping I might get a chance to speak with him face-to-face. I'm only here for a couple of days."

"Not for a while, I'm afraid." McKay stood up. "He's on assignment these days. Unfortunately, he won't be back this way for a while. How long did you say you were staying?"

"I don't know myself." Hauck stood up as well. "Too bad."

The Alpha manager looked at him curiously. "We like to think Weld County has its own austere charm, Mr. Hauck, but we know it's not on too many people's lists of their favorite places to visit. What brings you here, if you don't mind me asking?"

"I was out here to visit a friend Mr. Robertson and I may have had in common."

"Another time then, I'm afraid." McKay shrugged, feigning disappointment.

"I'm not sure that'll be possible. He's dead."

"My goodness, I'm sorry . . ." The oil manager looked surprised. "From around here? I could let him know."

"No, from Aspen," Hauck said at the office door. "And I think he does already. Know." Hauck kept his eye on McKay, searching for the slightest sign of recognition. The guy played his part out well. "Anyway, no bother. I'll be happy to find my way out. I appreciate your time." He put out his hand.

"Pleasure was mine," McKay said. "I'll make sure he gets this."

"Just tell him I'll just drop something in the mail next time."

"The mail?"

"He'll know what I mean."

On his way out Hauck stopped at a framed photograph he'd noticed on the wall when he was walking in.

An army photo. An entire unit, it seemed. At least sixty of them. Everyone in fatigues. *301st Air Division,* it read at the bottom.

Alpha Unit.

It was taken on an airfield tarmac, mountains in the background. The photo caption read, *Rasheed Air Base, 2009.* It looked like Iraq. In the back row, he noticed the person he had just spoken with. McKay. His hat off, a little younger-looking, with a bit more hair. Hauck thought he could make out a major's leaf on his uniform.

Alpha Unit. *What was that?*

Underneath Hauck saw a legend of names. He checked it, searching for the only one he knew. Maj. Randall McKay. He kept on looking until he found the other name he was looking for.

In the bottom row. Kneeling. A light-featured young man with a narrow, chiseled face, a hard jawline, light hair shaved close on the sides, military style, and a deep-set, expressionless stare.

Lance Cpl. John Robertson.

And next to him a smiling face in a floppy desert army hat.

Staff Sgt. Colin Adrian.

Alpha Unit had become the Alpha Group. *Crisis management solutions for today's energy and environmental issues.* Seeing no one around, Hauck took out his phone and bore in closely on the gaunt, narrow face. Robertson. And snapped the shot.

What the hell went on out there? Hauck stared closely at his face on the army photo.

In the field.

CHAPTER THIRTY-ONE

Back in his car, Hauck called in to Brooke at Talon. "I need another favor."

"You really *are* trying to get me in trouble, aren't you?" she said, only half in jest.

"I need you to look into the 301st Army Airborne Division. More specifically, into something called Alpha Unit. They were in Iraq or Afghanistan. I need to know specifically what they're about and what they did over there."

"Alpha Unit. The 301st Airborne. I'll get it as soon as I can. But Ty, I can't let you hang up just yet. Mr. Foley said he'll have my ass if you called in again and I didn't put you on. And I only half think that he was joking."

Hauck knew his boss was perfectly capable of doing

something like that, canning someone, simply to make his point to someone else. "Don't worry about Tom. I've got your back. Just get me that information as quick as you can. And Brooke . . ."

"Yes."

"This stays between us? Not anyone else in the company."

"That goes without saying, Ty."

"Especially Foley."

"So I guess you did, after all . . .?" He could hear the tiny smile in her voice.

"Did what?" he asked

"Get involved."

"Let's just say something's got my attention out here. And you know how that always seems to go."

"Yes." Brooke sighed. "I do know."

CHAPTER THIRTY-TWO

Dani hung with Trey's buddies Rudy and John Booth at the café in town, until they said that they had to head back to Carbondale. John played in a band and had a gig tonight in Glenwood Springs. They asked if she wanted to ride back with them.

"No. My stuff is in my uncle's car," she said. "He texted he's on his way."

She gave them both a hug. It had been a tearful ceremony. Both John and Rudy had asked to say something at it. They'd lost one of their own. Dani had her doubts, of course, about what had happened. But she didn't share them. At least, not until she knew if they led anywhere. She and Ty had already crossed the line a bit with Allie and Trey's father.

"We'll see you back in town." John Booth waved.

After the guys left, Dani stuck around the café. The waitress came up, a woman of about fifty, her dark brown hair in an old-fashioned bob. She was cheerful. Everyone seemed to know each other in here. Small town.

"I see your friends have left. Can I get you anything else?" she asked.

"How about a refill on the coffee, thanks . . ." Dani checked her watch. Ty had texted he was on his way. This wasn't exactly Starbucks, she acknowledged to herself. Lattes and macchiato would be a foreign language here.

"Never seen the lot of you before. What brings you all to town?" the waitress asked as she came back with a pot and refilled Dani's cup.

"We came for a funeral," Dani said.

"Oh," she said. "Chuck Watkins's boy?"

Dani nodded.

"So sorry to hear about that. I knew him a bit, growing up, before he went off. Seems like he died the way he lived, though. He was certainly not one to hold back."

"No, he wasn't," Dani agreed, smiling.

"I don't think he ever came back much after he left. I know he and his father never quite saw things eye to eye. No farmer, that boy. . . . We knew that the minute he got out of these parts he wasn't coming back." She took out a rag and wiped down the table. "Not that many people here would disagree with him."

191

"Disagree about what?"

"You're not family, are you?"

Dani shook her head. "Trey was a friend."

"Well, he's an honorable man, Chuck. His father. And nobody's fool. Everybody here respects someone who makes a go of it with what they're given. That farm's been in the family for a long time."

"The drought here has clearly cost him."

"Like it's cost a lot of people . . . But you have to move forward," the waitress said. "Look around, things are changing here. We have opportunities now."

"You talking the oil?"

"Honey, all the sugar beets and potatoes a man can plant in a lifetime won't match a minute's worth of what that land can really produce. I don't know why God saw to put it all here. Four years ago, this place was just a dried-up patch of dying cropland. Now we have schools, parks. People staying, not moving away. Jobs."

"I saw the park. And the football stadium. And I've seen this logo around a bit. RMM?"

"You'll get used to it if you spend a day here." The waitress laughed. "Resurgent Mining and Mineral. And bless them. You can ask anyone here, they'll tell you."

"Tell me what?"

"Like I said, every man's entitled to live his life as he sees fit. But one thing you don't want to mess with"— the waitress folded her rag in her apron—"is a town's future."

192

Dani noticed her boss behind the counter, who seemed to be giving her the eye. There was something almost eerie and swept under the surface about what was going on in this place.

"Never mind anyway . . ." The waitress saw her boss looking at her. "I've probably said enough. Why anyone who knows me ends up calling me Gabby. Let me know if you need anything else, honey, okay?" Then she looked back at the grill. "Junior, that stack of blueberries ready for table six yet?"

CHAPTER THIRTY-THREE

Hauck turned onto Route 34 on his way back to pick up Dani.

It was clear Alpha was keeping what Robertson did for them under the radar. The guy had taken someone's identity, an army friend from his old unit. He received his mail at an abandoned house—who knew who owned it? He worked amorphously in what they referred to as "the field."

Yet he was down in Aspen last week, where whatever fell under the job description of "senior field coordinator" intersected tragically with Trey Watkins. Maybe with that hot-air balloon as well. He had served with his boss, McKay, in Alpha Unit, in Iraq and Afghanistan. Hauck had been up against this type of resistance before, many times. He knew when he was being stonewalled and told to butt out.

Those were precisely the times when he knew it was time to dig deeper.

Halfway back to Templeton, on the stretch of the road that followed the river, he noticed one of those gleaming, eighteen-wheeler oil tankers—identical to the ones he and Dani had seen yesterday—about a quarter mile behind him and coming up him fast.

He realized he was almost at the very same spot where yesterday they had seen them pull onto the main road from the river.

The shiny exterior of the long, cylindrical tanker glinted sharply in the sun.

RMM—that was the logo on them, he recalled.

It was a gold mine. What did McKay say, a hundred thousand barrels a day? Seven million cubic feet of natural gas. A hundred gold mines. Against it, a bunch of dried-out crops and farmers . . . How could they even compete? The fancy park, the state-of-the-art football facility. Templeton was bought and paid for, and the check read "RMM." Everyone was grabbing their share of the Wattenberg field.

Everyone except Chuck Watkins maybe.

Hauck glanced again in the mirror and saw that the big oil rig he had seen a quarter mile behind had now pulled within a couple of hundred yards. He was nearing the turnoff where he had seen them come up from the river, by his best guess, a half a mile or so up ahead. That's where this one would likely be turning into, he surmised. To whatever well was down there. He thought of going down there to check.

As he neared, he saw an identical rig pull up at the intersection. It pulled out, slowly at first, its turning radius swinging it wide into the oncoming lane until it righted itself a hundred yards or so in front of Hauck. Hauck slowed. Gradually, the tanker built up speed, ten to twenty to thirty miles per hour.

The rig in his rearview mirror had now made up most of the gap on him. It seemed likely it would turn onto the same road to the river where the one in front of him had just come out from.

The one that was just ahead of him now . . .

Hauck didn't notice a blinker on. And he didn't seem to be slowing. Hauck sped past the turnoff.

Maybe fifty yards behind him now, the large oil rig did as well.

And it continued to pick up speed and narrow the gap until it was right on Hauck's tail. The one in front of him was cruising along at around thirty. Hauck was suddenly sandwiched between the two giant rigs.

"Take it easy, pal," Hauck said, glancing in the rearview mirror. "What's the hurry?"

Hauck looked ahead to try to pass. The traffic was light and they were on a straightaway with a dotted line, but as he swung into the oncoming lane and hit the gas, the oil rig in front of him sped up as well. For a moment, Hauck found himself completely in no-man's-land. He looked behind. The truck behind him kept up its pace as well. *They are playing possum with me!* He didn't dare try it. He squeezed back in lane in between the trucks. For a second they just kept their speed.

Having fun? Hauck glared in his mirror behind, trying to make out the driver's face.

The truck behind him honked. Hauck caught a glimpse of the driver. White. Baseball cap. Reflective sunglasses. He honked again.

The truck in front began to slow.

That was when it dawned on Hauck that these assholes weren't playing a game with him at all.

So here's the welcoming committee, he said to himself. Courtesy of Alpha and RMM.

That sure was quick.

The rig in back picked up its speed again. With mounting alarm, Hauck thought for a second that he was about to be dead-on rammed. He sped up, hugging the Colorado license plate of the rig in front. They were all cruising along at fifty. He glanced behind. He noted to himself that if the guy in front of him suddenly stopped . . .

Hauck's blood started to tighten.

He was in one of those compact, four-cylinder SUVs. Not a lot under the hood. He saw a clear path up in front of him now and decided to gun it and make a run for it. He gave it everything he had.

He shot out into the oncoming lane. His speed was

up to seventy now. Eighty. He pulled alongside the truck in front. Ninety. The sonovabitch picked up his speed as well. Keeping pace.

Asshole.

Hauck kept the pedal to the floor and got about halfway past when he saw a filmy object on the road far ahead and realized he couldn't risk this. He immediately hit the brakes, letting the front truck shoot by him, and ducked back into his lane, barely squeezing in as the creep behind him was tight on his tail.

Seconds later, a UPS truck whooshed by. What Hauck would have met head-on if he'd continued to pass.

Now, it was crystal clear what was going on.

The road curved along the river now and he couldn't pass. The cab behind him was virtually on top of him. He was trapped. They were toying with him. He *hoped* they were only toying. This was a game of cat and mouse, and clearly he was the one with the big ears and long whiskers. His heart began to beat with some urgency.

They could flatten him at any moment.

Doing sixty, Hauck glanced at the road's shoulder on the right. The road was slightly elevated, with a drop-off of three to four feet between the shoulder and a dried-up field. Enough to send his car into a deadly roll if he went over. The sonovabitch in back had pulled up on his tail. Hauck had the sense the guy was about to ram his rear. He kept on looking behind him and then ahead, his pulse going as fast as the car. He had to do something. And do it now. His nerves picked up as he glanced at the side of the road. Behind him he heard the rumble of the truck's engine hitting another gear.

His car was a rental, and he was on the hook for it, but hell, he decided, as he saw it coming right on top of him, a thousand-dollar deductible was a whole lot better than his life.

He jerked his wheel sharply to the right, forcing his SUV onto the pebbly shoulder, where he spun into a shaky, screeching turn, trying to hold it together. Spraying gravel, he tumbled over the three-foot embankment, his SUV nosediving into a ditch, then righting itself with a huge bounce that nearly flung him out of his seat. He came to an abrupt stop in a cloud of dust and flying pebbles.

Hauck's heart flew into his throat. *"Sonovabitches!"* Dust was everywhere. He watched the other two rigs drive off down the road, the drivers probably laughing to themselves over the radio. They could have easily killed him if he had rolled. He couldn't see if the trucks had kept going or stopped. If anyone was coming back for him. His breaths were heavy in his chest and his heart was pulsing, seeming about three times its normal size.

He had an urge to gun the car and turn around and head back to Greeley, and give McKay a sense of how he appreciated the escort.

CHAPTER THIRTY-FOUR

Flashing blue-and-red lights came into focus. A white-and-blue police SUV drove up at high speed.

The committee chairman, Hauck said sarcastically.

It slowed as it came in sight, slowly bumping over the elevated shoulder, and pulled up next to him, about five feet from Hauck's car.

The driver stepped out, khaki uniform, bald on top, short red hair on the sides. The requisite shades. Above the gold shield on the door it said, TOWN OF TEMPLETON, COLORADO.

And beneath it, CHIEF OF POLICE.

"You all right, mister?" The cop stepped over to Hauck's vehicle.

"Fine." Hauck lowered the window. "Just a friendly driving lesson from those two rigs that probably just

201

sped right past you going around eighty. Guess I flunked."

"*Yeah.*" The chief cackled amusedly. "Those big ones sometimes act like they're the only ones on the road. You really have to watch yourself out here. Glad I was coming by."

Yeah, just coming by, Hauck snorted to himself. McKay was probably on the phone to him the second Hauck left his office. "Thanks. You the chief there?"

"Until they take the job away from me . . ." The policeman grinned. "Riddick," he said. "So where you heading, if you don't mind me asking?"

"Back your way," Hauck said. "I'm picking up my niece."

"She lives here?" Riddick asked, almost as if he knew.

"No. We only came in yesterday."

"Not much to see in Templeton but onion fields and the potato festival. And that's in July."

"We came for a funeral," Hauck explained.

"Ah . . . Chuck Watkins's boy. Real sad . . . Tried to be there myself. You're sure your car will make it out of there? I could run you back if you need to."

"I'll be fine," Hauck said, giving the engine a rev. "However, if you come across those two again, I wouldn't hold it against you if you'd give them each a choke hold from me."

"You wouldn't, would you?" The chief chuckled again. "Just consider yourself lucky. What did you say your name was again?"

"Hauck."

"I've seen a lot worse, Mr. Hauck. I once knew this guy, he was driven straight off the road by a couple of those mothers a few years back. Almost flew right into the river over there. Nearly drowned. That was when there was a whole lot more water. Wish I could remember his name . . ." The cop tapped his forehead. "Doesn't work quite like it used to, know what I mean? Not that that matters, but I suspect you'll be leaving soon, now that the boy's in the ground?"

"Sooner or later. There's something about this place I'm starting to like."

"Yeah? And what would that be?"

"I don't know, the hospitality?" Hauck said.

If smiles could shoot things, Riddick's would have to be licensed by the NRA. "So I could run you back. Last chance. Never know when another of those rigs will come up again. Out of the blue."

The offer had more of a feeling of a threat to Hauck, than an invitation. "Won't be needed. And like you said, you were headed in the opposite direction anyway. I wouldn't want to hold you up."

"So I was." The chief laughed again, but this time without mirth. "Well. I'm glad you're okay . . . Maybe pull over next time, when you see them come up on your tail."

"Be sure of that," Hauck said.

Riddick went back to his vehicle and opened the

driver's door. "Ah, I remember now . . . That name I couldn't recall. Who got run off the road up here. It came back to me. It was John," the chief said. Hauck saw his face reflected back in the guy's shades. "John Robertson."

He let the name sink in.

"But that name wouldn't mean anything to you, would it now . . .? You're just passing through."

"Nothing at all." Hauck didn't need it explained further. "Anyway, I hope he's okay."

"Who?"

"Your friend. Robertson."

"To my knowledge . . ." Riddick scratched his head. "Haven't seen him in a long while." He climbed back into his car. "Funny thing, though, the longer you stick around this place, the more you learn anything can happen here."

"I'll be sure and keep that in mind."

CHAPTER THIRTY-FIVE

"Well that sure took a while," Dani said with a roll of her eyes. She was waiting on the street outside.

"Ran into a bit of a speed bump on the way," Hauck said apologetically.

"*An accident?* Look at your car, Uncle Ty. It's a mess." It had picked up a new layer of dust.

"Not an accident." Hauck shrugged. "Welcoming committee."

"You didn't run in to Robertson, did you?" Dani's eyes lit up with alarm.

"More like from the friendly folk at Alpha and RMM."

Dani looked at him, then at the SUV again, its wheels all covered in dust. "Is everything okay, Uncle Ty?"

"I'm fine. I could use a coffee, though. Maybe something to eat."

"Park over there then. I think I know just the place."

Inside, over a coffee and a bison burger, he told her about what he'd found in the mailbox at Robertson's abandoned property that led him to Alpha.

And then his meeting there with McKay. The run-around they gave him at the mere mention of Robertson's name. "They're some kind of energy consulting company. He's got some vague job there, though he's never around. Coordinator of field activities."

"What kind of 'field activities' brought him to the Roaring Fork River?" Dani snorted cynically. "Was he looking for oil there?"

"I don't know. But the Alpha Group seemed to have originated as a military unit in Iraq. The 301st Airborne. How that ties into the energy business, I have no idea. But I saw a photo of the unit on the wall, and both McKay and Robertson were in it. As was their pal Adrian, who was killed. I'll find out what the connection is. I have my office working on it now."

"So what happened on the road?" Dani asked again. "Look, you're cut, Uncle Ty!" She put a napkin to his forehead and dabbed at a small cut under the hairline, where his head must have nicked the wheel.

"Just a little warning."

"Uncle Ty, you're bleeding and your car looks like it's been in the Sahara to Cape Town rally. What do you mean a little warning?"

Not wanting to worry her, he told her about the two

trucks; the same as the ones they saw yesterday; and being caught between them and how they'd pretty much driven him off the road; he tried to make light of it as best he could.

"My God, they could have killed you, Uncle Ty! We have to take it to the police."

"I think I already did. Take it to the police." Hauck told her about his meeting with the local chief. "Any reason you think the police here are going to be sympathetic to some outsider who they hope will be out of their hair by tonight and who claims he was mishandled by a couple of RMM boys getting their jollies? That was all planned, Dani."

"Planned?"

"It was a message. To butt out. On Robertson. To get my ass out of town."

"But you could have been hurt."

He smiled. In the past couple of years he had been beaten within an inch of his life, dragged from a speeding car in London, dangled over a rushing river in Croatia, and still carried the scars from having been shot a bunch of times. "I'll be fine."

"That waitress . . ." Dani leaned forward and nodded toward the one she'd been speaking with earlier, her voice almost in a whisper. "I spoke with her while you were away. *RMM* stands for Resurgent Mining and Mineral. It's a big energy exploration company out of Denver. I googled it while I was waiting for you. They're the big honcho here. The ones behind all the parks and fancy bleachers. You ought to see the senior center and the town hall as well. Apparently Trey's father seems to have pissed them off in some way. A lot of the townsfolk here seem to resent him."

"Why is that?"

"Not sure. I got the impression he was somehow standing in the way of the oil and gas development that's going on here. She clammed up pretty quickly once she got going. I think her boss over there gave her the evil eye. But she did say, 'One thing you can't do is stand in the way of a town's future.'"

"Can't stand in the way of the truth, either, when it's ready to spill out."

His cell phone vibrated. He took it out and saw that it was Brooke. "Hopefully, this will make things a little clearer."

CHAPTER THIRTY-SIX

"I think I got what you want," his assistant said. "On the 301st Airborne. And Alpha Unit . . ."

Hauck excused himself and stepped outside. He leaned against the window on the old brick façade overlooking the dilapidated Main Street. "Go ahead."

"They were a Special Forces group in Iraq and Afghanistan, specializing in what they call PsyOps. Do you know what that is?"

Hauck shrugged. "The use of psychological tactics to influence the mind-set of the enemy or a local population in war . . .?"

"That's part of it. I was told this sort of thing has been going on since World War II, when we began dropping leaflets to encourage the resistance against the Nazis. In Iraq, though, you remember how during the Surge it came out how we started buying off Sunni tribal leaders to disaffect against Al Qaeda? And the same in Afghanistan?"

"Yes."

"Well, these are the guys who created and implemented that strategy. It was their job to influence not only the opposition, but the local populations as well. They did it with leaflets and disinformation, then ratcheted it up to spreading cash around, building hospitals, things like that. Performing lifesaving medical operations on kids. Anything that would win over the locals and paint a positive image of the United States. And underscore atrocities committed by the Taliban."

"Propaganda, basically," Hauck said.

"Propaganda, yes, in regards to information and branding. That's apparently what's referred to as 'white' PsyOps. The standard, informational stuff. Then there's what's known as gray. That when they start to set things up themselves, messages that they want promulgated widely. I was told an example of that was the toppling of Saddam Hussein's statue in that square in Baghdad during the early days of the war. It was always seen to have been a spontaneous event, but now it turns out it was fully staged and choreographed by the PsyOps people. Cameras and all."

"I didn't realize that," Hauck said. His gaze was caught by a sleek black SUV that pulled up across the street, its windows tinted, in contrast to the dusty Ford 150s and beat-up GMC Yukons that were everywhere else in town. "I thought that was all legit."

"I guess that was the point. But there's a whole other aspect to this PsyOps thing as well. The part that isn't in the brochure. The dirty-business side. As in bribing and paying off key tribal leaders to switch sides. And going in and kidnapping and eliminating any bad actors who quite didn't see it their way. One night someone goes to bed in his hut with his family, someone stirring up the townsfolk about maybe drone strikes or innocent people being killed. Come morning, there's only an empty blanket and a teapot in the tent where he used to be. Or the whole family's found dead in their beds and no one's heard a peep."

"I figure that's what they call black PsyOps," Hauck volunteered.

"You got it. The 301st Airborne was the army's PsyOps division in Iraq . . . And you asked about Alpha Unit . . ."

"Let me guess. Alpha Unit was the part of it that handled the black kind of stuff. The dirty work."

"I guarantee no one goes around talking about it," Brooke said. "But bingo."

Sonovabitch . . . "Crisis management solutions to technical and environmental problems . . ." These bastards did all the black-stuff work. In Iraq and here. McKay. Robertson. Bribing local leaders. Killing and kidnapping the opposition.

211

Hauck leaned back against the window. *What the hell would they be up to here?*

"That it?"

"You asked me about how it had morphed into this consulting company in the energy field. The CEO is a James Stengel. Formerly Army Colonel James Stengel, of the 301st. Senior commanding officer of . . . I bet you can fill in the blank?"

"Alpha Unit."

"Much of the senior management seems to be composed of people who were part of the team in Iraq and Afghanistan. And as I think you already know, they seem to have found a niche in the energy business now."

Softening the opposition. Buying off the local populations. The dirty work, Hauck reflected. *Like geology . . .* McKay had said with kind of a wry grin. *Just not in a lab.*

"You got a client list for them?" Hauck asked.

"Let me look. I'm on their website now."

Hauck checked out the black SUV again. The front passenger window had cracked a bit. He could almost hear the camera clicking away.

"Okay I'm there . . ."

"Who's at the top?"

"Let me see . . . Nebula Exploration and Gas. They're one of the big ones. They're a drilling and site management firm up in the Bakken Field in North Dakota. I only know that because my sister lives up there."

"Who's next?"

"Dillard Oil. You know them?"

"No. But next . . ."

"Next is a mining and exploration company out of Denver. It's called Resurgent Mining and Mineral."

"Yeah," Hauck said, glancing at the black SUV up the street, "they're all over the place here."

"You want me to find anything on them?" Brooke volunteered.

"Not sure I'll need that." He looked at the car. "I think they already found me. However, there is one more thing, Brooke. There was a balloon crash in Aspen three days ago. Five people killed. There's an investigative team there looking at it. I want you to have one of our people check in on how it's progressing . . ."

"Progressing?"

"If they found anything suspicious in the wreckage."

"You sound like you're getting in pretty deep out there, Ty."

"Tell Tom I haven't forgotten about him. And thanks, Brooke. I'll be in touch again."

He hung up and looked back up the street, but the black SUV had moved on.

CHAPTER THIRTY-SEVEN

Back inside, Hauck sat back down at the table. Dani stopped texting and put down her phone. "Who was that?"

"My office."

"Okay." She waited. "*And* . . ."

"And I don't want you playing detective anymore, Dani. You said it yourself, when you heard what happened to me on the road. Things are heating up."

"That's not fair, Uncle Ty. I can take care of myself."

"The truth is," he said, looking at her with concern, "it would make me feel a lot more comfortable if you could head back home."

"Home?"

"You said a few friends came up for the funeral. Any chance you can drive back with them?"

"And then what about you?"

"I'll be along soon. In a couple of days. When I see what's happening."

"You can't just shut me out of this, Uncle Ty. I'm the one who brought it to you."

"Yeah, and look where it landed you. In jail."

"You're still gonna need me, if you're intending to go back to Trey's father. And besides, my friends already went back. They left a couple of hours ago."

"Oh." Hauck gritted his teeth, disappointed. "Then I want you to stay at the motel and hang out on your iPhone tomorrow. I've got some business to attend to."

"What kind of business?"

"I'd rather not share it, Dani."

"Why are you suddenly shutting me out, Uncle Ty? What's changed?"

"What's changed is that there's some dirty business going on here, Dani, and it's not just the oil. RMM is using military-trained PsyOps teams—those are people who are trained to twist behavior, interrogate bad guys, intimidate the local populations in Iraq and Afghanistan. Of which the Alpha Group is a key player."

"Iraq and Afghanistan?" She screwed up her brow. "What would they be doing here?"

"I don't know."

"You think Trey was killed now, don't you, Uncle Ty?"

Hauck edged toward her. "You mind keeping your voice down just a bit?"

"But you *do* . . .!" She dropped it a level, but the wide-eyed look on her face reflected her shock as what he just said sank in.

He nodded. "I'm starting to think that's a possibility. Yes."

"And you think it was this guy Robertson who did it? Right?"

He nodded again. "He was part of a black ops unit of Alpha back in Iraq . . ."

She sat back, and blinked. "I was right. Oh my God. I almost didn't really want to hear this. So what are we going to do?"

"What are *we* going to do . . .? You're going to watch TV or listen to your iPhone and chomp down room service."

"They don't have room service where we're staying, Uncle Ty."

"Then we'll switch to somewhere that does. Either way, you're staying put, Danielle. That's our deal."

"You're starting to sound like Wade now . . ." She sat back, narrowing her eyes, letting it all sink in. Then she looked back at him. "You're going to RMM."

He didn't answer.

"You are, though. You're going to just walk in there? Like, *Here I am?* With what you now know?"

"The truth is, we really don't know anything. Other than these people are here and something murky is going on. Besides, RMM's a huge energy conglomerate.

216

They won't want to make a scene. Anyway, that's kind of what I do."

"What do you have, a death wish or something?" She stared at him.

"It's sort of like navigating rapids," he said with a widening grin, "but on land."

"That's really funny, Uncle Ty," she said, sitting back. She clenched her fingers into a fist and tapped it against the table several times as if in disbelief. "I can't believe Trey was actually murdered. I know I said it from the start, but now that things are coming out, I can't believe it's real. So we're staying?" She turned to him.

"Yeah, we're staying." Hauck nodded. He took her fist in his hand and squeezed. "One more day."

CHAPTER THIRTY-EIGHT

Resurgent Mining and Mineral was in a modern, redbrick office building on the outskirts of Greeley, close to the government buildings and the courthouse.

It was a huge oil and gas exploration company, based in Denver. Hauck looked it up the night before. It did upwards of six billion in sales in the past year and was listed on the New York Stock Exchange. It operated everything from coal to mines to hundreds of oil and gas wells spread over the central mountain states. It also was a partner in various pipeline projects in Canada.

Hauck parked in the lot and went in through sliding-glass doors. The lobby was a two-story atrium with oversize photographs of the company's interests. He went up to the woman at the curved reception desk and asked to speak to Guy Stafford, who was listed on the RMM website as the general manager of the Wattenberg region.

"I'm sorry, but Mr. Stafford is in Denver today. Did you have an appointment?'

"No." Hauck slid across his card. "I'm a partner in a global security firm back east. I was out here on other business and was hoping to speak with someone about what we do."

"Let me see if Mr. Moss is available. He's our regional VP of operations. I think this might fall under him. You can wait over there."

Unlike Alpha, with its cramped waiting area and brochures, Resurgent had a plush, nicely decorated section with a watercolor over the couch, and its annual report displayed prominently on the coffee table. A flat-screen monitor was on the wall, with a video showcasing the company's activities. Hauck watched for a few minutes, an actor he recognized going through all the precautions the company took in the drilling of its wells, the redundant layers of steel casings the well hole was encased in to protect the surrounding land, and the partnerships it created with the local communities.

"*At RMM,*" the actor said, "*we like to think of ourselves as a tenant in the local community, one that takes pride in it, and leaves it in even better condition than when we arrived . . .*"

Hence the fancy football field and all the government buildings, Hauck said to himself.

"Mr. Hauck." The receptionist stepped over to him. "Mr. Moss can see you now. Celia will take you back . . ." She walked him over to another nicely dressed woman, who brought him up a wide staircase and then down a corridor lit by a long glass picture window with a view of the far-off Rockies. "You're lucky. Mr. Moss just freed up for a few minutes. It's rare for him to see anyone without an appointment." Was there anything she could get for him? she asked. *Coffee? A soda?*

"Thank you," Hauck said, walking down the long corridor. "I'm fine."

She dropped him off at a spacious office with wide windows and the same expansive view. "Right in here . . ."

A middle-aged man in a shirt and tie, the sleeves rolled up, a bit round in the belly, stepped up from behind his desk. "Thanks, Celia. Wendell Moss," he said, introducing himself with a firm handshake. The kind of reassuring, midwestern demeanor you might expect from someone in a pilot's uniform stepping out of an airline cockpit.

"Ty Hauck."

"Yes, I know who you are. We don't exactly get many celebrities out this way. Especially in our neck of the woods. We once brought in a couple of the Denver Broncos and took them out on-site, kind of a motivational thing. Signed a bunch of autographs for the guys . . ."

"Well, I'm not sure any of them would exactly treasure mine," Hauck joked, suspecting that word traveled quickly between Alpha and RMM, and that the conversation about his visit there with McKay had already been had. "Nice of you to carve out a couple of minutes . . ."

"Not a problem. So what brings you out our way? Surely there's not much going on here for a man such as you."

"Your secretary gave you my card?"

"Have it right here. Talon. Security outfit. I'm sure I've heard of it."

"We're a large, international firm, with interests in several sectors of the security business. Digital protection. Foreign countries. One of the prospective firms we were looking into is called the Alpha Group. You know them?"

"Alpha . . ." Moss motioned him over to a small, round conference table. "They handle some advance marketing and technical matters for us. The kinds of things that need some massaging long before the first drill bit goes in the ground."

"Can you tell me exactly what you mean?"

"Oh, site planning and community dynamics. Boring stuff." Moss waved. "I'm sure they'd be happy to tell you themselves."

"Actually I already visited there," Hauck said, certain that Moss already knew. "And they were kind of vague.

I think they used the phrase 'It's like geology, just not in a lab . . .'"

"Yes." He grinned. "I've heard that before myself. Let's just say, they don't tell us where the oil is, just smooth over the pesky, administrative details of getting us to it. From that point on is where we come in."

On his credenza Moss had several photos. A pretty, blond wife. A boy and a girl. Playing soccer, biking. A few framed awards and citations hung on the wall.

"Alpha has its roots in the military, doesn't it?" Hauck volunteered.

Moss looked at him. "Yes. I think it does actually."

"So how does a U.S. Army PsyOps team solve technical problems for a huge oil and gas company like yours?"

The oilman smiled, the slightest shifting in his gaze. "Well, the short answer to your first question is, there are veterans all over this industry. In RMM as well. Much of what we do involves very challenging and sensitive work, both technically and environmentally, and that kind of training comes in handy."

"Yeah, I guess it's not exactly good optics to be sinking drills in the ground uselessly," Hauck said.

"Or a good use of money. But today, we don't quite do that. And when I used the word *environment* I was actually speaking far more broadly. First, for us, we have to identify the deposit. There's a lot of new science that enables us to pinpoint that much more accurately than in years past. Soil testing. Three-D imaging. Then we have to extract it, in both a cost-effective and environmentally friendly way. Not just for the money or the *optics* . . . as you say"—Moss focused on Hauck's choice of word coolly—"but for our own charter as well. We take our connection to the community very seriously here, Mr. Hauck, I can assure you of that."

"Yes, I saw the video downstairs."

"Then you get the picture. There are several advancements in drilling technology going on today you may have heard of. Horizontal drilling. Dynamic fragmentation . . ."

"Fracking?" Hauck volunteered.

"Yes, as it's more widely referred to. These techniques allow us to tap into deposits that were heretofore unreachable, drill multiple arms off each well site, which makes it cleaner and more community friendly. So it's important to work in concert with the local population—the town, the government—to make sure our goals are all aligned. Alpha assists us with this. Tries to show them that our gain is their gain too. Not only in terms of drilling leases, which can be lucrative, of course. Far more so than all the potatoes and corn seed they can grow in a lifetime. But for the community as well. In our trade, there is a certain winning of the local hearts and minds that becomes necessary."

One day some bad actor stirring up trouble just disappears during the night from their bed . . . Hauck recalled Brooke saying. *Black PsyOps.*

Hauck wondered if Moss was speaking of Chuck Watkins.

"We're not just some big, bad oil and gas company trying to take away their way of life, Mr. Hauck." Moss smiled. "Way too many regulations. It's just not done that way anymore."

"By winning the local hearts and minds," Hauck said, "I assume you mean the fancy new football field, the parks and new police station . . ."

"And the schools and the medical centers . . . Anyway, all that's only the short answer to your question. The long one would probably take all day and. . . ." Moss glanced at his watch.

"I appreciate your time."

"Look, Mr. Hauck, let me lay my cards on the table. I know who you are and what you've done . . . RMM is a firm that appreciates one's service for their country. Perhaps you'd like to see that firsthand."

Hauck chuckled. "I think I may already have."

"Sorry . . ." the oilman said.

"RMM's appreciation. Yesterday I was run off the road by a couple of your big rigs. On my way back from my visit with Alpha."

"*Our* tankers . . .?" Moss acted surprised.

Hauck shrugged. "Big, bright letters on the sides. *RMM.* Impossible to miss. Then the police chief drove up and kind of convinced me Templeton wouldn't be the best place for me to put down roots."

Moss gritted his jaw and grabbed a pen. "I'm sorry. I didn't hear about that. I'll make a point of looking into it."

"Not to worry. No harm, no foul."

"But at the least, not a very nice way to repay your interest in their company, was it?" Moss smiled circumspectly, giving Hauck the impression he didn't for a second believe the reason for Hauck's visit here.

"The same occurred to me."

"Anyway, what I was referring to," the RMM executive said, "was to drive you out myself and have you meet Hannah."

"Hannah?"

"Hannah One. She's the biggest-grossing well in the entire Wattenberg field. Over five hundred barrels a day. There's also a Hannah Two and a Three. C'mon, you can come with me." He stood up. "I'll drive you out, if you're free."

Hauck stood up as well. "Perfectly free."

CHAPTER THIRTY-NINE

The Wattenberg field was as "oil dense" as any in the country, Moss explained on the ride out. Two to four times more so than the larger and much more well-known Bakken field in North Dakota.

They took Moss's BMW 535i, which was parked in an underground garage. Along the same row of cars, Hauck spotted two sleek, black Yukon SUVs, identical to the ones he saw watching him in Templeton yesterday.

"Feel free to move the seat back and crack the window if you want." Moss put a pair of sunglasses on that he had in the driver's console. "Hope you don't mind if I smoke?"

Hauck shrugged. "Your car."

"Trying to give it up. For the kids. But old habits are hard to kick. Picked it up in flight school."

"The service?" Hauck detected a military demeanor in him as well.

"First Gulf War." They got back on Route 34 in the direction of Templeton. Moss put the window down and blew a plume of smoke out the window. "I told you, a lot of us in this industry are veterans."

On the trip, the conversation shifted to the land out here. The dry, arid shelf on what was known as the Niobrara shale field, which until ten years ago no one even suspected was a jackpot for oil. "It took state-of-the-art seismic imaging to even get a sense of what was down here. Now it's one of the largest oil and gas deposits we have." Moss chuckled. "The damn Apaches are probably kicking themselves, right . . .?"

"Question?" Hauck turned to him. They drove along the river in the direction of Templeton.

Moss flicked an ash out the window. "If I can."

"Are you familiar with someone at Alpha named Robertson? First name John."

"*Robertson . . .?*" Moss shook his head. "Can't say I am. He works out here?"

"Far as I can tell." Hauck took whatever Moss said with a grain of salt. The RMM man knew why he was here, and he knew what Moss was trying to get out of him. "I thought maybe he worked on the RMM account."

"Lots of people do. What's his job?"

"Senior coordinator of field activities."

Moss nodded. "In this business, 'field activities' is a pretty broad job description, Mr. Hauck. It could mean most anything. Rig work. Site management. At Alpha, they tend to focus on the population side, not the sites. So he could be the point person for what they do."

"This guy's skill set back in Afghanistan seemed a bit more extensive than standing up in front of a town meeting."

"What do you mean?"

"PsyOps. Special Forces training . . ."

Moss look a last drag, stamped his cigarette out in the ashtray, then lowered his window again and flicked out the butt. "You know, I'm beginning to get the impression you're not so interested in the Alpha Group for your company at all as you are in this guy."

They drove along the same stretch of road where Moss's truckers had forced him off the road. "Anyway, your police chief seem to know him."

"My police chief?"

"Riddick. After your guys ran me off the road. It was just up here . . ." Hauck was expecting Moss to slow down at the road from the river where he had seen the line of trucks come out the day before, but he didn't. He kept on going. "Even he brought his name up."

"Riddick?"

Hauck nodded.

Moss just shrugged. "Well, I don't know him." He accelerated past the turnoff.

"What about someone named Watkins?" Hauck decided to ask.

"Watkins. Is he at Alpha, too?"

"He's a farmer. In Templeton."

"What's your beef with him? He try to run you off the road, too?"

"No." Hauck smiled, meeting Moss's eyes through his shades. "His son died. It's why we're here."

"Oh. I didn't mean to be so glib. That's too bad."

"Apparently Watkins was interfering in some way against the oil development in town, so I thought his name might have come up. He seems to have made a lot of the local townspeople upset."

"Sorry, I don't get the chance to meet many of the local townspeople. But many of them are resistant to what we do at first. It's natural they feel threatened; they think we're going to leave their town like some barren landscape out of a Mad Max movie after we suck out whatever we came for. But soon they start to realize that neither is true. Every once in a while there's an outlier, but they usually all come around. They usually figure out on their own they can make more in a month with us than they can in a decade growing sugar beets. Of course, it's part of our job to persuade them of that."

"Field work," Hauck said. He thought he was getting the picture.

"Anyway, we're here . . ." Moss put his turn signal on to make a right. There was a dirt road that cut right

229

through someone's crop field. Hauck saw a gate about fifty yards up the road, a guard in the security hut. Moss slowed and waved familiarly at the him, the guard waving him through. "Mr. Moss . . ."

"Sam."

A white sign read, PRIVATE. RMM OIL AND DEVELOPMENT COMPANY VEHICLES ONLY. VIOLATORS WILL BE PROSECUTED. THEN ANOTHER SIGN FARTHER UP THAT READ, LOTS AB-42. ORDINANCE A-6. TOWN OF TEMPLETON, WELD COUNTY. TOM FLACK, COUNTY SUPERVISOR.

Hauck asked, "What's all that?"

"RMM gobbledygook. 'Hannah' sounds a little easier. Nice and natural, right? You wouldn't even know it's here."

"I'll give you that."

"Still, you wouldn't believe what's going on over a mile under us."

Ahead, Hauck saw something glint in the sun. His first thought was that maybe it was the well, but as they got closer, he saw that whatever it was was moving.

And coming toward them.

Coming into focus, it turned out to be another convoy of trucks. The same metal tankers he had seen coming out on the road from the river and that had tried to run him off the road the day before. Polished and shiny. Heading toward the main road.

As they approached, Hauck felt a strange tension inside, thinking for a second if this had all been some kind of elaborate scheme by the RMM man to get him out here alone to drive home yesterday's point. He looked at Moss, who had a vague look of amusement. "Look familiar?"

Hauck nodded. "Yes. They do."

Moss smiled. "You seem worried, Mr. Hauck."

"Not at all." But he was. He was out here alone. Who knew if they were armed.

Moss pulled over to the side.

Six gleaming stainless steel tankers. *RMM* plastered on the sides.

Moss waved to the first driver as they went by.

Hauck felt a wave of relief inside. He said to Moss, "Looks like Hannah's doing pretty well."

"Five hundred barrels a day. Twenty-four/seven. All of which, five years back, would have been completely unobtainable. Wouldn't have even known it was here. But anyway . . ." Moss pulled his car back on the dirt road. "Those aren't for oil . . ."

"Not for oil . . .?" Hauck glanced in the side-view mirror and saw the last one rumble away. "What's in them then?"

Hauck caught his own stare reflected in the RMM man's sunglasses. "Those are for water, Mr. Hauck."

CHAPTER FORTY

"Water . . .?" The answer took Hauck by surprise. He looked at the RMM man, confused.

"A well like this uses upwards of a hundred thousand gallons of water a month," Moss explained, "along with a mixture of sand and a few chemicals we call proppant. It's part of the hydraulic fragmentation process. What you're seeing there is the by-product of what has been pumped back out."

"And where's it going?" Hauck turned back around. Six tankers. That had to be thousands and thousands of gallons. Of by-product.

Moss shrugged. "It gets recirculated through a treatment plant that's down by the river."

So that's where they were coming from. The trucks were carrying water from the river. Up to the wells. Then they headed back with the contaminated liquid. He and Dani had had it all wrong. "And then what?"

"And then it gets put back." Moss turned his BMW through another wire gate, this one open. "So here we are . . ."

He pulled into the fenced-off well pad area, filled with several large prefab-looking structures: military-beige cylinders with tubes running to and from them that looked like they held pumps; a couple of Quonset huts; several large earthmoving tractors; and a built-up platform with a massive trestle rising from it.

There was virtually no sound other than a steady, hissing pumping: *Ka-chung. Ka-chung.*

Moss parked next to some other cars. They got out. Hauck stared at the impressive setup. Moss took two helmets from a storage bin. "C'mon, I'll give you the five-dollar tour."

He pointed out the water storage tanks, the drab, beige cylinders that were indeed pumping stations, as Hauck had surmised. How the water was fed into the well opening through flexible copper tubing and pumped down. Moss pointed out the blowout preventer, which, he explained, controlled the well pressure and protected against any blowback and surface release.

"C'mon up here." He went ahead of Hauck, up to the platform where Hauck could peer into the well opening and the casings, which were around six feet in diameter and went miles down. Moss waved hello to a couple of the workers. "We put in seven levels of protection inside the well. Copper, steel, concrete, reinforced steel. Not a chance in hell any of this leaches into the surrounding soil."

"How deep?" Hauck asked, peering into the black opening.

"Seven, seventy-five hundred feet. What we're doing now is fragmentation on Hannah Three, which runs over in that direction." Moss pointed. "I'll show you when we go inside. You can see that the water is mixed with the proppant mixture over there, mostly sand, to make something that bites when it's heated up and blasted into the shales down there. It's superheated over here"—he pointed to one of the domed, enclosed structures—"then fed down into the well, until it branches off from the main well hole and goes out horizontally. So instead of having to drill twenty, thirty vertical wells like this off one site"—Moss put his hands one above the other about an inch apart—"in horizontal drilling, the capturing tubes stay in contact with the shale deposits that run horizontally under the ground. The drill tube is perforated, and when you blast these incisions at various points with the superheated mixture, it creates fissures in the shale, from which the oil or gas flows more readily. Back up here, it's separated through these valves from the water-chemical mixture. That's how we get oil today." He shouted over the steady drone. "None of this would have been possible eight, ten years ago."

Hauck was impressed. It was clear they did have multiple layers of protections to prevent anything harmful from seeping into the surrounding soil. They had even built up berms and protective ditches surrounding the well pad so that if anything came back up to the surface it couldn't escape.

"So where do you get all the water from?" Hauck asked. "You said what, a hundred thousand gallons a month?"

"We buy it on the open market just like any other commodity. And locally we have some leases . . ."

"But it's totally dry here. The river's down. Look at the fields . . ."

"Everything is for sale, Mr. Hauck." Moss smiled. "For the right price. Now c'mon, let's go inside the office. I'll introduce you to the guys."

In one of the two domed Quonset huts, Moss introduced Hauck to some of the technicians seated behind computer screens.

"This is where we operate the drill." Moss put his hand on a worker's shoulder. "Where we pump in the water, build up the temperature, even pinpoint at which exact spots we're going to inject the mixture into the shale. It's all controlled by these 3-D configurations. See . . ." Moss pointed to a screen where there was what looked like a multicolored cross section of what was under the earth. "This is seven thousand feet down. Real time." He pointed to a depth gauge to back him up, like a reverse altimeter. "Here's the shale deposit." Moss ran his finger along a lighter, almost milk-colored shadow amid various striations of gray and black. "This and this are layers of surrounding rock. You can see the drill tube . . ." He pointed out a long red line that ran under the 3-D rendered shale line. "I can't tell you how it's done, these guys are a lot smarter than me, but if it shoots the water and sand mixture, let's say right here, or *here*"—Moss placed his finger on various spots— "it essentially loosens up the oil or gas, and that's how we're able to get at it."

"That's pretty good, Mr. Moss," one of the seated technicians said, as he turned around and grinned.

"Thanks, Francisco . . . Here, this is interesting," Moss said to Hauck as he picked up a multicolored, laminated chart similar to the three-dimensional image Hauck had just looked at on the screen. "It's a 3-D seismic image. This is how we evaluate if there's the prospect of oil down there. These trucks on the surface emit sound vibrations that travel thousands of feet below the earth's surface, and then the readings are run into a 3-D seismic volume, like this, which gives you an image of the different masses that are down there. This mass is rock." Moss pointed to a dark striation. "And this is shale." He indicated a wispy, lighter band that ran through the rock.

"Kind of like reading an X-ray," Hauck volunteered.

"Very much like that. You can see the different

masses . . . So we know with a much higher level of probability what's down there before the first drill bit hits the earth. And over here is what's down there now . . ."

He took Hauck over to a different screen, where he saw a computer rendering of the main well, its many protective layers inside it, and then farther down, how it suddenly branched off horizontally. "Hannah One," Moss said. Thousands of feet down, there were two other horizontal channels that fed out in other directions. "Meet her cousins, Hannah Two and Three."

It resembled the branches of a tree. Perfectly straight ones. With various colors in the cross section, representing different layers of rock. "How long does it take to drill one of them?" Hauck asked.

Moss shrugged. "Twenty-one to twenty-eight days, depending on if we can go day and night. Previously, we'd be sinking wells into the earth all over this area if there was a high probability of oil. The Wattenberg field we're in has what we call the EUR, the estimated ultimate recovery, of some fifty-five million barrels."

"That's a lot of money at stake."

"It is, but let's be clear, it's not just about the money." Moss leaned back against the workstation. "Or being able to run your air conditioners twenty-four hours a day and drive around gas guzzlers. We're not just talking lower gas prices anymore. The real number that matters is the percentage. The percentage of domestic to imported oil. That's what we're really doing

237

here, Mr. Hauck. What's really at stake. It's about independence. The independence from the Middle East. Economically and politically. Trust me, Mr. Hauck, what we're doing here is a lot deeper than simply pleasing our shareholders. We're talking foreign policy, and national security."

National security . . . The battle for hearts and minds, just like in Iraq and Afghanistan. That's how Alpha fit in, Hauck began to see. Shifting the battlefield. The new football fields, fancy parks. Town centers. *Inform. Persuade. Influence*. As lethal as if they'd sent in the Special Forces commandos to take out a bad actor in the night.

The last thing you wanted was for anyone to get in the way.

"So what do you think?" Moss's smile had returned. "Impressive . . .?"

It was clear to Hauck he was getting the tour designed to push him off why he was here. Moss had already been alerted about him. Before Hauck even showed up today. "Very."

It was Moss himself who had said it: *I was using the word* environment *far more broadly* . . .

What the hell had Trey Watkins's father done?

On the drive back, Moss's conversation grew more personal. Who was Hauck up here with? What else he'd done with his time? How long was he planning on staying? They got back to the RMM lot. Moss asked where Hauck had parked and drove him over to his car.

238

"Sorry I couldn't have been more helpful on the Robertson thing. Hope you enjoyed the tour, though."

"Thanks. It was very interesting." They shook hands and Hauck stepped out.

"Next time through," Moss said, "I'd like you to meet Mr. Stafford, our regional general manager."

"Maybe that can be arranged," Hauck said, watching Moss's expression slide. "I'm not sure I'm leaving so soon."

CHAPTER FORTY-ONE

Dani was going stir-crazy. Growing worried, too. He had left around ten and it was already after three. She'd called. She sat around watching Oprah and Ellen. She called again.

Finally he knocked on her door.

"I was worried. I didn't know what happened to you," she said, shifting on her bed, her arms around a pillow, the TV on. "You left for RMM at ten. That was over four hours ago."

"I got waylaid," he sheepishly replied.

"*Waylaid?*"

"I went to see Hannah."

"Lucky you."

"Hannah's a well, Dani," he said, noting her perturbed expression. "It's where those trucks we saw on the road

240

were heading the other day. And I found out a few things you might want to know. The first is, those tankers we almost ran into weren't filled with oil after all."

"What were they for then?"

"Water. Lots of water."

"Okay. And what's so great about that?"

"Water is how they get the oil out. They—"

"Fracking. I get it, Uncle Ty. I think I told you that when we drove up. I know the process."

"Dani, look around . . . What's the one thing you don't see around here? The place is in the middle of a two-year drought. And RMM needs thousands and thousands of gallons of water. So where do you think it comes from?"

She nodded. "Those trucks coming up from the river . . ."

"That facility we thought was a well, well, it isn't. It's a pumping station. For water. They're literally draining the river. And they might well be dumping it back in once they're through with it. You want your potatoes irrigated with fracking wastewater?"

She shook her head. "No, not really."

"Neither would I. I'm starting to see how Alpha fits in to all this." Hauck sank into a chair across from her. "Their job is to eliminate any organized or lingering opposition before the oil companies come in and do their thing. They come up with a strategy, just like they did in the war: persuading the local population, buying

241

any resistance off. E.g. the fancy football fields, health centers, and municipal buildings. And maybe turn the screws on anyone else."

"I thought they handled issues relating to the environment," Dani said.

"It *is* the environment. They're just using the word a lot more liberally. Meaning anyone—a town council, a building ordinance, or even a stubborn individual who is standing in their way, or maybe stirring up trouble . . ."

"Trey's father." Dani nodded, starting to get the picture.

"I think I'd like to pay him another visit, if your friend Allie is still there."

"I think she's heading back tomorrow."

"Up for it?" Hauck winked.

"I'm up for anything that gets me out of this dump you made me hang out in all day." She wheeled around and put her feet into her sneakers. "You know you could have called. After what happened on the road, when I didn't hear back for all this time, I was worried. That wasn't nice."

"You're right." Hauck tossed her her Whitewater Adventure sweat shirt, which was flung over the chair. "Won't happen again. My bad."

CHAPTER FORTY-TWO

They drove back out to the farm, sure that Trey was killed for some action aimed against his father. They got there at around 4:30, hoping to catch Watkins at the end of the day.

This time, there were only a few cars in front of the house and a few hands milling around. They knocked on the front door. Trey's mother, Marie, a warm, but no-frills-looking woman in her fifties with graying hair and no makeup, opened it, and let them in.

"Mrs. Watkins . . ." Hauck said.

She wasn't rude, but she wasn't welcoming, either. Dani went into the bedroom to speak with Allie. Hauck asked if they could speak to her husband one more time.

"He's out by the barn. But I'm not sure he'll want to speak with you. He was upset after the last time. We

243

all were. Now that our boy is buried, can't we just let him lie in peace?"

"If I could just have a couple of minutes, Mrs. Watkins, that's all I ask."

She tossed a rag on the table. "Wait here. I'll see."

She went out back. Hauck stood looking out the window at the barn. Hay bales were being stacked, hands transferring them into the big barn. That's what they were farming now. All the land would give them.

The room was a kind of sitting room, with old, uphol-stered chairs and a wear-worn couch, close to the kitchen. The place had the cozy smell of biscuits baking and there were flowers placed everywhere in all this drought, probably from the funeral. Their daughter, Kelli, who lived in Greeley, came out from the kitchen. She was pretty, in trendier jeans and a red knit top. "You can see how it is here," she said, with a hint of apology. "She might be right, though. It may just be better if you leave them alone."

"I'm not trying to cause anyone any pain, Kelli. But there are some things you all should know."

"You're not a cop?"

"No. Not anymore."

"So then why are you digging into this? Why are you putting yourself on the line? What's your interest in Trey?"

Hauck was struggling for an answer when he heard the screen door in the kitchen open.

Chuck Watkins came in, in jeans and a work shirt and a Caterpillar baseball cap. He stopped, removed a work glove from his hand, and put it on the table. "I don't mean to be unneighborly, Mr. Hauck, but I'm pretty sure my wife made it clear just how we feel."

"All I want is just a couple of minutes," Hauck said. "If that's—"

"I don't have a couple of minutes. What I have is twenty acres full of undersized potatoes and beet root that need to be watered best we can. And a whole bunch of hay to stack and bring in. I told you the other day, there's no point in trying to make some case here. We're the ones who have to live with what happened to Trey, not you."

"I know that." Hauck took a step forward. "But your son—"

The bedroom door opened, and Dani and Allie came out from where they'd been talking.

"My son died from an accident, Mr. Hauck. Not from anything else. The police in Carbondale confirmed that to my satisfaction. The parks investigators looked into it too, and didn't find any differently. So I don't know who you are or what you think you have, but all it's going to do for us is bring up a lot of questions that will never be answered and just upset everyone around here, who are already pretty upset. So I'm asking like I did the first time, to just let us alone now and leave."

"I want to show you a photo, if I can . . .?" Hauck

245

told out his phone and scrolled to the shot he had taken yesterday at Alpha of Robertson in the 301st Airborne. He narrowed in. "You recognize this person?"

Watkins shook his head. "No."

"His name is John Robertson. Do you know that name?"

Watkins shook his head again, but this time after a slight pause.

"I know what it's like, sir, but it's important you hear about RMM and some of the contractors they're using . . ."

"You know what it's like? You've both been in town all of about two days and you've got it all sized up. Well, I'm glad we're such a learning experience for you, Mr. Hauck."

"I know you were standing up against them in some way. RMM. I know they use contractors whose job it is to break down local opposition to the wells. They're trained by the U.S. Army, Mr. Watkins. It's called the Alpha Group. They all did questionable stuff over there, and now they're here, and what else you ought to know is, there was someone who was an operative for Alpha who was on the river at the same time Trey was—"

"That's enough!" Watkins's voice made a few people turn, then he lowered it. "Our son is dead, sir. Isn't that enough? He lived in his own freewheeling way and that's how he died. Why does there have to be anything else to it?"

"Mr. Watkins, I found Trey on the river." Dani came forward. "I know better than anyone what kind of whitewater he could handle and how he—"

"I said, that's enough! I know you were his friend, miss, and I appreciate that, and what you're trying to do. But I'm asking you to leave my house now. Both of you. I don't want another word."

"Dad." Kelli stepped toward him and put a hand on his shoulder. "Just listen to them, please . . ."

"Chuck . . ." said his wife. "Maybe you should."

"*Marie!*" His hand met the tabletop, causing the glassware to shake, his eyes ablaze. "Don't you say another word," he said to her. "Just don't." He turned back to Hauck. "If you had any sense you wouldn't be looking around this mess in the first place. You'd do the smart thing and just be gone. If we had any sense . . ." He stopped on the word, as if something inside had stopped him, and his voice softened. "I appreciate what you're trying to do. But just go back home. Please . . . You find anything, take it to the people who can do some good. Just let us alone. That's all I'm asking now. I know you think you have the answers . . ." Watkins was a proud, tough man, but Hauck saw tears come into his eyes. "But just go. Please . . ."

The entire house seemed to stand still like it was in the grip of fear.

"C'mon, Dani," Hauck said. He looked at her and could see she was bursting with frustration. "I'm sorry

247

to bother you again. All of you. *Ma'am.*" He nodded to Watkins's wife.

Dani said, "Mr. Watkins, if you only let us—"

"Dani, please, you heard him." Hauck took her by the arm. She took a futile glance around the room, ending on Allie, who nodded back at her with a look that conveyed something like, *Thanks. It's best. I'll see you at home.*

At the door, Hauck turned back. The farmer was still standing there with his hands balled around his cap. "I do know," Hauck said. "I lost a daughter myself. She was five. So I do know how it is."

Watkins just stared with an empty and impassive expression.

"So, Mr. Hauck . . .?"

Hauck looked back.

"They say it'll get better. With time."

"Which part, Mr. Watkins?" Hauck looked into the farmer's hooded eyes. "The grief or the guilt?"

As soon as they were on the porch, Dani grabbed onto Hauck's arm. "Something's going on here. How can you just leave and not make them see it?"

"Because I can, Dani. That's all there is to it. You don't understand." He went down the steps to their car.

"Uncle Ty, listen, please . . ." She caught up to him. "Allie told me inside, something's not right here. She said she heard Trey's father and mother arguing. She heard her tell him something like 'You're not responsible.' 'You're not responsible,' Uncle Ty . . . Allie was sure she

248

was talking about Trey." She latched onto Hauck's arm and swung him around. "We can't just leave. *She* wants to know the truth."

"Then let her find it. We're going home. We're sticking our noses into something where we don't belong."

"What do you mean we don't belong . . .? What's happened, Uncle Ty? Why are you suddenly agreeing with him?"

He pulled the car door open, the blood heating up inside.

"Mr. Hauck . . ."

They heard the front door open behind them. Kelli Watkins came onto the porch. She came down the steps and over to them. "I'm sorry about my father. He's not that way. Really. You can see, he's toiling his whole life away, and look what's happening . . ."

Hauck said, "You don't have to apologize. I—"

"I'm not apologizing. I know you both felt from the start that Trey's death wasn't an accident, and I don't want to get my father in trouble, or put anyone else in harm . . . But if my brother was the victim of something"—she looked up at him—"then I don't want to keep it quiet, either."

"I think he was, Kelli," Dani said to her. "It's just that no one wants to hear."

"*I* want to hear." She looked at Dani and then at Hauck, and pushed the bangs away from her eyes. "My father was always a courageous man. And look what's happened.

You don't know the truth of what's really happening here. My father and a few other townspeople got involved and . . .

"Just look around," she said, her gaze swept over the parched, brown fields. "You can see what we're struggling with here. None of them grew up with a nickel in their pockets other than this land. Now look at it. Then this thing comes like a gift from God that can save us. This was a quiet town, Mr. Hauck. Like some Norman Rockwell painting. Now it's turned people against each other. To my dad, it was like making a deal with the devil to sell your soul. And now we all see the cost, what's happened. The real cost . . ."

Hauck put his hand on her shoulder and squeezed. Tears came into her eyes.

"Look around at this shit, Mr. Hauck. God knows why anyone would want to give their lives up to save it. Other than just their own will and stubbornness." She wiped the tears away with her arm. "And look what it's cost us now."

"Kelli, if you want us to just go home, we will."

"I don't want you to go home." She shook her head and looked up at Hauck, a fire of something, maybe a last hope, flickering through her watery eyes. "Everyone goes home. I'm sorry for what you said in there, about your daughter. I wouldn't blame you if you did go. We've been afraid of the truth, because of what might happen next. But I loved Trey, and if something bad did happen, well then I damn well want to know. And the people who did it made responsible. He was a good kid, whatever my father feels." She turned to Dani. "You knew that, right?"

Dani nodded. "Everyone did."

"You go back now and not look into it." Kelli shrugged. "I don't know who will."

They stood here looking at her.

"So actually there is someone . . . Someone who you can talk to. In Greeley. She's a lawyer. She might be the only one left who's not on RMM's payroll. But you have to understand, you'll be going up against a lot here, Mr. Hauck, both with RMM and the town. They may be simple folk here, but trust me, they don't take kindly to someone getting in their way. We see that now."

"What this person's name?" Hauck inquired.

"Jen Keeler. She's with some environmental group. I could find out for you."

"Keeler . . ." Hauck said. "Won't be necessary." He squeezed her shoulder in a bolstering way.

They got in their car. Kelli took a step or two toward the house as Hauck started the engine, then she turned back to them and Hauck came around.

"So you gonna stay or leave?" Kelli asked. The hot wind whipped her hair and she pushed it off her face. Her eyes seemed to convey that she had seen this picture before.

"Everyone leaves . . ." She shrugged with an air of futility. "Or ends up being part of them."

CHAPTER FORTY-THREE

Hours later, Hauck lay on his bed at the motel. The Golf Channel was on the tube. Some obscure tournament in Dubai with a lot of European players he had never heard of. After a couple of beers and some decent Mexican, he'd left Dani a while back and went back to his room.

You gonna stay or leave? Kelli had asked him.

It had taken him two visits to see it. But standing at the door, looking into Watkins's haunted eyes, he saw the very same thing that had been etched onto Hauck's own countenance ten years before. The same cast of grief and helplessness and rage.

Guilt, too.

They always leave.

Hauck's thoughts traveled back to a place they rarely did now.

Ten years ago, he had been behind the wheel of his Ford Bronco when he backed out of his garage in anger and over his five-year-old daughter, Rachel, who had been playing with her sister in the small yard in front of their house and had chased a ball into his path.

To this day, the remembrance of that impact, and the high-pitched terror of Jessie's scream, still sent a shiver of anguish down his spine.

He was in a fit of impatience after a spat with Beth, which like most spats, could be traced to the most trivial thing, and had ended up costing them both the thing most dear to them.

That moment changed the rest of their lives.

But today he'd seen it again. Like it had happened just yesterday. Only a person who felt it himself with such immediacy would recognize it so plainly for what it was.

Leave, Kelli had said to him. *I wouldn't blame you if you did.*

So what if Watkins had done something that led to his son's death? Who cared if it was easier for him to live with it as some kind of unpreventable accident? Who was Hauck to force his way in and try to shine the truth on it? Truth is fungible, people say. Look at any conflict. There's always a different side if you dig deeply. A different truth. This wasn't his fight.

Does it get easier? Watkins asked him at the door.

Which part? The pain or the guilt.

He should just go back, Hauck tried to convince himself, like everyone was telling him to. He had a life on hold. An important job. A girl. If he was so looking for an answer, those could show him the way.

But that was before the latest text had come in from Brooke, just before he and Dani went to dinner.

That the team looking into the balloon accident in Aspen *had* indeed found something. A tiny hole in the nylon—most of the fabric had been consumed in the flames—ringed with microscopic traces of sulfur and potassium nitrate.

Gunpowder.

Which meant that the tragedy wasn't what everyone had thought. An accident. Someone had shot a bullet into the shell. It was just like Dani had said. A part of a cover-up that was aimed at the person Dani was headed to see that morning. Who'd caught sight of something on the river the day before, when Trey died.

That made things different now for Hauck. For Watkins, too, whether he liked it or not.

Five more people had died.

When he told Dani about it she wept and Hauck put his arm around her. He knew how hard it was when your worst fears turn out to be true. Even ones you carried from the outset. He went back to the room and lay down, and thought about Naomi. He needed to talk to somebody. This thing was growing. Whoever had done this not only had the means, but the will. He checked the time. Ten thirty P.M. Well after midnight back east. She'd long be asleep. Most days she was up at five A.M. for a run before work.

He wrote out a text to her.

Miss you.

Then his thoughts shifted to Jessie. His older daughter was sixteen now. She'd been seven when the accident occurred. She lived with her mom and her stepfather in Brooklyn. Hauck saw her every few weeks, though less frequently now, now that she was dealing with boys and AP classes. He figured she'd be asleep as well, but he thumbed out a text message to her. He needed to feel a part of someone.

Just letting you know I'm thinking of you.

Then he put the phone down and closed his eyes. He felt sleep coming over him.

Next to him, his phone jingled. A text coming in. Jessie had written back: "Thinking of you too, Daddy."

Which made him smile.

So late? he wrote back. *What are you doing up?*

He waited a few seconds until her answer came in. "I'm with a guy."

He bolted up, sleep rushing out of him, until he heard the phone jingle again: "Hahaha! Just doing homework, dad. It's exam time. Gotcha, tho!"

He wrote back with a wave of relief, just happy to feel her close. *Yes, you did.* He closed his eyes again and flicked off the TV.

The phone jingled again: "When you coming back, Dad? I miss you."

I miss you too, honey, he wrote back.

It had been three months.

What are you going to do? Kelli had asked him. *Stay or go?*

He knew his answer in his heart, even if he hadn't made up his mind.

No. It doesn't get easier, he could have told Watkins. It doesn't go away. It never does.

It only hides for a while.

He wrote out a last message. Something that made sense to him at least. Then he put the phone on the table and closed his eyes.

He was staying.

I am back, honey.

THE FALLS

CHAPTER FORTY-FOUR

Wade Dunn leaned back at his office desk, the phone to his ear. It was going on eleven; only the two or three staff manning the night shift were still around. He dialed the number and waited for the person he was calling to pick up.

"*Wade . . .?*"

"The very same," he said with a chuckle, doing is best to appear upbeat. "How're you doing, Dani?"

An hour ago he'd gotten the call, the one that was tearing his stomach into shreds. It was an old lesson, one he knew he should've learned before. You open the door and let people in, in this case the wrong people, they never let you go. It just keeps getting deeper and deeper.

"Wade, it's late." Dani sounded tired. "I can't really talk right now."

"I just don't want you to think we don't follow up on our guests when we let them out of jail here. We're a full-service operation. So where are you?"

"You told me to get out of town, so that's exactly what we did. I'm with my uncle."

"So where'd you go? Hiking? Fishing? Down to the sand dunes maybe?" He knew exactly where they were, of course. That's what was behind his call.

"Actually, we're up in Greeley. We came for Trey's funeral."

"You did, huh?" He acted surprised. Though he already knew that, as well. He knew most everything about what they'd been up to since they arrived. Who they'd seen. Who Hauck had spoken with. "The funeral was yesterday, Dani, wasn't it? Heard a couple of people went up there from here."

"Yes, they did."

He held his breath for her next answer. "So why you staying around . . .?"

She paused. "What's the issue, Wade? I thought you wanted me as far away from there as possible."

"What I wanted," he said, "was for you to keep that pretty little nose of yours out of things that weren't any of your concern, Danielle. And I hope that's what you're still doing. Are you?"

"Am I what, Wade?"

"Are you puttin' aside all those crazy notions you had? You and that famous godfather of yours. I figured

260

this was kind of a reunion for the two of you, and you don't want to be dragging him into something all pointless and foolish."

"I don't know, Wade, all of a sudden there's a lot that doesn't seem so foolish anymore."

"Hmm, guess I know what you're taking about." He exhaled. "The balloon thing. Guess you've heard by now? So you were right on that, Danielle, they did find some possibility that there might have been foul play. Though I stress the words *possibility* and *might*.

"But at the same time you oughta know that both sets of customers on that balloon only booked the day before, so it seems whatever it was, if it turns out true, wasn't aimed at them. More like someone here looking to do some mischief, God knows why."

Dani said, "It wasn't some mischief maker, Wade. You know damn well who it was aimed at."

Wade felt a bitter taste on his tongue. "You ought to come back now, Danielle."

"First you want me as far away as possible, now you want me back. I'll be back when we're ready to come back, Wade. Some things are starting to come out up here."

"I just want to watch out for you, Danielle. Whether you know it or not, I always have."

"Why do you need to watch out for me, Wade? Tell me what's going on."

"Just leave it all up there, darlin', whatever it is you

think you're finding. Come on back here and go down the river like you always did. And let that uncle of yours, or godfather, go on back home."

"I think it's too late for that now, Wade. I have to go now. You're sounding a little strange. You sure everything's okay?"

Okay . . .? No, they weren't okay. Nothing was okay anymore. He had a boy in the VA hospital who barely knew his name and had to learn how to put one foot in front of the other again. He had no money left in the bank but that he had to lie and look the other way for. He had a ruined, corrupted life that was falling apart a little more every day, save one last thing, the last thing he could hold on to—and that was the sliver of trust he had left with Dani.

"Nah, just worried about you," he said, "that's all. A stepfather's allowed to feel that way, ain't he? You never get too old for that, or too far away."

"I wish you'd just looked into it, Wade. I know you know now that I was right. About Trey, and Ron. And I can't just come on back right now. I can't just go down the river, as if nothing has happened. There are a lot of people dead. And a lot of questions that need to be answered."

He had the bottle in front of him. The bottle of Maker's Mark he kept in the drawer. As a test of his conviction. He took it out every once in a while. To gauge his strength. This time he felt his hand shake, running his fingers down the bottle.

"Take it easy, Danielle," he said, a sense of sorrow sinking in. "Do the smart thing, and come on back. Y'hear . . .?"

She hung up. Or he did. It wasn't clear who.

Wade unwrapped the foil on the bottle and pulled out the cork.

I can't protect you up there anymore.

CHAPTER FORTY-FIVE

"Ty . . ."

Hauck grappled for the phone on the night table: 6:05 A.M. The voice on the other end took him by surprise. "Tom . . .?"

"Always thought you were an early riser, guy," his boss, Tom Foley, said with a chuckle. "Didn't mean to be waking you up out there on vacation . . ."

Foley was about the last person Hauck wanted to have to deal with right now. And the word *vacation* felt like it had been marinating in sarcasm for a week. The morning sun shined in through the shades. He rolled over, forcing his brain to alert. He was usually up at six anyway. "No. I'm fine."

"Hell, if I didn't know how much you actually

missed us here, I'd be thinking you've somehow been avoiding me."

"I've just been out of earshot, Tom. They don't have cell phone service half the places I've been."

"*Aspen . . .?* I was out there myself not too long ago and I distinctly remember mine working just fine."

"I'm just doing a favor for someone out here. I won't be out here long."

"And when you're done with that . . .? When we heard you'd left the Caribbean, Ty, we were all actually figuring that we'd be seeing you back here."

Hauck hadn't decided anything, anything further out than learning whatever he could about Watkins and how that connected to Alpha and RMM. "You will, Tom. Soon. But listen, as long as you called, maybe there is something you can help me with. We've got a large oil and gas client at Talon, don't we? I've never worked with them myself, but I've seen a few of the presentations."

"Global Exploration. Yes, we do. Very large. They're out of Houston. We handle some of their employee protection details in Saudi Arabia and Nigeria. Some cyber-work back home as well. Why?"

"I'm looking for whatever you can tell me about an outfit named the Alpha Group."

"*Alpha Group?*"

265

"They do consulting in the oil and gas field. A lot of ex-military personnel it seems."

"Can't say I've heard of it. But what are you doing all wrapped up with them?"

"I'd rather not tell you why just now, Tom. I'm just doing a favor for a friend."

"That's becoming kind of a second career with you, isn't it?" It was a friend of his who was killed that had started him on the Gstaad Group case. "I hope you understand what's at stake here, Ty. There's a lot of big things in the works. Not just here, but internationally. You share in all that, if you remember, Ty. I brought you in as a partner quicker than anybody."

"I know that, Tom. And you know I appreciate it. I just need a bit more time."

"I thought that's exactly what we've given you these past two plus months . . . Time."

"You know I put my salary on hold, Tom. I'm not taking a nickel. Just bear with me a little longer."

"You have to make a choice, son. I know the money thing isn't what gets you, but there's an awful lot of it at play here. And I know you don't relish the role of being in the limelight either. But whatever it is you're doing out there, it can't be worth what's on the table here. Get on a plane and come on back. Hell, I'll send one out for you. Say tomorrow . . ."

"Just tell me whatever you can on Alpha, Tom. And thanks for hanging in there with me. I appreciate it."

"I don't want you to appreciate it, Ty . . . I want you to earn it. When this is over, and I hope it's quick, I'm looking forward to seeing you back here."

"Soon, Tom." Hauck climbed out of bed. "I promise. Soon."

CHAPTER FORTY-SIX

Hauck knocked on Dani's door and she answered through the crack. She was in a T-shirt and panties and her hair was messed.

He said, "You want to come along so bad, come on."

"Come on where . . .?"

"I got an address for Jen Keeler. I'm going to have a little breakfast and then head over."

"*So we're staying . . .?*"

"One more day."

"Give me fifteen minutes to shower and get ready and I'll be there," she replied, excited.

"Ten," Hauck said, backing down the hallway toward the lobby. "I eat quick."

Half an hour later, Hauck having finished a cereal with some syrup and a banana, and Dani taking a yogurt and granola in the car, they headed into Greeley.

The Weld County Open Range Initiative wasn't situated in some fancy office complex like RMM and Alpha. It was a storefront in a strip mall, between a pawnshop and a package store. And despite the big-sounding name, the office was tiny. There were a couple of desks. Posters and newspaper clippings on the walls. A young gal with red-and-green-dyed hair, big glasses, and tattoos running down her arm was manning the front desk, sorting papers from the copy machine. "Can I help you?"

"We're here to see Jen Keeler?" Hauck said.

"Is she expecting you?"

"No, she's not."

The girl looked at them warily. "You're not with the CSRC, are you?"

"The CSRC?"

"The state regulatory council. They come around here twice a year, get taken out to a steak dinner by the oil companies, and basically rubber-stamp their safety forms. There's a group in the area now."

"Do I look like I'm with the CSRC? We're actually here about Charles Watkins."

"Oh . . ." The girl put down her stack of papers. "We were so sorry to hear about that. And sorry for the third degree, as well. We get a lot of cranks and rabble-rousers in here who want to close us down. Or upset the townsfolk about us."

"No worries. His daughter Kelli told us to stop in. Tell her my name's Hauck."

Jen Keeler was tall, thin, boyish in shape, her shoulder-length blond hair in a ponytail, a red shirt worn out of her jeans. There was kind of a look in her eye, a glint of determination that said that while her office and staff might be small, her energy and commitment were high, and she was not a person to be trifled with.

"You from the press, Mr. Hauck?" she asked, as they sat in front of her brief-filled desk. "Monica said this was concerning Charles Watkins."

"Friends." He shook his head. "Actually friends of his son, Trey. Or Dani was. He died in a rafting accident last Thursday in Aspen."

"I know about it." Jen nodded. "I'm sorry."

"I saw you at the funeral Wednesday," Dani said.

"I was there." Jen shrugged. "I didn't know Chuck's son. I've only known *him* for just a few months. But it's clearly had an effect. It's kind of derailed everything."

"*Derailed . . .?*" Hauck asked.

Jen put down a paper. "What's your interest here, Mr. Hauck? As I said, I didn't know Chuck's son. It's a terrible thing to happen on any level, but it was damn poor timing for us here. It's hard enough just to take small steps forward, and then something tragic happens like that, and sets it all back. It's kind of how things work here."

270

"Watkins's daughter Kelli suggested we talk with you."

"Kelli did?"

"She thought you could explain some things to us. Like why a lot of the town had turned against her father. What sort of business did you have with Mr. Watkins, if you don't mind me asking?"

She looked back at him. "I'm actually thinking that's more like the question I ought to pose back to you, Mr. Hauck."

"Dani here is from Carbondale, Ms. Keeler. She was a rafting friend of Trey's. She was actually the person who found him. He was killed at a spot that should have been a cakewalk for a person of his ability level. So we were kind of thinking, and there's a growing stack of evidence to back this up, that maybe what happened to Trey up there wasn't much of an accident at all."

"I see." The lawyer stared back at them, sizing them up. Hauck noticed a gleam in her eye, that she understood precisely what he meant. "Monica, hold any calls," she called out to the front room. "Mr. Hauck, Dani, why don't we step into the conference room?"

"I'm a lawyer," Jen Keeler said in the cramped, window-less conference room stacked with briefs, after they brought her up-to-date on everything going on. "If you hadn't figured that out yet. But one with an advanced

271

degree in environmental science from Colorado State. Normally, I don't take on litigation. Mainly I do watchdog work; try to make the energy companies accountable in the face of the major threats to both the water-table levels and contaminants in the soil. Not to mention how that affects the things we eat—crops, livestock."

"From fracking?" Hauck volunteered.

"Fracking's one aspect. The Wattenberg shale deposit is a mile and a half belowground. So that's the only way the oil and gas are able to be captured up here."

"You said you don't normally handle litigation. But you were representing Watkins?"

She reached across and pulled a large stack of papers and folders toward her. "I was. Among others."

"Why?"

"Why were we suing or why did I choose to represent him?"

"Both."

"As to the first question," Jen said, "it's because there were no other lawyers between here and Denver who would agree to do it. Most of them already have retainers with RMM, and that's hardly accidental, of course. The one or two that were willing to listen to him eventually had to recuse themselves . . ." She gave them a cynical smile. "A sudden matter of conflict of interests . . ."

"Meaning they were bought off." Hauck picked up what she was saying.

"Call it whatever you want. One day they're nice and

helpful. Next day, they're recommending someone else. It's what we deal with here."

"And then the same thing would happen to *those* lawyers . . .?"

"Funny how that kind of things spreads like a virus in these parts." Jen smiled sagely.

"You said 'others.' So there was more than just Watkins in the suit?"

"At first. I can show you. It's all a matter of public record." She went through the folders and pushed one across to Hauck.

Hauck leafed through it. There were seven names. Fisher. Loney. Price. Samuelson. Whyte. Vasquez.

Charles Alan Watkins, Junior, at the top.

"So as to the second question," he said, "what the suit was about, I assume you're an environmental activist?"

Jen grinned. "I've certainly been called a whole lot worse. Pinko. Traitor. Opportunist. Whore. Dyke. We've had to replace our windows here a number of times. We've had to work in our parkas when our heat was suddenly turned off in the middle of winter. I've had my tires slashed; even had my car run off into a snow ditch."

"Ha, I knew we had something in common." Hauck grinned.

"Already?" Jen laughed. "Welcome to the neighborhood, Mr. Hauck. You certainly made your presence known here quick. I call myself someone who stands up for individuals who are being railroaded by larger interests. Surely no one else is doing that here. I get that today it's all about jobs and energy independence, and that's fine. I want those things, too. Trust me, everybody's rubber-stamping anything that comes before them today in the name of lower oil prices and job creation. I just want to make sure that once these wells run dry, and one day they will . . . we haven't handed over our towns and way of life to people who weren't operating with the same ideals in mind and without any governance over it.

"So that's my speech. What's yours? And you better say it very quietly if you're peddling the idea that Watkins's son was, what, murdered. I hope you have someone who can back that up."

"There was an operative from Alpha who was there at the river at the very same time," Hauck said. "And then he left, immediately after." They told her about what Rooster said he saw, and how the balloon he was operating was brought down with traces of what could be gunpowder on it.

Jen shook her head and blew out a blast of air. "I can't say I didn't have my doubts . . . One day Chuck is all full speed ahead. He even got six of his fellow farmers and ranchers to sign on. Then this terrible thing with his son and . . ."

"And what?" Hauck asked.

"And suddenly there's a toe tag on it. Dead as a body at the morgue. There were a lot of law clerks in Greeley and Denver who'd put a whole lot of time in pro bono on this stack of files. I thought we had a good chance."

"Where was it being heard?"

"We were taking it to the state appellate court in Denver after the local judge," she chortled, "no surprise, ruled we had no standing to bring up the case. By all means check *his* vacation fund. Chuck was looked up to by the farming community here. Third generation. He backs out, the rest find an excuse to back out as well."

"So it's all dead now?"

She put her hand on the stack of files. "Everything's just sitting here. Decorating the office. All it takes is a nod from the right person and we can have it back on track."

"That right person being Watkins?"

"Any of them, actually. Anyone who wants to stand up. But Chuck would be first on the list."

"I was up at Hannah the other day. Someone from RMM, Moss, took me for a tour."

Jen nodded. "Yeah, they're good at that kind of thing. He show you all the fancy 3-D imaging?"

"And the levels of safety they stringently maintain. All the concrete and steel reinforcing to prevent the oil or gas or chemicals from leaching into the soil."

"And, to be fair, much of that is absolutely true. But

275

how do you explain a farmer in Mead who can light a flame in his well and the whole thing goes up like a giant blowtorch?" Jen reached over and tossed Hauck a couple more bound documents. "Or a rancher in Keenesburg, less than a quarter mile from a well site, whose cattle are dying on their own grazing land and the toxicology report says ammonium persulfate poisoning. That's one of the chemical agents they mix with fracking water to loosen the shale. Along with hydrochloric acid."

Hauck paged through the top file a minute and then tossed it back on the table. "So no court in the region was willing to hear your case, so you were going to take it to Denver because of the environmental threat?"

"Not the environmental threat," Jen said. "That kind of suit would take years, cost millions . . . Even if we had a chance of winning. What *we* were filing was an injunction against the town. Templeton."

"The town . . .? I don't understand."

"They were the defendant. And it wasn't over oil, at all . . ." Keeler pushed across a document with Watkins's name in bold capital letters at the top. "It was over water."

CHAPTER FORTY-SEVEN

Trey Watkins.

Rooster.

Trey's father pushing Hauck away.

RMM. And the gleaming metal tankers chugging toward Hannah from the river.

It all came clear to him now.

That's not oil, Moss had said. *It's water*.

Water that kept the wells flowing. Water that ran the fracking process, which could reach the shale.

"The town is selling off its water supply to RMM," Hauck said, pushing back his chair.

"Out here, water flows *up*hill, Mr. Hauck," Jen said, "to money. Yes, RMM and other firms have locked up what used to be farmland for exploration and drilling. But wells are one thing. Nothing happens without the water. And these days, there is none. It's the water they've diverted away that's the biggest threat to the way this place used to be."

Hauck gazed at Dani, everything sinking in. She asked, "It's legal for a town to sell of its water supply?"

"Not the essential water supply . . ." Jen shook her head. "That's governed by law. But what becomes classified as excess water, yes. And look around at what they're dealing with here. You see the fields. The so-called excess water they're selling off is precisely what the farmers need to irrigate their crops.

"In normal years, farmers and ranchers paid an average of thirty dollars for an acre-foot of water," she explained. "That's about three hundred and twenty thousand gallons. In a drought year, when water is scarce, that can rise to as high as a hundred dollars per acre. Today, oil and gas exploration companies are paying as high as one to two *thousand* dollars per acre. That's treated water from city pipes, runoff from the Rockies; what's already low, but sitting in reservoirs near Greeley. And from the Poudre River in Templeton. It's like a bubble. The farmers can't compete. They're being systemically starved, between the weather and the oil development companies, who for that same acre of water can get a thousand times the return as on a field of crops. Farmers and ranchers can't produce their crops or graze their cattle, so there's no choice but to lease out their land for something."

"How do they get this massive supply of water?" Dani asked. "Where does it all come from?"

"There are auctions," Jen said. "Just like there are for land. A single well can use up to five million gallons. Statewide, the mining industry is consuming up to thirteen billion gallons per year. To put it in perspective, that's enough to serve a population base four times the size of Greeley, which is a city of close to a hundred thousand. Or to make all the man-made snow at every ski area in Colorado for the next ten years. And the demand keeps growing. Cash-strapped cities are balancing their budgets by selling off whatever water they can do without.

"Farms are being forced to shut down. Those that remain trade high-end corn and potato crops for low-revenue ones like alfalfa and beet root or hay that can be produced without much water. The energy companies are locking up supply with long-term agreements. Town managers make themselves look good by balancing their budgets. But it's the farmers and ranchers who are truly being starved."

"So you and Watkins and a few of his fellow farmers got together a class action suit and were suing the town to stop them from selling off their supply to RMM?" Hauck said.

"You can see why it scared them." Jen nodded. "Take away that water in abundant supply, those hundred-million-dollar wells are basically just giant holes in the ground."

"So they were pressuring Watkins to stop, but he kept on."

"Until his son was killed. He said he was being harassed, but he kept on ahead with it. I figured it was the kind of way we were all being harassed. Who could ever have imagined this? I was suspicious when I heard what happened, but I had no proof. And even if I did . . ." Her exhale conveyed her futility. "Their interests are vast, Mr. Hauck, and their will to use them just as undeterred. There are the people in the white hats in this town and the people in the black hats, and you best not forget who's who."

Hauck shook his head. "Oil companies just don't operate in their own sphere above the law. BP had to deal with that in the Gulf. Tobacco companies had free rein and then they were forced to obey the law."

"BP faced a government that had an interest to make them pay. Here, they've completely bought off all the channels that could possibly redress them. Lawyers. Local judges. Half the state legislature. Hell, even the state land councils and water boards are basically just rubber stamps with all the public pressures of jobs and energy independence.

"But what they're really doing is systematically raping the town . . . The way of life here. And in its place they're constructing football stadiums and senior citizen centers. And fancy new vehicles for the police to buzz around in. Yes, there *are* jobs—mostly for people from out of state. Engineers and field workers. The people here get jobs serving them coffee and sandwiches. Once those wells dry up, these will become basically ghost towns. Ghost towns, with a fresh coat of paint slapped on them. And it's happening all around these parts. Watkins and a few others finally said, enough. Now look what's happened . . .

Hauck said, "What about the county prosecutor here in Greeley?"

Jen Keeler smiled skeptically, as if it was something she knew and Hauck would soon find out for himself. "Good luck with that one. Take a guess who his largest campaign contributor is. It's also been in the financial papers that RMM is involved in some sort of takeover conversation. Profits from the Wattenberg field are all this company is about right now, and they're sprinkling them back around here pretty strategically."

"It is like the Wild West," Dani said. "The guy with the biggest herd runs the town."

"And the saloon." Jen Keeler grinned. "Whoops, I meant the stadium."

Hauck met her eyes. It was clear what he was up against.

"What about back in Carbondale?" Jen said. "That's where the crimes of record took place."

"Accidents," Dani said. "The police chief there wouldn't even open an investigation."

Hauck shrugged. "There's no real proof anyway.

281

Other than this Robertson guy being on the river at the time of Trey's accident. And that won't add up to an indictment."

"So now it's your turn . . ." Jen pushed aside the documents and looked back at Hauck. "What's your stake in all of this? Your business card says Talon. Partner. Back in Connecticut. You probably have a life back there. A family. Look at this place. It's mostly scrub and dirt and wind. And people you'll never see again in your life. Why do you want to take this on?"

"You mean other than the six people who have died?"

"Six people you never met. You probably don't even know their names."

"You're right. I don't. Maybe it's not so easy to answer, but like you said earlier"—Hauck grinned—"I could ask the same question about you."

Jen Keeler gave him back a smile of complicity. "You're taking on a lot here, Mr. Hauck. These people might wear suits and ties, root for their kids in soccer, and go to church on Sundays and drive SUVs, but, trust me, they're as ruthless and single-minded as you'll run into. But I'm pretty sure you already know that, don't you . . .?"

"I think I do." Hauck smiled. And stood up.

Jen stood up, too. "And, trust me, the ones in the cowboy hats aren't a whole lot better."

"I'll keep that in mind."

Jen walked them out and to the door. "I hope you

know what the hell you're doing . . . You seem like a nice guy. These aren't people you really want to mess with."

"People have been known to say that about me, too."

"Monica, say goodbye to Mr. Hauck, the last remaining white knight in the Wattenberg field."

The tattooed girl waved. "Nice to meet you, Mr. Hauck."

Hauck put out his hand. "Thanks for your time. I have a feeling we'll be seeing each other again."

"Stay safe," Jen said.

"Everyone's telling me that these days." He was about to open the door, when he saw something out the front window through the shades. In the parking lot of a farm supply depot across the street.

A black SUV, the windows dark.

"So, tell me," he said to Jen, "who drives a new, black, tinted-out Denali out here? I've seen a few of them in town."

Jen spread the shades with a finger and peered out. "Those are the men in the black hats, Mr. Hauck."

CHAPTER FORTY-EIGHT

The man behind the darkened window in the black SUV saw Hauck staring out at him. He picked up his phone and called in to his office.

"Mr. Moss," he said, his eyes trained on the Open Range Initiative storefront, "it's Hale. You asked me to stay on our subject. I thought you'd want to know, he and the girl have been meeting with someone I think you'd find interesting."

"Who's that?" Moss, at RMM's headquarters, inquired.

"The Keeler woman."

There was a groan on the other end, followed by a troubled sigh.

"They've been inside for about half an hour," Hale said. "I can see them through the window. I think they're coming out now." He watched them step out of the storefront office. He saw the subject look across the street, fix directly on him. From behind his sunglasses, around fifty yards away, Hale was sure he could see his target smile. The hair rose on his arms.

"I think I've been spotted. You want me to stay on him?" he asked.

"No," his boss replied. "Let him go."

"You're sure?"

"I'm sure," Moss said with a sigh. "Come on back. I think it's time to explore more persuasive measures anyway."

Moments later, Moss told his secretary to hold his calls and patched into Randy McKay at Alpha. "Are you alone?"

The Alpha man excused himself a moment and replied, "You can talk."

"Our friend has made a connection in town that may turn out very unfortunate. Jen Keeler. He's been meeting with her this morning. How do you imagine that happened?"

"If he dug, it was only a matter of time," McKay said.

"Well, I give him marks for persistence. But he's clearly misread our hospitality. I don't think our first attempt on the road made much of an impact on him."

"I can arrange something more persuasive," the Alpha man said.

"Where's John?"

"I told him to lie low while this fellow was poking

around. But if he's needed, I can assure you, he's close by."

"Well, maybe it's time," Moss said. "The guy's so interested in water rights, what do you think, maybe he'd be up for a little swim. Just remember, this isn't some OSHA functionary coming around with a clipboard and pen. You know what his résumé is."

"It's not our policy to underestimate anybody," Randy McKay said. "You can be sure I'll pass along your request to the right personnel."

"I'm confident you will," Moss said, and hung up.

McKay turned back to the person he'd been speaking to before the call, sitting across his desk. "We have to arrange something for our nosy new friend in town. Moss thinks maybe he's ripe for a swim. But remember, this guy's no lightweight."

John Robertson nodded. He stood up. "Neither am I."

"Well, remember, he found you, even with the insurance we had in Aspen. So make sure there are no trails."

"I understand," Robertson said, heading to the door.

"Oh, and John . . ." Robertson turned. Moss shrugged before he picked up the phone again. "It's your call, of course, however you see fit. Him, or the girl."

CHAPTER FORTY-NINE

Back in the car, Hauck didn't see any sign that the black SUV was following them. He stopped in an alley, took out his phone, and asked Dani to excuse him for a couple of minutes.

Naomi picked up on the third ring. "Hey, stranger . . .!" She was clearly happy to hear his voice. "Are you still on the boat?'

"No. I left it in St. Kitts. I'm actually in Colorado."

"*Colorado?*" There was a pause. "I might have thought you could've given me a heads-up if you were coming back?"

"It was a quick thing, Naomi. And I don't know if I'm even really back. I had to do something for a friend. It was kind of an emergency . . ."

"Hang on a sec . . ." Hauck heard her speaking on

her end, telling a colleague to give her a minute. "Okay I'm back, sorry."

"Sounds like you're pretty busy back there."

"You might say. The new health-care bill has brought with it about a hundred new ways to screw people that we're looking into. So what's in Colorado?"

He gave her the quick version of the call he'd gotten from Ted, and having to pull Dani out of jail.

She said, "You never told me you were a godfather. I actually think that sounds kind of sexy."

"I guess there's still one or two things I haven't fully revealed about myself."

"Well, if I weren't at my desk with about a hundred briefs around me and six in staff who can pretty much hear everything I say, I would let you know what I really think about that. Maybe I should find something to do out there and requisition a government jet. The mountains sound heavenly about now."

"And if I wasn't in the plains with nothing around but oil wells and a two-year drought, I'd tell you to do just that. In the meantime, though, I think I'll save you from having to appear in front of the House Oversight Committee about the plane and let you know why I called. I need some help with something."

"Buzz killer."

He brought her up to speed. Everything he had just told Jen Keeler: Trey, Rooster, Robertson. Alpha and RMM.

"I know RMM," Naomi said. "It's a big oil firm that's been in front of the Justice Department on some antitrust issues."

"Yes, but that's not what this is about. Oil. Or, at least not directly. I'm actually calling about something else. Water."

"*Water?* You mean like run-of-the-mill H2O?"

"Kind of like that. Except I'm really talking water rights here." He took her through what Jen had explained, from the drought that was afflicting the region to the huge amounts of water that were required for the fracking process. To the scarcity that had driven those prices through the roof. "There's a bidding war going on out here, Naomi. The oil and gas companies are buying everything they can and locking in long-term supplies that are killing the farmers."

"This isn't exactly something I know a whole lot about, Ty. A town selling off its water rights is legal?"

"Excess water rights, apparently. And in a drought, that's precisely what farmers need to irrigate their crops."

"It all sounds bad," Naomi said, "but so far it also all sounds entirely legal. And this all connects to your niece and what happened in Aspen *how . . .?*"

"The kid who was killed on the river, Naomi . . . his father is a local farmer here who was leading a suit against the town to restrict them from selling off their excess water to the oil companies. Which puts him in the cross fire between RMM and the town."

289

"Why the town?" Naomi asked. "Someone was being paid off?"

"The whole community is, in a way. You should see what the exploration companies are putting up to gain their support. High school football stadium scoreboards that look like MetLife Stadium, beautiful parks, senior citizen centers . . . in the middle of nowhere."

"And so you're suggesting what, Ty, just so I understand? That this friend of your goddaughter was murdered?"

"I'm starting to think so. To influence his father to drop his suit. Which is precisely what he did. Now that doesn't sound entirely legal, does it? They're sitting on some of the richest concentrations of oil and natural gas in the country. The Wattenberg field."

"So where is this suit now?"

"Where you might expect. Dead. The father backed down."

"Look, I'm sorry about all this, Ty . . . I mean, I get it. It's sad. And it's got to be really devastating if you're a farmer out there. But if you think this kid was murdered by some oil company to influence a lawsuit, isn't this more for the Justice Department or local law enforcement? I'm in financial fraud."

"Let's just say the local law enforcement here is about as helpful as talking directly to the oil companies themselves. And where it happened, back in Carbondale,

290

isn't exactly cooperating, either. And if this was simply just about the murders, I'd agree. The problem is, I just don't have the proof.

"But what I do have is someone trained by the U.S. Army in black ops over in Iraq and Afghanistan who was there at the very same time that kid was killed. And I have a witness who claimed they saw something suspicious out there who's now dead as well along with four others. And with RMM spreading money around here like they were printing the stuff, you can only imagine what the enthusiasm is for getting any kind of investigation off the ground."

Naomi sighed. "I see what you're up against. I admit is sounds shitty, but we're not exactly the Better Business Bureau here. We're Treasury. Financial terrorism."

"Murder. The intimidation of potential plaintiffs in a lawsuit. The manipulation of public resources . . ."

"I'm just being honest here, Ty." Naomi exhaled. "Anyway, what is it you'd like me to do?"

"I was hoping you might pressure someone in Justice to take a look. Just the threat of that could get these companies to back off. Or maybe use your own resources to look into it as unfair practices or something, on the water issue."

"We're not exactly a business fairness panel here. That's what the courts are for."

"I've already told you what kinds of things take place

when they do try to address it that way. Besides, these energy firms have given all the local lawyers either jobs or retainers. So they have to recuse themselves."

"You're starting to sound like you're out there staring at black helicopters, Ty."

"SUVs, maybe," Hauck added darkly.

"What does that mean . . .?"

"I already had a run-in with a couple of them. That's what they're driving here."

"Ty, the Justice Department isn't going to stick its nose into a local murder case, even if I did have some sway over them, which I assure you I don't. I'm the head of one, poorly funded investigative unit here at Treasury. And if you're looking for me to send out my own people, I barely have the resources to look into the things we've been charged to do. Not to mention I would need to see a lot more proof and specifics about how hundreds of people have been harmed by their actions."

"I have a copy of the lawsuit I mentioned."

"Okay. How many plaintiffs were signed on?"

Hauck exhaled, knowing his answer wouldn't exactly bowl her over. "Seven."

"*Seven?* Now there's a good ol' prime number for you, huh . . .? Look, I have to go. Seems to me you got your goddaughter out of jail, which is really what you went out there for. All you can do now by digging around into this is put her and you at risk. I know how you

292

look at this and how you want to help. But you should just come home. You could come here. You could sail your boat right up the Potomac. We could jog on the mall in the morning and—"

"I'm not sure they let private boats sail up the Potomac, Naomi. For obvious reasons."

"Then sail it up Long Island Sound; that's fine with me, too. It's just not your fight, Ty. Come on back and see what you can do from here."

"I'm not sure I can, Naomi. At least not just yet."

"And why is that?"

"Because it's gotten personal."

She paused. "It always seems to get personal, Ty. For you."

Hauck overheard voices interrupting her again. This time, she came back. "Sorry, I've got a staff meeting, Ty . . . Look, I'll make some inquiries, that's all I can say. Not just because it's *you,* and because you have this cool goddaughter you've never told me about. But because I know that anything you get involved in this deeply probably should be looked into. Even if I'm not the right one. How's that . . .?"

"You're a doll. Have I ever told you that?"

"Now there's far too many people in here now to tell you that yes, I think you have. I'll check into it. That's all I can promise. But I wish you'd come home, Ty. You can still fight the good fight from here."

"You're breaking up," Hauck said. "I can't hear you."

"Good Lord," Naomi chortled, "can't you come up with anything a little more imaginative than that?"

"How about that you're the best. And I kind of miss you. In my own way."

"And I kind of miss you, too, Ty. And I might a whole lot more if I knew I could keep you alive."

"Message received."

"Did it work?"

"Sorry, I'm getting that interference again . . ."

"Didn't think it would." She blew out a resigned breath. "Take it easy out there, my charming white knight."

CHAPTER FIFTY

"I want you to stay here," Hauck said, dropping Dani off back at the café on the main street in Templeton.

"Where are you going?" she asked.

"Back out to Watkins's one more time."

"So what do you want me to do in the meantime?"

"I don't know . . . Make some calls. Keep your ears open. Hopefully, I'll be back in an hour."

"An hour? Please don't leave me hanging like you have lately."

"I won't. I promise."

"Okay. And watch your back. Don't let any trucks creep up on you this time."

"I'll see what I can do."

Hauck made the drive out, along the river and brown, fenced-in fields. He thought about what Naomi had said to him: *Come on home. It's not your fight. You've done what you came out to do.*

Even Jen Keeler had questioned what his stake was here. Truth was, he hadn't met a single person, other than Watkins's daughter, Kelli, who even wanted him to stay. It wasn't just the people who'd been killed. Like Jen said, they were only names. People he had never met. But what was clear as the sky was the look on Watkins's face two days before. At first, it just told him to go, to let them get on with their grieving. And then it told him something more, something painful and familiar and close enough that even after all these years it still shook him.

Maybe it never went away, he thought, turning onto the gravelly road along the fence of Watkins's farm. Hard as you tried to cover it up or paint over it. Maybe when he got up every morning and looked in the mirror even now, that was what he still saw. Stared at. The guilt he still felt.

No, it doesn't go away, Hauck should have told him. It never does.

It just hides.

He spotted the farmer in the fields on a tractor with a couple of workers, the portable sprinklers drizzling a thin sheet of water on a row of crops. They were digging a makeshift irrigation ditch. The man was tough and Hauck knew exactly what he must be carrying inside him. What he was burying.

296

Hauck left the car along the road and climbed through a gap in the wire. Watkins was backing up his tractor, pulling away a large rock from the earth. Two or three farmhands were helping. When he spotted Hauck in the field, the farmer's face turned sour. "Lupe, Diego, take a few minutes," he said to the hands. "I'll be back in a second." He put on the brake and jumped down from the open cab. He said to Hauck, "Guess working with these guys, my English must be out of practice. I thought we made it clear—"

"I know why they killed Trey," Hauck said.

"—not to come around here anymore . . ." The farmer's voice trailed off. "Do I have to call the police on you, mister, or what?"

"They did it to get you to back down. From the lawsuit you were filing against the town. I spoke with Jen Keeler. She showed it all to me, the suit, the other names on it. And it worked. You did back down, right? And there's not a person in this world who would blame you for having done it. Not one."

"So you've been here for all of two days and you think you've got it all sized up, huh . . .?" Watkins's eyes shone with intensity and he took off his cap and crumpled it against his side.

"I know one thing I've got sized up," Hauck said.

"What's that?" The farmer glared.

"What was on your face the other day. I told you, I lost a child as well."

297

"And I'm real sorry for that, Mr. Hauck. I am. But you and I are different people, and there's nothing that's happened here that's even about you."

"My little girl"—Hauck stepped up to him—"she was playing in our driveway and I backed over her after an argument with my wife. I was impatient and my mind was elsewhere. She was five. It cost me my job and my marriage, and about three years of my life, until I realized, it was all just an accident. A stupid, tragic accident that should never have happened and that I didn't cause, no matter how many times I told myself that I did."

"Why are you going through this with me, mister?"

"Because I know what it's like to look in that mirror. I know what it's like to feel responsible."

"You want absolution, Mr. Hauck . . .?" Watkins took out a rag from his pocket and wiped his hands. "I'll see you in church on Sunday. Trey was a grown man and we're all different here. So don't come around and tell me you know what I'm feeling or what you think you saw . . ."

"There was a contractor RMM uses with military black ops training who was on that river the same time as your son. I know about the intimidation and the paying off, and the whole town being in the oil company's pocket. I know about how they're sucking the whole region dry of water. And I know what you were trying to do."

"I'm going to call my boys over now, if you don't

just turn around." His crew had heard the ruckus and one or two stood up waiting for the sign. "You're on my property and I'm asking you nicely, one last time. So which is it, Mr. Hauck? What do you want me to do?"

"I want you to continue on with that suit. I can bring people in who can protect you."

"Protect me . . .?" Watkins laughed. "*You . . .?*"

"You want to spend the rest of your life carrying around the belief that your boy died for nothing? Like I have all these years. That he wasn't worth grieving for. They killed him, Mr. Watkins, sure and clear. Because what you were doing threatened them. But it won't be for nothing if you stand back up. If the other people stand up with you. I want to help you carry it through."

"You want to help me, son . . ." Watkins spat in the earth. "Leave."

"You asked if it went away? What you were feeling. Well, I carried the grief of my daughter's death around with me for years. But it wasn't just grief. That was just a mask. It was guilt. And shame. And it ate me up. Like poison inside. Because I felt responsible. And that's what I saw on you, Mr. Watkins. You can't bring your son back, there's nothing you can do about that now. But you can make what happened mean something."

Watkins's hostility seemed to shift. "What could possibly mean something anymore?"

Hauck stepped up to him. "Stopping them."

"You come here and talk to me like you think you know."

"I do know," Hauck said. "I know everything you feel."

The farmer's eyes lost a little of their hardness and his fist opened around his cap. He gave Hauck a vague nod, looking past him at the fields. "They said if I ever brought it up again, they would . . ."

"They would what?" Hauck asked him.

"They told me I ought to be happy." He sniffed. "'Cause I was actually lucky."

"Lucky how . . .?"

"Lucky that they took the one that I didn't . . ." He gritted his teeth, mashing something in his jaw. "That if I kept at it, there were two more and they'd go after them, too. The ones I did . . ."

"The ones you did *what?*" Hauck kept on him.

The farmer twisted his mouth. "Loved. The ones I loved. Is that what you wanted me to say?" His Caterpillar cap hung from his fingers.

"*Who* said that, Mr. Watkins?" Hauck looked at him.

Watkins averted his eyes. Shame had now come into them. "You know what they did, so just be done with it. I have two more."

"Who?"

"I didn't exactly ask his name." Watkins let out a long, deep breath. "He called my cell phone. A day after it happened. Kelli picked it up. He told her it was concerning Trey, so I got on. We all thought it was just a crazy accident to that point. That boy was always going to end up like that one day anyway . . . He just said, 'Told you it was time to rethink that suit, old man.'"

He looked at Hauck. "They'd warned me before. Tried to buy me off. Saying my land might have oil value. I didn't want their money. They talked about my son's scholarship. To CSU. They said they could take it away. Like that. That they gave a lot of money there and had friends . . . They had friends everywhere. I kept on going. Then they said, 'We're telling you one last time.'"

Watkins spat on the ground. "I'd have strangled that sonovabitch with my own hands if he were in front of me. But what was I to do? Nick's got it all in front of him. He's got football practice starting next month. Kelli, too. She's just getting married.

"I'm not a weak man, Mr. Hauck. I lived my life and can take what comes. But how can I put them in danger like that? Think whatever you want, but you'd have done the same. Any father would. I can't beat them. You can't beat them. You can stand there and think you can. But you can't. You can stand up to them, maybe. If you want." His eyes had lost their fire. "But you can't beat them."

Hauck nodded and put his hand on the man's shoulder. "We can."

"You come in here, stirring up all this hope . . . You

301

say you know who it was? This Robertson. The one who killed Trey."

"I don't have proof. They have him out of sight. He was in the same unit in Iraq as a lot of the Alpha people. Part of a PsyOps unit. And he was there."

"PsyOps, huh . . .?" Watkins nodded. "You know he'd settled down. All that wildness. You met Allie. She's a good girl. They had Petey and . . . For the first time, he had a real life ahead of him . . ."

He stepped back toward the tractor. "I'll talk to the others. I'll see how they feel about things now. Not sure if they'll be willing to recommit. Couldn't blame them. But people here, they can be funny about things, you know . . . when you put their way of life on the line."

"Mr. Watkins . . ." Hauck took a step after him and put out his hand.

He heard a muted *phfft* go past him. Watkins groaned and jerked to the side.

A burst of crimson exploded on his shoulder.

Without even looking behind, Hauck leapt and threw his body over the farmer, dragging him to the ground. The workers all shouted and scurried away as another shot clanged off the tractor.

Hauck screamed, "Get down! Get down!"

He huddled there, the farmer breathing heavily underneath him, and tried to calculate where the shots had come from—someone was obviously using a sound suppressor—hoping he was out of sight there and the

302

next one wouldn't tear into his back. He tried to roll Watkins toward the cover of the tractor. A third shot whooshed in and kicked up dust at their feet. And then a fourth. Hauck inched Watkins closer to the tractor. "You okay?"

"I think so," the farmer said, glassy-eyed. "But I can't feel my arm."

Hauck rolled him over and saw that Watkins's shoulder was covered in blood. He looked behind him, calculating where the shots had come from, peering over the hood of the tractor, and saw a car out on the road about a hundred yards away, the shooter leaning on the hood with a rifle.

He ducked back down as another shot pinged off the hood of the tractor.

The workers were flat in a ditch, jabbering in Spanish. Watkins sat up against the wheel, his hand on his bloody shoulder. "Damn."

"*Chuck! Chuck!*" Marie Watkins bolted from the house, shouting. "Oh my God, what's happening?"

"Marie, get down. Get down now!" the farmer hollered, grimacing.

"He's been shot, but he's okay," Hauck yelled back. "Call 911!"

"Oh my God!"

"Do it, Marie! I'm all right," Watkins yelled again. "Do it now!"

She ran back inside the house.

"I'm losing a lot of blood," Watkins said, staring at Hauck with a dazed expression. "We have to stop it. Otherwise I'll bleed out."

Hauck ripped off his shirt from over his tee. He balled it up and stuffed it into the wound. "What's the most pleasing thing you can think of?" he asked Watkins.

"Easy." The farmer chortled. "Rain."

"Then I would think of Noah," Hauck said, "'cause this'll hurt." He pressed on the wound, hard. The farmer grimaced and turned away.

"You see combat?" Hauck asked.

"Huh?"

"You seem to know your gunshot wounds."

Watkins shrugged. "Mekong Delta. Hue."

"Then I guess you know what to do. *Here . . .*" Hauck put the man's hands on the balled-up shirt that was growing moist with blood. "Press. I have to make sure this guy doesn't come after us."

"How you gonna stop him if he does?"

Hauck looked up in the tractor cab and saw the keys in the ignition. "Come after him."

Suddenly the sound of a wailing siren pierced their ears, from the direction of the farmhouse. It went on and on. You could probably hear it all over the county.

"Tornado warning." Watkins grinned. "Smart gal, huh?"

"Real smart." Hauck nodded. He heard a car engine

start. He got up and peered out over the tractor hood and watched the car he had seen the shooter on drive off, heading down the long road back to the main road and Templeton.

"I can't believe after what those sonavabitches did they would try to kill me, too," Watkins said, sucking back the pain.

"They didn't," Hauck said, taking over the shirt and pressing to stop the blood flow, "try to kill you."

"Well they sure did a damn good impression of it then." Watkins winced.

Hauck realized that if he hadn't taken a step toward Watkins, that would have been his head. "That was for me."

"Well, I told you you should've been in that car of yours, on that road and gone. You know they were wrong," the farmer said, his eyes growing a bit glazy. Marie Watkins came running across the fields.

"About what?" Hauck said, folding his shirt over and pressing the other side down.

"Trey. I did love him, Mr. Hauck. I loved them all."

"I know you did," Hauck said. "I saw that, too."

The siren continued to wail. Marie Watkins arrived, fear in her eyes. "Chuck, Chuck, are you all right?" She saw him on the ground. "Oh my God, Chuck!"

"He's been hit in the shoulder," Hauck said. "I think the bullet went right through him. I think he'll be okay."

"The police are on their way. I told them there was shooting."

"*Riddick?*" Watkins rolled his eyes with a sarcastic snort. "That'll kick me over the edge for sure."

Suddenly a thought rose up that sent terror through Hauck's blood.

Dani . . .

He'd left her in town. By herself. If they'd come after him in this way, right out in the open, what would they do to her?

"I need to go," Hauck said. "My niece may be in danger. I left her back in town."

"Go on, go!" Watkins said, gritting his teeth, "I'll be all right here."

"I need something from you first . . ." Hauck looked at Marie.

"What? Anything."

"I need a gun."

306

CHAPTER FIFTY-ONE

Dani was at the counter at the one café in town. There were only a couple of tables filled, the conversations ranging from the Wounded Warrior Basket Drive next week to the prospects of rain to the Colorado Rockies.

She ordered a club sandwich, and sent a couple of emails to Geoff and her roommate, Patti, and went over in her mind what Jen Keeler had told them. The mystery was filling in. They now knew that Trey was killed to force his father and the other farmers to back down from their suit against the town. The only question now was what could be done about it. They knew that bringing in the local police would be about as effective as filing a complaint with RMM's customer service department.

And then there was Wade. Something just didn't sit right with her. How he'd dragged his feet from the start, hidden the fact that he'd impounded the film from the park that implicated Robertson. How he'd called her just the other night, sounding strange, vague. Almost drunk, she thought. *Do the smart thing, and come on back* . . .

The smart thing. Meaning what?

It seemed to come to her all at once.

They'd gotten to him, too. Just like they'd gotten to the people here. The police and the lawyers.

They wanted to come after Trey and they'd somehow bought Wade off. He was a walking, talking advertisement for a payout even from a couple of hundred miles away.

That was why he'd sounded so helpless on the phone the other night. *Do the smart thing, and come on back.*

Because she and Ty were in danger here.

She checked the time. Ty had been gone for well over an hour now. *Typical* . . . The little bell jingled when the front door of the café opened and Dani turned, expecting to see him come in. It was another man. She went to text Ty again. The man looked around the small café and came up to the counter. There were three or four stools open but he took one next to her. He was in his twenties, nice build, short hair, with a scruffy beard and muscular arms, wearing a South by Southwest T-shirt over his jeans.

He smiled affably. "This seat taken?"

"No." She moved her bag and phone closer to her. "Sorry."

"No worries." The guy had nice, green eyes, though there was something about him that seemed vaguely familiar. Maybe she had seen him at the funeral, she thought. Or around town somewhere.

She hit redial again, set to step outside if Ty picked up, but his voice mail came on again. She clicked off the phone, having already left a message.

"So what do you think, the chili or the bison burger?" the guy next to her asked.

Dani shrugged. "I don't know. First time here myself. Well, second, actually."

"Same here. I don't find myself in town much during the day. But we shut down the well site today, so they gave us the afternoon off."

Dani turned toward him. "You work on one of the wells?"

"Betsy Three South. Seven days a week. Think I'll go with the burger. You don't see fresh bison on the menu everyday." He seemed pleasant and polite in a midwestern kind of way. "Been pretty much spending twenty-four/seven out there."

"That's crazy. For how long?"

"I don't know . . . For over a month now. Gotta feed the beast while it's hungry, as they say."

"Or thirsty, I guess." Dani smiled.

309

"Or thirsty." The guy grinned back. He ordered from the waitress, along with a Diet Coke.

"So who do you work for?" Dani asked.

"Freelance mostly. Betsy's a nat gas well. Man, it feels good just to get these hands out of the dirt. So what brings you here? I've never seen you before around town."

"Just visiting," Dani said.

"Well, then you're lucky." The guy grinned, flagging the waitress. "The only thing I get to visit is a hydraulic compressor valve that separates natural gas from mud and water."

"Well, not that lucky," Dani said. "I came for a funeral."

"Oh, sorry. Meant no disrespect."

She smiled back. "That's okay."

The waitress came over with his soda. The guy took a glance toward the front door.

"So what sort of work do you do there?" Dani asked.

"Valve hand. On the water flow," he said.

"For fracking?"

"That's the only way to get the product out," he said. He took a sip of his soda and sighed.

"I actually always wondered," Dani said, "where all the water comes from for something like that. You need a lot of it, right?"

"Four to five thousand gallons a day. I don't know, you'd have to ask the bigwigs at the company on where it all comes from. I know much of it comes from the river."

"Yeah, I saw trucks coming up from there. On the way back to Greeley."

"That's right. They have a pumping station down there. I think the company also has other sources. What do you do?"

Dani said, "I guess I kind of work with water, too. I'm a whitewater guide."

"Cool. Whereabouts?"

"The Roaring Fork River. Outside Aspen."

"Very cool." His bison burger came. He put some onions and a pickle on it. "Sounds like a fun life to me."

"Ever been there?"

"Once." He took a bite. "Not too long ago. Mmmm . . ." He took a bite. "That was the right choice. So, hey, maybe I could show you if you've got some time . . .?"

"Show me what?"

"Where all that water comes from. That water facility down by the river. You seem to be interested."

"I don't know . . ." Dani shrugged. Maybe she had let it go too far. "We're actually leaving later today. Besides, I thought you said you've never been there."

"Hell, won't take more than an hour." The guy turned to her. "C'mon now, have a little pity on a guy who's been out in the fields for a month. What do you say?"

What Dani would have said, had she not noticed two things that sent a tremor of caution running through her, was that she'd heard better pickup lines in grade school. But her eye went first to the guy's hands, which were clean and smooth and trimmed down to the quick, and didn't look like the hands of any oil field workman who'd been out in the field for a month.

And the second, since he kept glancing, was that a black SUV had pulled up on the street outside the café.

"So what's your name?" the guy asked. His smile seemed to shift, no longer innocent and friendly. Now like there was something behind it. Almost professional.

That was when Dani placed where she had seen those hard, detached eyes.

"I'm sorry, I've gotta go," she said, reaching in her bag for some bills.

"Dani, isn't it? So what's the rush?" he said. The man put his hand over hers, restraining her from going into her bag. A chill ran through her. Suddenly she saw who it was. Her mind hurtled back to the grainy photo Ty had shown her that he'd taken at Alpha. To Trey's twisted and bloodied body she had found in the river.

"I'm John," the guy said, still smiling, but the smile now frozen and empty. "John Robertson. Heard you were trying to find me, Dani." He winked. "How about we just say, lunch is on me."

CHAPTER FIFTY-TWO

Dani froze, bolts of fear rocketing down her.

Her heart went from beating a mile a minute to a dead stop. She took hold of her bag and tried to slide off the stool and away from him, her eyes never leaving his. Trying with everything she had not to show him the dread that was ricocheting in her chest.

"Why the rush, girl . . .?" Robertson tightened his grip. "Now that you finally found me, you don't like what you see? So, listen up, here's how we're gonna do this . . ." The easygoing drawl hardened into a veiled command. "We're going to walk out of here, nice and friendly like, and we're going to get in that black SUV you see outside. Try something even remotely foolish, like yell or try to get away, and I'll crack your arm in two right here, and I assure you, no one in here will do as much as lift a finger to help. So are we good . . .?" He lifted her hand back out of her bag. "And no point in checking to see if that uncle of yours is gonna come to the rescue. 'Cause he ain't, I can assure you. I'm afraid he had a bit of an unexpected situation himself a few minutes ago."

Dani froze. "What have you done with him?" Worry springing up in her.

Robertson made a kind of chirping noise. "Now don't you worry about him, darlin'. You just come along. Nice and easy now. Now nod to me that you understand what I'm telling you and we'll get going."

"You're hurting me," Dani said under her breath, trying to wrestle her arm free.

"Just say you understand." Robertson squeezed her even tighter, on a pressure point that made her feet buckle. "Or you won't know what hurt is."

She looked back at him, both in pain and terror. She didn't know what they had done with Ty. *Please let him be all right*. But one thing was clear. Clear as anything she'd ever felt in her life.

She couldn't get in that car.

Once she did, she knew she was as good as dead.

"I understand." She finally nodded, and ripped her arm away. She looked around. Everyone behind the counter was working and the customers at the couple of tables still occupied seemed to be minding their own business.

"Good, then," he said. "So we're gonna walk out

314

of here, kind of arm in arm, just like we were gonna go take that trip I talked about. And we'll get in that SUV parked outside and no one will know the difference. So get on up now . . . and don't make a move to run. Or I'll crack that arm of yours like a twig. Just follow me."

Robertson slowly stepped off his stool, and Dani desperately tried to make eye contact with the waitress and then the cook behind the counter. Maybe they sensed what was happening. But if they did, it was just like Robertson had said. Everyone was just going about their business.

"Something wrong with the burger, hon?" the waitress asked, seeing Robertson put some bills on the counter. "I could pack it up to go."

"It was perfect," Robertson said. "Something just came up."

Dani caught her eyes. She gave her a look of alarm. *Can't you see what's happening? Call the police. Do something!* But she didn't seem to understand. She only looked back at Dani without it registering, taking the cash. "Next time then."

"Like I said," Robertson chuckled, "no one's gonna even lift a finger . . ."

Dani got up. The pressure on her arm pretty much forced her. She grabbed her bag. Two tables were occupied in the back of the café. It wasn't clear to her if anyone actually saw what was going on. One or two seemed to be purposely averting their eyes. Others just continued on with their conversation.

"Nice and easy now . . ." Robertson said in her ear. He locked his hand on her arm and led her toward the door.

Dani's heart was in a frenzy.

He's going to kill me, she told herself. *Just like Trey. And maybe Ty. Poor Ty . . . Oh, please don't let that be true . . .* She desperately wished she could find a way to contact him. He hadn't called her back, which only made the possibility seem worse. *Something could well have happened to him.* Her legs slid, wobbly and without strength, passing tables, people not looking or just going on with their normal business, not knowing anything improper was going on. *Can't they see!*

She thought of screaming out. They were ten feet from the front door. They couldn't all just sit there and let him take her. Blind to what was happening. Just like with RMM. And if they saw, well, then Robertson couldn't just do what he said, like what he had done to Trey. Too many people. As she walked, everything in slow motion, Dani's eyes darted around to anything she could use against him. There was silverware on every table, knives and forks, but she knew she'd never get a full grasp on something in time—and even if she did, Robertson was a trained special ops guy. She'd never have a chance to use it.

I'll break your arm off right here, he said.

She also saw those old-fashioned metal napkin dispensers on every table, the edges pointed and sharp.

Six feet. Robertson dug his grip into her arm ever harder. "Almost there now."

She couldn't let him take her.

As they reached the door, it suddenly opened, and a woman stepped in, maybe in her fifties, in a blue blouse and open sweater vest. She gave them a smile in the doorway. Robertson smiled back as if nothing was happening.

Once she was out that door it was over for her. This was her only chance.

Now.

Her heart pounding, Dani lunged and reached for the table closest to the door, grabbing on to the napkin dispenser, and swung it up with her free hand as Robertson, one hand on her, held the door.

She hit him with the sharp edge in the forehead just above the left eye.

He shouted out, letting Dani go, the hand he had around her shooting up to his eye.

The woman screamed as Dani wrenched out of Robertson's grasp, flinging her against him.

Then she bolted out the open door.

Outside, she almost ran headfirst into the black SUV pulled up there. There were two people in the front seats. She knew she had only seconds before Robertson, momentarily staggered, would come out after her. Even fewer before one of the two in the SUV would realize what was going on. The café was mid-block. Even though it was the town's main street there was virtually no one milling around and a only few vehicles on the street. She looked desperately for a police car. For anyone she could run to. The passenger door to the black SUV opened. A man stepped out.

Dani took off down the street.

She ran past the storefronts, a knitting supply shop and a State Farm insurance office. At an alley, she glanced behind her. Robertson had now come out of the café, a hand to his head, and the guy from the SUV came up to him.

They pointed toward her.

She had to find a way out of here now.

She sprinted down the alley, which was behind the storefronts on the cross street perpendicular to Main Street. She had about fifty yards on them. They hadn't even made it to the alley. She tore past the backs of the stores, searching frantically for a place to hide, her blood pumping feverishly. She knew she had to try Ty again. She only prayed he was somehow okay. She stopped and looked behind her; she saw two men turning into the alley. A back door was open to one of the shops and Dani ran in, locking the door behind her. It was an outdoors store, selling clothing and camping equipment. She pushed her way through a back storage room filled with boxes and garments on racks, toppling them

318

in her panic, and then ran through a short hallway and into the main store. A female clerk looked toward her, hearing the agitation. "Ma'am, can I help you?"

Dani didn't even know what to say. She was too panicked to even remain there the few seconds it would take to either call Ty or tell the woman what was happening.

"Call the police!" she said to the woman. "Please. There are two people chasing me."

Suddenly, she heard pounding on the door in the back. *"Call them!"*

She bolted out the front.

She found herself on the street that was perpendicular to Main Street. The stores were even older and less busy there. She didn't know if Robertson and the other man had come through the store, but there was another alleyway a couple of stores down where they'd be able to cut through and intercept her. She heard the two men coming down the alley, shouting. She ran across the street. She came upon a small side street and headed down it. She passed a bakery and a small crafts store with cheap, beaded jewelry in the window. She pressed against the building, keeping her breath still, fumbling in her purse for her phone. She grabbed it, finding Ty's number in her recent history, and punched at the keys, frantic, clumsily, until finally pushing the call icon with both thumbs to make sure it went through. Heart racing, she peered around the corner and saw the two men come out onto the street. To her surprise, Robertson wasn't one of them. They both had to be from the SUV.

Where the hell had Robertson gone?

To her anxiety, Ty's voice mail came on. *Dammit, no* . . . Under her breath, she started to tell him what had happened.

Suddenly they seemed to spot her across the street and pointed.

She ended the call.

There was a row of hedges on the right and a chain link fence that separated her from the parking lot of a Kroger food market. She sprinted down the length of it, not knowing where to go. She spun around the corner. It was a small parking alley: garbage cans and dumpsters, and a garbage truck making its way down the street, one man driving, the other throwing the contents of each receptacle into the compactor. Dani didn't know if she could outrun them anymore. The truck chugged down the narrow street ahead of the guy loading the trash, a black guy with a bandana around his head who had stopped to chat with a store worker. Dani ran up to the truck while his back was turned. The men pursuing her couldn't be more than a couple of steps behind.

Seeing no other way out, Dani pulled herself up on the truck out of the sight of the chatting garbage man. She climbed up a short metal ladder, basically a footstep and a rail for the workmen to hold on to during the ride, and hoisted herself up onto the rim of the truck's compactor and scrambled onto the top. For someone who'd been rock climbing since her teens, it was an easy task. The driver heard nothing from the cab; the truck's engine was running and the compactor was churning loudly. Dani lay there, glued to the sloped roof of the truck, breathing heavily, her heart almost pounding its way out of her chest.

She was petrified to even look up. She shifted onto her side, and maybe a block away, across from the food market, she saw the new police department, one of those modern redbrick buildings that seemed so out of place here. She remembered what Ty had said about his encounter with the chief. But they were still the police. They couldn't just hand her over to people who were trying to kidnap her. The truck began to move with a jerk and loud rumble, the guy who was loading the bags catching up and slapping the side for it to move onto the next store. Dani rolled onto her side and found her phone. She pressed Ty's number again. *Where is he? What happened to him?*

She hit REDIAL.

The line connected again. *C'mon, please, Ty, pick up.* She heard it ring. Once. Twice. Three times. *Please . . .* she begged.

To her amazement, this time she heard his voice.

"Where are you?" he asked. "Are you all right?"

"*No!*" she said, terrified. Her heart beat madly and she peered down the block. "I'm not. I'm being chased in town. Thank God, you're all right. I ran into Robertson and he said you were—"

"*Robertson?*"

She saw the two men turn down the street.

"I can't talk," she spat in a whisper. She pressed herself against the truck, afraid to even look up. "They're here. They're—"

"Are you able to stay there? Just tell me where you are. I'm on my way."

"No, I can't stay," she said again, her voice cracking. "I'm in town." The loud churn of the garbage compactor concealed it, her body quaking in fright. "Please don't hang up, Uncle Ty. I'm scared."

"I'm here."

Below her, the two men had come up to the truck. Dani flattened against it, the hot, steel roof. They stopped, not seeing her anywhere, probably assuming she had run to the end and turned onto another street. To be certain, they started opening trash cans, kicking them over, peering inside dumpsters. Looking under the cars.

One of them came up to the garbage worker. "You see a girl run down here?"

"Girl . . .? Just Becky. From the secondhand store . . ." He threw the contents of a can he was carrying into the mouth of the churning compactor, just a few feet below Dani. She held her ears from the deafening noise.

"You go on ahead, and I'll check if she ran into any of these stores," the one said to his partner. "She can't have gone far."

He ran ahead. The truck continued down the street. The other pursuer remained behind, kicking the cans to make sure they were empty. She caught sight of him jumping up and looking in the dumpsters.

The garbage worker held on to the side of the truck and it began to rumble away.

Dani pushed herself forward. "Are you still with me?" she asked Ty on the phone.

"Yes. I'm on my way in."

"I'm—" To her horror, she saw that the truck's sloped back and the growing distance between her and her pursuer meant she could be visible now.

The man kicked aside the top of a metal can in frustration and stepped out in the wake of the advancing truck. He looked up.

Their gazes collided.

"Oh, God."

"*There she is!*" he yelled, pointing at the truck. He ran after it, about thirty yards behind. His partner came back from up ahead, screaming at the driver to stop, then clawing his way up the side.

The truck jerked to a stop.

She was trapped. In a second or two, they'd nab her.

There was nowhere to go, but . . .

The one behind her hooked on to the back of the truck and began climbing, his partner slowly making his way up the side. Dani threw her phone in her bag and got to all fours, and as they reached the top, leaped off the truck's roof, landing with a thud on the hood, and then jumped onto the ground. She hit the cement hard and rolled from the impact, coming to a stop against the wire fence. The men climbed down after her. She scrambled to her feet and started to run. The police station was just a block or two away. They couldn't just follow her in.

Her two pursuers made it to the ground.

Dani sprinted. She made it as fast as she could to the end of the alley and swung around across the street. The police station was only a hundred yards away now. Remembering what Ty had said, she didn't know if this was the smartest thing, but what other choice was there? However corrupt they might be, they were still police. They couldn't just hand her over. Ty would come and they would figure out what to do.

She took a glance behind and saw the two men catching up. Fifty yards. Her heart pounded. She darted in between two cars and ran out into the street. It was just ahead of her now.

Thirty yards.

She looked around one last time and saw the two men slow to a stop. *She'd made it.* Whatever would happen, she was away from them.

Suddenly there was a screech. From out of nowhere, the black SUV pulled out of the food market lot and blocked her way.

Dani virtually crashed right into it.

A second car sped out of an alley, wedging her in, in a V.

"*No! No!*" she cried out, slamming her fist against the side. She spun quickly around to try and break free.

The rear door of the SUV opened and someone took her by shoulder and pulled her in.

He had the same gray T-shirt she had seen just minutes before with a skeleton on it and the letters *SXSW*. A bright red gash over his eye.

"So I owe you that trip." Robertson winked, slamming the door shut. "Man, if I didn't know better, I'd think you weren't so eager to go."

CHAPTER FIFTY-THREE

They bound her hands with a nylon rope that dug deep into her wrists, and almost seemed to enjoy it when she winced, maybe a smirk of payback for the welt above Robertson's eye.

Someone Dani hadn't seen before in a white, short-sleeve shirt and tie was at the wheel. She let her head fall back against the headrest—nervous, spent, completely out of breath.

And scared. She knew what they had done to Trey and those people in the balloon. Robertson sat next to her in the back. It gave her the creeps just to feel their legs come together when the car turned. They drove through town without seeing as much as a police car on the road and got onto Route 34 toward Greeley.

"Where are you taking me?" she asked.

"Don't you worry your little head about that," Robertson said. "You'll find out soon enough. Just enjoy the ride."

"I said, where are you taking me?" she asked again, with defiance.

He rubbed the mark above his eye. "You were asking about the water supply, so we thought we'd give you a look, firsthand. Up close and personal, as they say." He ripped her bag away and pawed through it quickly, and tossed it to the floor underneath his legs. "Don't think you'll be needing any of this now."

Trepidation and uncertainty pulsed through her, where seconds ago adrenaline had held her together. She watched the familiar landmarks go by. On the edge of town, Robertson took out a walkie-talkie and spoke into the receiver. "Cargo's on board. We're on our way out to the Falls. Everything set up there?"

A scratchy voice came back. "All ready. Whenever you arrive."

"*The Falls?* Where is that?" Dani asked warily. She knew she was in extreme danger now. "What do you mean, are you 'set up'? People know I'm here. They saw me."

"Don't ask so many questions," Robertson said, stowing the walkie-talkie. "Trust me, you'll need every breath."

Inside, her stomach tightened into a knot. She inspected her bound, useless hands, the binds digging into her. Up ahead of them, she spotted a black-and-white state police car on the side of the road. State, not town. *Beat on the windows*, she told herself. *Scream.* There had to be some way to contact it as they passed.

"Up ahead . . ." the driver glanced behind and said to Robertson, alerting him to it.

"I see it."

As they got close, to her dismay, Robertson reached over and forced her down against the seat, well below the windows, which were darkened anyway, so that no one could possibly see in.

Or hear.

"Help! Help me! Goddammit, help me!" Dani screamed in vain, her pleas muffled into the leather.

"Scream all you want," Robertson said, releasing her when they'd passed. She sat up and looked behind. The police vehicle had made a U-turn and receded into the distance the other way. "Go ahead, exercise those lungs of yours . . . Trust me, you'll need every breath."

A feeling of deep helplessness set in. *What were they going to do with her . . .?* Her only hope now was Ty, and there was no way to contact him. She eyed her bag on the floor next to Robertson. Suddenly it dawned on her she had never turned off the phone from when she had called him on the truck. It was a long shot, but what if he had kept his on as well? Maybe there was a chance he was hearing everything that was happening to her. And tracking where they were taking her. It was the

328

only shot she had now. "Where the hell are the Falls?" she asked, trying to direct him to where they were heading. "Greeley?"

"Don't ask so many questions." Robertson just looked straight ahead.

"*Please . . .*"

Finally he snorted brusquely. "The two of you are fools. You're lucky they don't let me do what I'd like to do to you. For *this*." He tapped the red mark over his eye. "You come up here and think this is all some kind of game. You think you're playing with kids, huh? You more than anyone should have known. You saw what happens . . ."

What happens . . . She realized what he meant. "You're talking Aspen?" she said, praying that the cell phone was somehow live. "Trey."

C'mon admit it, she said inside. *Say it.*

"You should've just done what you came up here for and left. The two of you." He looked back ahead. "That's all I'm saying."

"I know you killed him. I know you were on the river. I saw the tape."

"*Tape . . .?*" Robertson turned to her with renewed interest in his eyes.

"The ranger station keeps a running record of who goes in and out. Your car is on it. You do anything to me, and people will know. Everyone knows I was looking for you up here. They'll put it together."

He shook his head. It was clear he didn't know. "Useless piece of shit . . ." he muttered disgustedly under his breath.

Useless piece of shit . . . Dani realized that he had to be talking about Wade. That's why Wade had dragged his feet the way he did. Why he went and hid the tapes.

"Anyway, nobody knows," the Alpha man sniffed. "So don't worry yourself. And even if they did . . . it doesn't lead anywhere." He looked at her and shrugged with a philosophical smirk. "Least it won't anymore."

They were going to kill her. That much was clear. Just like Trey. Fear pounded up inside her. She felt tears in the backs of her eyes, tears of helplessness and fear and the total futility of her situation. She didn't want to show them to him. This bastard who had killed Trey and Ron and those others. She blinked them back as best she could. She begged herself not to give him the victory of seeing her cry.

"They'll know," she said back defiantly. "They'll all know."

"Hard to prove much," the Alpha man said with a shrug, "when there's not a trace in the world of anything left behind. And where you're going . . ."

"Where I'm going, *what*? What are you going to do with me?" she demanded again.

"Like I said"—Robertson looked away again, "just enjoy the ride."

The next few miles went by mostly in silence, heading

east toward Greeley. Dani's thoughts drifted. To her mom. How painfully she had deteriorated at the end—and Dani wasn't even there. How sad she would be, wherever she was, to know Dani wouldn't get to live out her life. Then she flashed to Wade. *The worm.* To betray her like this. To betray everything. So that's why he impounded the tapes. They weren't evidence; they were insurance. Insurance against getting caught. She gritted her teeth in disgust and looked out at the tops of wells as they passed by.

Bastard. They owned him, too.

The thought of him just looking the other way filled her with a deflating sense of sadness. Once, he was like a father to her. Until he just watched her mother die and took the house, her jewelry, whatever money they had. How helpless he had sounded the other night when he called. He knew what they were going to do to them, if they stayed. And he just hung up that phone.

He probably didn't even raise a voice to stop it.

Suddenly they slowed. The turn signal went on. Dani's heart jumped. She saw they were turning at the very spot where what they thought were oil tankers had pulled out onto the road, where she and Ty had thought there had been a well by the river. Ty had said there was some kind of water facility down there.

They called it the Falls . . .

Dani said, "I saw the trucks coming out of here," hoping against hope that somehow Ty might still be listening. "From down by the river."

331

Robertson ignored her. He just instructed the driver to loop down to the "plant." He seemed to suggest that someone would be waiting for them there.

"What's down here?" Dani pressed.

"Don't you worry about it?" Robertson said. He spoke into the walkie-talkie. "You'll find out soon enough. We're on the road now," he said into the receiver. "Are we all clear?"

"Roger that." A scratchy voice came back. "We're ready for you."

Ready for what? Dani's heart picked up with mounting dread.

The road was dirt, hard packed, and wide enough for the large trucks she and Ty saw to get through. It swung around to the left and then made a steady grade downhill to where Dani caught a glimpse of the Poudre River. The sign read, MID-RIVER HYDRO TREATMENT CENTER. She saw a building ahead. Actually, more of a large cylindrical tank made of beige-painted concrete, maybe four stories tall. A couple of attached huts were built out of it, and four of those large steel tankers were pulled up nearby. *They're not for oil, but for water,* Ty had told her. *Water.*

They looped around in front of the building. There was only one other car around, a blue Audi; otherwise it seemed deserted. If people generally manned this facility, they surely weren't around now. Maybe that was what they meant by, *are we clear?* The driver made

332

a sweeping turn with the SUV and pulled up next to the Audi.

The car locks went up.

A man in a plaid shirt stepped out of the Audi. He had a high forehead, bald on top, and sunglasses.

"What happens now?" Dani asked Robertson.

"*Now . . .?*" He opened his door. "You're a water girl, right? So, hey, now you ought to feel right at home."

Dani saw a rounded concrete conduit maybe four feet in height stretching from the base of the cylindrical tank; then it went into a berm, presumably down to the river.

Robertson stepped out, and the man in the plaid shirt came up to him. Dani couldn't hear what they were saying, then Robertson came back to her vehicle and opened her door.

What were they going to do to her?

"What is this, some kind of water treatment station?" Dani asked warily.

"You'll find out," Robertson said. "Out."

She didn't move, her wrists clasped, and held on to a strap on the seat in front of her.

"Get her out." Robertson signaled to the driver. The man in front came and yanked her by the cord binding her wrists and Dani tumbled out of the car onto the ground.

"Ms. Whalen, I'm truly sorry it's come to this," the man in the plaid shirt said as he stepped up to her. "It's not the kind of methods we usually use, but you've proven to be quite a nuisance, against all our warnings. Both here and back at home."

What warnings . . .? she thought. Then it hit her. *Wade?*

"So, like most potential stumbling blocks, maybe it's better just to get them out of the way up front. You know how these sorts of things only come up and bite you later on."

"Who are you?" Dani asked.

"Not to worry about that. You've got far more crucial and immediate things to be concerned with about."

"You won't get away with it." Dani glared. "He'll get you. I don't know what you thought you did to him, but he's alive. He'll bring you down."

"Well, that's something you needn't be worrying your head about right now," the man said. "Leave that as our problem. Take her up." He nodded to Robertson. "I'm told you've wanted to learn about the water supply for our work here. I think it's time you got to see it for yourself."

"He's going to kill you!" Dani yelled as Robertson dragged her toward a closed security door. The Alpha man headed back to the Audi. "You'll rot in hell. He'll kill you all!"

"By all means cling to whatever fantasy makes you feel good right now," the man said back.

She fought, as Robertson kicked her legs out and dragged her to the door. She saw the rounded, concrete tunnel that seemed to run down to the river. She also saw a dam, one she'd never noticed from the road, the water table high on the Greeley side, water cascading through openings at the top and no more than a trickle on the Templeton side. *The Falls*. Robertson keyed in a code on the door lock and it opened, a buzzer going off. He wrestled Dani inside.

It was a huge metal tank, at least forty feet high. The sealed door clanged shut, echoing throughout the chamber. There was a metal staircase leading up the sides and catwalks on every level, and an escape door that led outside halfway up. Robertson pulling her by her binds, they began to climb.

"So since you wanted to know so badly, this is how we divert water from the river to the wells. It's consolidated by the dam, then pumped in here through that underground conduit you saw outside, where it's transferred to the trucks, which take it around to our active wells. You already know it takes quite a supply to keep the fragmentation process running . . ." He pulled Dani up, one step at a time, their footsteps clanging on the metal stairs, echoing through the empty chamber. There was about eight to ten feet of sitting water at the base below ground level.

"What are you going to do with me?"

A buzzer went off, the noise slicing through her. It kept repeating, five times. *What was going on?*

Then it stopped. Suddenly she heard a sound and saw the water level below her begin to swirl.

And slowly rise.

Water began to rush in.

"That's coming in from the river." Robertson kept pulling her up. "Through that conduit outside. Now come on along . . ." he said, the way you might to a child, "or I'll punch your lights out here and just throw you in. Up to you. I promise, it'll only make it worse."

"Please, don't. *Don't,*" she said, fear rippling through her. "You don't have to do this."

They were on the second level now, above the water level, which, to Dani's mounting alarm, was rising. It suddenly became clear what was going to happen. The current of the river water sloshing around was pouring in through multiple conduits. She looked up to the top.

"Ten minutes." Robertson saw what she was thinking. "Until the water goes all the way up. Fifteen max."

"People will find me," she said, fighting against him as Robertson kept dragging her up. "They'll know I'm here."

"No one's going to find you. When you get carried up to the wells, you'll end up in an underground drainage pipeline we use to divert the tainted fracking water. All mud and slough. It'll take as much as an earthquake for you to turn up one day. No one will ever even know."

"*Please,*" she begged, pulling back from his grasp and looking into his eyes. "Please . . ." Knowing as she said it that this was the man who had killed Trey, and who had likely shot down that balloon. It was all falling on deaf ears. A professional.

"We gave you enough warnings. We told you to stay away."

She kept pulling against him. *"Please."*

Robertson forced her up another flight of stairs. There was a door there, the door she had seen outside leading to an emergency outside staircase. The only way out. That was how he was going to leave. She suddenly knew she was going to die in here. She'd drown. Deposited like waste in some deep, underground chasm. No one would ever know what happened to her.

They stopped at the landing in front of the door. "End of the line."

They stood above the swirling water. The level had risen to about twenty feet now, increasing rapidly. No more than ten feet below them now. Thrashing and bouncing against the walls like whirlpools as it poured in from the multiple pumps. Close to half the tank was filled. Dani searched around frantically for any other way out.

"There is none." Robertson yanked her over to the railing. "No other way out. Now, c'mon, don't make the job tougher than it has to be."

She knew now that Ty wasn't going to come in time. She'd tried to alert him, but who knew if he'd even heard. Maybe he was dealing with his own situations. Maybe he wasn't even alive any longer. She willed herself not to cry so that Robertson wouldn't see her crumble.

"He'll kill you." She looked in Robertson's face. "You know that, don't you? He'll kill you for doing this."

"You keep saying that." The Alpha man smirked through his light beard. "And maybe, someone will one day. But in his case, I don't think so. He's just one man."

"Be sure of it." The fire in her eyes softened into a resolute smile. "He will."

"Well, here's what I am sure of . . ." With a grunt, he threw her forward and forced her chest over the railing.

She looked down at the black, swirling water. *This was it.*

"You know this kind of reminds me of a joke I heard once . . . Bad timing, I know, but let's call it payback for that gash back at the restaurant. Two black guys are fishing off a bridge. They both have to take a pee. One opens his fly and his thing drops all the way into the water. 'My, this water's cold . . .' he says, and beams at his friend with pride. So his friend opens up *his* fly and his drops all the way to the water, too. 'Yeah'—he smiles back to his buddy, 'and it sure is deep.' It sure is deep." He laughed. "Get what I'm saying."

Dani spun and tried to strike him in the face, her fists locked together. But Robertson avoided it easily and hoisted her up by the waist. "You're right. Maybe it wasn't so funny after all. Enjoy the swim."

He pushed her over. Dani let out a scream. She fell, hitting the surface in a ball, the water cold and oily and metallic. She kicked up to the surface, her arms in front of her. Robertson was still standing over her, leaning over the railing, a satisfied smirk on his face. He gave her a wave.

She knew she had to conserve her strength. Thrashing around in the ice-cold water could easily sap it. She brought up her knees and pulled off her unlaced Converses, tossing them back in the water, and flutter-kicked to the side of the tank and held on to a railing there.

The water kept rising, the river pouring in. The first thing she had to do if she had any chance was to get her hands free. Her wrists were bound with a synthetic boating rope. She dug at the knots frantically with her teeth, trying to loosen them. Robertson just kept watching her from above, amused; the whole thing was almost like an entertainment to him. What did it even matter if she got free? In minutes the tank would fill completely. In a short time, she was going to drown in here anyway.

Heart pounding, she glanced up. The water continued to rise. She gauged she was about twenty feet from the top.

Twenty feet. Maybe all of eight minutes.

Finally the water rose to within a foot or two of Robertson on the catwalk. "Don't stay in too long . . ."

He waved. "And watch out for that current. I hear it's a doozie." He laughed and opened the outside door, which Dani saw had pressurized sealed mechanisms, and locked it behind him, completely sealing her in.

She was trapped now.

Frantically, she dug even harder at her binds. Water splashing over her, going into her mouth; she managed to loosen one just enough that she created a small space and wiggled her wrist free. She looked up at the ceiling one more time, and saw it getting closer. She had to climb to a higher rung. Finally she got it free enough to squeeze one wrist through, then she feverishly pulled at the other knot, the water making the cord a bit soggy, which made it harder to loosen, until she pried her other wrist through.

She was free.

But free for what? *To rise up with the water to the top of the tank and drown.*

The catwalk where Robertson had just been standing was now underwater, so Dani swam across, took a breath, and dived down to the spot where the door was. It had a sealed window on it. Dani tugged at the bar, trying to open it, but it wouldn't budge.

It was locked from outside.

She was in a massive tank with no way out, and the ceiling was coming closer to her with every second.

Panic began to set in. There was nothing she could do but ride it all the way to the top. Maybe there'd be a bit of air space up there, enough to breathe for a while. But ultimately, she'd give out. They would drain the tank to recover her body. Even if she miraculously lasted until they checked, they would kill her then.

She looked up and saw she was within ten feet of the top now. There had to be another way out. There had to be.

Then something flashed into her head. Maybe something she had learned in college. In Geology 101. Or was it physics? About water in a vacuum: the displacement and different levels of unequal pressure balancing.

How certain oceanic canyons were made.

She thought that maybe there was a chance that could be at work here. If it wasn't, she would surely drown. But if she stayed where she was, she knew she'd be dead in a few minutes anyway.

Please, let this work.

Dani sucked a huge gulp of air into her lungs and dove, scissor-kicking against the current, until she made it all the way down to the open, conduit valves where the river water was pouring in. Maybe forty feet below.

If she could somehow fit herself through the opening, there might just be air pockets in there.

It seemingly took a full minute to swim her way down. Only someone strong and trained, who knew how to swim against fast currents, would have even made it. The wide, open pipes were about six feet from the bottom, the resistance even stronger there, water pouring in. It was like a huge Jacuzzi jet battling against her. Treading water, her lungs starting to strain, she tried to gauge the width of the open pipe.

Three feet across at most. Enough to squeeze herself through, she prayed.

Her lungs were aching now. She moved toward the opening and the current flung her back.

Don't panic. It had been over a minute now and the water was blowing forcefully all around her, dozens of gallons pouring in every second, hurling her back into the tank. It was like trying to climb up against a water-fall.

Pain started to rip her insides apart. She flutter-kicked and came at it from the side. She didn't have much time. Maybe only one last try. She clenched her teeth, air bubbles escaping.

This had to be it.

Dani locked on to the rim of the large pipe and joyfully saw what she was praying to see.

Water was streaming in, but it hadn't filled the inside of the conduit completely. The water in the tank hadn't displaced against the greater pressure coming in and filled the space.

That meant there were air pockets in there.

Possibly even a way out.

It had to be close to a minute and thirty seconds now. Her lungs now felt like they were about to explode. She threw herself into the conduit, grasping for anything

342

she could hold on to to keep her there, and turned herself upward. It was agonizing. She couldn't take it for another second. She prayed she was right, because otherwise she'd give out. She pushed through the cascading current just as her lungs gave out. With a last gasp, she opened her mouth and sucked whatever was there.

It was air.

Thank God . . . She breathed, gasping, heaving, inhaling the desperately needed oxygen deep into her aching lungs. Hanging on, she squeezed herself in, wedging her feet against the interior pipe rim. Water beat at her furiously; but there was about eight inches at the top of the pipe that hadn't completely filled. And that wasn't all. The valve was open. The thing had to lead somewhere. To the river, she assumed. Maybe she could make it through. She visualized when she saw it outside; it couldn't be much longer than a hundred feet or so. But each of those feet would be a battle, she knew, fighting the current; fighting for oxygen. She had no idea how much air could possibly be trapped in here. Only that it wouldn't last for long. She gulped in three huge breaths, saturating her lungs, and then a last one, ducking back in the pipe, and tried to swim against the formidable current. The force of it hurled her back. She tried again, scratching on the sides for something to grasp on to. She fell back again. It was too strong.

She couldn't make it, she realized.

Then she heard something that sent a spasm of terror flashing through her.

The buzzer. Sounding again. The same buzzer she'd heard when the water first began.

Four, five times. Which meant maybe Robertson was at the controls. Or there was some kind of auto control now that the tank was close to being filled.

Which turned Dani's fright into outright panic.

As the water neared the top, the valve might close. *She'd be trapped in there.*

The current against her suddenly eased slightly; maybe it was part of the flow control as the water level reached the top of the tank. She forced herself back in. It was slow going, foot by foot, exhausting on her legs and thighs, and she grunted and screamed out in frustration, hurled back close to the opening into the tank.

She hit her head against something.

She felt above her. It was a metal rung. On the top of the pipe.

This time instead of swimming she rolled onto her back and lunged forward, using the rung to propel her.

She found another one.

And another.

Every five feet or so, maybe used for maintenance work in case of a leak somewhere. It was hard to even make the distance between them with the current beating against her and her strength tiring out.

But she had to go on. There was no other choice. The valve could be closing soon.

And if they were stopping the water flow, that buzzer also meant that the valve to the outside could close at any time, too. Which petrified her. It was black and creepy in there, like a zero gravity chamber—no sense of space or direction—but Dani willed herself forward. Rung by rung. The current against her weakened. Which to her meant the valve to the outside might be shut and whatever air was in here was coming to an end. She increased her pace, kicking and lunging and gasping for air at every rung, her fingers locking around them, pulling herself through, not even knowing if there'd be a way out at the end or if she'd die in here.

She had no idea how far she had to go, only that her strength was giving out. It was dark and gritty and smelled of river sediment and metal. Something slithered against her back and she screamed. Some kind of scaly fish going by.

Oh, God, God . . . she moaned, shutting her eyes. *One more rung. Keep going.*

What if she was wrong? What if this went on for a mile and she wouldn't have the strength to get to the end? What if when she got there the valve was closed? She would die in here—this dark, wet grave. She decided she'd just let herself go and be carried by the current back to the tank and drown. She thought of her mom. The strength she had shown. Until the end. *She* didn't give up. Dani's arms grew weary. But she couldn't rest. She gulped in air, and water poured into her mouth. She coughed it out. The conduit might be endless. She could just lie back and go to sleep in this narrow, black grave.

One more. She reached out and pulled herself forward. Her fingers slipped off and she fell back into the water. She caught herself and reached back up high.

Just one more.

Then she saw it.

She arched her head back, unable to fully tell if it was real or not.

A ribbon of yellowy light, shimmering up ahead.

Maybe it was just an illusion. Maybe it was the end for her. What they say happens when you die, when the light comes toward you.

One more. She pulled herself forward, her arms like deadweights.

The light seemed to grow brighter. It gave her new strength. Renewed will. She pulled. Faster. If there was light, then there had to be an opening of some kind. It grew brighter. Closer.

It had to be.

The water levels were growing higher here. They were filling the pipeline. Dani had to summon the last of her strength and battle toward the light. She gulped in a last lungful of air and kicked, propelling herself forward by grasping on to the rungs. She didn't even look ahead. How far was it? She felt the water getting colder. That was a good sign, right?

One more rung.

Then something happened. The cold water seemed to envelop her and she burst free. She flailed her arms and suddenly there were no more rungs. Bright light swept all around her. Water was everywhere, and cold.

She was in the river.

She wanted to scream for joy.

She was in the river. Probably directly underneath the dam. Her legs bounced off the silty bottom. She propelled herself up. It wasn't far. She broke through the surface, even brighter light all around her now, knifing at her eyes. She gasped—beautiful, sweet air entered her lungs. She was too exhausted to be ecstatic. She coughed and gasped and dragged herself over to the shore. She crawled along the pebbly bank, rolling onto her back and letting the sun wash over her. Beautiful and warming. *She was free.* She looked up and saw the dam about fifty yards behind her. And then she felt fear again. *What if they realized she had escaped? What if they were looking for her?* But then, exhausted, unable to summon the will to do anything about it, she shut her eyes. She was still breathing heavily and her arms were too tired to move. She should probably find some cover. Just in case they came after her. But she couldn't move. She just lay there, she didn't know for how long—exhausted and spent, pinned to the soggy soil. Inside she was joyously laughing.

She'd made it.

But then she felt the sun blocked out on her face. She opened her eyes, feeling someone there, panic rising up in her all over again, and she saw a figure shadowed in the glare standing over her. Instinctively she pushed herself back in the sand.

No. Don't let it be them. Please don't let it be them. Please . . .

"Are you all right, lady?"

Dani looked through the glare.

It was a boy. Two boys. Standing over her, Fuzzy through the haze. Maybe thirteen or fourteen. With fishing rods.

"Are you all right?"

"Yes," she said, barely able to spit out the words. "I'm all right. I'm all right. Do you have a phone?"

"*I* do," one of them said. He went in his pocket.

"Dial this number." She racked her brain to recall it from the screen. "Nine-one-seven. Three-two-four. Six-nine, six-zero. Please."

Her head fell back. As the consciousness rolled out of her.

Ty's number.

CHAPTER FIFTY-FOUR

The motion of the car jostled her awake. Dani blinked open her eyes and looked out the window, trying to get her bearings. She moved with a sudden start, not sure for a moment where she was, and then spun, staring.

Ty was behind the wheel.

"It's okay." He reached over and gave her arm a reassuring squeeze. "You're with me."

She blinked alarm still in her eyes. "Where are we?" she asked, trying to clear her head. She tried to put together the last thing she recalled.

Two boys.

"On our way home. We're just heading up into the mountains. How are you doing?"

"I'm fine." She nodded fuzzily. "Fine."

349

It all tumbled back to her. The tank. Robertson. The conduit leading to the river. It scared her all over again. She shook her head in defiance. "Ty, we can't go home," she said, pushing herself up. Every muscle in her body ached. "Robertson. He tried to kill me. He had someone with him. His boss, I think. From Alpha. Or RMM." She described the man with the high forehead and balding top.

"McKay." Hauck nodded. "He was the head of his unit back in Iraq."

"They basically admitted to killing Trey. They also said they tried to kill you, too. They threw me in this tank and let the water in. It filled all the way up. It was terrifying, Uncle Ty. You don't know what I had to do to get out."

"You're safe now," he reassured her again. "You're with me."

She could see they were on I-80 west of Denver, heading into the mountains. The last thing she remembered was clawing her way out of the river to the bank. The sun in her face. Then the fear back again. Someone standing over her. The boys. She looked at Hauck. She nodded, for the first time really trusting that she was safe. "I knew you would come."

"You did it. I followed you from what you said on the phone. I only wish I had gotten there sooner."

"I told them you would. Ty, please, we can't just go back." She faced him. "You don't know what they did

350

to me. They almost killed me. I can't believe I'm even alive."

"It's not even up for conversation, Dani. You're out of it now. It's my fault. I never meant to put you in any danger. I should never have let you stay."

"I'm all right. I am. It's just—" She tried to sit up, but her head ached and she still felt in a daze. She sat back and tried to clear her brain; remember all had happened, every terrifying second: the water rising, having to will her way out of that conduit, not sure if the valve would close. But it all just flickered through her consciousness like a movie on fast-forward, flashes of fear as if out of some horrible nightmare. "I was so scared. I was sure I was going to die. I thought you were—" Tears rushed into her eyes again.

"You don't have to go through it," he said. "Just rest. Get some sleep. We'll talk about it when we get home."

"No, I want to," she said. "I have to."

"Idaho Springs is up ahead. Do you want to pull off and eat something?"

"I don't know. I don't think so."

"There's some water in the console next to you. You ought to drink some."

She looked at the plastic bottle there and couldn't help but smile. "Water's about the last thing I need right now."

He smiled back. "Sorry. We'll stop." There was a turnout on the highway up ahead. Scenic view. "You

351

can tell me, but only as much as you want, okay. You don't have to go through it all now. You should just rest. We can talk about it later."

"If I don't go through it now, then it's like some dream that wasn't real."

Hauck pulled off the road and parked as far from the other cars as he could.

Dani looked at him and shook her head. "But it was real."

Horrifyingly real. And it all rushed back. Every terrifying detail. Things she had stored and didn't know what for. Why it was important. Robertson sitting next to her in the café. The South by Southwest T-shirt he was wearing. The friendliness in his eyes that suddenly changed.

"I didn't recognize him. He just started to talk. Something seemed familiar, but I couldn't put it together. I'd only seen that grainy, black-and-white photo on your phone. He had this growth on his face now. He tried to get me to get into one of those black SUVs. I hit him . . ."

"You hit him?"

Dani nodded. With kind of a disbelieving grin. "With one of those pointy metal napkin holders, as we went out the door. Right here . . ." She pointed above her eye. "It left quite a welt."

Hauck chuckled, admiringly. "The guy's a trained military operative."

"I can handle myself. Besides, I didn't have any choice. I knew I couldn't get in that car."

The rest she went through, feeling her heart quickening again. The chase through town. How she hid on the garbage truck—"when you called me I was pinned on top of it; they were all around." How she leaped off and almost made it to the police station.

"They tossed me in the back of one of those black SUVs. I realized I still had my phone on from when you called, so I just hoped, prayed, you'd hear." Her heart was beating rapidly. "It was the only hope I had."

"That was smart." Hauck smiled. "It led me right to you. Then when the kid called . . ."

"Robertson told me you were dead at first. I thought I would ever see you again." Anxiousness rose up in her again.

"But I'm not. I'm here. It's okay, Dani. What exactly was that place they took you? Some kind of water treatment facility?"

"Where they pump the water out of the river and send it up to the wells. You saw the dam?"

Hauck nodded.

"They're sucking the river dry, Uncle Ty. The one side had water they were capturing. The other . . . the Templeton side . . ." She shook her head. "The building there is basically a huge water tank. They locked me inside. Robertson dragged me up a couple of levels and pushed me in. I did my best to fight him off. Then they opened the valves and it started to fill."

Her eyes filled with fear again as she recalled it, and grew wide. "It was like the whole Pacific Ocean was coming in on me. I somehow managed to get my binds off. And I rode it to the top. He said they were going to toss me down some drainage pipe in the hills where they dispose of the fracking waste." Her eyes now filled with rancor. "*Fuck him . . .!*"

"So how did you get out?"

She shrugged. "He left. He just left me there to drown." Then she told him how she remembered this one thing, from college, about how water levels balance. And how she went down, her lungs bursting, and swam into the conduits, hearing the buzzers go off again, sure that the valves would close behind her and she'd be trapped.

Hauck put his hand on her arm. "You don't have to go through anymore. I'm so sorry I put your life in risk."

"It's okay. It's . . ." Her eyes grew moist again and she sank like a weight across the seat and into his arms. This time she began to cry. He just held her there, against him, telling her over and over he would never let go of her again, that she was safe, and stroking her. His beautiful, courageous goddaughter who had been entrusted into his hands, and he had let her down. "You're safe." He just kept stroking her hair. "You're with me now."

She just kept shaking. Then she looked up. "They told me you were fucking dead! I thought you were dead!" Her eyes were raw, her cheeks mashed with tears. "I told them you would get them. I said to Robertson, as he was about to throw me in, 'You know, he's going to kill you for this.' That's why we can't go back home. We have to do something or arrest them. We know what they did now."

He took a napkin from out of the console between them and wiped her tears. "Maybe we should leave this part out when we describe how things went to your dad."

It made her laugh, sniffling back the tears. Then she grew serious again. "Wade's involved. They basically said that to me. They just never thought I'd be around to tell anyone. When he called the other night he sounded so weird and helpless. Now I know why. Because he knew what they were going to do. He couldn't protect me any longer if we stayed. They got to him, Uncle Ty. I don't know how. Money. Kyle. Something. That's why he didn't act on any of the evidence. Why he sat on those tapes . . . We've got to report this. I can finger Robertson. And that other man. And Wade . . ."

"It's just not that easy, Dani. We can report a crime, but then we'd have to go back. The Templeton Police Department has jurisdiction there. You'd have to make a deposition against them."

"Damn right I'll make a deposition. I'd do it laughing in their faces."

"And we'd have to find a lawyer there who'll go to trial. And be around there. And face a jury of people from the town. I'm not going to risk that. Not till I know that whoever the state attorney is there will bring charges up. And then you'd have to testify at trial . . ."

"So what are we going to do? Just let them get away with it? Like they wanted?"

"First, I'm taking you back."

"No. Uncle Ty, we can't—"

"That's all there is, Dani. I should have done this days ago."

She stared, more fragile than he'd seen her before, the courage and the rancor and maybe even a little belief in him draining from her face. "All we've talked about was me. They told me you were dead. What about you?"

Two hours ago, a bullet had narrowly missed his head, plowing into Watkins. Hauck started the car up and backed out of the space. "I'll be fine."

"What do you mean, you'll be fine? You're sure?"

"I'm sure." Hauck pressed the accelerator and turned back onto the access road, melding back into traffic.

"They killed Trey, Uncle Ty. They killed the others, too. And they tried to kill me. We can't just go back," Dani said again. "We can't just let them win."

He switched lanes. Carbondale was still two hours away. He looked back at her. "Who said anything about letting them win?"

CHAPTER FIFTY-FIVE

The call came in from higher up. McKay was already at his desk back at the office.

"So how's our situation?" Moss inquired. McKay detected a ripple of nerves in his voice. The RMM executive was an oilman at heart, West Texas through and through. Who turned a blind eye to the kind of tactics McKay employed. Still, he had hired him.

"Nothing you'll have to worry yourself about anymore," McKay replied.

"And that means . . .?"

"It means it's not a problem anymore. No one who saw anything that could lead back to you. No more mouths running off that can get us in trouble. You don't have to know any more. I assume that's what you wanted to hear when you said to handle it my way."

"Yes. I guess it was." The oil executive blew out a breath. "And not a day too soon. Just to be clear, we *are* talking both of them, aren't we?"

"I'm afraid Mr. Hauck is still at large. But he's useless now. He has nothing that connects directly to anything we need to hide. In fact, it may have even worked out better for us. Call it a bonus . . ."

"Bonus?"

"The farmer. Watkins. Apparently the old man took the shot intended for Hauck."

"Is he dead?"

"Let's just say I don't think you have to worry about any pain-in-the-ass lawsuits anymore. I didn't think you'd be crying to hear that."

"Good. This will all make the process go a whole lot smoother." Moss exhaled, relieved. "I'll pass the word upstairs. I'm sure there'll be something in this deal for you and your team."

"We do aim to please, Wendell," McKay said, with pride.

His cell phone vibrated. Another call coming in. "Hold on." McKay checked the screen. "That's my man now." He put the RMM executive on hold and went on his cell. "John . . .?"

"We've got a problem," Robertson said.

"What kind of problem?" McKay felt a flutter in his chest.

"She's gone."

"Who's gone?"

"The girl. We drained the tank. She wasn't in it. We searched everywhere. Somehow the damn bitch managed to get out."

"Someone just doesn't get out, John. Are you sure you locked the containing door?"

"Of course I locked the door. Anyway it wasn't opened. That tank was airtight. The only thing I can even think of is maybe through one of the water ducts out to the river. But that would be . . . We searched the area. All I can say is that she's gone."

McKay thought for a second about what this meant. Everything he had just told Moss was untrue. Everything the man was probably now drafting in an email, assuring his superiors about it being smooth sailing from here on in. But it was even worse. She had seen him. His face. A rare mistake, but one he thought came with zero risk. If she was talking to the authorities now, they were totally screwed . . .

"What if she talks, John? *I* damn well would. We're the ones she can pin it on. We're the ones who have everything on the line."

"I know that, Mr. McKay."

"Find her. We don't let people down, John. Either here or back overseas. That's not just a phrase, you realize. It's a commitment. It's what we stand for. And now we're about to let a whole lot of people down. Important ones. You find her. Both of them. And when you do, you do what you have to, and do it right this time. This isn't Alpha anymore, you understand that? This is us. This is one big, giant shit ball now."

"I understand."

He hung up. McKay's stomach ground as tight as powder. He took in a breath and got back on the phone with Moss. "You're on your cell, Wendell?"

"I am."

"It might be a good thing to destroy it. Take it apart. Remove the chip. Maybe toss it down one of those wells of yours. Today, if you can manage the time."

"What's wrong?" the RMM man asked, hearing the sudden change in tone.

"What I told you before, about that problem we discussed . . . I'm afraid I may have been a little premature . . ."

CHAPTER FIFTY-SIX

They made it back to Carbondale just after five P.M. Before heading to Dani's, they stopped to pick up Blu where he'd been staying for the past four days.

As soon as he saw her get out of the car, he bounded up and smothered Dani with kisses, his paws up on her chest, almost as if he sensed what had happened. Dani put her head against him, knowing that was true. "Oh, Blu, baby, you sure are a sight for sore eyes. You have no idea how close I came to never seeing you again." He eagerly hopped in the back of Hauck's SUV, his tail wagging happily.

They all went back to her ground-floor unit in town. Dani's roommate was still on the West Coast. Exhausted, Dani sank wearily onto her couch, Blu climbing up, one leg at a time, and resting his chin on her thigh.

"Who can you call?" Hauck asked her.

"Who can I call for what?" Dani replied.

"Who can you call to come and stay with you? Or better, who can you go stay with? I don't want you here alone."

"C'mon, I can take care of myself, Uncle Ty. I'll be fine. Honest."

"I saw that, but not for the next couple of days. You've been through a lot. You haven't even started to deal with what just happened. You need to take it easy and regain your strength. Personally, I'd take you to the hospital . . ."

"I don't need to go to the hospital." She shrugged. "I suppose I *could* call Geoff."

"Your Aussie boyfriend?"

"He's not my boyfriend," she said defiantly.

"Okay, your friend. Your boss. The one who's called you a couple of times up in Templeton. The one you're not supposed to be canoodling with."

"Okay." Dani finally gave in. "Yes. Him."

"Call him then. But you can't just stay with him. Wade might know."

"No one knows . . . Besides, he lives in Glenwood Springs. That's fifteen miles away."

"Find some other place. Somewhere they can't trace. Otherwise you can go visit your father in Chile."

"Uncle Ty, don't you think you're taking this a bit too far . . .?"

"Just find a place, Dani. For once, just trust me, please."

"Okay, okay . . . If I had a phone maybe I could. Mine's still back in that asshole Robertson's car. Shit, along with my wallet and my license and all my credit cards. And my river guide ID . . ."

Hauck sat across from her. "If I told you back in that tank that you could get out, but you'd have to leave your phone and credit cards behind, what would have been your answer?"

"I would have said, can't I just take my river ID with me, please . . .? All right, I hear you. I'll find a place."

"Now." Hauck tossed his phone over to her on the couch.

She glared at him. "I mean, just what is it you want me to say, Uncle Ty? 'Someone tried to kill me and I'm too scared to stay at my own place right now'?"

"I don't care what you say. Say you've missed him. Say you've been away three days and you need it bad. Tonight. Whatever you want to say. Just make the call."

She rolled her eyes, pouting, but picked up his phone. She started punching in the number. Then she stopped. She looked up at Hauck, like a wave of new concern had come over her, her eyes reflecting something more serious. "What are we going to do about Wade?"

"I'll handle Wade."

"I don't mean about *that*. I'm not scared of him. For God's sake, the man was my stepfather. He practically

363

raised me. I mean, I can't just go on here as if nothing has happened."

She was right. Wade complicated things. "You just call."

She dialed the rafting company and Geoff did come on, and he seemed to be as happy to hear from her as Hauck had hoped he'd be, not to mention just as worried not to have heard anything from her these past few days. Apparently he'd left some messages that had gone unreturned.

All she told him was that something was going on and she really needed a place to be that night. It didn't seem to take much convincing. He said he'd come by and pick her up when he closed things up around half past six.

"He said he has a friend's house up in Snowmass. The guy's out of town, okay. Happy?"

"You know, the same people who put you in that tank know the way up here," Hauck said, putting it back in his pocket.

"Well, now if you'll excuse me I'm going to jump in the shower. I don't think I've ever felt slimier in my life."

"That's a good idea."

CHAPTER FIFTY-SEVEN

Hauck stepped out on the back deck, which was bordered by two other ground-floor units. He sat in one of those mesh infinity chairs, reclining all the way back, and took a sip of a beer he found in the fridge.

There were two ways Alpha could go on this. They could figure he and Dani had gotten the message and wanted to get as far away from this mess as they could. Like any sane person likely would.

Or they could make sure they covered all their tracks. He and Dani still knew about Trey and how that tied in to Rooster's balloon mishap. They could finger Robertson and McKay in what had happened today at the river. If he were them, Hauck decided, he'd want to make sure that there was no trace left to follow and no one to turn them in.

But they wouldn't just follow them back up here. It was too soon. Too obvious. Fingers pointed at them.

Besides, they already had someone up here to do the work.

But he knew they'd come. No doubt about it. Eventually. These sorts of things, these kinds of people, they always did.

His cell phone chimed. He took it out and checked who it was. The readout said Washington, D.C.

"Hey," Hauck answered, shifting back in his chair.

"Hey back," Naomi said. "So how did your day go?"

"Typical," Hauck said back with a snort.

"Typical as in, just another day at the office? Or typical of someone who's pushing back against a very powerful company and is probably getting in way over his head."

"You decide. Right now I'm staring at a beautiful snowcapped peak."

"Where are you?" Naomi asked.

"Back in the mountains. We left."

"Well, that's the best new I've heard all day. You finally came to your senses?"

"If that's what you call having a bullet go right by your head and your goddaughter being drowned to within an inch of her life, yes, I did."

"Oh my God! You're both okay?"

"Yes. She's all right, too. Just a bit shaken."

"What are you trying to do, Ty, get her killed? Over fucking water rights . . .?"

366

"Yeah." He rubbed his head. "She got sort of a crash course in that subject today. At least now you know what I meant by 'typical.'"

"Ty, are you trying to just scare me or does this just come out naturally? I got in touch with an assistant AG at the Colorado attorney general's office today. I've had some dealings with him in the past on some banking litigation the states are signing on to. I ran the whole water rights thing by him, how local supplies are being bought up or diverted for outside commercial means and he immediately went: 'You mean energy companies?'"

"I get it. It's not exactly secret out here."

"He said that was mostly governed under local ordinances, so I asked, what if people were colluding to divert them unfairly. Like companies paying off politicians or town managers. Or diverting water that the community needed. As in a drought."

"And . . .?"

"And he basically just laughed. He recommended I contact the state's department of environmental affairs. Department of Violations and Policing, or some bureaucratic office like that. You can only imagine where that will get you."

"Yeah." Hauck grunted with frustration. "That'll take two years."

"He asked, just for argument's sake, which company I was referring to, and I told him RMM."

"That must have made him laugh even harder."

"No, that made him go silent. For about a minute. Then he went into this speech that the energy trade is responsible for almost a third of the job growth in the state, and RMM a good portion of that. And that they're tied in with half the politicians in the state and have built more in terms of infrastructure for the towns—new schools, parks, civic centers—than all the public money combined. He pretty much said in the current administration you'd have better luck taking on the NRA to cancel a gun show in Fort Collins than get an inquiry into RMM."

"What about murder and bribery?" Hauck sighed sarcastically. "Aren't those crimes?"

"I asked that. I had to be a little vague, Ty—I mean, I'm financial fraud, not Justice."

"I understand."

"But I said, just for argument's sake, if, say, a capital felony had been committed, and it led back to an oil company in an attempt to cover up the improper granting of water rights, what would be the disposition of the state to look into that?"

"And he said . . ."

"He said that it isn't actually up to the state. That it's up to the local police authority and district attorney where the crime was committed. So then I said, what if *they* declined to act on it? What if it all fit under the heading of conflict of interest? Or more, like they were all under their thumb. And just to fill out the hypothetical, what if we were talking RMM . . .?"

Hauck was silent.

Naomi said, "That's when he laughed again."

"Yeah, the humor's hard to miss." Hauck took another chug of beer.

"Look, off the record, he said the best path would be to give this to the local press or TV and let them investigate it, until the local jurisdictions would be forced to respond to it. I'm sorry. You picked a big fish to fry here. Especially in this state. I wish I could have been of more help."

"You did great, Naomi. It's about what I expected. Thanks."

"So what are you going to do now?"

"I really don't know."

"You're going to go back there, aren't you?"

"I don't know."

"Ty, you heard the reaction I got out there. No one wants to touch this. The proceeds mean too much to the state. What happened today . . . was this basically a way to tell you to stay clear?"

"Either that, or to kill me. Or Dani. It was hard to tell."

"Ty, don't joke. I'm honestly worried about you. That has to matter to you. I'm worried you'll do something foolish and I'm going to hear about it on the evening news."

"It does matter to me, Naomi." He put down the beer bottle. "It's just that, this does, too."

"More than me telling you to back out . . .?"

Hauck stayed silent.

"I guess I get it," she responded kind of dejectedly. "You know I'm not your wife. I'm not even sure if I'm your girlfriend. But I do have a stake in you, Ty. You have to acknowledge that."

"I do acknowledge that, Naomi." Hauck glanced at his watch. It was almost six P.M. "I know this is rotten timing, but I have something I have to do."

"Stay safe, Ty . . ." He could hear she was frustrated. "Let me hear from you that you are."

"I will."

They hung up. Hauck didn't like the manner in which they did. He took his car keys and knocked on Dani's bedroom. "I'll be back in a little while," he said. "Geoff will be here in a couple of minutes. Don't let anyone else in but him."

"Where are you going?"

"I have to see someone about something."

CHAPTER FIFTY-EIGHT

The police station had thinned out for the night shift when Wade Dunn finally stepped out the door.

He was dressed a khaki police shirt over jeans, a cowboy hat, and the same python boots he'd been wearing when Hauck had met him before. He chatted in the doorway with one of the officers on his staff, gave him a laugh and an amiable poke on the shoulder, then headed over to his vehicle, which was parked in the spot marked CHIEF.

Hauck went up to him.

Dunn's demeanor changed—maybe surprised to see Hauck back and in front of him. Or maybe just rolling around in his head in a moment of panic exactly why Hauck was there. His eyes finally brightened in recognition.

"Hey . . .! Hauck, isn't it? Dani's godfather? I see you're back."

"That's right." Hauck stood in the way of the police chief and the green-and-white official SUV.

"Your trip over so soon? I heard she took you up to her friend's funeral up outside Greeley. Not much to see up there but potato fields and a few oil wells. I'm afraid you didn't get to see our state at its best."

"I'd have to agree on that." Hauck nodded. Dunn was either completely out of the loop or a ridiculously bad actor. Hauck figured the latter.

"Look. . . ." The chief glanced at his watch. "I'm afraid I have to be over in Glenwood in a couple of minutes. AA meeting. Not telling you anything everyone else here doesn't know. I'm one of the hosts tonight."

"I'll walk you over to your car."

"Car's right here, actually. So how's my girl? She was taking her friend's death pretty hard."

"She's okay. She had a little run-in up there today."

"Run-in? Anything I can do?"

"There might be, now that you bring it up. I think she realizes now she may have gotten in a little over her head in some of this business. Like you warned me, she gets pretty riled up about things."

"You can take *that* to the bank and cash it." Dunn grinned with a shake of his head. "Always been her way." He stopped at his car. "So, uh, like I said, I—"

"Those photos . . ." Hauck looked at him.

372

"*Photos* . . .?" Dunn stared back, playing dumb.

"I think you know what I'm talking about. From the ranger station the morning Trey Watkins was killed. Dani said you took them."

"Well, I wouldn't quite call it 'took 'em,'" the chief snorted officiously. "They're part of an investigation. I just can't be showing them around."

"So you're opening an investigation? The Watkins family will be glad to hear that."

"I merely meant that they're part of the official record now. Police property. Depending on what we decide to do," the chief said, backpedaling. "You used to be in this line of work. I figure you understand."

"I do understand. Same way I understand you're pretending you don't know exactly what I'm talking about, and that your name didn't come up in a curious way while we were up there . . ."

"*My* name . . .?" Dunn took out his key and clicked open his door. "It did?"

"By the same man whose car was in those photos you have in there." Hauck looked at him directly.

The chief blinked, his runny eyes locked on Hauck, trying to convey the full measure of his authority. "I'm not exactly sure just what we're talking about, Mr. Hauck."

"Some bad things have happened, Chief, and a lot of them seem to find a path back to you. You and some really unfriendly people up there. I guess the only question is what we're going to do about it now. Dani's a good girl. You know that as well as anyone. I know you have feelings for her in some way. But I also know . . ."

"You also know *what*, Mr. Hauck?" Dunn took off his hat and stared at him hard now.

"I also know you seem to be a man who's willing do what he *has* to do, when it all comes down to it."

"When *what* comes down? I'm not sure I catch your meaning."

"What inevitably will, Chief Dunn. What always does when people get in over their head."

Dunn nodded, twisting his mouth, and ran his hand along the close-cropped sides of his scalp. "I'm thinking there's a threat in there somewhere. Which is a crime, as you likely know. If you weren't Dani's godfather and I wasn't late for this meeting . . ."

"No threat," Hauck said, "there." He put his hand on the driver's door. "Here's the threat, and I want it to sink in carefully before you take whatever your next step is in this mess. One you'll likely not be able to walk back from."

"You're treading a very narrow line here, mister"—Wade stared at him—"whatever résumé you come with."

"Anything happens to that girl," Hauck said, "either by you, or by someone connected to you, even someone I just may think is connected to you . . . Say,

374

someone who just might show up in town, kind of like what happened to that Watkins boy last week, and she has a similar accident on the river, or maybe doesn't show up for work one day and simply disappears. Or even if she just slips on the ice during ski season and chips a nail. You hear me, Chief, a single hair on that kid's head is out of place . . ."

"And what?" The chief chuffed back a smile. "You'll hold me responsible?"

"Oh, I won't hold you responsible . . ." Hauck kept an arm on the car door, blocking his way. "I'll come back out here and I'll kill you. Myself. I'll put that fancy gun you carry around in your mouth and blow the back of your head into a hundred pieces. And you can take that one to the bank and cash it. Just so we understand. And any time you feel like arresting me, Chief, for threatening a police representative . . . you be my guest. There's a lot of things that don't look so kosher out here that if I was a sixty-year-old ex-drunk on his last job I wouldn't want to be getting out."

Dunn twitched. He blew a blast out of his nostrils, his last pretense of crusty resolve receding into a pallid nod. He put his hat back on. "I don't think it'll come to that," he said. Hauck took his arm away and Dunn climbed into his car. "So where is she? Dani. Don't get all riled up now. I just want to say hello and make sure she's okay?"

"Maybe better left unsaid." Hauck shut the door. "I hope that meeting goes well, Chief . . ."

Dunn just sat there for a moment. He sniffed into a smile Hauck couldn't quite read. "I read up on what you've done. Back east. I know, maybe you've gone up against some bigger folk in the past, bigger than those oil boys up there. But let me tell you," he said, his eyes twinkling, "I bet your last dollar you've never run up against none who want what they want with more resolve."

"I'll consider us both warned then," Hauck said back.

"It's been nice having you out here, Mr. Hauck." Wade smiled and started the engine. "Not sure I'll be seeing you again." He pressed on the accelerator and the SUV roared to life.

"You never know . . ." Hauck slapped the door shut. "But next time I hope it's for a foot of fresh powder."

CHAPTER FIFTY-NINE

Around 6:30 P.M. Geoff came by and picked up Dani. She still wasn't happy to leave, but she finally went, reluctantly, Blu trailing along. Geoff seemed like a good guy who genuinely cared about her. His said his friend's house was empty for a week and Snowmass was twenty-five miles from Carbondale, and no one would have any idea she was there. He promised Hauck he wouldn't mention it to anyone.

Hauck drove into Aspen and checked into the Hotel Jerome. He figured as long as he was out here, while he figured out his next step, why not enjoy the stay. The Jerome was a famous, redbrick building on Main Street, a holdover from Aspen's nineteenth-century mining heyday. Its brass-trimmed, Old West-style lobby combined the charm of old Aspen with a trendier, modern-day style and crowd.

Besides, Hauck had been there before and liked the bar.

He checked in, sent out some clothes to be express washed for the next day, took a long shower, and put on the one clean shirt he had left. Then he headed down to the bar. He ordered a Stoli on the rocks with olives. He was able to finally decompress from all that had happened today.

"Crazy day?" the bartender asked. He seemed in his forties, handsome, fit. His idea of a crazy day was likely when his mountain bike suffered a flat.

Hauck shook his head and laughed. "You don't have any idea."

He noticed four women at a table in bright-colored tops, short leather jackets, and stylish jeans. The sound of southern accents. Texas, he was thinking. Probably a girls' weekend. One of them, a pretty brunette in a leopard-print top, seemed to glance over a couple of times, catching his eye.

His mind drifted to Naomi. She was the third woman he had gotten involved with in the past five years. First, there was Karen. Together they had searched for her husband, Charlie, a hedge fund manager who had engineered his own disappearance in the smoke and chaos of a Metro-North train bombing. After a year together, she'd gone back to Virginia to take care of her dad, which had pretty much broken Hauck's heart at the time. Then Annie, who still had her restaurant in town, and her son, Brandon, who had Down syndrome and whom Hauck still took skating every once in a while.

Then Naomi. If you could even call what they had being involved.

The brunette in the drapey leopard top kept looking his way. They were probably out in Aspen for some fun. He signaled to the bartender for another. Hauck needed a meal badly. He'd have him recommend a restaurant.

His cell phone sounded.

Hauck looked at the screen and saw that it was from Talon.

It was awfully late back home. Maybe Foley had come back with something on Alpha after all. He took the phone and went to an empty corner in the bar area where no one would hear. "Tom, it's after ten back there . . ." he answered.

"Well, things don't just stop just because you're lazing your way out there in Colorado."

"Not exactly how I would describe it," Hauck said, "but . . . Any chance you found out anything on what I asked?"

"To be truthful," his boss replied, "I can't say I tried."

"Oh." There was a seriousness in Foley's voice. This had the earmarks of a different kind of conversation altogether. "What's going on?"

"Ty, I have to be frank. I've spoken with the executive committee. We all feel this sabbatical of yours has to come to an end."

"I'm sorry that's the way you look at it, Tom."

"How else are we supposed to look at it? We've extended ourselves for you a good deal now. We've tried to be flexible. We're running a business here, son, not a wellness clinic. I know you went through a rough patch and you had a little soul-searching to do. But that time is up now."

"Sounds like there's an ultimatum coming here . . ."

"Call it whatever you want. I would simply say it's a reality check. We want you back to work here. Tomorrow. The day after, the latest. This thing you're on out there has got to come to an end. If not—and the choice is yours, son—we'll have no option but to nullify your partnership agreement with the firm. You're an asset here, Ty. But only if you're here. I've sent you an email putting all this in writing, so there's no misunderstandings."

In writing . . . "No misunderstandings, Tom. Except only a couple of days ago you were willing to check into Alpha for me, and whether you knew anyone out here who could help. What's changed?"

"What's changed is that it's time to put this whole thing behind you, Ty, that's all. And come back home."

"Six people are dead out here, Tom. If you knew what happened today, you'd—"

"Look, that all sounds bad and I'm sorry for them," Foley said, cutting him off. "I really am. But there are agencies to look into that. Police. We have our own things to get done here, and we've met, and we're united in how we feel about it. You find your way back here, and let's get on to doing great things. Or we revoke your agreement—I think we're long past the clause that says you execute your job 'in a timely, accepted manner'—and that's that. I'll give you the night to sleep on it. As long as you realize, there's an awful lot you'd be throwing away. Do I need to repeat any part of this, Ty?"

"No, no need to repeat a word of it, Tom. It's all perfectly clear." Hauck knew that Foley's patience had been running thin. But revoking his partnership? Forcing him to come back. Tomorrow? Something surely had changed. "I guess how I'm reading it is, it was okay to go off and get myself shot up and my life threatened when it involved company business. But it's not okay if there's nothing to be gained."

"I'm not exactly sure that's quite how I would put it, Ty. I tend to think of it as doing the smart thing for your career and keeping that young niece of yours, or whatever she is, safe, which is where I might put my priorities right now."

Hauck didn't reply.

"I'm sorry it's come to this, Ty. Is there any part of what I said you need me to go over?"

"No, Tom. I think everything's perfectly clear."

"Then I'll look forward to your reply. Say by noon. Tomorrow. I know you're two hours behind out there."

"That's awfully considerate of you, Tom."

"If we don't hear from you by then, we'll consider our agreement void. Think long and hard on it tonight, son. I hope you make the right choice."

After they hung up, Hauck sat there, his stomach hollow, his skin tingling, then sank back against the bench. The choice was to walk away from Alpha. His promise to Watkins and Dani. From making Robertson pay for what he'd done. Because he damn well knew that if he didn't, no one else would lift a finger to. Or walk away from Talon. His career.

I hope you make the right choice, son.

He thought about how Kelli Watkins would feel. *They all leave. Or become part of them.*

And Chuck Watkins, who'd just taken a bullet meant for Hauck.

He got up and went back to the bar. The group of gals had left. The bartender came up again. Hauck indicated another drink.

"The pretty brunette over there said they'd be at Justice Snow's later if you wanted to come by. It's a hot spot here in town."

"Thanks."

He sat back at the bar. His insides were buzzing like a tuning fork. *We've all met and we're pretty united.* Hauck didn't exactly have a graduate degree in corporate shrewdness. *What had changed?*

Then it struck him. A shot to the belly at first; then

it wormed up like something heated in his bloodstream until it was a throbbing in his head. He thought back to the first time Foley had called him out here. Or Brooke.

"Take that young niece of yours or whatever she is and . . ."

He was pretty sure he had never mentioned Dani. To either of them. All he'd said was that he was out here for a friend.

The bartender brought his drink and Hauck downed it in a couple of gulps. *What the hell did Foley know?*

"You gonna join them over at Justice's?" he asked. "Fun times."

Hauck shook his head and motioned for a check. "Room service."

CHAPTER SIXTY

He got the answer he was looking for just a few minutes later.

An NBA playoff game was on that he wasn't paying much attention to, and he had just picked through a pretty fair burger. He was surfing around on his phone—answering an email from Vern Fitzpatrick, the head of the Greenwich police force, his old boss, who wanted to see him, and a couple of business-related things that he forwarded on to Brooke.

At the same time, going over his conversation with Foley.

If there was one thing he'd learned in the time he was on the boat, it was that what drove him wasn't the money. Or the fame. Or power. He'd surely been on enough news shows. *I hope you make the right choice, son.*

He thought back to a time when he was the happiest, and it somehow took him back to when he was working for the NYPD, on the fast track to detective, his whole career ahead of him, with Jessie and Rachel, his two young girls, his family whole and together, immune from harm.

He could never go back to that, of course.

He'd been happy when he was drifting around the Caribbean with Naomi, no plan or destination. But he knew that was more of a postponement than a life. And he knew he could never go back to that, either.

And he was happy when he went up against the Gstaad Group, a force much more powerful than himself, and whom no one had had the will or the courage to take down.

He had.

Or the other times in his life he'd stood up when no one else did.

And Hauck saw it now. Clearly. As if for the first time. Just who he was. Stripped of the high-arcing career and all the TV interviews and fleeting fame. Out here. In a place he had no connection to. Alone.

He saw that he felt most alive, most infused with purpose, when he went up against them.

Against those forces no one else would.

What he was doing here.

It wasn't very complex. It wasn't even remotely heroic, no matter what they said.

All he'd ever wanted to feel was the sense that he was doing some good.

He leaned back and watched some Indiana Pacer guard do a crazy-ass dunk on a fast break. His whole life wasn't so much more than a big, transparent cliché. *There are those in the white hats and the black hats*, Jen Keeler had told him, *and don't confuse the two.*

He didn't. He'd never confused them.

There was never much doubt about which hat he wore.

The game turned into a rout and there was nothing more he could occupy himself with online. He scrolled down Google News before calling it a night. He had to make up his mind about Foley's ultimatum, but something told him that he already had, and that he had for a long time, weeks, while his soul and body mended. He just hadn't admitted it to himself maybe. Until now.

Flicking through the headlines, something caught his eye.

Normally he might have breezed right by it, but a single word grabbed him, pretty much punched him, listed under Colorado Business news:

"RMM Agrees to Be Acquired by Oil Conglomerate."

He opened the link. The oil and gas exploration company had agreed to be taken over. Jen Keeler had said they were in talks for this. Whatever they could pump out of the ground only improved the bottom line.

And for that, they needed all the water they could get. The stock had jumped sixteen points that day.

But it was something else that caused Hauck to stop, that gave him the answer he was searching for, and changed the course this whole thing was heading in.

What's changed, Tom?

In a way, it even made him chuckle with mock respect.

It explained Foley's ultimatum. Why Talon's board had gotten together. Why it was so urgent that he come back. Why it had to be done tonight.

It also explained how his boss knew about Dani.

The company acquiring RMM was Global Exploration. Talon's client.

CHAPTER SIXTY-ONE

So that's how Foley was getting his information. And why it was all so important. Why it had to be acted on now. He needed Hauck out of the way. What Hauck was trying to do was only stirring up things up out here. Things that could screw the deal should they come out.

I've spoken with the executive committee. We're united on it.

Bravo, Tom, you played your role to a T. Hauck couldn't help but give him a sardonic applause.

His phone sounded again. Hauck checked the screen. *Geoff Davies.* He pressed the answer button.

Dani.

"How're you doing?" he answered.

"I guess all right. It's all kind of like a dream, what happened today."

"I know."

"But I'm glad I'm here. With Geoff. You were right, I couldn't have been alone. I just called to say thank you."

"You're welcome. Call any time, my rates are pretty fair."

Dani laughed. Hauck was pleased to hear the lightness back in her voice again. Then she said, "I just wanted to say thank you for being there for me, Uncle Ty."

"Hey, you were the one who made all the difference, Dani, not me."

"I didn't mean just for today . . . I meant, for coming out here in the first place. For just caring. I've been thinking, since my mom and dad split, the truth is, I haven't had anyone in a while. Someone I could count on. That I trusted. My dad was always off somewhere. You know how busy he is with his work. Then Mom got sick, and it was more me taking care of her than anyone. There was Wade. But even back then I knew he was always out for himself. Plus he had Kyle, who got hurt and needed so much attention."

"I understand."

"No," she said, "I don't think you do fully understand. I always felt like I had to be so tough and independent of everything. And everyone. To prove I could handle whatever came at me. Maybe that's why I stayed out here and why I do what I do, when everyone else is starting to put their lives together. And I kind of saw all that today . . . in that tank. I saw all I was, was just alone. And scared. Not scared to give up or to let people down. Scared to die. I just wanted to get out of that tank and live."

"Anyone would have been just as scared, Dani. And wanted the same thing. Put me at the top of the list."

"You're never scared, Uncle Ty."

"No," Hauck said. "That's not true."

"What are you scared of?"

He had been to the edge many times. Scared of losing the people he loved. Scared of letting them down. Scared sometimes that the bastards would win. "Just things."

"But there was one thing I had faith in," Dani said, "the whole time I was in there. And in a way, that's what kept me going."

"What was that?"

"*You*, Uncle Ty. That you would be there for me. That if I could just hold on, you'd come. And you did."

Hauck felt a wave of warmth travel through him. "Like I said, you were the one who led me to you, Dani."

"Maybe. But there was something else I knew, and I just wanted you to know it. And it gave me a little peace when I wasn't sure I would make it through."

"And what was that?"

"I knew that you'd get them. I told them that. That one day, no matter what happened to me, you'd kill them for what they did to me."

390

Hauck smiled inside. She could have been his own.

She said, "I was right about that, wasn't I, Uncle Ty?"

"Yes." Hauck drew in a breath and nodded to himself. "You were right."

That was exactly what he was going to do.

Dani said, "I just wanted you to know that. All of it."

"I'm glad we got to spend that time together, Dani. Though a part of me wishes we had just gone to see the hot springs."

She laughed again. "So what are we going to do . . .?"

"*You're* going to rest up and keep out of sight. That's all."

"And what about you? I thought tomorrow we could get together and have breakfast? And talk about what's next."

Hauck blew out a breath. "I'm afraid I'm not going to be here tomorrow, Dani. I was going to call you and let you know. I just hadn't made my mind up until a while ago."

There was a pause. It was filled with anticipation. "You're heading back there, aren't you?"

He didn't reply.

"To Templeton," she said.

He wasn't sure what to say, or even how to explain it. Only that he didn't want her to come along.

"Ty, I know you are."

"I have to, Dani. There's stuff to finish there. Stuff you don't even know."

391

"I'll go with you," she said quickly.

"You can't."

"I'm the one who got you into this. I'm—"

"It doesn't matter how I got into it, Dani. I'm in, that's all that matters. There's nothing more you can do. None of this would have ever come out if it wasn't for you. You put it all together. You saw through Wade. You knew Trey and you saw what was happening when few people would have. That's your skill. But it's time for my skills now. It's just how things work out sometimes."

"Do you even have a plan?" she asked.

"The makings of one," he joked, trying to break the tension.

"I'm not sure the 'makings' of one is going to be enough this time."

"I'm sure it'll evolve, as it goes along."

"Please don't joke, Uncle Ty . . ." Hauck got the sense that she was crying. "I'm scared for you. I can't help it. I don't want to lose you."

"You won't lose me. But I need you to stay safe as well. I want you to stay out of sight with Geoff until you hear back from me. And don't go out. I'm going to email you a number. It's a friend in D.C. If you don't hear back, you tell her everything. She can help. And please don't let Wade know that you're even here."

"Okay." He heard her sniffle again. "I don't even know if I'll see you again."

"You will."

"Promise me . . ."

Hauck drew in a breath. An honest one. "I can't promise something I can't keep, Dani."

"You have to."

Hauck closed his eyes and could almost feel the tears rolling down her cheeks.

"Promise me something else then?" She sniffed.

"Name it."

"When you nail him, Robertson, remember to give him a knee to the balls for me. And Trey."

Hauck laughed. He shut off the TV to get rest for tomorrow. "I'm not sure how that will all play out, Dani. But I give you my word I'll sure try."

ONE MILE UNDER

CHAPTER SIXTY-TWO

Hauck's first stop upon arriving back in Greeley was the Weld County district attorney's office.

He asked for the DA, Littlejohn, but was told he was in Denver for the day. ADA Adams was around, but at the courthouse. He should be back in an hour. Hauck told the receptionist he'd wait.

He stepped outside. He took out his phone and dialed up Chuck Watkins. The farmer's wife called him in from the fields. She told Hauck she'd tried to keep her husband resting, but he just kept insisting he was perfectly okay. Hauck was glad to hear he was back at work. After asking Watkins about his arm, Hauck asked him, "Did you have that conversation we spoke of with your friends?"

Watkins said he had.

"And are they back in?"

"Some. Maybe."

"What about you?"

The farmer paused. "I guess between my land, my son, and a little dignity, there's not a whole lot more left these bastards can take from me."

"So I guess I'll take that as a yes," Hauck said.

"I expect you will."

"You know, maybe it would be best to have your wife go and stay with your daughter in Greeley for a few days. The minute they get word of this, there's going to be trouble."

"Funny, she was just asking about going there," the farmer said with a full understanding of what Hauck meant.

"I'll be seeing you soon."

The hour passed and finally a young ADA finally stepped out of the elevator, a thick messenger briefcase slung over his shoulder, accompanied by a female colleague, who had an armful of files.

Hauck got up. The ADA looked just a few years out of law school. Hauck had stopped by before he left the first time up there and was told that none of the crimes were committed in his jurisdiction. "I thought I told you I would discuss what you said with my boss and if there was anything to discuss further, we'd be in touch," Adams said.

"What you said was to come back when there was

something to follow up on that happened in your jurisdiction."

"And . . .?" The ADA looked exasperated.

"Something has."

The prosecutor excused himself and led Hauck into
his small, cramped office, stacks of briefs piled high on
the desk and credenza. He dropped his satchel on his
desk and tossed a Dunkin' Donuts coffee cup into the
trash. "Okay." He motioned Hauck into one of the two
chairs in front of him. "Let's hear what you have."

"The last time I was in I was with my niece, Dani.
Actually, my goddaughter."

"I remember." Adams nodded.

"She was abducted yesterday afternoon. In Templeton.
In the café on Main Street."

Adams showed surprise. "Abducted . . .?"

Hauck took him through what had happened. From
being chased through town and picked up off the street,
forced into the car and bound, then thrown into the
water storage tank. How the conduits to the river were
opened and she had to make her way through them
against the flow, and how she'd come within an inch
of drowning.

The young ADA's eyes widened.

"It was only by a miracle she made it out. I found
her on the riverbank. This all happened about the same
time someone took a couple of shots at me on Charles
Watkins's farm. I'd say mine was a pretty lucky escape

as well—not quite as lucky for Mr. Watkins, who was hit in the shoulder. But I'm only here to focus on Dani's situation right now."

"You're saying all this happened yesterday?"

Hauck nodded.

"Did either of you file a complaint with the police?"

"I'm going to give that question a little more credit than it probably deserves." Hauck forced a smile. "Given the circumstances, I felt pressing a case against them from here was the last thing that was in her best interests."

Adams nodded, giving the impression that he understood, slumping back in his chair. "So where is she now?"

"Safe. She said she'd be happy to give you a full deposition of what took place. If it was brought to trial I'm sure she'd be delighted to come back and testify. With some assurances, of course."

"You mean that we'd prosecute?"

"And adequate protection," Hauck said.

Adams tapped his fingers against his desk and nodded. "You said you only wanted to focus on Ms. Whalen's situation. Why?"

"Because she can identify who did this to her. The two people at the water facility were a John Robertson of Alpha Group, who, by the way, was the same person I described last week who was on the river in Aspen at the time Mr. Watkins's son was killed.

"The other was a Randall McKay, also of Alpha, who I believe is Mr. Robertson's boss."

Adams made some notes. "We'll have to hear her story in full, of course, before we could even contemplate taking this further. And I'll need to discuss this with my boss." The pallor on his face seemed to say that he was unsure whether this was the case of a lifetime or the one that was going to cut short his once-promising career. Hauck wondered where the next position could be, a place lower down the rung than Greeley.

"Just to be clear," Hauck said, remembering what Jen Keeler had told him, "isn't RMM a contributor to Mr. Littlejohn's last campaign?"

"This isn't the Wild West, Mr. Hauck." The ADA grew annoyed. "No matter what you think."

Hauck got up. "You claimed that your office wasn't beholden to anyone, Mr. Adams. Here's your chance to prove it." He took out a card from his wallet. "Here's how to reach me."

He thanked the ADA for his time. He hadn't come here expecting anything more. In fact, he had gotten exactly what he came for.

Within the hour, about as long as it took for Adams to reach his boss's ear, he figured what he'd told them would get to RMM.

CHAPTER SIXTY-THREE

His next stop was at Jen Keeler's. There was a staff meeting going on inside, but when she heard Hauck was in the office she stepped out.

"I'm glad to see you," she said, her eyes indicating it was true. "I heard you had some trouble up at Watkins's farm the other day. Everyone had the impression you had gone."

"I'm not so easy to be rid of," Hauck joked. "Anyway I hear he's doing okay."

"He's a tough one," Jen said. "So what brings you back?"

"That lawsuit you showed me the other day. Watkins's . . .?"

She nodded.

"I want you to dust it off and get it started again."

"Nothing would make me happier." Keeler's eyes brightened. "However, it's not mine to file. It will take one or more of the defendants to agree to it. Preferably Mr. Watkins, of course, as he's the lead complainant."

"I think you'll have that within the day. What happens when you get the go-ahead?"

"We'll file an immediate motion with the state. And have a copy delivered to RMM's headquarters. To let them know they're served."

"That ought to stir the pot pretty well."

"You see the papers today?"

"You mean about the buyout?"

Jen nodded soberly. "Then you know what a lawsuit like this now will do . . .?"

Hauck smiled. "I thought that's exactly what you were trying to do, Ms. Keeler."

That gleam in her eye, the one between skepticism and growing trust, became even brighter. "You know the farmers here, they've had a lot of false hopes in the past few years . . ."

"Get things rolling," Hauck said. "I'd like that lawsuit in their hands as soon as you get the call."

CHAPTER SIXTY-FOUR

Hauck finally made the drive back out to Templeton and Watkins's farm. There was a flurry of activity as Hauck drove up. The farmhands were bringing in some equipment, boarding up the windows, corralling the horses, as if a storm were coming in. He spotted Watkins in back, his arm in a sling, spreading out bales of hay from a small flatbed. They were building the bales up as possible cover.

"How's the arm?" Hauck asked, as he went around the side.

Watkins stopped his truck. "Not as good as it would be if you hadn't showed up the other day. The doc said it went clean through. Two of my hands decided to stick around. The others have family. I told them to go. I don't know if they can shoot, but I figure, three is better than one, if it comes to that."

"Four," Hauck said. "And we can use every hand we can get. What do we have for weapons?"

Watkins climbed down and took Hauck inside. There was a locked wooden case on the wall. He pulled it open. Inside, there were four hunting rifles with scopes. A Remington hunting rifle with an illuminated scope. That was good. There was a Winchester pump-action shotgun that would be of use at close range, and Hauck hoped it wouldn't come to that.

"Here, I owe you this." Hauck took out the Colt 9 mm he had taken the other day.

"Hold on to it. Not exactly Fort Bragg . . ." the farmer said, "but I've bagged a few choice elk in my day with that Remington. And that shotgun's not much fun for anyone within ten feet if it comes to it."

Hauck checked the action and sights on the Remington. Good to three hundred yards.

"Listen, there's something else going on." Hauck told him where he went before Jen's, to the DA. And about what had happened to Dani yesterday.

"I'm really sorry to hear that." Watkins winced with a mixture of disgust and anger. "How is she?"

"She's okay. She's back at home. She actually wanted to come back up here."

"Good kid," the farmer said. "I'm sorry she got caught up in this."

"She's the one who put it all together. Without her, Trey's death would still be just another accident. And

405

RMM would just be another oil company on the news. I guess you heard?"

"I read the news." Watkins nodded. "Anyway, I'm sorry she had to find Trey, though maybe that's the way it was meant to be. Maybe we would have all been better off if she hadn't."

"I guess we'll see."

"So let me ask . . ." The farmer looked at him. "You back here because of me and the rest of us and RMM? Or you here because of what they did to your goddaughter?"

Hauck checked the action on the Remington. "Can I go for a little of both?"

"Well, I don't care. Whichever it is," the farmer said, "you're here."

It was almost dark when they got the defenses set, including the stacked bales of hay from behind which they could shoot. They punched out the window at the top of the barn, which afforded someone with a rifle a 180-degree perch. The old combine that Watkins used to harvest grain was revved up, the thrasher blades whirring. It could discourage someone from advancing on them.

Two of the farmhands were all that was left. They all had a dinner of chili and bread that Marie had thawed. Hauck sat up high in the barn, with the Remington, looking out over the road and fields. Some Mexican music was playing from the barn. Hauck knew enough Spanish to recognize it as a love song. And about death.

It seemed to fit.

It grew dark. This was when they would come. He heard footsteps on the stairs coming up in the barn. No one knew what to expect. There was a nervous feeling in the air.

The farmer stepped up to Hauck's perch, holding the shotgun in his one good hand. "You sure they'll actually come?"

"Once they hear Dani's safe and that she's willing to testify. And about your suit . . ." Hauck rolled over on his side and kept his eyes on the dark road. "My experience is that they always come."

Watkins looked at him. "Just why are you back here, Mr. Hauck? The truth this time."'

Hauck shrugged. "I don't know. I've tried to answer that myself a hundred times in the last few days. The best I can come up with is, there must be something about it I like."

"*Like?*" Watkins shook his head. "You're long on courage then. But I'm afraid it'll make for a short career."

Hauck grinned. "It just seems to stick in my gut when I see people using their power to step all over others. Especially when they hide behind some shiny government shield or a corporation. There are a lot of people who just get trampled upon on the way. I've found people are just waiting around for someone

407

to take the first step. So I must like it. 'Cause I'm here."

"I know you were a cop and all," the farmer said. "But me, I got something I'm fighting for here. Our lives are at stake. To me, it's not just what's right. I lost my son. It's personal."

Hauck thought of Dani, who'd become as close as if she were his own, and what she'd been through. "Trust me, it's personal for me, too."

Watkins smiled. "It's enough to shake the idealism in anyone, isn't it, Mr. Hauck? Anyway, only one thing I ask of you here . . ."

"If I can."

"You just point out the sonovabitch who killed my boy. That a deal?"

"All right. But just so you know, I have my own gripes against him, too."

"Best shot then." The farmer nodded. "You know, more I think about it, I think we're here for the same reasons, Mr. Hauck."

"And what's that?"

"Strip away all the idealism, all the wrongs, we're really both just here to kill a man."

Hauck smiled. "Seems a good time for you to call me Ty."

"Chuck, then."

Up in the distance Hauck saw two sets of lights heading toward them. He yelled out, "Two cars coming

408

in!" and checked his rifle. "Take your positions. Here they come."

"Lupe! Miguel!" Watkins hurried back down the stairs. The music cut off and Hauck saw the two farmhands scampering around outside. One had a couple of improvised Molotov cocktails—made from heating oil in beer bottles stuffed with a rag. The other jumped in the cab of the large combine and started the engine.

The lights grew closer. Hauck trained his sights on the driver in the first car. He had night sights but they weren't very good. Maybe for a buck creeping around the woods at a hundred yards. The rumble of the engines could now be heard.

"Here they come!" Hauck said. His heart was beating fast. "Hold your firing till I give the go."

He steadied his shooting elbow on the window ledge and followed the lead vehicle in. He thought, though, that something didn't figure. If it was Robertson, he wouldn't have made such a visible show. These guys were all trained. Unless this was a diversion, and the main attack was coming elsewhere. He rolled around to the other side of the window and scanned both sides of the fields, searching for signs of activity.

There were none.

He brought the rifle back. His pulse picked up as he watched the lead vehicle, which he now could make out as a flatbed truck, stop along the fields maybe a hundred yards short of the driveway. His finger tensed softly on the trigger. "Everyone get ready . . ."

The doors opened. Two men stepped out. Hauck followed them in his sight, squinting into the sight. The first wore a cowboy hat. He didn't recognize either of them, and they didn't exactly look like an elite team. They both had rifles. Two more got out of the pickup truck behind them.

Hauck trained in on the lead person, illuminated through the yellow night sight. *Where was Robertson? Where was McKay?* "Just give me a reason," he muttered softly, boring in.

Then, the man in the cowboy hat called out, "*Chuck! Chuck Watkins . . . It's Ben. Early. Milt Yarrow is with me. Don Ellis and Fred Barnes are in the truck behind us.*"

"Hold your fire!" Watkins shouted, coming out from the house, waving his arms.

Hauck lowered his gun. The names were familiar somehow. Then it hit him. The class action against the town he had read at Jen Keeler's.

They were all part of it, too.

"Word was you were a little undermanned here and might need a little help." Ben came up to Watkins and extended his hand. "We thought we'd lend a hand."

They also brought ammunition and other weapons. Hauck figured by now RMM and Alpha knew about his visit to the DA. Kidnapping charges, along with attempted murder, wouldn't exactly be the kind of publicity they'd be seeking now, enough to derail any merger. Tomorrow, they'd find out about the new class action suit. And once Global Energy learned of it, the sparks would fly. The guys at RMM had dug themselves a hole and they couldn't let that just sit. Hauck thought he'd give anything to see Moss's reaction to it.

The others stayed in the house and opened a few beers to settle their nerves. He sat up in the window, watching the road and the fields.

Could be anytime, Hauck decided. Maybe tonight. He sat back and settled his eyes over the dark fields.

But they'd come.

More likely tomorrow.

CHAPTER SIXTY-FIVE

Wendell Moss leaned against the railing at the Trixie One well site. The reassuring *ka-chung, ka-chung, ka-chung* of the pump bobbing at three-second intervals was as natural a sound to him as a hymn in church. The sound meant that product—either oil or natural gas—was being pumped back up the well. But, sadly, Trixie was on her last breaths. In the past months, her production had sunk beneath the economic costs of keeping her running. That was why the crew was down to two men who were sucking the last barrels dry and preparing the concrete mixture that would be pumped down the wellhead in a day, forever sealing it off. Moss wiped his forehead in the afternoon sun.

Ka-chung.

He lit a smoke and reflected that he'd basically given

his whole life to RMM. He'd worked for them the past twenty-two years, straight out of what was known as West Texas State University back then, as a young geological engineer. He'd shuttled his family around to dusty hellholes more times than he could recall. Living in excuses for towns that barely had a Dairy Queen; at various makeshift communities in the Bakken up in North Dakota and the Powder Ridge Basin in Wyoming. Over the years, he'd gotten his hands so black from soot and oil he doubted he could ever clean them again. There was more oil in his veins, he always joked, than blood cells. He had started out on the clock, then salaried, then earned a few bonuses, which allowed him to buy a house in Midland for the first time in his life. And now with this merger he finally had enough vested in options and stock to make what even a happy wildcatter would call a killing. It was *his* wells that were delivering the cash flow to make it all happen. His babies, in the Wattenberg field. And now he saw it all slipping away. Because of some stupid kid on a river, and a farmer that had no sense. And no one was going to take that away from him. He'd earned it, every godforsaken penny. He flicked away an ash and looked at his rough hands. He'd given too much.

He wasn't naturally a man with an urge for violence. Not like these Alpha boys. They'd do anything to get the messy work done. That's what he paid them for. He went to church Sundays; sat in the stands Friday night cheering on his girls in soccer or his boy Blaine in foot-ball. Twenty-two years, he never hit his wife once, or even raised his voice in anger at her.

Yet here he was.

He could have stopped this all a long time ago, he reck-oned, but he'd turned his head away at just the time he should've looked straight, and had trust in the people who knew how to handle this sort of thing.

Maybe too much trust.

Water—Moss knew they could have trucked it in from any of a hundred different sources. Not as profitably perhaps, or as quickly, and that was part of what made the numbers look so sweet. They'd invested millions in that recycling plant. Bought off the fucking town. And no bunch of farmers in overalls and cowboy hats was going to take that away from him now.

It was too late anyway.

He heard the sound of the car coming up first, tires grinding over loose dirt and gravel. The dark blue Audi, winding up the narrow road through the chain link fence, came into view. Moss took a last drag. The car came around to a stop, kicking up dust, its sides grimy. Randy McKay stepped out. In a plaid shirt and khakis, he looked like any old guy who might be filling up at the next pump or in the checkout line at Kroger.

"There used to be a joke," McKay said as he came up to him, "one wildcatter saying to the other, 'Let's

414

go somewhere quiet we can talk and not be disturbed. How about one of your well sites?'"

"Trixie's given it up with the best of them. Now don't go raggin' on her. See this . . .?" Moss took out the new class-action suit that had been delivered to him today.

Lifting his shades, McKay unfolded it and looked it over. He scanned the first couple of pages and shook his head and sighed. "Thought we had this all put to bed."

Moss took a drag and blew it out. "It's not just the suit. The suit we could settle in a day, if we'd wanted. Hell, it was all just a matter of money anyway. Just didn't seem right to have this kind of thing lingering in the face of a merger. But it's no longer just the suit, is it now?"

"No." McKay shook his head. "It's not."

"It's about saving our damn hides. I heard from the grapevine this sonovabitch Hauck went to visit the state's attorney today in Greeley. He told them about what happened at the Falls. Littlejohn says if the girl comes forward with this, his hands'll be tied. Our fingerprints are all over this mess, Randy. It's all there in black and white."

McKay handed him back the suit. "I know."

"This could sink the merger, if it comes out. Hell, this could sink the whole damn company. It's time to end it. Both of them—him and the girl. And this time, make sure the job gets done right."

The Alpha man nodded. "I know what you need me to do."

"I hope you do." Moss glared at him with sagging but unmistakable eyes. "Tonight. Before she goes to the DA. Before she goes on record with what she knows. They talk, and it doesn't matter how much oil we pump out of the damn ground. We're both gone."

McKay nodded. He put down his aviators and headed toward his car. "I'll be in touch."

"By the way," Moss called. "We're closing Trixie up for good tomorrow. Lots of concrete being pumped down. Tons and tons of it. I suspect, no one'll know if something was buried in there for a thousand years."

"Thanks for letting me know." McKay started the Audi up, and drove away without a wave.

Moss looked back at the well. *Ka-chung. Ka-chung.* Goddamn water, he spat on the dry soil. He flicked his butt to the ground and stamped it out with his shoe. Two-thirds of the planet's covered in it, and this is the one godforsaken place we bid it up a hundred times what it's worth.

CHAPTER SIXTY-SIX

Wade pushed the tray across to his son, Kyle, at the VA hospital in Denver. Three years earlier, Marine Specialist Kyle Dunn's supply truck had driven over an IED in the Helmand Province in Afghanistan, blowing off his right leg and arm, rupturing his spleen, puncturing his kidney, and rattling his brain against the sides of his skull like ice in a blender. A diffuse axonal trauma in the brain forced him to have to relearn everything from taking a step, to feeding himself, reciting the alphabet again, or even taking a piss. Pretty much everything he knew how to do as a five-year-old.

He was doing well, the doctors claimed. He could now speak sentences and align numbered blocks in order and pick up a fork, a huge step from where he was a couple of years ago. But, truth was, he might require care for the rest of his life. Wade generally made the drive down on Sundays to visit. He and Kyle's mother were long divorced and she sent him money whenever she could, off in Florida and working on a cruise ship somewhere.

"C'mon," Wade said, "take some of this soup. You best eat something, son."

Kyle shook his head and pushed Wade's arm aside. "Not now. Not hungry, Dad."

"Okay, okay. Maybe the nurse will have some better sway with you," Wade said.

Once, Kyle had been a handsome, athletic boy, all-state in wrestling and head of the Why Not? Society, a volunteer group in Pitkin County, who won a full ride to CU in Boulder. But he dropped out after his freshman year to sign up with the Marines. His own little Pat Tillman.

But like with Tillman, who put his NFL career aside to sign up with his brother, it all came crashing down. Though Kyle managed to survive.

The prognosis was hopeful, but slow. Agonizingly so. And costly. The VA paid for most of it. But what if he was never able to walk or live alone again for the rest of his life? Or if he couldn't hold a real job ever again, which seemed likely?

Then there would be all the supplemental things. Like an aide to live with him when he got home. Wade surely couldn't. And a customized van to drive, so he could get around. And a home that was retrofitted for his needs. And people to continue to help him speak; and head doctors so he could tell them about the horrible images swirling around in his brain that caused him to just turn away in midsentence and stare into space for hours.

Who'd cover that?

Wade knew that, he'd lived his life in the wrong. He'd crossed the line. Not once. Many times. The Watkins boy was just one example. He was a lot like Kyle. Athletic. In the prime of his life. And then there were those people up there in that balloon—the terror they must have felt as it burned up around them and all came crashing down. He never really actually knew what was going to happen to them; he was only told to look the other way and handed a big, fat envelope of cash. When he looked at Kyle, sometimes it made it all seem okay. The things he'd done. Easier to swallow.

"Come on, what do you say we check out the Rockies . . ." Wade picked up the remote clicker. Kyle liked watching baseball. He could watch anything he didn't once play, which caused him too much pain. Wade flicked on the TV and found the channel. "Look, De La Rosa's pitching. He's good. You like him, right?"

Kyle nodded, the inkling of a smile. "Good r-run," he said, then stared vacantly.

"*Run?*" Wade questioned.

419

Kyle thought about it a little longer, screwing up his brow, then turned to Wade. "E-R-A."

"That's good, Kyle. Good. Yes, he's got a mighty fine earned run average. He does."

Wade's cell phone chimed. He pulled it out and took a look at who it was. There was no one he really cared to hear from these days.

His stomach dropped. He'd prayed he'd never hear from this person again. But inwardly he always knew it never was over, once you stepped over that line. He let it ring several times, and thought about just letting it go to his voice mail and pretending he had gone away somewhere. For good. Like maybe Africa.

"I'll be back in a second, son," he said to Kyle, and stepped out into the hall. He put his back against the wall and answered. "Chief Dunn here."

"Bet I'm the last person in the world you were hoping to hear from," the caller said, with a smirk in his voice that cut through Wade like a knife through butter.

"Yes, you could say that's true. What do you want?"

"We need you to do something. And you're still on the payroll, Chief."

"You already made me do something," Wade said. "And I did it. You've got no cause to keep calling me."

"You think you got all that money just to look the other way like some mall cop. Or put a few photos under lock and key in your desk drawer? You know more than anyone how your son has that private room

420

and all that fancy attention up there. And you better not forget why."

"I can't talk. Not here," Wade spat back under his breath, smiling briefly and waving familiarly to one of the doctors as he passed by.

He wished he had the balls to just hang up and tell them to go fuck themselves. That the debt was paid. But he knew very well that the debt was only beginning, and that, down the line, he would need all they promised him. And anyway, these weren't exactly the kind of people you said those kinds of words to and hung the phone up on.

"Go ahead, hang up if you want . . . It can all go away in an instant. All the specialists, that fancy van you got lined up for you. Poof! Gone. Is that what you want to happen, Chief?"

Wade squeezed his fist into a ball, but didn't say a word.

"Didn't think so. So if I were you I'd put away the big, brash attitude that doesn't get you anywhere, and just listen. Comprende . . .?"

"What is it you need? I destroyed those photos like you asked."

"That was only Part One, Chief. Part Two is that I hear your stepdaughter's come back home . . ."

"Is she? I didn't know." Just the sound of Dani's name sent a spasm through his bowels. He flashed back to what Hauck had warned him. And he didn't seem like a man to be trifled with either. "I haven't spoken with her. She doesn't check in with me."

"She knows things, Wade. Things that could be very problematic for us. Problematic for us all. Because if we go down, you go as well. Just as hard. You know that, right? In fact, they might be more interested in you than any of us. Greedy small-town cop who had to sell himself and his office out."

Wade sucked in a breath and chuffed back, "I know that."

"So she needs to be dealt with, Wade. And you're our man in Havana, as they say . . ."

"Dealt with?" The grinding in his stomach worsened. "Dealt with how?"

"C'mon, Wade, you're a smart guy . . . How'd you get to be chief? Just that it has to be done. And soon. Tonight. Tomorrow. You understand. I don't care how. Just that's it's done. This is what it is. Don't matter whether you like it or not. You have to find a way."

Wade felt as if some huge gristmill was grinding his insides into powder. This is what he always knew would happen, the moment he saw that money hit his account. The moment Dani first came in to see him, telling him how he had to get involved . . .

He'd tried to tell her. A dozen times. If he told her any more clearly, he might as well just admit what he'd done. But she was too damned stubborn to hear what he was saying. *God damn her. God damn her to hell . . .*

"I can't. You hear me, I can't. I can't do that for you. Find someone else."

"There is no one else, Chief. This is what it is."

"I said I can't!" Wade pressed his back and the sweat was cold all over him. "I can't do that."

"You know, you should've thought of all this a long time ago, buddy. Before you walked around with all that money stuffed in your pockets. That's what it was all about, Wade. Right? Not your son. Not your step-daughter. But you . . . Right? You should have thought of all that then."

"How do you know she's even here? How do I find her?"

"Hey, that's your problem, old-timer. I mean, you are a cop, aren't you?"

"She's my stepdaughter, goddammit!" He looked up and down the hall. A few people turned. He shifted away and curled the phone close to his lips and brought his voice down. "It's not human. You can't make me. I just can't . . . ." He stared into Kyle's room. "I won't."

"I see your situation, Chief. I really do. So let me phrase it in a different way. . . . That boy of yours, I know how you feel about *him*. He's your flesh and blood, right? He's put in a lot of work to make his way back. After what he's been through."

Wade didn't like where this was heading.

"He may be out soon—four, five months. That's what this is all about, right . . .? You. Us?"

423

Wade grit his teeth, both angry and increasingly worried. "Yes."

"So you disappoint us on this, I give you my solemn oath of God that that scrambled brain of his will get a pillow over it one night. And soon. We'll put a rag in his mouth and a knife in his ribs and I promise, he won't know whether to fucking gag or scream. You hearing me? Anyone can get in there. You know that, right? A fool could. And you already know where we stand when it comes to doing what has to be done. We don't have to prove that to you, do we, Wade?"

Wade closed his eyes and squeezed the phone, hoping it would crumble. "No. You don't."

"Good. So you think about your son, and go do what has to be done. And this is the last you'll have to hear from me. We'll all be square. Otherwise I may just have to drop by up there with a load of flowers. Your boy likes flowers, doesn't he, Wade?"

"No." Wade seethed. "Don't."

"What I thought. So you just remember who your own flesh and blood is, Wade. He is. Not her. Maybe think of it that way. You've got two days. Two days to find her if she's there, and do what has to be done. She trusts you, right? So you figure out the way. I mean, she's your goddamn stepdaughter now, isn't she?"

The caller hung up. Wade's heart had sped up like an amphetamine had been injected in it. Sweat clung to him. He put the phone in his pocket and went back inside. He sank down in the chair next to the bed.

Kyle looked at him. "Who was that?"

"No one, son. No one important." He'd stepped over this line a dozen times in his life. With his ex-wife, Dani's mom. With the booze and the pills he'd taken and going into that evidence locker, which cost him his reputation and his job. With Trey.

A dozen times, and maybe just a little bit, each time hurt a little less. Kind of like drinking, he thought.

What was one more?

"C'mon, Kyle, so let's check out that game. What do you say?" He flicked on the overhead TV and found the broadcast. "Bottom of the sixth. Four to two, Rockies . . ." Wade said. "De La Rosa's still in there . . ."

Kyle nodded, his eyes glazy, staring straight ahead.

Wade reached and wrapped his fingers around his son's hand. His flesh and blood. "Whaddya say, let's root 'em in, okay? Ball and a strike. What're thinking here, fastball or a slider? I'm thinking slider. What do you think, Kyle?"

CHAPTER SIXTY-SEVEN

When they came, as Hauck already figured, they didn't exactly march through the front door.

It was just past nine, that next night. Hauck had taken a break at the barn window. The one thing he wanted more than anything was to hear his daughter's voice. A last time, if things didn't go well. He punched in her number and she picked up on the third ring. "Hey," he said.

"Dad?"

"Sorry if I woke you. I just wanted to hear your voice."

"You didn't wake me. It's Friday night. I was just watching *Girls*. With Carrie."

"*Girls?*" Hauck said. "Isn't there a lot of sex in that?"

"Dad, please. There's sex everywhere today. Would

you rather I be watching *Game of Thrones*? Or maybe *Ray Donovan*?"

"I was just saying . . ."

"Hold on, let me put it on pause. Where are you?"

"Still in Colorado," he replied. "For a short time more."

"You ever going to come back here? Mom says it's because you have a beard. She says you've gone native."

"I lost the beard. Didn't do much for me, I thought. Made me look old."

"I kinda liked it actually. Send me a new pix."

"Okay . . ."

"So you want to give me a date when I'll see you again? Like, maybe, before I leave for college? That gives you a year."

He laughed. "Soon, I hope, honey."

"You keep saying soon. Dad. What's going on? You're sounding a little strange."

"I just wanted to hear your voice. That's all."

"I think you just have this dad antennae, to catch me doing something I shouldn't be."

"Yeah, kind of a police thing, I guess. We all—"

The power suddenly shut off. Outside, the house went dark. People started yelling. "Power's down!" "What's goin' on?" "*Chuck!*"

This was it, he figured. "Jess, I gotta go."

"What's happening there, Dad? I hear a lot of shouting . . ."

"I just wanted to say I love you, Jessie. Don't be worried, doll. I'll see you soon."

He hung up. He placed the phone on the ledge, rolled himself underneath the window, grabbed his rifle, and looked out. Two vehicles were coming up through the fields, their lights out, barely visible. He could make out four to five of them in them through the sight, with automatic weapons and even night goggles. Two of Watkins's neighbors scampered around, ducking behind a wall of hay bales from the barn. Murmurs and whispers spread around like wildfire. These were farmers, cattle raisers, not soldiers. Everyone was scared.

Hauck kept cover behind the third-story window and looked through the sight.

Below him, Watkins ran into the barn with his shotgun. "You see 'em?"

"I see them," Hauck confirmed. "There's at least four in the fields. Tell your friends not to do anything foolish; don't start a war. You know the police chief, Riddick?"

"Thirty years. But we don't see eye to eye on much."

"Well, this might be a good time to give him a call."

He looked back outside and saw an SUV coming down the road. It was black, almost blending in in the darkness, its headlights shining. This car they wanted everyone to see. It came to a stop around fifty yards from the house. Hauck trained in on it. The rear door opened and someone got out. Fatigue jacket. High forehead. Under a military-style baseball cap. Balding on top. Hauck had seen him before. The guy from Alpha. The one who told him Robertson wasn't around much. McKay.

One of the two who Dani said was at the river.

He stood behind the open car door, presumably for cover; it was probably bulletproof. "I'm Randy McKay," he called out. "From Alpha. Some of you here know me. And what we've done for you. And the town. And you know why we're here, right . . .? We just want one man. Just to talk with him, that's all. There doesn't need to be any bloodshed. We can all just put away these guns."

Below Hauck, whispers shot back and forth amid the ranks.

"Anyway, I've got good news. Truth is, you've all already won. I just spoke with Wendell Moss, head of operations for RMM. He's agreed to negotiate all water rights for farmers in Templeton in exchange for dropping the lawsuit. He guarantees full access to whatever reserves they have. For your fields. For anyone who needs it. They're even prepared to talk about restitution for lost crop yields over the past six months. That's up and beyond anything you could have hoped for. It's a win-win, don't you agree? No reason that a single drop of blood should be shed here. Just hand over who we came for, and we'll be gone. And you'll all be back in business."

There were murmurs up and down. Hauck heard, "That's a damn good deal. We're back in business." "That's a whole lot better than we could've ever gotten on our own . . ." "Chuck, do you hear what they said, we've won."

"What'd the police say?" Hauck called down to Watkins, who was standing behind the door.

"Said all their cars were a little busy right now." The farmer spat, as if disgusted.

Hauck wasn't surprised. "Kind of a waste of thirty years, no . . .?"

Watkins chuckled. "And a helluva lot of taxes."

"Mr. Watkins . . ." McKay shouted. "You can step out while we talk. Don't be worried."

"No worries at all," Watkins shouted back. "But if you don't mind, I'll wait for you."

McKay remained behind the car door. "Congratulations, you've won a helluva victory for your friends here," he said loudly. "Without a drop of blood spilled. What do you say?"

Watkins came out from around the barn. He went over and ducked behind the large combine that was set up below. "Not a single drop of blood . . .?"

"That's a promise. We'll be gone in five minutes once we have what we want. You have my assurance on that. And what I'm proposing has no conditions. All you have to do is get back in your cars and leave. You're all witness to it. All we ask is one thing."

"*Hauck* . . ." the farmer said back.

"That's right. He's not one of you anyway." McKay came out from behind the open door and seemed to be speaking to everyone. "He's only come here to stir up trouble. Look at you all now. Huddled here. You're not with your wives and children. You're readying for a fight. *He's* not gonna be here once this all quiets down. He's gonna leave and you'll be high and dry.

"But we'll be here. To make sure your fields have all the water and irrigation they need. Even before it gets allocated to our own wells. So which is it? *Him?* And a fight. A fight you can't possibly win. Or this deal. The very deal you've sought for the past two years. Even better . . ."

"C'mon, Chuck." Hauck heard murmurs below. "We can't pass this up."

"We've won, Chuck. We have to listen to him."

Who was this Hauck? Hauck knew they were all probably asking themselves. They'd didn't know him. He'd only been in town a few days, and since then the shit had hit the fan. Most had only met him the night before. They hadn't been shot at like Watkins had. Or had their son taken from them. They were just farmers. And now they were getting the deal they had put their asses on the line for.

"Not one drop of blood, you say . . .?" Watkins called back. Hauck thought maybe the farmer was weakening.

"You have my word," McKay confirmed. "We just want to talk to Mr. Hauck."

"Seems to me, you're forgetting just one detail . . ." Watkins said.

431

McKay stepped forward. "I'm listening . . ."

Watkins slowly elevated the barrel of his shotgun in McKay's direction. "My son."

Someone scampered over in a crouch to McKay and spoke to him, as the Alpha man stepped back behind the door. Hauck focused in through the night sight. He had a beard—what Dani said—and his face was hidden under a military-style cap. He hoped it was him; hoped as much as he could without ever actually seeing him. Robertson.

"What's done is done," McKay shouted back. "We can't take back the past. I'm sorry about your son. But all we can do is make his death mean something. Which it can here, sir. I think you know what I mean?"

"Yeah, I know what you mean," the farmer said. He turned to his friends. "Any one of you who want to take this deal and leave, go ahead. I can't keep you here. To me, seems they're just buying us off all over again. But he's right. It's what we wanted. What we put our necks on the line for. Anyway, I appreciate you boys standing here with me. But anyone who wants to go, now's the time."

"Chuck," one of them said. "I know it's personal to you, but to us, it's what we've been fighting for. We've got businesses. And families, too."

"I understand."

"So put down your gun, too. Take what he's offering. They only want to talk with him anyway. We understand

432

he stood up for us. But you heard him. It's not like they're going to kill him."

"Yeah I heard him as well," the farmer said. "You all better just go."

"I'm sorry, Chuck . . ." Two of them lowered their guns and stepped out from behind the combine. "*We're coming*!" They put up their hands. Two others, Milt and Don, stayed a few more seconds, trying to reason with their friend. "Chuck, please . . ."

"I'll be all right," the farmer said. "You guys head out."

"We'll call Riddick," Don said.

"Yeah, you do that," Watkins said. "Tell him I want a rebate on my town taxes. He'll know what I mean."

The two looked back at him one last time. Then they came around the bales. "We're coming out!" They stepped out with their hands visible.

"You men made the smart choice." McKay stepped out to greet them. "Just head to your trucks and go on home. Don't you worry about anything. We're just gonna talk it all through. Man to man."

"We'd like to stick around if that's all the same," Milt Yarrow said. "And see how that goes."

"I told you to get in your trucks and go." It almost sounded like an order. "That's the deal. Unless any of you want to reconsider. Go on. You can talk with your friend here in the morning."

One by one, they all took a last look at the house and loaded into their trucks. They started up their engines starting up, slowly backed out onto the drive, and headed down the road, glancing behind as they drove.

"You boys, too," Watkins said to his hands. "I appreciate you staying. But it ain't your fight, Miguel and Lupe, any more than it was theirs. Go on."

The two hands said goodbye and thanks, in broken English. Lupe handed Watkins the two improvised Molotov cocktails. Then they scampered away into the dark fields.

"So now I guess it's just us," McKay said.

"And now I got *you* an offer," Watkins called out.

"Go ahead," the Alpha man said. "We're not looking to make this any more difficult than it has to be."

"You give me Robertson, I give you Hauck. How's that?"

McKay smiled. He seemed to think over the proposal, maybe just long enough to make Robertson sweat a bit. Then he shook his head. "No deal."

"What I thought. Well, you want him so bad, you might as well come and get him then." The farmer glanced up at Hauck. "But you're going to have to come through me."

McKay stood there without making a move. He just nodded. The person next to him in the fatigues waved his arm, and the two Jeeps out in the fields began to close in, the Alpha men ducking behind them.

McKay shook his head. "If that's how you feel about it then."

434

CHAPTER SIXTY-EIGHT

The first sound was a spurt of gunfire directed at Watkins that didn't penetrate the hay bales. With his good arm he hurled one of the improvised explosives toward McKay, which shattered on the grill of the black SUV.

A small fire erupted.

Hauck squeezed on the trigger. He advanced a second round into the firing chamber of the single-shot hunting rifle, and fired again. The man next to McKay buckled, the car window in front of him shattering. A burst of automatic fire came at Hauck from out in the fields, bullets illuminating the darkness like tracers zinging into the barn window. Hauck spun and threw himself down. This was a mismatch, it was already clear. The others running off meant McKay could do anything he wanted to them now. He peered back out the window and saw one of the teams in the fields scurrying toward the house. He grabbed his handgun and sent four, quick 9 mm shots at them. Hauck heard a howl, and saw one of them come up hobbling, throwing himself behind the vehicle for cover.

Two down. That evened the odds just a bit. Hauck put another round into the Remington's chamber.

Watkins had run inside the farmhouse and was firing back at them from window to window. Rounds clanged loudly off the advancing Jeep. Hauck peered out the barn again and saw McKay with what looked like an M-16 scampering in a crouch toward the house. He ducked behind a baling machine. Watkins knew the layout. He wasn't a fool. Maybe he'd be able to lure him inside.

Hauck took his handgun and the rifle and got ready to climb down to get over to him.

One of the Alpha men had sprinted in and made it as far as the combine in front of the barn. Hauck leaned out the window with the 9 mm and tried to get off a shot, but a sharp burst of automatic fire came back from behind the Jeep from the guy with the wounded leg. One round grazed Hauck on the arm, like a fiery poker. Another felt like the poker was thrust in his right shoulder. He shouted out, spinning backwards, the 9 mm falling to the ground. Hauck threw himself behind the window. "*Shit.*" All he had now was this stupid hunting rifle. A bolt of pain immobilized his right arm and shoulder. Blood seeped from his shirt. He felt for his back and saw blood there as well. It must've gone through.

"Wait out here," he heard someone shout to the guy behind the Jeep who had shot at him. "If he jumps out that window, cut him to shreds."

The next thing he heard was the sound of footsteps front around the front and the barn door thrown open. Someone stepped in. Hauck pushed his back against the wall, hidden by the wall of hay bales.

Whoever it was crouched behind the inside tractor. Hauck moved away from the ledge, his arm limp, as an extended spray of gunfire shredded the spot around the window where he'd just been.

"You wanted to meet, Mr. Hauck, well here I am . . ." the guy called out.

Robertson.

"Don't be so shy . . . I'm easy to talk to. Your niece certainly seemed to find it that way." He slithered his way around the tractor and the wall of hay bales, intermittently spraying gunfire up in Hauck's direction. Hauck scrambled down onto the stack of bales, a trail of gunfire following him. He was safe for the time being, hidden behind the bales. But he was also trapped in here. And outmanned.

"You ought to just come out." Robertson jammed in a fresh ammo clip. "It makes me mad as hell when I have to go dig someone out. Did a lot of that back in the day. Overseas." Hauck heard him going along the wall of hay below, looking up, spraying sporadic gunfire whenever he thought he saw a shadow or

437

something moving, sending Hauck to the floor, his arm on fire.

"Taking fathers away from their families . . . Not fun work. But trust me, that was only the start of things. But you already know all about that, right . . ."

Hauck crawled along the top of the stacks of bale. There were maybe fifty or sixty piled high in three-foot cubes. A metal hook that was probably used as a stacking device hung loosely from a pulley maybe ten feet away.

"Why am I telling you all this . . .? I guess, so you know this kind of shit is nothing to me. It's what I do. Look at the Watkins boy. And your niece, right . . .? Only she was a wily one. I'll get my chance again. But let me tell you what your best chance is . . ."

He unleashed a prolonged burst of gunfire up at Hauck, shredding hay bales a couple of feet away. Hauck crouched behind them in a ball, his shoulder throbbing, and tried to figure out how he was going to get out of here alive.

"To me, your best chance is to throw down whatever you still got up there and come on out while you can. And here's why . . . You like a good steak, Mr. Hauck? You know, right off the fire, smelling like hickory chips. Mmmm, I sure do. Well, that's exactly what's about to happen to you. A burnt piece of meat, Mr. Hauck."

Gunfire erupted from what seemed inside the main house, then Hauck heard a single shotgun blast. Watkins. Hauck hoped the farmer had hit home.

"So check out what I have here, Mr. Hauck. I know you can see me. From between one of those bales . . ." Hauck leaned through a crack in the stacks and saw Robertson, at least his arm, high in the air, holding up one of the Molotov cocktails the Mexicans had made.

"It certainly didn't do a whole lot of damage outside. That's for sure. But I bet in here, with all this hay, we'll have a totally different result. Probably all go up in one big *whoosh*. Tons of smoke. Suck all the oxygen out. Not to mention the heat. One big ol' barbecue. Take about three or four minutes, I suspect, for the whole place to go up. You willing to burn to a crisp in here, Mr. Hauck? For some ol' farmer you only know a couple of days? Who's probably dead now anyway. Or some kid on a river you never even met? So I was saying . . . short of jumping out the window from up there and having my guy outside shoot you up like a duck with one wing, your best chance, seems to me, is to just show your face and save us all the aggravation and the mess. I'm sure Mr. Watkins would appreciate saving his barn, too. If he's still alive, that is . . ."

Hauck quietly loaded a round into the hunting rifle, his right arm barely cooperating. He knew the moment he jumped out from behind the bales he'd be a dead man. He slid on his belly over to the loading hook, its point resting in a bale just a few feet away. The thought came to him that maybe he could ride it down and surprise Robertson. Hauck knew he'd get just one shot.

But blood was matting through his shirt and it was more likely he'd end up on the ground in pain than hit his mark. In fact, he wasn't sure he could even hold on.

"So what do you say, Mr. Hauck? I'm the one doing all the talking." Hauck heard the action on Robertson's rifle pulled back. "You're leaving me no choice."

The Alpha man stepped back and took out a lighter and lit the fuse rag stuffed inside the bottle, which sprang up in flame. He held it above his head it while the rag burned down. "Last chance . . . I'm afraid, things are going to get a little thick under the collar now . . . Only thing I can say is, you shouldn't have brought these to the fight if you didn't want to see them used . . . So buckle up now. How about we all yell at once, '*Fire . . .!*'"

Robertson hurled it against the wood pallet supporting the bales of hay.

There was a whoosh. The oil in the broken bottle exploded in flame. A flash of yellow and orange lit up against the hay. Smoke immediately started to rise.

Hauck could make it back to the window and jump, like Robertson had said. It was maybe twenty feet. The remaining Alpha man was out there. Hauck would have only one shot—if he could even hold on to the rifle in the fall. He'd be a sitting duck.

Below, flames shot up. Dark smoke quickly began to rise. As well as the temperature. Hauck's shoulder hung limp like meat on a rack. He had no idea what had happened inside the house, if Watkins was dead or alive.

He just heard the crackle of flames and felt the heat against his skin. He knew he had to get out of there. Smoke was already seeping into his lungs. He'd have this one chance.

"Think I'll just step back a bit and watch the show, if that's okay . . .?" Robertson called out, pulling back the action on his M-16.

Suddenly Hauck heard the siren. The same emergency call he had heard the other day. *Watkins!* So he was still kicking. The barn was engulfed in flames now. Robertson stood back against the tractor, his gun readied, waiting for Hauck to show himself. Which had to be soon. Hauck grabbed the Remington with his good arm and took hold of the loading hook. He drew it back as far as he could, positioning himself with his back against the barn wall and his feet against the row of hay bales third from the top. Then he let the hook go. It swung as if on a pendulum right across the barn, hitting the top of the tractor with a resounding clang.

Robertson spun toward the sound with his gun raised.

Hauck pushed with everything he had against the bales. In a minute or two the entire barn would be a fireball. Straining, his shoulder in agony, the row of bales began to give way. It dislodged the ones above it like a house wall about to collapse, the whole thing suddenly caving in as Robertson looked up, seeing it all just a second too late, the heavy bales tumbling down on him like boulders in an avalanche.

Hauck leaped down.

Robertson fired at him, a wild spurt from under the rubble as he tried to extricate himself. Hauck dug his gun through the bales, trying to locate Robertson's body. The hunting rifle would only give him this one shot. Robertson kicked a bale off him and Hauck fired. The Alpha man yelped, the bullet seeming to graze him on the side, not the direct hit Hauck needed. Hauck drew the rifle back and frantically went to load another round into the chamber, while Robertson tried desperately to kick himself free. Robertson's gun snaked through the bales and Hauck realized it would take too long to load and fire again, his other arm a mess, so he tossed the Remington aside, diving where Robertson was trying to break through, and grabbed on to the shaft of the M-16 and tried to wrench it away.

His shoulder felt like a molten hot rod was being stuck in it.

He seized the stock and swung it hard into Robertson's jaw. The Alpha man grunted and fell back, his mouth filling with blood. The fire had reached the roof now. Outside, the signal continued to wail.

They wrestled for control of the gun, Hauck realizing he couldn't hold on much longer. A burning bale of hay fell off the wall and came to rest close by. Robertson squeezed his leg around Hauck, trying to wrestle him off. Hauck felt himself start to slide. He knew if Robertson managed to get on top and got the gun free, it was over for him.

442

With everything he had, he forced the rifle over Robertson's head, both of them straining to hold on to it with both hands. The Alpha man grunted as his arm brushed the hay bale that had tumbled down that was caught on fire.

Robertson strained to pull the gun back toward him, but Hauck kept pushing it farther away, closer to the burning bale.

Hauck knew he couldn't hold on much longer. The Alpha man tried to head-butt him, seeing what he was attempting to do. With a final thrust, all he had left, Hauck jerked the rifle upward, pinning Robertson's arm against the flaming bale. The Alpha man screamed, the smell of seared flesh immediately noticeable.

He let go.

That's when the other Alpha man who'd been stationed outside ran in, hearing Robertson's distress. Hauck wrestled the gun out of Robertson's singed arm and rolled off him.

"Take him out. Shoot him," Robertson shouted at this team member.

The man hesitated. He was around fifteen yards away and Hauck and Robertson were pretty much entangled. If he fired he could hit either of them. Flames were darting in all directions; smoke was filling the barn. The guy pointed the gun and said to Robertson, "Get away from him. Let him go!"

Hauck kicked Robertson free and squeezed. A burst

of four rounds shot out and the Alpha man fell back, his stomach dotted in red. Robertson dove toward Hauck and made a desperate lunge for the gun. Hauck swung and struck him in the head with the shoulder stock and Robertson slumped back, bloodied in the face. His arm almost dead, Hauck scrambled up to his feet. He pointed the muzzle of the gun at Robertson, who just lay there, breathing heavily. "So who's steak now, asshole."

Robertson held on to his burnt arm. "Fuck you."

Just take him out, Hauck said to himself. What you promised Watkins and Dani you were here to do. The miserable shit had locked Dani in a tank of rising water. If this situation was reversed, he wouldn't hesitate a nanosecond to do the same to you.

"Go on," Robertson said, his contempt fading into a look of final resignation. "It's what you came back for, isn't it? For me. So go on. Do it, dude. If you have it in you."

Hauck stepped up and placed the muzzle of the gun squarely over the Alpha man's chest. One burst and it was what he deserved. What else was there to do? Turn him over to Riddick? RMM would have him out by dawn. Then who'd be next? Him? Dani?

The man was right. It was what you came back here for . . .

The Alpha man lay there smirking. "Not so easy, is it? Just to kill someone. Goes against everything you have inside, right, detective?"

Hauck pressed his boot on Robertson's throat and

444

dug the muzzle into the his cheek. "You're wrong." His finger tensed the trigger. "Doesn't faze me one bit."

He was about to squeeze when he heard a shout come from outside the barn. *"Hauck!"*

It came from the direction of the house. Hauck recognized it as McKay. He slowly took his foot off Robertson's chest and stepped back, the gun still trained on him.

McKay said, "Something out here you ought to see . . ."

"Don't listen!" Watkins's voice rang out from the same location. "Just do what you have to do."

"Count of five . . ." McKay called back. "Then I fill his head full of holes. And we come after you."

"Do it, Hauck," Watkins yelled again. "That's the sonovabitch who killed Trey. That's why we're here."

"Seems you missed your chance, huh, old buddy . . .?" Robertson cackled, sizing up the situation.

"One more word, it'll be your last," Hauck said, jamming the muzzle into the Alpha man's forehead.

"Okay, okay . . ."

Hauck looked out through the flames outside and saw McKay holding Watkins by his collar, a rifle to the back of his head. The siren was blaring. The fire had reached the roof of the barn. It was starting to split apart. They had to get out of here.

"Three seconds . . ." McKay came back. "I'll blow his head apart like an eggshell. And I don't bluff."

"Get up," Hauck said, kicking Robertson over.

Watkins hollered from outside. *"Don't!"*

"Get up," Hauck said again. "Give me the slightest reason, and this is where it ends for you."

With a grin, Robertson slowly pushed himself up to his feet, his arm smelling of burnt flesh.

Hauck prodded him in the back with the muzzle. "Now move."

They stepped out of the burning barn. McKay was behind the combine, holding Watkins. He smiled, in the way a desperate killer might smile who had brought all the pieces of his plan together. Hauck pushed Robertson forward until they were about ten yards away, the gun tip dug into his back.

"You're either one foolish man or a very unlucky one," the Alpha boss said smiling. "Violence always seems to follow you."

Hauck met his gaze. "I was thinking similar thoughts about you."

"So here we are."

"Seems like a standoff," Hauck said. "So how do you want to play it?"

"Oh, no standoff." McKay shook his head. His look of satisfaction and control sent an uncomfortable feeling down Hauck's spine. McKay motioned with his chin for Hauck to look around.

Behind him, one of the men Hauck thought was down came from around the barn.

"No standoff at all."

CHAPTER SIXTY-NINE

"How badly do you want to lose your man here?" Hauck said, the rifle pressed into Robertson's back, glancing at the other man circling behind him, his own gun trained on Hauck.

McKay dug his M-16 into the base of the farmer's skull and shrugged. "How bad do you want to lose yours?"

The numbers didn't quite add up. It all seemed pretty foolish now, coming back, but Hauck was long past any regrets. He'd been to the edge before. Nowhere to go. And he knew sometimes you just had to play it out. People often faltered. Lacked the will. Though it seemed McKay had been here, too.

Hauck smiled at him. "So is this what they meant in the brochure by 'environmental challenges' . . .? Using the word broadly, of course."

447

McKay chuckled. "No, I admit, this one's a bit beyond the mission statement. But we do whatever the job calls for. So here we are."

The siren continued to sound.

Watkins gave him an imploring look. "Hauck, I told you, do what you came here to do. I can't live with it, the other way."

"Shut up, old man," said McKay, swatting him on the back of the head with the gun butt. "I know you a bit," he said to Hauck. "Maybe more than you think. We both believe in the things we do. I know that one of them for you is what seems like doing the right thing; otherwise you wouldn't even be here. And for us, it's getting the right things done, and so these wells, the energy independence they bring, it's what we believe, at all costs.

"But you also don't believe in people dying when they don't have to. Otherwise you would have blown John here's head off back in the barn. Any more than you can let this ol' farmer of yours die here needlessly, too. He's already lost enough, don't you agree? Am I right on all that . . .?"

The man behind Hauck stepped around at a bad angle looking for a clear shot, and Hauck kept dragging Robertson by the collar, so he would stay somewhat shielded. "Don't make yourself into something fancy, McKay. You're basically just hired killers. But you've got the floor . . ."

"You know what we want. Drop the gun. We'll let ol' Chuck here go and go about with his life. Back to his family. You heard what I offered before. He's already got what he wanted."

"Don't listen to him, Mr. Hauck. That's not what I want at all." Watkins tried to flail at McKay and the Alpha man kicked his legs out from under him, sending him to the ground.

"But you know what the one difference is between us, Mr. Hauck." The Alpha boss shrugged with a slight smile. "It's that in our world, people are dying all the time . . ."

"There's one more"—Hauck jammed the muzzle into Robertson's back—"difference. I also believe people have to pay. And as you hear, I don't think my friend Watkins here would be so happy with me if I just handed him over to you. Would you, Chuck?"

Watkins shook his head. "No."

"And of course there's one more thing . . ." Hauck raised the barrel of the gun to Robertson's head.

McKay said, "What's that?"

Hauck looked across at him. "The girl."

"The girl . . ."

"She has to live."

"You're right, the girl . . ." McKay nodded, but his eyes lost their amusement. "That does complicate things a bit."

Behind Hauck, flames rose into the sky; the barn was

about to break apart. The fire flew up in waves with a bellowing whoosh. Hauck felt the heat press against his skin. The siren continued to wail.

"People are gonna hear that. They're going to be coming here," he said to McKay. "Let him go. He's already lost enough. It's me you want anyway."

"Do what we're here to do," Watkins seethed, trying to wrangle out of McKay's grasp.

"We both know what this is about now. And it's not the water. Not anymore. Let him go."

"Well, you're right about that." McKay dug the tip of the muzzle into the back of Watkins's skull. "So I'm giving you to the count of five . . . Then things start. We see where they fall."

Hauck looked at Watkins, the farmer's worried but steady look saying that somehow this was okay. This was right. *Kill the sonovabitch who killed his son.* Hauck shifted with Robertson. He decided the better odds were to shield himself with him from McKay and go for the Alpha man behind him first.

Suddenly he heard a rumble. His gaze shot toward the road. Three or four cars were coming up it toward the farm. Maybe neighbors, seeing the flames. Or Watkins's friends, the ones who had left, hearing the siren.

"Take a look," Hauck said. "It's over, McKay. What are you going to do, shoot him in front of everyone? Maybe kill them, too, to cover it all up? And then me?

Robertson? The guy behind me? We're all gonna die for this?"

The vehicles stopped about a hundred yards from the house. A few people stepped out. Hauck saw Milt and Don. And Watkins's farmhands came back from the fields.

"It's over," Hauck said again. "No way to keep this quiet now. Put the gun down."

The Alpha man looked at the people arriving at the scene. "Oh, it ain't over . . ." He shook his head, gritting his jaw. Beams and planks collapsed into the fireball. Three of his men were lying dead somewhere in the fields and the barn.

"Get out of here," the Alpha man hissed, giving Watkins a kick with his boot. "You just hit the jackpot, Chuck. Get lost."

Watkins looked at Hauck and wouldn't leave him behind. "No."

"Get going, I said. And you do one thing to interfere, everything we talked about goes away. For all of them. You hear . . .? So get along. Now!"

"Go." Hauck nodded. "Warn Dani." He was about to say, call the Aspen police, but then he stopped himself as not to give it away.

"Count of three . . ." McKay tensed on the trigger. "You want to die so bad, old man, stick around. But I don't see how that helps the rest of you in any way. So get everyone out of here now."

The farmer looked at Hauck with futility in his eyes and pulled his arms away. He started to walk toward the cars, looked back at Hauck again, then picked up his pace into a labored trot. Ahead, people were gathered, watching, waiting. It looked like his friend Milt had come back for him. And Don. Everyone just stood there watching.

"So what're you going to do now, McKay?" Hauck grabbed Robertson by the collar and jerked him backward. He tried to keep the Alpha man who was circling behind him in his line of sight. His arm felt useless. It took everything he had just to keep the gun level now. He felt his legs weakening, too. Blood came down his side.

"Look at you, soldier," McKay said laughing. "I think it's over for *you*." He stepped away from the cover of the hay bales, narrowing the distance between them. The other Alpha man crept in closer behind Hauck. "You want to start shooting, shoot. Truth is, though, I really don't see any way you get out of here alive."

Hauck heard a crash and the barn imploded in flame. With a blast of heat, beams and planks and burning embers collapsed onto themselves with a freight-train-like roar.

Startled, Hauck turned, his strength ebbing. McKay seemed to nod, and the Alpha man behind Hauck closed in. Hauck backed away, grabbing on to Robertson, but Robertson managed to wrap his foot behind Hauck's leg and spun him backward, Hauck stumbling.

452

There was a tussle for the gun, but Hauck had no strength left to fight him. It fell out of his hands. He stood there, barely able to keep himself up, staring at Robertson, whose smirk had a lot more life in it now.

"Shoulda done it while you had the chance . . ." Robertson said, grinning. "My turn now."

The rifle stock came up, clubbing Hauck on the side of the head, his legs buckling and darkness rushing in.

"That's what you fucking get for messing around in my mailbox, asshole," was all Hauck heard before he blacked out.

CHAPTER SEVENTY

Hauck blinked his eyes open. He had no idea how much time had passed. The vehicle he was riding in drove through a chain link fence gate, which closed behind him. He struggled to get a sense of where he was. The car continued up the darkened road, then swung around. He saw a hut, two large round tanker trucks, lights canting into the car from a tall trestle. His head throbbed, and as he went to rub it, he found that his hands were bound in front. Across from him, Robertson was at the wheel, across from him. Hauck pushed himself up and heard a click in his ears from behind. The muzzle of a gun pressed against the back of his head.

"Welcome back. One wrong move and it's lights out," McKay said, behind him. "Just so we understand."

Hauck nodded. He realized he was riding in one of

the black SUVs he'd seen around. In spite of the circumstances, which were about as dire as they got, there was enough irony to still make him chuckle. "Always wanted a ride in one of these," he said.

"Unfortunately, we've arrived," the Alpha boss said, "so the strobe lighting and party bar will have to wait for another time."

"Shame," Hauck muttered. It was clear to him there was no way out. His hands were bound. His left arm barely felt attached and there was blood all over his shoulder. He couldn't even do what Dani had done days before, be tracked by his own phone. It was somewhere back in the barn. Melted cinders by now.

They drove up to the black trestle in the center of the well pad; it was about twenty feet high, lit up by a series of floodlights. The pump head, which Hauck recalled Dani telling him was known as a "horse head" on these old wells, bobbed up and down in three- or four-second intervals.

"Welcome to Trixie One," McKay said. "I hear you're already acquainted with Hannah, her cousin. She's been quite a girl. Three hundred and sixty barrels a day. Seven days a week. For eighteen months now. Unfortunately this is the end of the run for her."

"Sorry to hear that," Hauck said.

"For you, too. Pull up here," he instructed Robertson. "I'll get the well cap open. Why don't you show Mr. Hauck around."

It was dark. There didn't seem to be anyone around. Hauck tugged at his wrists, testing the ties. But there was no give. At least he was alive. They could have shot him back at the farm.

Though he knew they hadn't brought him up there just to give him a second tour.

"You realize this is all gonna come falling down on you." Hauck turned back and looked at McKay. "You. Alpha. RMM. Global Exploration. People saw what happened back there. You can't buy them off forever. It'll all come out. And it'll bring down everything. The merger. The entire company."

"You're right." McKay nodded. "We can't sweep this one under the rug. Or down the well cap, as we say here. But these kinds of operations always carry the possibility of future surprise. It's like sinking a well. You never know how it will turn out; you only try to keep the odds in your favor. It's kind of an arbitrage, between what you can control and what is inherently uncontrollable. In our favor, experience tells me, the people back there will see quickly what's in their best interest. And that would be water, Mr. Hauck, all the water they need in this drought. And all the benefits that go with it. Basically a continuation of their way of life. The police, even the local prosecutors . . . the same calculus works for them as well. They know what they get with us and they don't know you. So we'll see how it falls out. Ultimately, our most important goal is to protect our client."

"And those people back there on that farm? Your people?"

"What people, Mr. Hauck? You mean *our* men? Trust me, that's already in the process of being cleaned up. Maybe a gas line explosion. Or in the fire in the barn. They won't be found. They all knew the risk when they signed up here. Isn't that right, John?"

"Part of what we signed up for, Mr. McKay. Just like back in the service. Only the pay is a whole lot better."

"And earned." McKay nodded. "So that only leaves one thing unattended to, in my view, and we'll see where the chips end up falling . . ."

Robertson turned off the engine in front of the giant, hissing pump head.

McKay jumped out from the back and opened Hauck's door. "You, Mr. Hauck. And where there's no body, there's often no proof of a crime, isn't that right? You're an old detective, I'm told. And I promise, where you're going, a hundred years from now there still won't be a trace of any part of you. Even an earthquake won't be able to alter that. Get him out there," McKay said to Robertson, opening his door. "I'll be inside."

A bright, intense light came up the road from behind them, momentarily blinding Hauck. Robertson shielded his eyes. Another vehicle, a black Jeep this time. One of the vehicles that was at the farm. The guy behind the wheel was the one who had circled behind Hauck there.

"Take the car and wait down by the road," McKay instructed him. "No one comes up. And I mean no one."

"Yes, Mr. McKay," the operative said. He executed a three-point turn and headed back down the hill.

"So, c'mon now, Mr. Hauck." Robertson swung around and took out a Colt 9 mm army issue. "Out of the car. I don't have to explain how this all works all over again, do I? I've heard you already had the tour."

Hauck didn't move, ratcheting through the possibilities of how he could remove the gun from this former Special Forces guy with his own hands bound and his right shoulder limp and aching. They weren't promising.

"I said, get out!" Robertson said again, digging the gun into Hauck's shoulder like a cattle prod.

Pain shot through him. He bent over. Robertson reached for the binds and dragged Hauck out of the car seat onto the ground.

"C'mon, get up now," Robertson said. "Quit being such an old hen. Everyone told me you were tough."

"Tough enough to have gotten that gun from you back at the barn." Hauck pushed up to a knee. "With only one arm."

"Yeah, well even my eighty-year-old grandfather gets a boner every once in a while. Don't dream on it. Won't be happening again."

He kicked Hauck forward, in the direction of the well, its large horse head pump bobbing up and down in a steady, hissing rhythm—*ka-chung, ka-chung, ka-chung*.

"Three hundred and fifty barrels a day," Robertson said. He pushed Hauck toward it with his boot. "Seven days a week. Three hundred and sixty-five days a year. For almost two years . . ."

Hauck got to a knee and forced himself up to his feet. Every time he put pressure on his arm to balance, he winced, pain shooting through him.

"But that's all she had. Sad, huh? We're closing her up. You see those trucks?" He motioned to two large round-bellied trucks. "Filled with cement. Enough to go down about a thousand feet below the water table and plug this mother up so that even a worm wouldn't have enough to breathe. Starting to get the picture now . . .? That's what Mr. McKay meant by no one will find you for a hundred years. Maybe a thousand. Tomorrow, you'll be like a fossil. What do you think of that, Mr. Hauck?" He pushed Hauck over to the wellhead, its pump sucking up the last barrels of whatever the old well had to give, its hydraulic coils dropping loosely below the bobbing horse head, up and down.

Ka-chung. Ka-chung.

"A hundred years from now there'll be some earthquake, or some reason to go down into this old chute, and it'll be like, who the fuck is this? You might even be famous. Kinda gets you thinking, right . . .?"

Hauck stood there, covered in blood and dirt, his right arm slumped. The opening in the wellhead was about three feet in diameter. Just enough for a body if the pumping tubes were removed. The area was protected by a circular railing. A beeper began to sound and suddenly the cap began to widen—McKay clearly at the controls—until it grew to around four feet wide, enough for a body to be stuffed down.

The signal stopped.

"Well, I'd like to say it all just ends here with you and we could all just go home and be done with it . . ." Robertson knelt and opened the well cap. "But, of course, that's not the way it goes."

Hauck said, "What do you mean?"

"I mean the girl, of course. Your niece. Or whatever she is. Cute one, though."

"Just let her alone," Hauck said. "Let it end with me."

"Well, wish I could. But it's all gone on a bit far for that now. Anyway, already in the works, I'm afraid, bro." He kind of winked, clearly enjoying the moment. "I thought that might be a thought you wanted to carry with you to where you're heading next." Robertson grinned, pushing up the brim of his army cap with the tip of his gun. "You didn't think we could just let her go now, after what happened, did you, ol' buddy?"

A well of anger and futility rose up deep inside Hauck. He balled his fists and dug his wrists against the binds, helpless. "Sonovabitch. Don't."

"Too late now. That man's in a real tight squeeze, I would say. That ol' sheriff there. Seems like what I told him applies to you as well. You all should've thought about all this a bit more carefully before you jumped in headfirst. Know what I mean . . ."

The horse head pump went down, belching steam. The hydraulic cables drooped as well, hanging loosely. Watching it, Hauck made the mental count to three before the pump went up again. One of the floodlights attached to the trestle canted over Hauck's shoulder, making a bright white cone on the ground.

"Anyway, I've run out of things to say, bro. You got anything . . .?"

Hauck had been to the edge several times, but had always managed to find a way. He looked back at Robertson.

"I didn't think so, *bro*."

"One thing . . ."

"What's that?"

The horse head bobbed up and down. *Ka-chung. Ka-chung.*

One, two, three seconds . . .

Hauck took a step sideways in front of the light.

CHAPTER SEVENTY-ONE

Chief Riddick sat in his office at well past nine that night. He waited glumly for the call. He hadn't spent the full evening here in years, but this wasn't like other times. Other times, they'd deal with fires, floods, twisters. Even the time Tom Early's son went off the handle and killed four people, making the national news.

This time was different, though.

Before, they all banded together against what was happening and everyone knew what to do. Those days everyone here seemed to share the same principles. This time it was like the slow creep of water over an alluvial plain. The bitter taste in your gut of being bought off. The slow erosion of your principles.

Like the river's bed: One day there's water there; the next there's not.

He couldn't remember when it first began. Maybe when that fancy new town hall was built. Or when the squadron of shiny new Broncos his men we're riding around in was first proposed, financed fully by RMM.

Maybe it was the day they all realized that due to the drought and the land, their town was drying up.

He'd known Chuck Watkins thirty years. Shit, he'd once dated his sister back in the day. He was a good man. But good men couldn't make it rain in July. Good men couldn't turn a parched patch of brush and dirt into millions.

Riddick knew there was bloodshed out there tonight. He knew bad things had likely happened. He knew that the minute Watkins called. It made his stomach feel as empty as if he hadn't eaten for days, to hang up on him. *No cars to spare right now. We'll get out to you as soon as we can.*

"Jesus, Joe, do you know what's happening out here . . .?"

Riddick knew he was leaving him out there to die. Twenty of ten; he looked at his watch. It'd been dark for forty minutes now.

Probably all happened by now.

Any minute he ought to get the call. Then he'd drive out to the ranch. Then he'd go out and bury it all.

His wife, Ann, would be ashamed of him.

There was nothing more he could do.

Suddenly his thoughts were interrupted by a commotion coming from out in the station. One of his young officers burst in, trying to restrain a group of people behind him that had the feel of a mob. Milt Yarrow was there. And Don Ellis.

And to his total consternation, Chuck Watkins came in.

"What the hell's going on . . .?" Riddick barely had time to stand.

"Where is he?" Watkins said.

"Where's who, Chuck?" Part of Riddick had to admit he was actually glad to see the old farmer still standing. Another part felt like this was the posse that might well take him outside to be lynched. "You can't just come in here and—"

"Where'd they take him, Joe? I know you know exactly who I'm talking about. McKay and that other guy from Alpha. They took him. They're going to kill him, Joe. We both know that. And I know you know exactly where they are. Now you may have sat on your hands in here tonight, when the rest of us have been shot at and almost killed. Like you've sat on your hands for the past three years. But he's the one damn person who didn't. Who stood up for us. And I don't intend to wait around here one more second trying to explain things to you because that second may well be his last. I know that there was once a decent person inside of you, if you can dig deep down and find him again. So where the hell are they, Joe? Tell me now."

Riddick had known Watkins a long time but had

never seen so much fire in him. In all of them. He'd always found ways to keep things together, even when that ugly lawsuit reared up and damn near tore the town in two. He'd hadn't had a damn thing to do with Watkins's son being killed, if that's what happened. Though inwardly, when he heard the news, he guessed he knew it was true. He knew it had all gone too far. He just didn't know how to stop it now. That slow creep of your principles washed away in the soil was now like a mudslide dragging everything down with it, and he knew, once he stood up and tried to turn it all back, everything would come crashing down and swallow him as well.

"Chuck, Milt, look, I—"

"You what, Joe? You don't have enough guts to do what's right? I'm not waiting one more second. Or for God's sake, maybe you intend to do what here, arrest us all? Taking their money was one thing. But I lost a son, Joe. And we almost lost a whole lot more tonight. What kind of town do we live in anymore? What do we stand for now?"

Watkins looked at him and Riddick as the last of that slide went over the edge. *"Where'd they take him, Joe?"*

CHAPTER SEVENTY-TWO

Hauck stepped to the right, the bright floodlights on the trestle beaming over his shoulder. He knew he had only seconds.

Instinctively, Robertson took a step along with him to give him a target dead-on. The cone of targeted light fell on him, blinding him momentarily.

He put a hand up toward his eyes.

Hauck shot his leg up, driving his foot into Robertson's extended arm, forcing his gun hand skyward. In almost the same instant Hauck bull-rushed him, lowering his shoulder and driving the Alpha man back against the iron well cap railing. Robertson emitted a grunt, his back bent over the bar. Hauck swung his elbows and struck him in his jaw, keeping his arm pinned, and pounded the Alpha man's gun

466

hand against the railing—two, three, four times, fighting back the searing pain that tore through his shoulder. Hauck knew that if the man's gun hand was freed, he could groan about his shoulder for the rest of time, a thousand feet down in that well.

Robertson reached around and peeled Hauck's face back with his free hand, digging into his eyes and nose, as if trying to tear them off. Hauck continued to ram the Alpha man's gun hand against the railing, twisting his wrist back at a severe angle until it was about to crack, summoning every sinew of his strength to try to break it, ignoring the pain in his shoulder and face.

The gun finally fell free.

Hauck's only hope was to get to it first. In his weakened state, with his hands bound and ribs aching, there was no way he could hold off the younger, more agile ex-Special Forces man for long. Robertson kneed him and swung around and came at Hauck from behind, wrapping Hauck's head in a viselike hold and trying to jerk it sideways, to snap his neck. Hauck tumbled over the railing, attempting to roll Robertson over with him.

If he gave Robertson leverage even for a moment his neck would break.

It worked. Hauck dove over the railing and Robertson fell over with him onto his back. Hauck reached for the gun; as he extended his arm his shoulder screaming with pain. He got his bound hands on the handle and spun but Robertson scrambled over and kicked it out of Hauck's hands. Grunting, they both lunged for it, and suddenly they were grappling. Robertson on Hauck's shoulders, Hauck's head hitting against the steel cap of the open well about a foot from the tubing pump that was churning up and down, the large horse head looming above them. The hydraulic belching in Hauck's ears roared like a train going through a tunnel: *Ka-chung. Ka-chung. Ka-chung.*

"You're fucking done now," Robertson grunted only inches away, his eyes ablaze. He dug his elbow into Hauck's wound until Hauck screamed, almost passing out, and then he rammed the back of Hauck's head against the metal well cap rim. He did it again, Hauck trying with whatever he had left to fight him off, but his strength was evaporating with every second, and the impact against his head was like being checked into the boards of a hockey rink over and over without a helmet. At some point he knew he'd black out.

Seething, Robertson kept ramming him.

The Alpha man was younger and stronger. He lifted Hauck up and drove him onto the well pad closer to the pump shaft, the heated tubing hanging loosely, bobbing up and down. As he got closer to it, Hauck realized that if he came in contact with it, besides the scorching heat, the force of the bolts and seals would surely rip his skull open.

The pain in his shoulder was almost unbearable now.

The Alpha man kept inching him closer to the rising and falling horse head. He was now no more than a foot away and he could feel the heat against him. He couldn't keep Robertson from forcing him closer. Above him, the giant horse head bore down on them and then back up, the hydraulic cables looping lower, almost within his grasp. The churning, hissing noise sounded in his ears, the belching of the well pump almost reverberating through him.

"Here's something you can take with you," Robertson hissed at him. "I'm gonna make sure she's dead. Tonight. How does that feel?" His eyes shone like fiery embers. He pinned Hauck's hands onto Hauck's chest and jerked him a few inches closer. From the corners of his eyes Hauck could see the pump tubing now only inches from his head, each earsplitting bellow from the well almost inside him now. It would only be seconds, and he would have Hauck up against the churning pump.

Hauck turned his face away.

He was almost directly underneath the enormous horse head now. Robertson raised up to put everything into one last thrust, and Hauck's arms came free. With the pump shaft inches away, he waited until the horse head bore down, Robertson getting ready for one final push into its path, then spun the Alpha man with whatever he had left, grabbing on to the hydraulic cables that were barely a foot from his head.

"This is for Dani . . ." Hauck said, looking into

Robertson's eyes, and kneed him in the groin. The Alpha man raised up in pain. The pump lowered again and Hauck grabbed the cable and looped it around Robertson's neck.

"And this is for Trey . . ."

In the nanosecond that the machine came to a stop, Robertson's eyes bulged as he realized what would happen next and his hands pawed madly at the cables.

Hauck looped them one more time.

The pump reared back up, dragging Robertson upward with it. The hydraulic cables straightened as the giant horse head rose into the air, snapping Robertson's neck with its force. It held him there, then three seconds later, drove downward again. Then back up, his body slack and immobile now, dangling tautly in a grim, deadly rhythm.

Up. And then back down.

Up and down.

Exhausted, Hauck lifted himself to his knees. He looked up at Robertson's inert body being jerked around like some crash dummy. "So how does *that* feel, asshole?" he said.

He knew he didn't have much time. McKay was still somewhere. He might well have even watched what had happened on the monitors inside. Hauck looked around on the ground, searching madly for the gun Robertson had kicked away. It had to be here somewhere . . . He was sure it—

470

Then he heard the sound of shoes crunching on gravel and a familiar click that was as emptying of all hope as it was unmistakable.

"Well done. I give you full credit, kicking his ass. And with one arm."

Hauck looked up. McKay had his gun on him, nodding admiringly toward Robertson. "Looking for this?" He kicked Robertson's gun about six feet away.

Hauck watched the gun skip out of his reach. All hope disappeared with it.

"It's not going to work," Hauck said, rolling back on his knees. "Too many people already know. Even if you kill me, it'll just bring everything down. There isn't going to be any merger." He looked at McKay, the gun pointed at his chest. "There's nothing left to protect."

"You may be right." McKay nodded with a resigned breath. "But you surely didn't think I'm going to let you just walk out of here. Not now." He came over and put his foot on Hauck's shoulder and pushed him back to the ground. Hauck grimaced. He bent and put the gun against Hauck's face, Hauck too exhausted now and with too much blood lost to even feel fear. Just that this was the end. He let his mind go. To Dani first—how he prayed she would somehow be safe after this, even though he was unable to save her now. And then to Jessie, who would never even know what happened to her father. How he died. He tried to summon the strength, but he couldn't. He grabbed a

471

fistful of dirt and just looked up at the wide moon, as good a sight as any to dream on.

He heard a voice. "Nothing personal, Mr. Hauck."

He wanted to stab one more time at the gun, but there was nothing left, only the dirt slipping out of his fist.

Nothing.

Suddenly there was the sound of tires on gravel and a blinding cone of light swept over him and McKay.

It didn't bring Hauck much elation. It was likely just the other Alpha operative coming back up from the gate. Which was what McKay must have assumed as he continued to press the muzzle of the gun against Hauck's skull.

But this light was blue and red. And whirling. And it seemed there were several of them, bouncing off the trestles. Everywhere.

Hauck heard McKay mutter under his breath. "What the fuck is . . ."

Hauck squinted into the glare. Suddenly he heard shouts, car doors opening. More lights and vehicles coming up behind them. Into the area around the well, with the horse head with Robertson's body attached continuing to drag him up and down.

For a moment Hauck thought it was likely just a dream, until the pressure against his skull suddenly lifted.

And then he heard someone shout, out of the glare

of rotating lights. A voice that was familiar, but which he'd heard only once before, so it took him a second to be sure.

"I don't think you want to go through with that, Mr. McKay. Enough's enough now, don't you think?"

Chief Riddick's voice.

"What the hell are you doing here, Joe?" McKay barked back. It didn't have the feel of a question, more of a command.

"Maybe something I should've done a while ago. Put the gun down now. No need to make it worse. It's all over."

More cars came up through the gate. Hauck rolled onto his side and squinted into the glare. McKay stood up, his fingers still flexed on the trigger. As many as twenty people were facing him. Three or four in uniform. Others, as Hauck narrowed his eyes in disbelief, he had seen earlier. Milt Yarrow. And Don Ellis. A lot of people pointing guns. Rifles and shotguns.

"You're making the mistake of your life, Riddick," McKay seethed in a voice like stone.

"Maybe. But in my view, I think it's more like I'm finally undoing it," the police chief replied. "You don't want to test my resolve here, Mr. McKay."

The Alpha man looked at the hopeless situation and dropped his gun.

And then people were rushing everywhere. Someone came up to Hauck out of the glare. Through the pain, his almost hallucinatory state of mind, he saw that it was Watkins.

Dirt and soot were all over Hauck's face and there was blood over his shirt. He gave the farmer a grateful smile, all he could muster.

"That him?" Watkins asked, gazing up at Robertson's still-bobbing body.

"Best I could do," Hauck said. He tried to stand, but couldn't, showing Watkins his bound hands. "Given the circumstances."

"Don't worry. Works for me. Here, let me help you up . . . If these boys took another minute to make up their minds what to do here, I'm not sure what we would have found."

"Chuck—" A bolt of dread shot through Hauck. He grabbed the farmer's arm, so spent and past all pain he could barely say the word. Though Watkins could have read it on Hauck's face, and seen the terror in his eyes.

"*Dani.*"

CHAPTER SEVENTY-THREE

Dani had stayed with Geoff at his friend's house up Elk Creek Road in Snowmass Canyon for two days now. She was officially going stir-crazy.

She'd spoken to Ty a couple of times and assured him she was perfectly safe and well taken care of. Snowmass was twenty minutes away from Carbondale. And even in the valley, where rumors of who was with whom and who had split up traveled like wildfire, only a couple of people at work even knew she and Geoff were together. And no one knew about Geoff's friend. Anyway, it was Wade whom Ty seemed so worried about. Wade, who had practically raised her, whatever he had done. He might've gotten himself in over his head in some mighty hot water, but in a million years, Dani was sure he would never actually come after her.

Still, she hadn't even left the house, even to pick up a new cell phone, or contacted any friends. She basically just sat around with Blu, watching TV, reading whatever was around the place, eating whatever Geoff brought back. Trying to be a good patient and get her strength back. And her wits. And stay out of sight.

Her battle in the water tank was like a nightmare to her now. She'd woken up both nights drenched in sweat, Geoff grabbing her thrashing arms. The first night she relived the chase in town: the terror of realizing that the person seated next to her at the counter was the person who killed Trey. Stabbing him with the dispenser, then fleeing into town, hiding on the truck, the frantic dash toward the police station just out of reach . . .

Then the two SUVs surrounding her.

Last night she dreamed of being back in the tank. Water levels rushing in on all sides. Crawling her way through that dark, creepy conduit, more like a murky, black, foul water-filled tomb. No exit this time. Realizing that her air was about to expire. She screamed, her hands pawing at something—the closed pipe cap. Or that's what Geoff told her she was doing when he woke her up. In her dream, she remembered trying to push her way out of the blocked opening, something bumping into her back. It was a body. A dead body that had brushed up against her in the dark. Its arms entangling with her in the dark. She spun around to get it off her and screamed out in terror.

It was Trey.

Even Blu came over to the bed, putting his snout next to her on the mattress, sensing something was wrong. Geoff held her and wrapped her close to him until she fell back to sleep. It had been a long time since she'd felt close enough to someone to let that happen.

In the two times she and Ty had spoken he somehow sounded different to her: kind of resigned, almost like something inevitable was going to happen. That didn't sound like him. He told her to write out a description of what had happened back at the river, leaving nothing out. He said one day the police would ask for it so to remember the details as best she could.

She just kept asking him what he was doing there and letting him know she was worried about him and that maybe she should come too.

Tonight, she was worried more than ever. She'd tried calling several times on the house line and he hadn't picked up. It was going on ten P.M. And that wasn't like him. She'd left a couple of messages, growing in concern. Geoff had gone off to town to pick up a pizza and some eggs for the morning. She was alone there with Blu. She had the TV on. She'd flicked from the Discovery Channel to the Vikings on the History Channel and now was just watching some rerun of *How I Met Your Mother* just to lighten the mood. It was an eighties chalet-style house, and every time she got up the floorboards creaked, and with everything going on, that made her a little anxious too.

She tried Ty one more time on the house phone, and when he didn't pick up, for a third time now, she officially began to go crazy. If something happened to him, how would she even know? Who could she even call? He said if she went a day without hearing from him to call this number in Washington, D.C. She went to the kitchen counter and pulled it from the pad.

It belonged to a friend of his. Naomi.

She thought she heard a car outside, the sound of tires crunching on twigs and gravel, and her heart eased with relief that Geoff had finally returned.

But no car light flashed through the windows, the way it did when someone came up the steep drive. She went and looked out. Nothing. Maybe just the wind, rustling through the trees.

It really did suck, being out here in this house all by herself.

The seconds started to go by slowly and no one came up to the house. *Just calm yourself, Dani. You're making yourself crazy. Take it easy.* The open living area was up on the second floor and had a deck off it with a view of the ski area, and Dani opened the door and looked out, but she didn't see any thing at all. She thought about calling Geoff from the house phone. He promised he'd be back in fifteen minutes. It was over twenty now. All the outside doors were locked. She opened the sliding door and stepped out on the deck. Blu got up and came out with her.

"What do you say, Blu, am I just getting all spooky here by myself?"

The Lab walked over to the railing and began to bark.

Jesus, it was enough to unnerve anyone, not to mention someone who had just been through what Dani had.

She went back in and shut the door behind her. And made sure she locked it, though who could climb their way up to the second floor? She checked the time: 10:35. *Geoff will be back any second. Calm yourself, Dani. No one even knows you're here.*

Blu began to whimper and let out a growl. He didn't like being cooped up here any more than she did. At least *he* got to go out once in a while. He didn't go far; just explored the woods and pooped and peed and then came back. Now he went to the top of the stairs leading down to the backyard. There wasn't much of a yard; the house was built on an incline and the woods and brush grew in pretty close to the house.

Dani said, "You want to go out, boy? I don't blame you."

The dog headed down the staircase and Dani followed him. She looked outside and didn't see a thing, and opened the door just a crack and listened, restraining Blu by the collar. Whatever it was, it was just her imagination, she decided. The only light was from the

479

moon, which was close to full. Feeling a little foolish, that she was making up dangers when there was enough real anxiety to go around, she finally opened the door wider and let him out. "Okay, boy, go ahead." He trotted out. Then, hearing Ty's caution in her head, she decided to be safe and closed the door back up. She stayed there awhile and watched the dog poke around. Normally this time of night he just sniffed for a bit, then did his business and came back in.

This night he was acting a little strange.

His sniffer must be going crazy, because he was making his way as if he was on the trail of something, through the plantings on the side of the house, and he whimpered a bunch of times and barked. Dani kept an eye on him through the glass. Must be an animal out there, she decided, as he barked and barked. Then he headed around the side of the house and out of sight. "Oh, come on, Blu, not tonight," she groaned impatiently. "Please . . ."

She waited a minute or so and then heard Blu barking up a storm around the side of the house. There was a stream that ran alongside; sometimes there were raccoon or deer. Up here there could even be mountain lions. Dani listened at the door and decided it was all going on too long. She grabbed his leash and stepped out and called for the dog. "Here, Blu, come on in . . .! You want a biscuit? *Biscuit!*" she yelled, which never failed to bring him in.

All she heard was his continued barking.

"Damn you, Blu," Dani muttered and, grabbing his harness, stepped out after him.

It was no big deal, she told herself. Clearly no one was out there. Probably just a creature. She went around the side of the house and found him looking out at the dark valley, barking. "C'mon, guy, let's go back inside." She pulled him by the collar. The big dog didn't move. She petted him to calm him down and took hold of him. "Not tonight, boy. Just not tonight . . ." she said, and clipped the harness around him and dragged him back toward the house.

He wouldn't budge. Just pulled against her, barking.

"*Blu!*" Dani yelled, trying to yank him away. "Come on. It's—"

Suddenly she did hear something. Footsteps. Coming from the front of the house. Like a boot crunching on the ground. Her heart came to a stop and her eyes darted. A couple of footsteps. Then nothing. The hairs on her arms stood up. She pulled the dog.

"Please, Blu, please . . . Let's just go," she said in almost a whimper. The dog started barking even louder.

She heard the noise again. As if it was coming toward her.

Shit.

This time it came with a beam of light, shining toward them from out of the darkness. Dani's blood froze. It canted off the house, the trees, all the time

481

coming closer. Now Dani pulled at Blu with all her might, but the dog weighed about eighty pounds, and when he made his mind up, he was difficult to control, and he wasn't budging. She knew she probably ought to just leave him out there—he'd be all right. But she couldn't. And whoever was out there had heard her; Blu was her protection. She stood there holding on to him as she heard the crunch of footsteps come closer and the light get brighter.

Suddenly someone stepped out from around the house, encased in darkness. Just enough that Dani saw the familiar boots, the uniform, and then the face, partially lit up by the light he was flashing around, which now shined directly on them, the dog on his hinds now, going crazy, growling, barking with everything he had.

"Wade."

She didn't know whether to be relieved or terrified. At first her anxiety eased, but when she saw what he had in his other hand, it rose up all over again. "What are you doing with that gun, Wade?"

CHAPTER SEVENTY-FOUR

For two days, Wade told himself he would only check to see if Dani had come back to the valley; which he prayed she hadn't and was somewhere else—somewhere far away—and he wouldn't have to go through with what they were pressuring him to do. That was tearing him up inside like razor blades right now.

His choice was, tell them to go to hell and risk what they would do to Kyle. Or follow through on it, a thing so bad he couldn't even hold the thought in his own stomach, and then be free of them but have to face what Hauck had promised he would do.

Either way he knew he could no longer go along with things as they were.

You let us worry about Mr. Hauck, the man on the phone had said. *You just handle your side of the business . . .*

His business. After going through it a hundred times, that seemed his only way out now.

Numbly, as if there were some kind of host inside him, something controlling his actions apart from his own conscience that he had no power over, he went by her apartment unit on Colorado Street earlier that day, and was relieved to see it all locked up. A few dog's toys were strewn on the back deck. He peered inside the sliding glass doors in back and didn't see any sign of life. No mess about. Nothing in the open kitchen. Clearly, she hadn't come back there yet, and that gave him a reprieve. Then he went by to see Trey's widow, Allie, and she said she hadn't heard from Dani since she left Templeton two days before. Wade figured that if Dani was back, Allie was the first person she would see. He drove out on Roaring Fork Drive to the rafting company Dani worked at. The gal there said she hadn't been in for three or four days.

So where had she gone now?

Back at the station, he sat at his desk, going through the motions. He took out the business card Hauck had given him that first time he came by. Talon Global Security. Partner. A phone number back in Connecticut.

And underneath it, his mobile.

You are a cop, aren't you? the bastard had taunted him. *That's your problem. You figure out what to do . . .*

He had a way of finding numbers. Most detectives could. There was the formal way, which required a warrant, and that's the way you absolutely went when you knew it was going to be run through the system. But there were less forthright ways, too. People who worked for the phone companies, who could assess anyone's account. Save a whole lot of time and trouble. And the chain of evidence didn't have to be particularly clean on this job. This situation wasn't going anywhere near the system. This time, he wasn't about to be arresting anybody here.

A couple of hours later Wade had a conversation over his cell and had gotten what he was looking for. In the last twenty-four hours, there were three calls to Hauck's cell phone from the same number in the local area code, 970.

The rest was easy. All you had to do was plug the phone number into Google and it came up right in front of your eyes.

Tom Whyte. Snowmass. And an address out on Elk Creek Road near Snowmass.

Wade didn't know who he was, but who else would possibly be calling Hauck from here?

So if the rest was easy, how come it sure didn't feel that way? He took off for the rest of the day, citing personal matters, convincing himself over and over exactly what it was he had to do. He came up with a plan, a sketchy one, he knew, but the best one that presented itself. What he didn't know was whether he could actually go through with it when the chips were on the line. It was either Kyle or Dani, and like the man had said, one of them needed him more than anything in the world and was his own flesh and blood. That was the way he had to look at it. He looked at his hands, hands that had shaken the hands of lots of famous people who had passed through Aspen over the years. Hands that had done a lot of things he was ashamed of, too.

Now they had to do one more.

He went to his garage and opened a Styrofoam box, then dug around amid the old clothes and personal effects, and pulled out that old bottle of Dewar's he'd kept there for years. More as kind of a test, knowing it was always there, and he'd passed it for these few years. He'd passed the test well. He undid the foil and opened the cork. He didn't even look for a glass. He just looked at it like the devil next to him in the room and took in two long gulps. The first liquor that had touched his lips in years.

He wanted to feel ashamed, but he couldn't. The whiskey was harsh and fiery, but it still felt like an old friend, someone almost forgotten through the years, but who had now walked through his door and all past affronts were forgiven. He took another large gulp and then one more, until he'd made his way through a quarter of the bottle. He felt it burn, like a truth that was long delayed, but clear.

Then he just sat down in his garage and stared. He could see it now. What he had to do. It wasn't much of a way out. Only the easier of two bad outcomes.

These hands had done a lot of things in his life he was ashamed of.

What was one more?

CHAPTER SEVENTY-FIVE

"Tell that dog to shut up!" Wade said, flashing the beam of light at Blu, which only agitated the dog further.

The Lab was on his hinds, pulling against Dani, going crazy now. He didn't really know Wade; he'd met him only one or two times. Maybe it was the uniform or the light flashing in his eyes. Or maybe only that Wade was even out here in the dark. Poking around with a gun.

"What the hell are you doing here, Wade?" Dani asked him again, her eyes going to his weapon.

"Who else is here?" Wade ignored her question, shining the light up at the house.

"No one. My friend will be back any minute, so unless you've got some reason to be here, Wade, it would be a good idea to—"

"Put the dog away, Dani. You're coming with me."

"What are you talking about? I'm not going anywhere with you, Wade. You're acting kind of weird. You seem like you're drunk. And you still haven't told me—"

"Not drunk enough that I don't know what to do," he said, cutting her off. The dog continued to try to get to him. Wade took a step back. "Shut him up, I said." He pointed the gun at Blu. "Or I'll take care of him myself!"

"Wade! Don't!" Dani yanked on the harness, pulling Blu as close to her as she could. "He's just scared, that's all. Can you blame him?"

"He damn well ought to be scared. I'm afraid you have to come with me, Dani. That's why I'm here. Don't make a fuss. It's all official business. *Here . . .*" He put the flashlight in a holster on his belt and took out a set of handcuffs. "Put these on."

"You're arresting me . . .?" She looked at the cuffs and knew that wasn't what he came here for. "How did you even find this place, Wade?"

"Doesn't matter. I'm just taking you down to the station, that's all. Some people in Templeton made a complaint. I have to do this, Dani. Just put these on or I will. We can discuss it there." Blu tried to lunge, continuing to growl. "And get your goddamn dog out of my face, or I'll take him down!"

"No." Dani pulled him back. "Who made a complaint, Wade? What people?" Blu almost lunged out of her grip, as if trying to protect her.

Wade's eyes flashed wildly. "You keep that animal

488

leashed or I'll shoot him, you understand? Right in front of you." He pointed the gun as if he was about to fire. "I swear."

"Wade, don't! Please. Put the gun away. He's only trying to protect me." She thought she could wait this out until Geoff came back. Which had to be in minutes. But then what would happen? Things could get a whole lot worse. The way Wade looked, the erratic gleam in his eye, if someone else suddenly drove up, Dani didn't know what would happen then. "Wade, tell me what's going on."

"Just do what I say, goddammit! For once, just do it. Get the dog inside, or you won't like what happens. Just get him inside." He kept jabbing the gun at Blu. "Or I'll shoot him right where he's standing, you hear . . .? I can do that. No one's gonna ever think twice on it. I swear."

"Okay. Okay," Dani pleaded. "Wade, please . . ." He looked like he might do anything with that wild look in his eye. Her heart was pounding out of control. "I'll bring him in. I'll come. I'll come. Just back off now."

She dragged Blu around the back. The door to the yard was still ajar. She didn't know what to do. She could run inside the house with Blu and lock the door. Then what? Wade might do anything. He seemed crazed.

"Put these on," he said, dangling the cuffs in front of her.

"Wade, please . . ."

"Put 'em on! Or, so help me God, I'll shoot him between the eyes. Is that what you want, Dani? You want to see

489

your dog die?" His eyes were wild and fiery. She'd seen him mad many times, but never, ever like this.

"Okay, okay!" she screamed back. "Okay! Blu, go back inside now, baby . . . please." She pushed open the door and tried to drag him inside. If she was going to lock herself in, this was the time. But Wade came around and put his hand on the door as the dog went back in, Dani letting him go ahead.

Then he shut it on him. Blu came back up with his paws against the glass, barking again.

Dani looked at Wade. "Wade, you're scaring me, please . . ."

"I think I told you to put these on."

"Wade, I'm not going anywhere with you. You know I can't."

"Oh, you're going . . . You're damn well going with me, or else I'll—" He took her arms and wrenched them around her back and slapped on the plastic cuffs, screwing them tight on her wrists, digging into her.

"Why are you doing this?"

"Because there's no damn other choice, Dani. There just isn't. That's why. Now c'mon." He took her by the arm and pushed her forward around the front of the house. She left Blu standing up in the window, barking. He pushed her down the driveway, Dani stumbling in the sandals she had on. About halfway down the drive she saw Wade's white police SUV, parked out of sight on the side. It had what looked like a parasail strapped on the top. She had a feeling of dread about what was going to happen. If she could stall him, Geoff might come back. He'd know this was something bad. Whatever he was, Wade wasn't a killer. He wouldn't just shoot them. Though he seemed crazy tonight and maybe he had been drinking, and she didn't know what he would do.

He said, "Get in," opening the passenger door.

"Wade, where are you taking me?" Dani demanded, fears springing up. "I know we're not going back to the station."

"I said, just get in, girl." He pushed her inside and slammed the door shut behind her. "You'll see."

"You have to tell me, Wade!"

He went around and climbed into the driver's seat beside her and locked the doors. She was trapped. Then he started the car up and slowly backed down the remaining part of the driveway, then went into a turn and headed back on Snowmass Creek Road toward the main highway. About a half mile down the road, a set of lights came up on them. Dani saw that it was Geoff, coming back, and when they passed she screamed out his name, futilely, pounding the window with her two fists in desperation, yelling "Geoff, Geoff!" as he drove by.

On Route 82, the main road in the valley, Wade turned west toward Carbondale. They stayed silent for the next few minutes, Dani desperately trying to figure out what she could do. Bound. Helpless. Trapped.

When they finally came to the turnoff for Carbondale, Wade passed right by.

"I thought we were going back to town?" Dani said, for the first time a real feeling of fear rising up inside her.

"You didn't give anyone any choice, dammit," Wade said.

"What do you mean, Wade?" He had the police radio on. There was a crackle from all the local departments coming in. A bar fight in Snowmass Village. An ailing car off the road near Basalt. "What do you mean I didn't give you any choice?"

He looked at her. "I told you not to stick your nose in it, didn't I? How many warnings did I give you? To just butt out."

"People were killed, Wade. My friend was killed. They tried to kill me up there as well a couple of days ago. And Ty. But you already know about all that, right? That's actually what we're doing here, isn't it?" Her eyes drilled on him. It was like he was being controlled by somebody or something. "What the hell have you gotten yourself into, Wade?"

"Hell," he said, continuing to drive. "Living hell. Nothing else to call it."

"And now you're going to do, what, climb deeper in it? Drag me in, too?"

"Don't blame it on me. You dragged yourself in, Dani. You've been in it since you walked in my office that first day."

"What are you going to do to me?" she pressed.

This time he didn't answer. He just continued down

82, occasionally turning up the police radio to listen to the chatter.

"Just sit there. Nothing you can do about it anyway. I can't let them kill him, Dani. I can't. I've done enough wrong. That's where I hold the line."

"What are you talking about? Kill who?"

She saw it in the tightening on his face. The predicament he was in. She knew only one thing would make him do this. "Kyle?"

He switched lanes, turning the radio up higher.

"It's Kyle, isn't it? What are they making you do, Wade? They're squeezing you, aren't they, and you're about to do something terrible? You don't have to do this. You'll regret it the rest of your life."

He put on his blinker. "Maybe I will."

He pulled off the highway at the outskirts of Glenwood Springs, and turned onto what Dani knew was Red Mountain Road for a while and started to wind into the hills.

She knew where she was. At the top was Cutter Point. She'd been up there once, with a bunch of paragliding friends. It was the spot they jumped from in Glenwood. There were houses on the road at first, on both sides, and past them, aspens rising into the sky as the road turned from paved to dirt.

There was nothing up there but a sheer drop.

"Where are we going?" Dani asked, trepidation setting in.

"Just shush."

"You have to tell me, Wade! Where are you taking me?"

"There's only one place up here, girl. I think you know that."

Her thoughts flashed to Ty. She didn't know if he was alive or dead now. Only that he hadn't answered her all night and she'd called several times. It was clear he wasn't going to save her this time. He wasn't anywhere near her. Even if he was alive. She wrestled against her cuffs. She tried to slip her wrist through, but it only made the clasps tighter. She'd been stupid, she realized. She'd been stubborn and foolish, and bulled her way into things she didn't belong in. Even Ty had told her that. She had dragged him in, too. And now she was going to pay. Wade had the flushed countenance of a trapped, hunted animal, looking for some way out of the box, but with a single-minded determination to do what he had to do.

He continued to wind up the road as it narrowed, putting on his brights.

"Please don't do this to me, Wade. You were married to my mom. We've known each other since I was a child . . ."

"Best just hold on, Danielle." The crackle of the police chatter grew thinner and less audible the farther up they climbed.

There was a time in her life when she had trusted him. He wasn't exactly loving—she wasn't *his*, Kyle was—but he was always fun and full of life. When she was a kid, he'd taken the two of them camping and rafting. She and Kyle. That's how she first got started. When her mom got sick, he'd taken her to her college back east, almost like a dad. And now he was taking her where . . .? To do what? *Kill her*. Doing someone's dirty work to shut her up. The car wound up higher and higher up the mountain. Dani knew it went two thousand feet up. There were no lights up here. Only the moon. There was a series of narrow switchbacks with only boulders to act as a guardrail; even by day it would make your stomach uneasy. Dani eyed the lock switch next to Wade. She thought about diving across and slamming into him when he slowed at one of the turns. Forcing the vehicle off the road. The car would surely roll. She didn't know how high up they were now, but there were still trees to block their fall. Then maybe she could make her way out and run for it.

Whatever he was going to do, she wasn't going to just go willingly. Without a fight. No way.

"Wade, I know they've gotten to you somehow. But you don't have to do this. We can take it to Sheriff Warrick. This isn't going to help you, Wade. Only suck you in deeper." She saw she was talking to a stone wall. *"Wade, listen!"*

He put his foot on the brake and slowed to about ten miles an hour as they went around a turn, the car wheels grazing the edge. The lights of the valley flickered far below them. Dani suddenly dove across him and

495

grabbed hold of the wheel and jerked it to the left toward the edge as hard as she could.

"What the hell are you—"

The vehicle lurched, its front wheels rolling off the embankment, teetering a second or two on the edge, just a foot or two from rolling off and tumbling down the mountain. It was her only chance. Dani kept the wheel pinned as Wade slammed on the brake, the vehicle hanging there over the darkness, front wheels spinning.

"You dumb little shit . . ." Wade said. He ripped her hands off the wheel and swung the back of his into her face.

Dani's head snapped back, and she felt the warm drool of blood running down her chin.

She tried to dive across him again, this time to unlock the lock switch and somehow get out of the car. But Wade blocked her and pulled her back by the hair and struck her again, opening her lip. Dani gasped with pain. He pushed her back over to her seat, keeping his hand pinned on her throat, his thumb digging into her larynx, causing her to gag.

"Wade! Wade, please!" she pleaded, trying to tear away his hand. Tears burned in her eyes. "What are you trying to do? You're hurting me!"

He kept his hand pinned there. Choking her. Driven by some uncontrollable urge in his ruined life to protect what he knew was now beyond protection. His rage seemingly built up from so many things. Anger. Shame. Guilt. Futility.

"Wade, please . . ." She shook herself free. "What's the plan?" Dani stared at him incomprehensibly. "What are you going to do, Wade? Tie me into that parasail up there and throw me over the edge?"

He just kept his hands on her.

"Who's going to believe it? Geoff'll know that's not how it happened. What are you going to do, kill him, too? People know I don't even do this, never mind drive up here and do it at night.

"And how did I even get up here? Geoff was out. My car's at my house. How are you going to figure that one out, Wade? It doesn't make sense. Nobody's going to believe it."

He stared like some mute, hunted animal.

"What's your plan, Wade? What's the goddamn plan?"

"I don't know what the fucking plan is!" he screamed. He took his hand away from her and pounded the steering wheel several times. "I don't have a plan!"

Dani looked at him, barely able to breathe. "Wade, please . . ."

She sat there, catching her breath. Tears rolled down her cheeks. She thought she had reached him. She waited for his breaths to calm. Then he turned the car back from the ledge and righted it on the road.

"Do that one more time I'll shoot you here," he said, and pulled out his gun.

He threw the car back in gear and continued climbing.

CHAPTER SEVENTY-SIX

"Sheriff Warrick, my name is Ty Hauck, and I was a police detective for years back in Greenwich, Connecticut. I'm here with Chief Joe Riddick of the Templeton police force up near Greeley. I know it's late, but we have a bit of an emergency here that involves Chief Dunn of Carbondale and we need your help . . ."

Riddick had done about everything he could going through the skeptical night duty officer to raise the Aspen sheriff so late at night. Hauck couldn't locate the number of the phone Dani had used to call him from earlier, his own phone no more than a mound of melted plastic back at Watkins's barn, but he recalled Geoff's name, Davies, and they were able to obtain his number, which they called, Robertson having told Hauck with relish that it was too late to stop it now, and, thank

God, Davies answered. Saying how she was gone—the house empty—and only the dog was there, barking up a storm. And that she would never have left without leaving him a note, and anyway, the only car there had been his. He was worried out of his mind.

Their next call was to the Carbondale Police Department looking for Wade. Hauck was told he was out, on personal matters—that he had been for much of the day—and left strict instructions with the duty officer not to track him down. Hauck pleaded with the guy that it was urgent, but he wasn't sure if the officer would do what had to be done against his boss with his career path on the line. That was when Hauck thought to bring in Aspen, which had the largest force in the valley.

"There's been a number of people killed, both here and back where you are, Sheriff Warrick. Trey Watkins and the people in that balloon. And I'm sorry to say it appears Chief Dunn's had a hand in them. But that's not why I'm calling now. What's pressing now is I'm pretty sure he's got Dani Whalen with him, who's aware of his involvement in these matters, and I believe he may have already done something terrible to her to keep her quiet. She's gone missing and we don't know where he is, and we need to find him, Sheriff, now—if it's not already too late."

"You think he's going to *what* . . .?" the Aspen sheriff asked.

CHAPTER SEVENTY-SEVEN

They were almost at the summit now. Dani recalled that the access road led to a flat cliff top, which during the day paragliders and base jumpers used as a jumping-off point. And a sheer drop of two thousand feet.

She eyed Wade's gun, but knew she couldn't get close to it. What was he going to do, shoot her up there and then roll her body off to the valley floor? At the top, there would be nowhere for her to run or escape other than over the cliff.

Dani's heart began to race. There was only a couple of hundred feet left to climb.

"I remember when I first met you," Dani said. She wiped the blood off her chin. "I was what, ten? You were a whole lot different than my dad, and I went, 'What the hell has mom brought home now?'"

He looked at her and tried to convey he wasn't into this. "Shut up."

"You weren't exactly a girl's dad," Dani went on. "You were into all this cowboy stuff and had this hard exterior. But I got to like you, didn't I? And I always thought you liked me. I kind of thought we had this deal. We didn't show we liked each other, but inside we really did. In a way, I think you turned me a little into the person I am today. All the rough edges. And stubbornness."

"I said, shut up!" He glared at her. "You were just a brat. You came with the deal."

"No, I don't believe you, Wade. We had good times. I can remember them. When you took me back east to school, all my roommates thought you were the bee's knees. With your python boots and turquoise ring, all the big movie actors you knew . . ."

He shook his head. "It's not gonna work, Dani. Please don't make this harder than it already is."

Dani saw that the tree line had thinned. Only another quarter mile or so of road. "I actually remember that I—"

A voice came over the radio. Up until then it had just been police cars and dispatchers talking between themselves. This time the voice was different.

"Chief Dunn. It's Dave. Can you hear me?" Dave Warrick.

Wade slowed. He seemed startled. He turned the volume up, but didn't make a move to talk back.

502

"Wade, we know where you are. You know as well as I do there's a tracking device in the GPS of all your cars. We know you're on Red Mountain. And we know who's with you."

Wade slowly pulled to a stop. They were only about a hundred feet below the summit. He sat there impassively. As if not knowing whether to go forward or turn back. Whether to reply or not. He closed his eyes.

"Wade, it's all over now." Warrick's voice crackled in. "The people who were pressuring you are either dead or in custody. There's no point getting yourself in any deeper. Or hurting people you care about. I spoke to someone named Hauck." At the sound of his name, Dani's insides soared. "He told me about Trey and those people in the balloon. Wade, I want you to stay where you are until we can get a car to you. Dani, can you hear me? Are you all right . . .?"

"Tell him I'm okay, Wade," Dani said. "Please . . ."

Wade opened his eyes back up. His face seemed to have a different cast on it now. Like some doomed, trapped inevitability. Instead of nodding, he just put his foot back on the gas again and continued up the mountain.

"Wade, you can't," Dani pleaded. "They know. It's over. There's no point going forward."

He just kept gunning the engine up to the last rise.

"Wade, I want you to answer me," Sheriff Warrick said. "We've been friends a long time. You were always

503

respectful to me, how things went, and I hope you always felt I was to you. I want to hear that Dani's okay. You have to let her do that now, okay . . .?"

Wade ignored him and kept the SUV going forward.

"Wade, let me talk to him, please. *Chief . . . Chief!*" The reply button wasn't on; there was no response. "Please, let me tell them that I'm okay and that you'll wait for the other officers. I'll be here with you. Kyle would want that, wouldn't he?"

Wade pushed the accelerator up the last rise, his eyes narrowed ahead.

"*Wade, please . . .?*" Dani said, more firmly. The SUV picked up speed. "Wade!" she shouted, becoming scared he was about to do something crazy.

Finally they rose up over the last bumpy rise to the top of the mountain. The stars were close and bright. Millions of them. A canopy of lights. A thousand homes sparkling brightly on the valley floor. Wade traversed slowly over the ridges and rocky growths as what was left of the road came to a stop. Dani's heart picked up. Wade pulled to within ten feet or so of the edge.

"Wade, please," she begged. "I'm scared. Don't!"

He stopped.

He swallowed slowly; Dani almost saw the lump in his throat crawl down his thick neck. He ran his hand across his scalp, knocking off his pride Stetson hat, and then when it fell in his lap, swatted it away in wordless rage into the backseat. He just sat there breathing,

504

composed but heavy. Warrick kept saying, "Wade, Wade, answer me."

Then he turned off the radio.

"I've done some bad things," he said, staring forward.

"I know. I know you have, Wade. But it's like with recovery, isn't that what you always said? It's never too little or too late. Let me tell them you'll give yourself up."

"I don't mean just about Trey. And Rooster. Though I haven't lost a minute of sleep over him. And those others . . ." He finally turned to her. "I never knew any of that was going to happen like it did. I swear."

She looked at him. "I believe you, Wade."

"I was talking about Judy," he said. "Your mom."

"What do you mean about Mom?"

He inhaled a deep breath that seemed like it had been inside him forever and then locked his hands behind his head. "She had time left. I don't know how much. But time. You could have made it back to be with her. But I . . ." He stopped. "She was taking a lot of morphine then."

Dani's eyes grew wide and she didn't understand. "What are you saying, Wade?"

"I took that from you, I know. Your last time with her. I increased her dosage. A lot. More than tripled it. She was in pain and I told myself I was doing the right thing. But we both know I was out of control back then. And scared. I was scared she wouldn't die. I needed money to pay back a few things. My lawyer. Some people who I owed things to, who would speak up for me." He swallowed again hard and then nodded as if finally making some peace with it himself. "You should've had that time."

"What are you saying, Wade, you killed her?"

"I just put her in God's hands, I told myself. But yes, you could say I did."

Dani blinked. "I always hated myself for not being back with her."

"I know you did." He nodded. "But now you see. It was me. That's why this seems right now. Now get out."

A wave of anger rose up inside Dani. Now it was her turn to look at him. "What seems right? How could you have done that, Wade? She loved you."

"Get out now, Danielle. Time's up." He took out his gun and cocked it back and pointed it squarely at her. "Walk over toward the edge. Sorry, but it doesn't end like you wanted it to, Dani. It just doesn't." He lifted the automatic door locks.

"What are you going to do, Wade? The police are on their way up now."

He said, "You want me to just shoot you here? I will. It's pretty clear I have nothing else to lose. Now go on . . ."

Dani remained there rooted to her seat.

"Count of three. And don't test me on this, Dani. Not this."

Confused, nervous, Dani fumbled at the door. She stepped out and just looked back at him. The killer of her mom. An accessory in killing Trey. So many things became clear.

His face had a cast of doom on it.

"Now close it," he said, keeping the gun on her and lowering the window. "Step back."

"Wade, please . . ." Dani shut the door.

"Now start to walk over. To the ledge."

Fear shot up in her. "What are you going to do to me, Wade?"

"Take a step, I said." He kept the gun trained on her through the open window. "Go on."

She did. She took a step or two, then she just stood there, Wade nodding and training the gun on her.

"Now walk over there." He swung the gun to indicate the cliff's edge. She stayed rooted, but her heart quickened its pace in fear. She didn't know if there was any reason left in him. "Walk over there, or so help me God I'll shoot you where you stand, Danielle. I will."

Tears of dread wound their way down her cheeks. She took another step back.

"*Walk!*" he shouted.

She started to move. She tripped in her sandals over a rough growth of scrub and caught herself. She backed away to a distance of about ten feet from Wade's car. She was maybe three or four feet from the ledge. A two-thousand-foot drop. She could start to run, but to where? And not in her sandals. She was trapped. She could feel the warm wind whooshing up the cliff face and beating into her. How could he want to kill her now? There was no point. She always thought he loved her.

He still had the gun pointed at her through the open window.

"Wait."

Dani stood there.

"Watch out for him," Wade said.

"Who?"

"He still needs lots of help. He gets whatever I have, of course, which ain't much. He'll just need somebody."

It took a second for what he was saying to break through her confusion and fear. "Wade, please, don't . . . What are you even thinking?"

"I lied before." His voice seemed to soften. "What I said about you . . . We always did have that deal. Being tough with one another. But I was always fond of you, Danielle. I tried to think of you as if you were my own. No matter what I've done, I did."

"I know." Suddenly the tears were burning in her eyes. And they were no longer of fear. "I did, too."

"I tried to warn you . . ."

Suddenly there were sirens in the distance.

"Don't let my son think ill of me, if you can."

Dani heard the V8 engine rev.

"Wade, wait!"

He looked ahead, and with a roar the white police SUV lurched forward and hurtled toward the edge.

"*Wade, no!*" Dani screamed in horror.

It shot off the edge, vaulting into the night sky, and seemed to hold there for an instant, like a hang glider catching the wind, about to soar.

Then it fell, nose forward into the deep abyss of the valley. Into the web of a million flickering lights. The valley Wade practically owned at one time, or at least that was the way it seemed, she thought later. If you could ever really own something like that, a man who never had a dime, only an off-color joke, a hearty laugh, or a slap on the back. Descending silently with a hundred secrets still buried with him.

Yet in his own way he had.

CHAPTER SEVENTY-EIGHT

Three days later, the United Airlines A320 touched down at LaGuardia Airport in New York and pulled up at the end of the runway with Hauck in it.

Three days of being treated for his wounds—two fractured ribs, a contusion on the back of his skull, and a clean through-and-through gunshot wound in the shoulder. And sorting things out with the various law enforcement agencies to come to the conclusion that despite two dead and one wounded at the farm, on top of the six dead in Aspen, he and Chuck Watkins wouldn't be charged.

In the end, the only charge that seemed even remotely prosecutable, but at the same time moot, was for unlawfully breaking into Robertson's mailbox, which the DA in Greeley seemed agreeable to ignore, only half jokingly, if Hauck promised never to come back to the state.

Randall J. McKay, from Alpha, was brought up on multiple counts of attempted murder, kidnapping, conspiracy to commit murder in the case of Trey Watkins, blackmail, and witness intimidation. Not to mention federal charges of illegally using military PsyOps tactics in the United States. Alpha Group agreed to discontinue all operations on the Wattenberg field pending a review of their business practices, and before that was even undertaken, several other energy accounts of theirs decided to walk away, and the firm collapsed. Several litigations against their management and board of directors were initiated.

Resurgent Mining and Mineral underwent an internal audit and Wendell Moss, their regional head of Colorado operations, resigned, pending charges against him of blackmail, conspiracy to defraud the justice system, and conspiracy to commit murder. The company expressed its "dismay and disappointment" at the tactics employed in the Wattenberg region, which ran against its "core philosophy to working hand in hand with local communities." The CEO said it would immediately take steps to ensure "that sufficient levels of water, either from local sources or beyond," would immediately be made available to the farmers and ranchers of Weld County, "who had been disadvantaged by their policies." In advance of what was anticipated to be several class action suits, the company pledged up front to invest the sum of $60 million to be put back into the affected localities, for RMM's role in compounding the hardships of the drought the past two years. At the same time the company insisted it had only worked within the wishes of the local municipalities affected, and that other than the actions of a few misguided managers, it had broken no laws. In Templeton, Police Chief Joseph Riddick tendered his resignation, citing reasons of personal health, pending a criminal review, and an outside lieutenant from Greeley was temporarily put in charge.

Two days after Hauck was taken away from Trixie One on a stretcher, a news release came over the wires that the proposed merger between RMM and Global had been put on hold.

RMM's stock fell twenty points that day.

On Hauck's second day in the hospital, a call came in from Vern Fitzpatrick, the chief of police back in Greenwich and Hauck's old boss, who'd tried to reach him before. When he heard Hauck was in the hospital and why, he laughed. "Every time I talk to you, life seems to be chipping a little more away," Vern said, recalling what had happened only months before after the Gstaad Group venture. "Bet you never thought when you left the force, that's when things would really start to get dangerous."

"Never did." Hauck chuckled. "That's true."

They talked about some people they knew in common; Hauck brought Fitzpatrick up-to-date on how he'd spent his past three months. Then he said, "So I know you didn't call in to hear about my trip to the Rockies . . ."

"No," Vern admitted. "I didn't." The chief paused for a second. "I guess you could tell the last time we saw each other, Ty, I'm not getting any younger. I've been running this department for almost twenty years now."

"And doing it pretty damn well," Hauck said. "Everyone respects you." Though Vern was right, the last time they had seen each other, at a retirement party for one of the department's longtime secretaries, Hauck couldn't help but notice the gray had turned to white, the crow's-feet around the eyes more pronounced.

"Thanks. That's actually kind of what I want to talk to you about."

Hauck shifted in his bed. "Okay . . ."

"I have a few things going on, beyond the usual aches and pains. I seem to have this irregular heartbeat now, they tell me. And this shake. You probably saw." Hauck had noticed the tremor the last time they met. "That's not getting any better."

"Have you gotten it tested?" Hauck asked. Vern was as much a friend as an ex-boss.

"I have." Then he switched the subject. "Marge and I were thinking about spending a little more time down south. We have this place, outside Charleston. Ever been there?"

"Never. I hear the eating's good, though."

"And the golf. Though I don't get down there near enough to confirm that myself."

"You telling me you're thinking about retiring, Vern?"

"Thinking seriously about it," Vern said.

"Wow. When?"

"Soon as I can groom someone into the job and replace myself."

"Well, yours will be big shoes to fill, Vern. Twenty years . . . The size of the force must have doubled in that time."

"Tripled actually. At least that's what I get reminded of, every time I go through the budget process."

Hauck laughed. "I bet it is. So what can I do? You want an assessment on who you have in mind? I'm sure Steve's up for it. He's next in line." Steve Cristafuli, whom Hauck had brought in himself, and who had replaced him as the chief of detectives. He'd held the job under Vern for two years now.

"Steve's not the answer, Ty. He's fine just where he is. He as much as said so himself when I asked."

"Okay. What about one of the other municipalities then? Mike Garvey's up in New Canaan and I always thought he has what it takes."

"You're right. He would be a good choice. But the reason I called you, Ty, is I was hoping you might think that this could be the right thing for you."

"*Me . . .?*" Hauck sat up in the bed.

514

"I don't know how things are in your new job . . . I know you're doing well. But I also know you spent a whole lot of time after that last escapade down in the Caribbean. And there are rumors . . ."

"Rumors? What kinds of rumors, Vern . . .?"

"You know how it is. People talk."

Hauck paused. He let the idea simmer around in his blood. "I've been out a long time. Close to three years. I'm sure things have changed. And things work a little differently in the private sector. And I've gotten used to that."

"I understand. But you're still the best man I can think of for the job. Everyone respects you. You know the place better than anyone. And maybe some of that private-sector savvy is a good thing these days . . ."

"You might be right on that," Hauck agreed.

"'Course, it's not the big glamour job like what you're used to now. And we can't even begin to offer you anything close to what you've been earning . . ."

"Money's never been the motivating thing for me, Vern. You know that."

"That's what I told the town council when I floated the idea to them. 'Why not ask Ty? We might be able to get him on the cheap.'"

Hauck chuckled back. "And what did they say?"

"Who?"

"The town council."

Vern didn't answer. "Think it over at least, would you? It's a good job. And a good life. You know that."

Hauck nodded. "It is."

"And something else to consider . . ." the chief of police said with a laugh.

"What's that?"

"It might be safer."

The farewells were tough for Hauck before he left to go back east.

Chuck Watkins came around with his wife. The farmer stepped in cautiously, seeing Hauck's head still bandaged and his arm in a sling. "So how's the shoulder?"

"Not quite as good as it was the day before I met you. How's yours?"

"Guess I could say the same thing. Played with my aim a little; otherwise that McKay guy would have never gotten the drop on me."

"So I suspected." Hauck said, twisting around. "The ribs hurt like a sonovabitch, though."

"Chuck." The farmer's wife nudged him forward.

"Okay, Marie . . ." Watkins took off his cap. "We want to say thank you," he said, and put out his hand. Hauck had to reach awkwardly with his left arm to take it, wincing. "Sorry . . ." the farmer said.

Hauck said, "I'm feeling like I'm the one who should be thanking you."

"It's mutual then. Though part of me does feel you owe me a new barn."

"Be sure and send the bill to RMM."

"You can be sure I will."

"*Chuck* . . ." Marie Watkins nudged him again.

"Marie, *please* . . ." Watkins glanced at her irritably. He cleared his throat. "Not just for what you did. For helping us all take a stand . . ." He squeezed his cap, as if he were wringing out the last drop of water from it. "What I meant was, thank you for giving me back my son. The way it was, I'm not sure I would ever have been able to think of him again without anger or even shame. *Now* . . . Now at least why he died means something . . . And I'm working on trying to forgive myself. Like you said you did with your little girl."

Marie Watkins interjected, "What my husband means to say is . . ."

"Dammit, Marie, if you could just butt out, I think Mr. Hauck and I both know what I'm trying to say . . ."

"I think we do, Ms. Watkins," Hauck said, with a wink to Chuck.

"See." Watkins shot a roll of the eyes at her. "Have to admit," he said, turning back to Hauck, "I quite liked what you came up with for that guy Robertson, though." His eyes lit up in admiration. "Got to thank you a lot for that one."

"No point in letting him hang around forever," Hauck said with a smile.

"Hang around . . ." The farmer laughed, the first time Hauck had heard him. "I kind of like that too."

The two of them shook hands, two unlikely partners who both knew they would likely never see each other again.

And Dani . . . She drove up the day Hauck was released and insisted on driving him back to the Denver airport. She looked nice, in a printed dress, her thick hair up. Pretty sandals. A little makeup on.

Of course, Blu was there in the back of her wagon. For most of the trip they just spoke about trivial things: How Hauck was mending. How long he was going to stay back east. She bet he was thrilled to go and see his daughter.

They drove down I-85 without saying what they really meant to say between them until the turnoff for the Denver airport, where Dani just pulled over to the side of the highway.

Hauck saw there were tears in her eyes.

"You going to be okay . . .?" he asked, and gave her a napkin from the fast food drink on the console.

"Yes." She nodded and dabbed her eyes. "No." The tears began to fall. He drew her into him with his good arm and held her against his shoulder. "I feel like such a jerk," she said, burying her face into him in a mash of tears.

"We're all jerks sometimes," he said, stroking her hair. "I'll always be there for you, Dani. You know that. Whenever you need me, you just call."

"Sounds like some stupid James Taylor song." She

nodded. Then she pulled away and looked at him, her eyes glistening. "Thank you."

"Everyone seems to be saying that to me today."

"Thank you for believing me. Thank you for saving my life. Thank you for making it through. If you hadn't, I don't think I'd ever have had a happy day for the rest of my life."

"But we did," Hauck said, smiling. "Both of us. So we don't have to worry about that, right?"

She blew her nose and nodded. "Right. My dad's flying in tomorrow. From South America. We're going to spend some time here and talk about a few things."

"Tell him something for me?"

"What?"

"Tell him this was just a bit more adventurous than he led me to believe. And next time, to call Tom Cruise."

Dani laughed again. "I will." She hugged him, and saw him wince from the awkward embrace. "Oh my God, sorry . . ."

"It's okay. I'm just not sure I can take a lot more of these goodbyes."

Then she wiped her eyes and looked at him.

"What are you going to do?" she asked.

"My old boss called. The police chief in Greenwich. He said he's retiring. They're looking at a few people who might fit the job. My name came up."

"You'd be happy? Doing that?"

He'd waited for the rising tide inside to tell him that

there was something bigger to do in his life, and the truth was, it just felt fine. "I think I would."

"You remember what I said to you on the phone? Before you went back up there. About your being here for me."

"Of course."

"Please stay in my life, Uncle Ty. Promise me."

"That's one promise I can keep, Dani. And I will."

They hugged again, gingerly this time, and Dani put her head against his chest. "I don't want to let you go."

"Then don't." With his arm around her, Hauck thought, of all the things that happened here, maybe this was the best.

Hauck's jet traversed over the tarmac and back to the gate.

When the seat belt signal dinged, he stood up and tried to pull his bag down with his good arm. He didn't have much with him. Only a couple of shirts and jeans. It seemed funny now, with what happened, that he'd figured he'd stay only a couple of days.

The man across the aisle, who had the look of a guy who'd been on the road for weeks, noticed the sling and helped Hauck pull his bag down. "What'd ya do?" he asked.

"Shoulder sprain," Hauck said. "Fly fishing."

"Must have been one helluva bass," the guy said with a laugh. "Those suckers can be tricky. Whatever you do, make sure you do the PT. That makes all the difference in the world."

"I will," Hauck said brightly. He took his bag from him and nodded thanks.

"Traveling or coming home?" the man asked, pulling his briefcase from under the seat and wrapping a strap around his shoulder.

Hauck thought for a moment. About the life he'd left behind here. About his daughter, Jessie, who was waiting for him here. He didn't know what was ahead for him. Talon was gone now. Wherever that led. *The head job in Greenwich, huh?* He tried to fit that on for size. He and Naomi had tried to plan a week when they could get together, but she was in Houston next week and had budget meetings after that. It had been a long time away. Months. And felt right, to step back out. At last.

"Home," Hauck said.

Acknowledgments

This is my first Ty Hauck book in five years, and it was like getting back together with an old friend. Though the setting is not a familiar one for Ty, the nature of his character, his dogged search for the truth, usually undertaken on behalf of someone else (generally female), his humble and overachieving way, and his unfailing willingness to put his life on the line have always made him kind of a white knight for me, an idealized version of who I aimed to be.

But I'm just a guy who sits at my desk with a keyboard and a computer, and writing a thriller is more often a battle in problem solving than a search for inspiration, so this is a good time to thank the handful of people who did truly help in getting this one done, and hopefully done well: Tree Trujillo, an accomplished rafter, for vetting my whitewater scenes (I knew taking my family on those crazy rides down the Snake and Kennebec Rivers would come in handy one day). Tim Hopper, chief economist at TIAA-CREF in Houston, for some timely info, over dinner in Steamboat, on the economics of the fracking process; and Roy Grossman, an early reader of many of my books, and whose perceptive comments helped make this one a whole lot better.

Also a nod of thanks to my longtime team at William Morrow: Henry Ferris, David Highfill, Lynn Grady, Liate Stehlik, Danielle Bartlett, and Julia Wisdom, who, despite a few bumps and spills over the years, have guided me on one of the most memorable rides of my life. And to Simon Lipskar of Writers House, who continues to guide me, wherever that leads.

Two articles that helped me in this book deserve mention: "Option for Drilling Pits Farmers Against Oil Thirsty Wells" (*New York Times*, September 6, 2012). And a blog post by Brendan Demelle on *desmogblog.com*, "Gas Fracking Industry Using Military Psychological Warfare Tactics and Personnel in U.S." (September 6, 2011).

The themes of this book are cover-up and vindication, but the story leads through fracking and horizontal drilling, and in writing it, I immersed myself in much of the technology and environmental impact. Normally I just say it's not for me to agree or disagree on such issues. I'm a thriller writer, not a journalist. It's merely a device. But if I had to take sides on this one, I think